THE
BENEDICT
BASTARD

Books by Cate Campbell

Benedict Hall

Hall of Secrets

The Benedict Bastard

THE BENEDICT BASTARD

CATE CAMPBELL

KENSINGTON BOOKS
www.kensingtonbooks.com

KENSINGTON BOOKS are published by

Kensington Publishing Corp.
119 West 40th Street
New York, NY 10018

All Kensington titles, imprints, and distributed lines are available at special quantity discounts for bulk purchases for sales promotion, premiums, fund-raising, educational, or institutional use.

Special book excerpts or customized printings can also be created to fit specific needs. For details, write or phone the office of the Kensington Special Sales Manager: Attn. Special Sales Department. Kensington Publishing Corp., 119 West 40th Street, New York, NY 10018. Phone: 1-800-221-2647.

Kensington and the K logo Reg. U.S. Pat. & TM Off.

eISBN-13: 978-0-7582-9231-5
eISBN-10: 0-7582-9231-7
First Kensington Electronic Edition: September 2014

ISBN-13: 978-0-7582-9230-8
ISBN-10: 0-7582-9230-9
First Kensington Trade Paperback Printing: September 2014

10 9 8 7 6 5 4 3 2 1

Printed in the United States of America

For the "little kids," with love,

Judy, Bo, and Sarah

Staunch companions on the journey

CHAPTER 1

Bronwyn fitted a cigarette into her holder, and looked around for some gentleman to offer her a light. The Cellar was crowded with partiers, a crush of people elbowing one another, stepping on one another's feet, shouting to be heard over the din. There were never enough tables, and chairs were crammed together any which way. She had a flint lighter in her handbag, but she decided it wasn't worth trying to reach under her chair to drag it out. In any case, if it was smoke she wanted, an abundance of it hung in the air, billowing against the low ceiling, dimming the lights in their stained shades. Her dress would reek of it in the morning.

Fortunately, her maid was a wizard at dealing with that. And had plenty of experience.

Bronwyn leaned against the brick wall, crossing her silk-stockinged legs and brandishing the Bakelite holder like a scepter. Johnnie pushed his way toward her through the throng, holding their drinks aloft in his two hands and turning sideways to fit his bulk between the chairs. He grinned as he caught sight of her. He evaded the waving arms and tossing heads, managing somehow to set the cocktails down without spilling. He collapsed onto a chair that was much too small for him, and dashed at the perspiration dripping down his cheeks. "Gosh!" he cried. His voice was barely audible above the tinny plonk of the player piano's keys. He leaned close to make himself heard, enveloping Bronwyn in a gust of gin-scented breath. "I think half the town is down here!"

Bronwyn picked up her cocktail and eyed it, tipping it this way and that.

"It's a Fallen Angel," Johnnie bellowed. "That's your drink, isn't it? A Fallen Angel?"

"It doesn't look like one," Bronwyn said doubtfully. "Gin and lime and crème de menthe? It should be green."

"Well—it's sort of green." Johnnie peered at the cocktail. "Willy said it was a Fallen Angel."

Bronwyn shrugged. "Never mind," she said.

"What?"

She waved her hand, and took a sip of the drink. It wasn't a real Fallen Angel, though Willy, the barman, had tried to make up for the deficit of crème de menthe by adding sugar syrup. At least here at the Cellar she could trust the gin. As she had laughed to Johnnie the last time, they could trust the gin at the Cellar because Willy made it in his very own bathtub.

"Come on, Bron, let's cut a rug," Johnnie said. He tossed back his own drink, which was probably straight gin—Johnnie wasn't the discerning sort, which was why he was content to squire Bronwyn Morgan around the speakeasies of Port Townsend. He jumped to his feet and reached for her hand.

"I don't see where," she protested.

"We'll make room, over there in the corner. Come on, we'll put another nickel in the piano. Everybody wants to see you do the Black Bottom!"

Bronwyn polished off the drink, grimacing at the bite of rough gin and sour lime. The taste didn't really matter. It would have been nice to have a real Fallen Angel, like the ones people drank in New York and Seattle, but gin and dancing were why she had come to the Cellar. Gin, awkward dancing, loud voices, bad music, bad company—they irritated her enough to distract her from the other irritants in her life. She got to her feet, and Johnnie gripped her hand to pull her through the crowd.

People nodded to her and spoke her name as she wound among them. Most of them called her Bronwyn, because she was by far the youngest woman in the place. There were a few—men mostly—who called her Miss Morgan. They were the ones who would no doubt mention having seen her, stirring afresh the embers of her father's wrath. She smiled brazenly at each of them, and flourished the cigarette holder. When the Black Bottom began, she threw herself into the steps, making her skirt swirl to show the satin garters clasped around her thighs.

She liked the Black Bottom, because it had no rules. The dancer didn't have to touch her partner—in the case of Johnnie Johnson, this was preferable—and she was limited only by her own talent for movement. Bronwyn knew her personal faults very well, assisted in her understanding by her father's frequent reminders, but she also knew her strength, and it was dancing. The foxtrot, the rhumba, the swooping steps of the tango, all came as naturally to her as walking.

It was what had first drawn Preston to her, at the Bartletts' reception three years before. She had been dancing.

On that day, in the summer of 1920, she hadn't worn garters or carried a cigarette holder. She had dressed in the most modest of afternoon frocks, a drop-waisted georgette with a scarf hem and a lace-edged collar with long points. She had recently cut her hair in the Castle Bob, and her mother had allowed her a touch of lipstick. She was sixteen, but she was certain she looked at least eighteen. She had just been accepted into the Cornish School, and she was feeling very grown-up, a young woman with the world at her feet and a shining future.

Now, at nineteen, she understood that the younger Bronwyn had been as naive as a kitten. She had believed that an older man's attention, the shine of admiration in his eyes, the way he watched her every movement, meant he had fallen in love with her. And she had—dizzyingly, breathlessly, passionately—fallen in love with him. He was a decorated war hero. His family was even wealthier and more respectable than her own. His dancing made her feel like a creature made of cloud, swirling as weightlessly as a puff of mist.

She was older and wiser now, and neither condition brought her much joy. She swung into the hip-thrusting motions of the Black Bottom, knowing that her father hated this dance. He said it was because he didn't like girls flinging themselves about, but Bronwyn understood it was the sensuality that offended him. She hadn't known the Black Bottom when she was sixteen. She wouldn't have understood it.

Someone put another nickel into the piano, and a Charleston began. Without bothering to see if Johnnie joined her, Bronwyn began the dance. It took more space than the Black Bottom, but people stepped back to give her room. The rhythm swept her up. She was adept at the sliding kick-step, the shimmy, the coordination of hands and knees and feet. Her heeled pumps skimmed the floor, and her beaded dress shimmered. Johnnie tried to keep up, but his big body was awkward, and his efforts made her laugh. She knew every step, having seen all the films, with a pianist beneath the screen inventing tunes to match the dance. Bronwyn had invented a few of her own steps, too, which would no doubt soon show up at someone's debutante ball or engagement party.

Someone else would have to demonstrate them, though. She wouldn't be invited to these events. Her parents had fooled no one by sending her to Vancouver. No one in Port Townsend would mention the matter in the presence of Chesley and Iris Morgan, but everyone knew their daughter was ruined. No matter how frantically she danced, no matter how many Fallen Angels she drank, she couldn't pretend otherwise.

Still, she couldn't hate him. She had loved Preston Benedict. She was still in love with his memory.

*   *   *

In that faraway summer of 1920, everyone Bronwyn knew was giddy about the new decade and the unfolding of a peacetime era. Port Townsend was recovering from the collapse that had threatened the city twenty years before. Businessmen were growing fat on the boom in lumber sales, and planning their profits from the new paper mill. The more daring among them padded their incomes by importing Canadian liquor for the speakeasies in Seattle. The boys who made it safely home from the war were celebrated as heroes, and had their pick of Port Townsend beauties.

Bronwyn and her friends read *Vogue* and *Harper's Bazaar* and planned their debuts. They cut their hair and rolled their stockings, and tried, in secret, to learn to smoke cigarettes. They liked to think of themselves as daring, independent women of the new century, but in truth, they were very like their mothers. They understood the rules of their social circle. Though they cast off their corsets and shortened their dresses, their magical girlhoods were meant to end, inevitably, in fairy-tale weddings.

None of the girls gave much thought to what came after. There would be honeymoons. They were expected to know how to choose menus and entertain guests. They would learn to manage maids and cooks and laundresses. To Bronwyn and her friends, marriage was just a grown-up version of playing house.

Their fathers treated them like dolls on a shelf, to be seen and admired until they would, one day, be plucked down and settled on a different shelf. Their mothers watched over them like swans over their cygnets, guiding their steps, protecting their good names, eyeing the young men to sort out the ones with the best prospects. Both mothers and fathers believed, as their own parents had, that the less girls knew, the better off they were.

The girls grew up in blissful ignorance of their own physiology. They were told their monthly periods were the curse of women. No one explained why, or how they were connected to the great mystery.

Bronwyn's view of romance was more Jane Austen than D. H. Lawrence, more *Snow White* than *The Scarlet Letter*. The union of men and women was a misty, magical idea, a fantasy of white silk and flowers, of veils and pearls and wedding cakes. She knew nothing of the realities of flesh and blood, of passion and pain, or of treachery.

Such a lovely June day it had been, when Bronwyn and her friends Bessie and Clara clustered near the French doors of the Bartletts' ballroom, giggling and whispering together. Their mothers were nearby, but the girls were doing their best to ignore them.

Bessie nudged Bronwyn. "Don't you just love a man in uniform?" Bessie was wearing a dress with a high collar, to hide the reddish freckles that so embarrassed her. Bronwyn and Clara had found a recipe for her, a paste of rye and tartar and oil of roses, but it wasn't working.

Clara said, "The Bartletts invited all the officers up from Fort Worden." She blushed as she said it, and turned her back on the knot of young men gazing around the room.

Bronwyn looked past her at the reception line, where the Bartletts stood with their daughter Margaret. The party was in Margaret's honor, to signal the end of her debut year. Margaret had always been plain, but she looked almost pretty today, powdered and pressed and coiffed. The officers bowing over her hand did indeed look handsome, the whole crowd of them, with their shining boots and polished buttons. Bronwyn was about to say so when Bessie whispered, "Who is *that?*" and the others turned to look at the stranger just entering from the garden.

Time suspended for Bronwyn. The soldiers in their uniforms faded from her consciousness, vanquished by this new arrival. He paused in the doorway, and her heart paused with him.

The afternoon sun burnished his pale hair to gold. His suit was the latest cut, broad shoulders, pleated trousers, a vest of taupe silk. In his breast pocket, just peeking out so everyone could see it, was a notebook and pen. He was not particularly tall, but his features were finely cut, and his eyes—oh! Such a clear, pale blue, shining even across the crowded ballroom.

Bessie hissed in Bronwyn's ear, "D'you know who that is? That's the newspaperman! The columnist!"

"What columnist?" Bronwyn whispered back. Her mouth had gone dry, and her heart resumed its beat, thudding hotly beneath her silken frock.

"With the *Times*, silly." Bessie poked her with an elbow. "He writes 'Seattle Razz.' Everyone's reading it!"

"*He's* the one who writes 'Seattle Razz'? But he's so *young!*"

Bessie shrugged. "Not so young, I guess. I mean, he went to the war and everything. Of course he doesn't wear his uniform anymore, but Mama says he was a captain in the British Army. Has all sorts of medals and things."

"Oh . . ." Bronwyn gazed at him in astonishment. She had never seen a more appealing man. He came into the ballroom with a step that was modest, almost diffident, as if he wasn't sure anyone would notice him. He touched his hair in an absent way, smoothing his forelock back with one finger. It didn't stay, but fell down again over his forehead, a strand of gold gleaming above those ice-blue eyes.

Bronwyn could hardly breathe past the melting sensation in her breast.

"And," Bessie went on, parceling out information like sweets from a box, "he's one of the Seattle Benedicts. You know, the ones who have Benedict Hall. On Millionaire's Row."

"Oh . . ." Bronwyn said again. It wasn't like her to be wordless, or to lose her composure, but this man was nothing like the callow boys she knew, nor even like the grinning soldiers lined up on the opposite side of the ballroom like puppets. He was just— just—*perfect*.

She could hardly bear to watch him bow over Mrs. Bartlett's hand, then take Margaret's. Margaret gave him a coquettish smile, confident in her lace-and-chiffon afternoon frock, her drab hair caught up with loops of pearls.

Pain shot through Bronwyn at the idea that Preston Benedict might take a shine to Margaret Bartlett. Perhaps he would even

ask her parents if he could court her. She was the proper age,
after all. Her family name was impeccable. Worse, she was looking her best today.

Bronwyn felt a sudden and staggering sense of loss. It made no
sense, since she hadn't even met Preston Benedict, but she
yearned toward him nevertheless. He flashed a smile at stupid
Margaret before he put out his hand to Mr. Bartlett. Bronwyn
wanted to push her way through the crowd and seize his arm.

She knew what her mother would say about him. He was not
only too old to be introduced to a young lady who was not yet
out, but he was a newspaperman. Iris Morgan maintained that a
real lady appeared in the papers only three times in her life: at
her birth, at her marriage, and at her death. She might make an
exception for a debutante event, perhaps a ball or a fashionable
tea. She would never, ever approve of her daughter being mentioned in "Seattle Razz."

A small band, trumpet, saxophone, and piano, began to play
from an inner corner of the ballroom. Young men glanced around
in search of partners. George Bartlett, Margaret's younger
brother, started toward Bronwyn, but Iris Morgan, appearing as if
from nowhere, stepped between them. Though she blushed at
having to assert herself, she said, "No dancing, Bronwyn. Not
until you're out."

"But, *Mother!*" Bronwyn cried. "Bessie's dancing, look! And
Clara!"

"I don't think your father would like it," her mother said,
glancing around as if Chesley might show up at any moment.

"You let me dance at Clara's birthday party!"

"That wasn't public."

"Mother, please! Just let me dance with George. It's his house,
after all."

Iris hesitated, gazing at her daughter, lifting a hand to smooth
a wrinkle in her collar. "I just don't know . . . I'm afraid . . . ."

"Mo-*ther!* You're always afraid."

George reached them at that moment, saying brightly, "Good

afternoon, Mrs. Morgan. You look so lovely—you could be Bronwyn's sister!"

"George, shame on you." Iris colored, and gave an embarrassed titter. "Such flattery."

It could have been true, though. Bronwyn and her mother looked much alike. Their honey-brown hair was dressed in identical finger waves, firmly fixed with flaxseed gel. Their eyes were the same hazel, sparkling with flecks of gold. Iris's skin had grown soft around her chin and throat, but it was still fine-grained and clear.

Bronwyn took advantage of the awkward moment by putting out her white-gloved hand for George to take. "Just one dance, Mother," she said. "Listen, it's the new foxtrot! Please."

Iris didn't exactly give her permission, but she sighed, and as she pressed an uncertain hand to her embroidered bodice, the young people made their escape onto the dance floor.

George wasn't much of a dancer, but he was better than nothing. Bronwyn danced the foxtrot with him, then a one-step and the Castle Walk. She felt her mother's worried gaze on her, but she didn't look back for fear Iris would make her stop. When she saw Preston Benedict watching, she pretended not to notice, but she made her steps smoother, her turns swifter, the movements of her head and hands as graceful as she could. Her skirt fluttered gratifyingly around her ankles, and the narrow scarf around her throat rippled like a ribbon of cloud.

When Preston cut in, George was forced to give way. A slow waltz began, and Bronwyn, her heart fluttering into her throat, took special care not to catch her mother's anxious eye. She floated away in Preston's assured clasp, and knew in her bones that her life would never be the same again. Her fairy tale had begun.

In the bliss of gliding across the dance floor in his arms, of feeling his cheek brush her hair, in the enchantment of being chosen over every other girl in the room, Bronwyn Morgan forgot that every fairy tale has its dark side.

CHAPTER 2

The new automobile had a distinctive smell to it, a scent Margot couldn't name. She sniffed it curiously as Blake closed her door and climbed into the driving seat. As he pressed the starter, Margot settled herself against the mohair velour, and removed one glove to caress its silken texture. "Do you like it, Blake?"

"Do you mean the motorcar?"

"Yes."

He glanced at her in the rearview mirror, and reached up to adjust the angle. "Well, Dr. Margot," he said, his deep voice noncommittal. "It's certainly a change."

"Green!" she marveled. "I can hardly believe Father could make such a racy choice."

"It's elegant, don't you think? It's called a Phaeton. The steering wheel is solid walnut."

"Very chic."

"Yes. I believe it's quite up-to-date." Blake smiled at her in the mirror as he put the automobile in gear. He pulled out into Fourteenth Avenue, and didn't speak again until he had safely negotiated the turn. "I recommended the black, but Mr. Dickson wanted something different from the Essex. I believe he hopes Mrs. Edith will bring herself to ride in it."

"But she rode in the Essex, didn't she? After the accident, I mean?"

"Only to go to the cemetery. And later, Steilacoom."

Blake was being tactful. For more than a year, Margot's grieving mother had hardly set foot outside of Benedict Hall except to visit an empty grave. Everything had changed when she learned her younger son was alive. Nothing would do for her then but to go straight to the state hospital where Preston was being held. Margot and her father feared Edith would break down when she saw how badly Preston was burned, and when she grasped the truth of the terrible things he had done.

They had misjudged her.

Edith made regular visits to see her son until he was moved to a private sanatorium in Walla Walla. That was too far for a day trip, whether by motorcar or by train. Edith was planning to visit, and frequently spoke of it. Margot doubted this was a good idea, but it was the only thing her mother took any interest in. She sent Preston packages from home, she bought him clothes and toiletries, and she kept his place set at the dining table in Benedict Hall, ready for the day of his return.

Margot suspected Edith would have responded the same way if Preston had gone to jail, which was his only remaining alternative. Edith had an infinite capacity for denial where her youngest son was concerned.

Blake interrupted her thoughts. "Do you like the new motorcar, Dr. Margot?"

"I do," Margot said. "It's quieter than the Essex. The upholstery is beautiful."

"Indeed. Very handsome."

"But green! It seems like a symbol for something. A sea change, perhaps."

"It has been a year for change," he said mildly.

"Blake, you're a master of understatement."

"Yes, ma'am," he said gravely, and Margot chuckled.

Curious eyes followed them as the sparkling automobile rolled at a majestic pace into the East Madison neighborhood. Small boys stared, and some pulled off their caps in awe. Women with shopping bags turned their heads. Blake behaved as if he didn't notice, but Margot smiled and waved, winning tentative nods. There was no room to pull over in front of the Women and Infants Clinic, so Blake was forced to stop the Cadillac in the middle of the road. An elderly Negro woman came out of the house across the street to gape at it. Blake tipped his driving cap to her, and she dipped a rather elegant half-curtsy, as if he were royalty. Even Blake had to chuckle at that.

Sarah Church came dashing out to meet them, her nurse's cape rippling around her. Blake opened the door of the Cadillac, and as she climbed in, he relieved her of the case of medicines she carried. She dimpled at him, and pressed her hand to his arm before she climbed into the back beside Margot.

She perched gingerly on the mohair upholstery, as if afraid her slight weight might mar its smooth surface. "Dr. Benedict," she breathed. "Your new motorcar is—I mean, it's just—"

"Isn't it, though? I think so, too, and so does your neighbor across the street." She smiled at Sarah, and patted the seat. "Come now, lean back. I've been assured we can't hurt the material by sitting on it. Let's enjoy this splendiferous ride while we gird our loins for battle."

"Are we going into battle?"

"I'm afraid so. I'm told Mrs. Ryther is something of a terror."

"It's hard to imagine that, considering the work she does."

"Perhaps you have to be a terror to take on such burdens. How many children does she have now?"

"Over a hundred, I believe."

Margot shook her head in wonder. "I'd be cranky if I had so many children to watch over. I suppose if she's difficult we should make allowances."

Margot leaned back, and gazed out the window at the sparkling day. It was good to be outside the hospital for a few hours, to be driving through the green-boughed streets of Seattle. Spring blossomed all around her, sprawling rhododendrons blazing pink and red, azaleas flashing their starry flowers against the layered greens of fir and pine, cedar and vine maple. Every year, May surprised her with its heady scents and glowing colors, as if the rains of winter had erased its memory.

Nineteen twenty-three was off to a fine start in every way, as far as Margot was concerned. Benedict Hall hummed with life, and it was hard sometimes to know who was where.

Cousin Allison was always in motion, rushing off to her University classes, racing back to snatch up her tennis racket or a stack of books. The family's telephone rang even more often than Margot's, almost always for Allison. She had taken to flopping on the floor, so the maids had to step over her legs, until Blake ordered a chair brought from the small parlor so the girl could sit properly for her endless conversations. He had issued strict instructions to the staff that they were not to eavesdrop on these telephone calls, but no one believed those orders had any effect at all.

Little Louisa had begun to walk in earnest, toddling at top speed wherever she went. Nurse followed with her hands outstretched, ready to pick her up when she fell, and trying to prevent her tumbling down the long staircase. Everyone in Benedict Hall doted so on the baby that Nurse had put her foot down about naps and bedtime and what she called "too much excitement." The excitement, Margot thought, came mostly from Louisa herself, who found entertainment in everything she saw, from the Irish maids' freckles to Hattie's long apron strings, which she liked to use for balance as she negotiated the kitchen on her fat, unsteady legs.

Frank had settled nicely into living in the Benedict household, and Hattie, delighted at his young man's appetite, exerted herself to make his favorite meals. Since he preferred simple dishes, mashed potatoes and roasted meats, Hattie's skills were shown to better advantage than when she strove for the *haute cuisine* Edith had ordered in the past. Ramona was too busy with the baby to fuss much over menus, and Edith had lost interest, with the result that the food in Benedict Hall was both plainer and tastier than it had ever been.

And Margot, somewhat to her surprise, loved being Frank's wife.

She thought about this as they turned north on Stone Way toward the Ryther Child Home. She had feared she wasn't suited for marriage. She feared giving up her independence, and she worried about diluting the single-mindedness that carried her through the daily challenges of her medical practice. She had found, however, that coming home to Frank in the evenings, sitting close to him as the family gathered to listen to the cabinet radio in the small parlor, climbing the stairs with him at night, sometimes even having time for breakfast with him in the morning, strengthened her. She felt as if she had a foundation from which she could accomplish nearly anything. She was Dr. Benedict all day, and at night if she was called out to a patient. But in the evenings and in the early mornings, at rare social events or when she and Frank slipped out alone, she was Mrs. Frank Parrish, and she liked it very much indeed.

She came out of her reverie as Blake pulled the Cadillac up in front of a large brick building. It had three floors stretching to either side of a formal entrance. Flowers and shrubs filled the front garden, surrounded by a picket fence. Ranks of clotheslines stretched the length of one side of the building. Four surprisingly small children were taking down dry clothes and piling them into a basket. They turned to goggle at the automobile, and at the people emerging from it and turning up the walk.

They did make a sight, Margot supposed. She was taller than most women, and she was carrying her medical bag. Sarah Church, with the box of medicines in her arms, was petite, and very pretty, with bright brown eyes and thick curling hair pinned up beneath her nurse's cap. Blake, leaning on his cane, insisted on accompanying them, saying he wasn't sure just what they would find inside.

And of course, Blake and Sarah were Negroes, while Margot wasn't. That alone would cause a stir.

They paused at the entrance to the house. Sarah said, "I did make a telephone call to Mrs. Ryther to tell her we were coming, but we might be a little early."

Margot nodded, and knocked briskly on the door.

It opened immediately. A young girl, aged fourteen or fifteen, wearing a voluminous printed apron over a cotton housedress, said in rehearsed fashion, "Hello, and welcome to the Ryther Home."

"Hello," Margot said. "Thank you." She smiled at the girl. "I'm Dr. Benedict, and this is Nurse Church, from the Women and Infants Clinic. And Mr. Blake, our driver."

"Yes?" The girl didn't move, and Margot wondered if her job was to keep undesirables from crossing the threshold.

"I believe Mrs. Ryther is expecting us."

A sudden, childish screech from somewhere in the house made the girl flinch, but she didn't budge, though more shrieks followed, punctuated by the crash of something like a stack of aluminum saucepans. "Mother Ryther is busy at the moment," the girl said carefully.

"It sounds like it," Margot said.

The girl's composure cracked just a little. She gave a small shrug, and pleated her apron with her fingers. "It's bath day. The little ones never like it."

Sarah moved forward, and Margot stepped to the side, out of her way. Sarah had spent the past year working with mothers and babies, and Margot was happy to let her take control of this interview. "May we come in?" Sarah asked directly.

The girl in the apron gazed at her, her mouth a little open. Probably she had never spoken to a Negress before. In this neighborhood, colored people were rare, unless they were servants. The Ryther Home couldn't afford servants. Mrs. Olive Ryther—everyone called her Mother Ryther, even the newspapers—cared for her charges with just three matrons to assist her. She was famed for wringing contributions out of every business and charity in the city, and even this sprawling house had been built by soliciting donations. "Buy a brick for the Ryther Home," had been the slogan. Margot was certain her father had paid for several.

Sarah was accustomed to a variety of reactions to her dark skin, and she was more accepting of them than Margot. She said now, in a matter-of-fact tone, "Mrs. Ryther will want to speak to Dr. Benedict. It's about vaccinations. And money."

The girl's gaze drifted from Sarah's youthful face to Blake's lined and grizzled one. She said in a distracted way, "I guess. I just don't—"

"Why don't you go and ask?" Sarah said. "We'll wait here. But do tell Mrs. Ryther it's Dr. Benedict, from the Women and Infants Clinic."

Margot added, with a touch of asperity, "And Nurse Church."

At the girl's puzzled expression, Sarah said gently, "That's me. I'm Nurse Church."

"Oh! I didn't know—that is, I thought because—" The girl's cheeks flamed an uncomfortable red, and she took a step back. "Wait, please." She shut the door with a bit more emphasis than needed, and Sarah cast Margot a rueful glance.

Blake gave his deep chuckle. "Like the Magi," he said. "Three strangers at the door."

"And bearing unfamiliar gifts," Margot said.

They stood on the sunny porch for several minutes, listening to the racket from inside the house. Occasionally, they heard the slam of the back door, and quarreling voices coming and going, presumably with more laundry to hang. "How do you suppose," Margot said, "these people manage a hundred children?"

"Strictly," Sarah said, and Margot saw she was serious. It made sense, she supposed, but she wondered what this Mother Ryther would be like.

Another girl, slightly older, opened the door again, and stood back to let them come in. "Mother Ryther will see you now," she said. She wore an apron, too, a short white one. Beneath it she was neatly dressed in a shirtwaist and a skirt that was a bit too long for fashion. Her hair was pinned up behind her head, and she wore wire-rimmed spectacles. "I'm Maisy Chisholm," she said. "Mother Ryther's assistant."

"How do you do, Miss Chisholm?" Margot said. "I'm Dr. Benedict, and this is Nurse Church. Mr. Blake is our driver."

The three of them trooped into the cool shade of the hallway, and the girl said, "This way, please, Dr. Benedict." She led the way down a corridor.

Margot glanced around curiously as they walked. The floor was bare wood, well polished. There were several doors, all closed. The noise went on unabated, and from somewhere came the aroma of soup on the boil. A carpeted staircase led straight up the middle of the house.

Their guide, seeing Margot's interest, pointed to it. "The dormitories are upstairs," she said. "These are playrooms and sickrooms down here."

"Sickrooms?"

"Yes. We separate children who get sick."

"That's wise, Miss Chisholm."

The girl executed a most superior sniff. "Of course, Doctor. Mother Ryther has been taking care of children for a long time."

Margot suppressed a smile. Maisy Chisholm couldn't be more than seventeen, but she was as sure of herself as any adult, or at least she behaved as if she was. Margot wondered if she had been one of Mother Ryther's orphans.

The young woman stopped and knocked on an open door. She said, "Mother Ryther, here they are." She stood aside, and gestured for them to go in.

A battered desk filled most of the small room, with two spindly, mismatched chairs facing it. Bookshelves and glass-fronted cabinets, all stuffed with books and magazines and what appeared to be photograph albums, crowded the rest of the space, and an enormous ledger rested on the desk's surface. Seated behind it was a woman much older than Margot had expected. She had a long face, sharp dark eyes wreathed in wrinkles, and gray hair falling out of its pins in a way that suggested she had put it up in a hurry. She held a fountain pen poised over the ledger, and a sheaf of paper in her other hand. She laid both down, and waved her ink-stained hand toward the mismatched chairs. "There are only two, I'm afraid. No room in here for any more."

Miss Chisholm introduced them, one by one, applying their correct titles. Mother Ryther scowled at each of them in turn, peering through a pair of round spectacles. She reminded Margot of someone, but she couldn't think yet who it was. Blake stood to one side, leaving the chairs to Margot and Sarah. Miss Chisholm withdrew, closing the door of the cramped office behind her.

"So," Mother Ryther said. "You want to examine my children. Inspect my home."

It was spoken like a challenge. Margot tried to choose her words carefully. "What we want, Mrs. Ryther," she said, "is to apply for funds on your behalf. They'll be supplied through Sheppard-Towner, but there are requirements to be met."

"Oh, yes, Sheppard-Towner," Mother Ryther said. Her lips pulled down, drawing deep lines around her mouth. "The Better Babies Act."

Margot disliked the jocular label. It was misleading, for one thing. The Sheppard-Towner Act wasn't just about babies. It provided aid and assistance to mothers as well as their children. The Women and Infants Clinic could not have existed without it, and though the clinic was barely a year old, Sarah and the physicians who assisted her had more work than they could handle. It was Sarah who had called the Ryther Home, and its unvaccinated children, to Margot's attention.

Sarah spoke in her pragmatic way. "Government money will help to provide medicines and supplies, and educational materials as well. I'm told you place a high value on education for your children."

With a deliberate move of her heavy body, rather like a great ferry turning toward a dock, Mother Ryther faced Sarah, and contemplated her for a moment that went on slightly too long for courtesy. Margot was just drawing breath to remonstrate when the old woman spoke at last. "Nurse Church," she said. "Fully trained, I presume?"

Sarah met the old woman's gaze with a level and unwavering one of her own. "Of course. I manage the Women and Infants Clinic."

"You're a properly registered nurse?"

Margot bristled, and drew breath again, but Sarah said, without rancor, "I'm a graduate of the University of Washington, Mrs. Ryther."

"That can't have been easy for someone like you."

It was too much. Margot rapped, "Nurse Church has my full confidence."

Mother Ryther ignored her. "I've never met a nurse who was a Negress."

Sarah's dimple flashed. "I must send you a biography of Mary Eliza Mahoney, then. She's also a nurse. My mother studied with her."

"Hmm." Olive Ryther gave a sharp nod, as if granting her approval. Margot saw laughter in Sarah's eyes and in her fleeting dimple. She herself couldn't see the humor.

Mother Ryther turned next to Blake, and Margot had to press her lips together to keep from protesting this examination of her staff. The interview was not going as she had planned. "Mr. Blake," Mother Ryther said. "Why did you feel the need to come inside? I believe the usual custom is for the driver to wait with the automobile, especially one as fine as your Cadillac."

Blake's deep voice reverberated in the small room. "Ma'am," he said, "these two ladies are in my care, just as your children are in yours. Meaning no disrespect, but we didn't know what we would find within your walls. We heard a good deal of shouting from the front door."

For the first time, the flicker of a smile twitched at the old woman's mouth. "Bath day," she said. "And housecleaning. Squabbles and stains seem to go together."

Margot leaned forward, and picked up her medical bag with a

decisive gesture. "All that's needed, Mrs. Ryther," she said, "is for us to inspect your dormitories, your kitchen, and your bath facilities. We want to assess the needs of your children. Vaccinations will be required, of course. Nurse Church will handle the paperwork."

Mother Ryther gazed at her through her spectacles. "I don't hold with vaccinations."

"Why?"

"Sticking my children with needles? Putting God-knows-what into their little bodies?"

"It's 1923, Mrs. Ryther," Margot said, striving for patience. She could feel the clock's swift ticking, the relentless passage of her one free afternoon. "Medicine has advanced a great deal, which you must know. Diphtheria, smallpox, whooping cough—our children don't need to suffer these anymore."

"Newfangled," Mrs. Ryther said.

"Hardly," Margot said. "Their efficacy is well proven."

"It doesn't make sense, injecting germs into children."

"You misunderstand," Margot said. "Vaccines are inactivated viruses and bacteria. They've been used for thirty years and more. I can send you the research, if you like. In the meantime, the governor supports our work, and wants your children to benefit as the ones at the Clinic do."

Mother Ryther was clearly an expert at the long, considering stare. She favored Margot with one now, and Margot's foot began to tap in irritation. Finally, the old woman said, "Dr. Benedict, the governor is a good man, but he doesn't know what's best for my children."

"No, he doesn't." This was Sarah, speaking crisply. Mother Ryther's eyebrows lifted. "But you turn to donations and assistance when you need them, don't you." It wasn't a question.

"It's good for the community to help," Mother Ryther said.

"No doubt," Margot said. "The question is, do you want us to help as well? If not, perhaps we should waste no more of your time." To underscore her point, she stood up, her bag in her hand. Beside her, Sarah also stood, though she left the heavy box of supplies on the floor.

Mother Ryther pointed to the box. "What's in there?"

Sarah seemed not to share Margot's impatience. She answered in detail, listing the contents of her box and ticking the items off on her slender fingers. "Thermometers. Two stethoscopes. A supply of vaccines and serums for common childhood illnesses."

"We can test any children you think are at risk," Margot put in. "We should also test for tuberculosis."

"What do you usually do about medical attention?" Sarah asked.

"What any other mother does," Mother Ryther said with asperity. "I call a doctor."

"Can you pay your physicians?"

"We trade," Mother Ryther said, with no evidence of embarrassment. "Milk and eggs and vegetables."

Margot had taken her share of such "trade," especially in the early days of her private clinic. Some of the offerings that had come her way were less than helpful, but she had accepted them just the same.

"Well, Mrs. Ryther," Sarah said, brusque and efficient now, as if the matter were settled. "Your children will fare better with preventive care than waiting until they're ill to see a doctor."

"And the government will pay."

"The government will help. But applications need to be made."

The old woman picked up her pen and toyed with it, glancing from Sarah to Blake to Margot, evidently in no hurry to make a decision.

Margot said, "The vaccinations will be required. There will be no money without them."

Mother Ryther's eyes flicked down toward the ledger on her desk. Margot could see now she was in the process of managing bills. Surely this woman felt the pressure of time just as she did.

Mother Ryther said, "And who is going to give these vaccinations? This nurse?"

"Nurse Church has been doing this work for some time now, Mrs. Ryther. We're lucky to have her. Her skills are excellent."

"Hmm. I suppose we'll see." Mother Ryther put her hands on her desk and pushed herself to her feet. She was wearing a long dress with a high collar, and when she stepped in front of the desk, Margot saw old-fashioned button-up boots beneath it. She moved stiffly, and her hand moved to her back, then dropped self-consciously to her side. As she approached the door, Blake opened it, and gave one of his small, formal bows. Mother Ryther, seeing this, raised her eyebrows at Margot once again, as if to warn her she wouldn't be charmed into compliance.

A new odor struck Margot at the top of the staircase of the Ryther Home. It reminded her a little of the hospital smell, that miasma of disinfectant and medicine, floor wax and bleach. In this case it was overlaid with the sort of aroma she associated with bodies. Young bodies, big and small, clean and very likely not-so-clean, healthy and—at least some of them—ill. Her nose twitched, and when she glanced down at Sarah, she saw Sarah's wide, delicate nostrils flutter. The noise was muted now—she could only suppose the bath day crisis had passed—but the house was full to the brim with the sounds of children.

"Usually most of the children are at school," Mother Ryther said over her shoulder. She walked steadily, but with a side-to-side gait as if her feet hurt her, or perhaps it was her hips. She was too old for such work, Margot thought. But who else would take on such responsibility?

"Today is a holiday," Mother Ryther said, "so we moved up bath day to keep them busy." She paused at a door. A torrent of voices poured out when she opened it, but when Mother Ryther put her head around the doorjamb, the room fell quiet. She clicked her tongue, once, the way Hattie sometimes did at Benedict Hall, and then withdrew, closing the door. She seemed not to notice the tide of sound rising again as they walked on.

"You may already know that we require all our children to stay in school until the age of fourteen. The boys learn a trade, and the girls enroll in business school. We rarely accept pregnant girls, because fortunately there are other places for them to go.

Our mission—" She stopped again to open a door. In this room there was only a murmur of conversation in light feminine voices. A girl greeted her, and she nodded, and closed the door again. "Our mission," she repeated, as she led them onward down the corridor, "is to give orphaned or abandoned children the same opportunity in life as those who grow up with their own parents."

She paused before a double door, behind which came the sounds of small children at play, mixed with the wails of at least one baby. With her hand on the knob, Mother Ryther said, "I believe these are the children you should meet first. They're the ones with the greatest need, because they're so young."

"How do you find them?" Sarah asked.

"Mostly," Mother Ryther said, her voice softening, easing into a tone of resignation and sorrow, "our children find us. Infants are sometimes left on our doorstep. Occasionally, the hospitals send newborns, either because they've been abandoned or because the mother died in childbirth." Margot winced at this. "Once in a while a poor mother comes in person, and either leaves her children, or takes up residence with us if she has no place else to go."

It was the first time she had spoken with any emotion, and she gave a slight shake of her head, as if to deny the hint of weakness. As she pushed the doors open, Sarah and Margot exchanged a glance. Blake, close behind them, with the box of supplies balanced on his hip, cleared his throat.

Mother Ryther cast a warning eye back at him. "Men are not generally allowed here," she said. "Some of our older girls help out here in the nursery, and we want them protected."

"Will you accept my voucher for Mr. Blake's character?" Margot asked solemnly.

"I will. This time." The wrinkled lips pulled down again. "Come in now, and meet my youngest children." Mother Ryther went into the room, and held the doors wide for the three visitors to pass through.

Margot's experience of nurseries was of two extremes. At Benedict Hall, little Louisa and her nurse dwelt in a beribboned haven of pink and cream silk, of puffy quilts and tufted pillows and pastel flocked wallpaper. At Seattle General Hospital, the nursery was all white, with cribs of white-painted iron, bleached sheets and pillowcases, nurses in long white aprons and starched caps. Only the floor was dark, the uniform brown of the linoleum that covered every hospital floor.

Here, in the Ryther Home, her first impression was of unrelenting drabness. Cribs and cots lined the walls, each covered in blankets clearly handed down from an earlier time, and washed until their colors had melded into one vague gray. The walls were dingy, though the house was only three years old. The curtains, hanging dispiritedly from their rods, were a sallow beige, and the linoleum floor was also beige. A bucket of diapers soaking in Fels-Naptha stood in one corner, its distinctive smell permeating the warm air.

The only color came from the children themselves. Margot counted fourteen of them, their hair every shade from blond, to red, to a curling head of hair as black as Sarah's own. There were no Negro children, but there were two that must, Margot thought, be Indian. The youngest was standing in a crib, the source of the wailing she had heard from the corridor. Tears ran down the child's cheeks, and its nose ran copiously.

Two teenaged girls in printed aprons were ferrying children back and forth from an attached bathroom, wrapping the clean ones in towels, seizing the reluctant remainders to work their clothes off and get them into the bath. It was obvious they had their hands full, but when the visitors came in, they lifted the current wet ones out of the bath and carried them to Mother Ryther. Four older children, five or six years of age, trailed behind them. Others, several who looked to be about four, and one silent, slow-moving child of about three, wandered aimlessly through a litter of toys and blankets. The remains of lunch were stacked on a sideboard, and a counter held a stack of boiled and folded diapers next to an enormous jar filled with nickel-plated safety pins.

The room felt chaotic to Margot. She drew a breath, unsure where to begin. She heard wheezing from somewhere, and it distracted her as she tried to locate the sufferer.

Sarah crossed the room with a quick, unapologetic step, smiling in friendly fashion to the two older girls as she passed them. She walked straight to the crib, and gathered the howling baby into her arms. From the pocket of her cape she produced a huge white handkerchief, and began scrubbing the child's face of tears and mucus.

One of the girls said defensively, "She cries a lot. I think she misses her ma."

Sarah said, "She should be held when she cries."

The girl said, "Don't do 'er any good to spoil 'er."

"It doesn't do any good to break her heart, either." Sarah settled the child against her, tucking the little head under her chin as if it were the most natural thing in the world. The baby clung to her with both arms and both legs, shuddering as her sobs began to subside.

Mother Ryther stood in the very center of the room, her arms folded. "That one came a week ago," she said. "A policeman brought her. He found her wandering down in the Tenderloin, and nobody to claim her."

Margot heard Blake draw a sharp, painful breath. She felt the same sorrow, but like Mother Ryther, she had learned long ago to discipline her feelings. Pity wouldn't help these abandoned children. Sarah's instinctive caretaking would. And medical attention, which was what Margot had to offer.

"I assume you deal with louse infestations, obvious infections?" she asked.

"Doctor," Mother Ryther said. "I've been taking care of babies for longer than you've been alive. The answer to your question is, Of course."

Margot accepted this without argument, though she could have cited a hundred cases in which years of experience seemed to amount to little. She turned to Blake. "Could you set the box of things on that counter, Blake? I may as well start with this child, and work up to the older ones."

She turned as she spoke, to indicate the area she meant, but

Blake was staring into a corner, his lips parted as if he had been about to speak, but was distracted.

Margot, another instruction dying on her lips, followed the direction of his gaze. Her heart gave a sudden lurch.

The child crouched near the wall. He held a toy in each hand, and he was staring up at the strangers with an intent expression at odds with the childish softness of his features. Two, Margot thought he must be. Certainly no older than three. His eyes were a clear, translucent blue, and his hair was a pale ash blond, almost white. Nearly transparent.

It was a thing Margot remembered about her youngest brother when he was small, the silvery color of his hair. The crystalline color of his eyes had never changed, even when he was an adult. The two together, and the shape of the child's chin, the silhouette of his head, made her shiver.

This little one could have been the identical twin of Preston Benedict when he was tiny. For long seconds Margot and Blake stared at him.

Sarah interrupted them by carrying the baby forward and laying it on a blanket on the counter, beginning to strip off its ill-fitting and stained shirt so Margot could begin her examination. Margot blinked, and made herself look away from the toddler in the corner. She took the stethoscope Sarah was holding out to her, and fitted the earpieces into her ears while Sarah unpinned the baby's wet diaper. The little girl's bottom and belly were red with rash.

Margot turned to her work. It was coincidence, of course. Preston had put the idea in their heads with his claims of a child. They would have known if it was true. Someone would have come to them. The Benedict name—and wealth—had that effect.

With the earpieces of her stethoscope in her ears, she bent to listen to the baby's heart and lungs. There was no time for pointless speculation. She had work to do.

CHAPTER 3

"Your eyes," Preston had said, "are so unusual. It looks as if someone sprinkled gold dust in them."

His white smile included both Bronwyn and Iris. They had withdrawn to one of the small round tables in the Bartletts' parlor, where the buffet was laid out with a grand silver tea service. Tiered plates held sandwiches and cakes. Iris had been anxiously twisting her handkerchief when their waltz ended, but Preston had returned Bronwyn to her mother with a respectful bow, and now was charming both of them, bringing cups of punch and a saucer of finger sandwiches.

Iris said in a voice so diffident it was barely audible, "Thank you, Captain Benedict. Please do sit down with us."

"Call me Preston, please, Mrs. Morgan. I took off the uniform months ago."

He pulled up a chair and sat down. Iris said, "I'm sure your parents are so very glad you're home safe."

"So they say," he said, with a light laugh that made the golden lock of his hair flutter above his eyebrows. He touched his pocket, where the pen and notepad were unobtrusively displayed. "I believe my father is relieved that I'm gainfully employed once again."

"Your column," Bronwyn said. Her cheeks felt warm, and she feared she was unbecomingly flushed. She picked up the cup of cold punch and took a sip.

"Do you read it?" he asked, with a sudden focus on her that made her cheeks feel even warmer. She bobbed her head, afraid of saying something silly. "That's marvelous, Miss Morgan. I do hope you enjoy it."

"Oh, yes," she breathed. "Yes, very much."

"How kind." He smiled into her eyes, and her heart fluttered in response.

Iris gave a small, discreet cough. "I was surprised that Anabel Bartlett invited the press to Margaret's party."

Preston's regard returned to her, and a faint, charming line appeared in his smooth brow. "Don't you approve, Mrs. Morgan? Gosh, I'm sorry about that. I assure you, I always do my best to keep 'Seattle Razz' respectful. This is such a *chic* event, don't you think?"

"Well—I suppose—"

"Oh, yes, Mother, it is," Bronwyn said suddenly. "Everything straight from Emily Post, right down to the sandwiches." She pointed to the ones on the plate in the center of the table. They were perfectly and quite unnaturally symmetrical, with paper-thin slices of cucumber arranged between buttered slices of bread. The crusts had been neatly cut off, and Bronwyn could imagine the leftover bits of sandwich lying around on the counter in the Bartletts' enormous kitchen. She wondered if the servants got to eat them, or if they were just thrown out.

Preston chuckled. "I keep a copy of *Etiquette* on my desk at the paper's offices," he said in a confiding way. "Although I admit there's more news when a hostess defies the rules than when she follows them to the letter!"

At this they were all smiling, exchanging confidential glances. Bronwyn felt infinitely sophisticated at that moment, she and her pretty mother sitting at a private table with the newspaperman, sharing an inside jest. He was not wearing gloves. When he put out his hand to pick up his cup, she followed the gesture, drawn by the even texture of his skin, the masculine shape of his fingers, the fine golden hairs that marked his wrist below snow-white cuffs. Her stomach contracted strangely as she remembered the feel of that cool, strong hand pressed against her back, guiding her in the steps of the waltz. The fabric of her dress was so thin it was as if his palm had touched her bare skin. He had breathed into her ear, "You dance like an angel, Miss Morgan!" and she had utterly, absolutely, believed him.

She said, "You won't find broken rules in Mrs. Bartlett's home, Captain Benedict. You'll have to dig up something else to write about. Do you want to hear the latest gossip?"

"Bronwyn!" her mother said. "Captain Benedict doesn't want to hear childish tales."

Bronwyn gave her mother a slow blink, lowering her eyelids in a deliberate way that told Iris the use of "childish" had irritated her. Iris shifted, pulling back slightly in her chair.

If Preston noticed this brief familial conflict, his face didn't reveal it. He said, with a confiding air, "Mrs. Morgan, truly, I love tales of all kinds! We newspapermen deal in stories, big and small."

His smile was an irresistible combination of shyness, as if he wasn't sure of his reception, and confidence, as if he believed in himself no matter what. Bronwyn watched her mother, normally so hesitant and suspicious, dissolve before his charm like a bit of ice caught in a sunbeam. He was terribly suave, she thought. It was no wonder the society dames of Seattle gave him *entrée* into their majestic homes, awarded him early notice of their announcements, and even told him their secrets. She supposed he knew many secrets, but was much too well bred to reveal them.

She felt, even then, as if she was meant to meet him. When he asked if he could escort them home, her mother and herself, she felt envious eyes on the back of her neck as she took his left arm and her mother his right. Bronwyn walked out with her head high, her feet as light as if she trod on clouds. She pretended not

to notice that the other girls—and their simmering mothers—
were watching as Captain Preston Benedict handed her into his
gleaming black Essex motorcar, and climbed in to sit opposite
the ladies, his Homburg poised on his lap. The driver, a tall
Negro who had taken off his cap and bowed to them as they approached, closed the door behind them, then got into the driving
seat and started the engine.

Preston said, "Can you direct Blake to your home, Mrs. Morgan?"

"Oh! Oh, yes, thank you, Captain Benedict. Just turn left
here, then right on Lawrence, and left on Monroe. We're at the
top of the hill."

"Of course," he said, and relayed her instructions to the driver,
as if he either couldn't hear Iris's soft voice, or as if he was trained
not to listen.

They all settled back to enjoy the stately ride up the hill. The
sun was setting behind them, gilding the snowcapped Olympics
as well as Preston Benedict's golden hair. Bronwyn said impul-
sively, "You must stay for dinner, Captain Benedict!"

Her mother said hastily, "Now, Bronwyn, you mustn't be
gauche. It's been a lovely afternoon, but I'm sure Captain Benedict . . . that is, of course you would be most welcome, Captain,
but you have such a long—that is to say—how will you get back
to Seattle?"

In his habitual boyish gesture, Preston pushed his forelock
back with one finger. "Well, actually, Mrs. Morgan," he said, then
stopped. "No, no, I wouldn't want to put you out, but—"

"I know!" Bronwyn cried. "You came over on the ferry, didn't
you? One of the Mosquito Fleet. The boat won't leave until the
morning. You can't go home until tomorrow!"

Her mother's fingers found her hand beneath the cover of
their skirts, and pinched. Bronwyn subsided, but Preston said,
with a small, self-deprecating gesture, "As it happens, the paper
is putting me up at the Bishop. Blake has a small room as well,
naturally."

The words were innocuous, mere courtesies, but Bronwyn understood what they meant. Preston wanted to spend more time

with them. With *her*. They had been fated to meet. She *felt* the connection between them, like a silvery strand of spider silk stretching from one to the other, and she could tell—she knew it had to be true—that he felt it, too, that he could no more bear to be separated from her, when they had just found each other, than she could.

Her mother gave a genteel cough. "Captain Benedict, of course we would be delighted to have you join us for dinner if you don't have other plans."

He touched his forelock again, then dropped his hand as if he hadn't meant to do it, as if perhaps someone—his own mother?—had told him to stop. It was endearing to watch. "So good of you, Mrs. Morgan," he murmured. "Of course, I have Blake to think of . . ."

Bronwyn sighed over such kindness, this noble concern for his servant. She had met so many men who gave no thought to anyone's comfort but their own, who would never for a moment put an evening's pleasure at risk for the sake of someone like this Blake.

There was a brief moment of tension, during which Bronwyn knew precisely what was running through her mother's mind. The driver was a Negro. Their cook, Mrs. Andrew, was a prickly, unpredictable sort of woman. She tended to bully everyone in the house except Daddy, and most particularly Mother. Bronwyn couldn't guess how Mrs. Andrew might react to Blake, and she supposed her mother couldn't, either. For that matter, she couldn't predict how Daddy would react to an unexpected guest, though someone from the Benedict family would surely command his respect.

She held her breath, awaiting her mother's ruling. She was uncomfortably aware of the slight stiffening of the driver's neck, the resolute way he kept his eyes forward, guiding the shining motorcar down Lawrence toward their own street.

Iris said at length, in a way Bronwyn knew took some courage, "Naturally, Captain, your driver is welcome to take his supper with our cook and the maids. I'm quite sure—" She coughed again, a tiny, rabbity sound. Bronwyn loved her mother, but she couldn't deny she was that sort of woman, shy and skittish as a bunny. She said, "I'm sure Mrs. Andrew will be delighted."

There was no certainty in Iris Morgan's voice. Bronwyn hoped neither man would notice.

Preston had been pleased with himself after this exchange. He had seen Blake's neck go rigid, and he could imagine this fluttery woman would think he was embarrassed. He had handled the whole thing with aplomb, he thought, painting himself as the concerned employer, the gentleman who put his servant's needs above his own pleasures. Of course, he didn't give a damn where Blake ate his dinner. He didn't give a damn if Blake had dinner at all. But that was something these two didn't need to know.

Idly, reflexively, he pushed his forelock out of his eyes, and saw the girl, the tender, lovely child, drinking in his every move.

The mother did, too, and that intrigued him.

It was the sort of thing he loved above all else. It was gratifying to be recognized as a hero, a champion of the underdog, a successful and popular man unaware of his own charm. The matrons and debutantes of Seattle saw him somewhat differently, because, through his column, he had power over them. They were careful around him, exerting themselves to please him, but wary.

These two, the mother and the daughter, were different. They were provincial, naturally, but their naiveté had its own appeal. It wasn't bad for a fellow to be treated with respect, after all. A man, making his way in the world with only his wits and his talent, deserved that.

It was what the pater didn't understand. It had been months since Preston went to his father's offices to share the good news of "Seattle Razz," but Dickson's reaction still rankled. It festered in Preston's heart, reminding him of his father's years-long preference for his older sister over him. It didn't matter that he had proved Dickson wrong, that "Seattle Razz" was a great success. Dickson Benedict found his younger son a disappointment, and he barely bothered to hide the fact. He couldn't grasp the impact such a column—wry, pointed, always up-to-date, with the most modern sensibility—could have on the city's society.

The mater admired it, but then, Edith Benedict had always been predisposed toward her youngest son. She understood him. He was her favorite, and naturally he enjoyed that, though she was a little obvious about it. Preston caught the looks that passed between his sister and older brother, or even between his sister and his father, looks that made him grit his teeth.

He had to admit his mother was not the only person in Benedict Hall who appreciated who and what he was. Hattie loved him, too, but Hattie was merely the cook, and not much of one at that. And a Negress. She was sweet, and she put herself out to please him, but she really didn't count.

These thoughts distracted him, and spoiled his mood entirely by the time the Essex pulled up in front of Morgan House. He felt irritated and restive, wishing he had never accepted the invitation. He had to watch Iris Morgan face down her cook's objections to having a Negro dine in her kitchen, and he hid his boredom behind a bit of fuss with hats and gloves and coats.

Blake, as always, pretended to dignity. Acted as if he was above it all. It was no wonder he and Margot were thick as two thieves. They were both experts at putting on a show.

It had been entertaining, though, and by the time he was escorted into a surprisingly elegant parlor, his good mood had returned, fed by the girl's obvious infatuation and almost equally by Blake's discomfort. He decided to exert himself, to charm the two Morgan women and even to be respectful to the paunchy little man who was the father of the house. Why not? He had an entire evening to kill in this tedious town. There was certainly nothing better to do.

CHAPTER 4

Bronwyn drank another Fallen Angel, and then another, determined to drown the memories that swam in her head. She danced again, and again, until unladylike perspiration ran down her sides and soaked her beaded headband. Johnnie gave up, retreating to their table to nurse his gin and wait for her to tire herself out. She danced with anyone who would join her, and when there wasn't a man free, she danced alone.

At length the player piano emitted a final tinny chord, and ceased playing. Bronwyn had no money with her, and it seemed no one else wanted to put in a nickel. The room spun gently around her, as if she had been doing somersaults, and reluctantly, she teetered back to Johnnie. He had ordered another drink for her, and it waited on the table. "You're some hoofer, kiddo," he said. "Get off your dogs, there. Have one more jolt!"

His slang grated on her ears. There had been a day when she wouldn't have dreamed of spending a moment in the presence of someone like Johnnie Johnson, but that day was a memory now, added to all the other uncomfortable ones. Johnnie had spent a lot of money on her tonight, and not out of sympathy, or even admiration. As she picked up the cocktail, she tilted her head and gave him an exceedingly polite smile, as if they were having tea instead of overpriced, illegal liquor. "Thanks so much, Johnnie. It's been a swell evening."

She saw by the sudden narrowing of his eyes, the forward thrust of his head, that he understood she was saying good night, and good-bye.

He wanted more, of course. That was why his wallet was wide open. It was why he had tolerated her dancing without him, why he was still waiting at this table when most of the bleary-eyed crowd had disappeared into the night. He put out his rough workingman's hand, and seized her wrist. "Think again, *kiddo*."

This time the word carried both disdain and danger. She heard it clearly, and she saw it in the slackness of his mouth, the flush of his heavy face. He was no more than a year, perhaps two, older than she, but anger and resentment and lust made him look infinitely older, nothing like the young man she had agreed to come out with.

With effort, she pulled her hand free, and his thick fingernails scraped on her skin. "I'm tired, Johnnie. I want to go home."

"You're tired? *Now* you're tired?" He leered at her, and thrust a thumb in the direction of the dance floor. "You weren't tired thirty seconds ago!"

Bronwyn shot to her feet. "I'm tired now, Johnnie Johnson. I said thank you for the nice evening, and if you're the gentleman you pretend to be, you'll now see me home!"

He lurched up from the table, sending his chair flying. The barman glared at them both, as if Bronwyn were as guilty of the interruption as Johnnie. Maybe she was, but it was too late to worry about that now.

Johnnie snarled, "I took you where I was takin' you already, Miss High and Mighty! You got that bitty nose in the air, you can just follow it home on your own!"

Bronwyn put her hands on her hips. "You're going to just leave me? Do you know what my father would say about that?"

Johnnie gave a bark of derisive laughter. "I don't think your father has anything to do with it," he said. "Those days is past for you, my girl." He laughed again.

Bronwyn picked up her cocktail glass and flung the remnants of her Fallen Angel at his face. There wasn't much left, and only a few greenish drops reached him, but it felt good just the same. "Don't you ever call on me again, Johnnie Johnson," she spat at him. "I'm still an Uptown girl, whatever you may think."

"Ha," he said, wiping the drops from his cheeks. "You can't kid a kidder, my girl! What do you think all your snooty girlfriends think of you now? You're fast, that's what you are. You're fast, and everyone knows it!"

Willy forestalled the rest of their argument by calling from behind the bar, "Closing time, ladies and gents! Drink up!"

Bronwyn spun on her toes, and marched past the handful of remaining customers to the door. Johnnie shouted after her, "Hey, princess, gotcher carriage out there?"

She heard titters of laughter, and though her neck burned, she lifted her head higher and walked with a determined step. When she reached the doorway she paused. The lights from the street above shone down on her head. Deliberately, she drew a fresh Lucky Strike from her bag and fitted it into her cigarette holder. A man near the door jumped up, grinning, and struck a match to light the cigarette.

Bronwyn drew on it, and blew a cloud of smoke back into the room before she turned, the cigarette holder poised at a jaunty angle, and went out into the night. She maintained her attitude as she climbed the stairs, and walked up Water Street with smoke trailing behind her until she left the glow of the streetlights and reached total darkness. There she pulled the cigarette out of the holder and threw it into the gutter.

Johnnie wasn't the first to think because Bronwyn Morgan drank Fallen Angels, and because in the eyes of the town she *was* one, she would open her knees for any man. As if one lapse had determined her entire life.

It had, though. At this inescapable thought, all the elation of alcohol and dancing drained away from her in an instant. One lapse had determined her life and stolen her future. It had left her with nothing but ruins.

She shouldn't be here in the lower town at all, she knew, and especially not at night. The businesses were shuttered, but the alleys were alive with loiterers. There were men too drunk to make it home, and sailors loath to return to their uncomfortable bunks. There were streetwalkers calling out to the men who could still stand and might have money in their pockets. Bronwyn gripped her handbag and hurried her pace, pursued by an occasional catcall. Every stone and curb bit her soles through her soft shoes as she half ran until she reached Monroe. There, panting, she began the long hike up the hill.

The moist air from the Sound filled her lungs, and cooled her burning cheeks as she trudged along the steep street toward home. There were no footsteps behind her. Johnnie must have given up. She felt now as if she hadn't drunk a thing. All the feelings she had tried to submerge welled up again in a tide that nothing could stem. In the darkness, spring flowers glowed faintly against the dark shrubbery, peonies and rhododendrons and azaleas, their beauty mocking her misery.

It was her own fault for bringing out the clipping once again. She should have burned it the moment it came into the house.

Daddy had carried the copy of the *Times* home in his Gladstone bag after a business trip to Seattle. When he unpacked the bag to bring out the perfume and taffy he had brought home for his wife and daughter, he took out the paper and laid it on the Westinghouse radio in its place of honor on the sideboard in the breakfast room. Absently, knowing her mother didn't like anything on top of her brand-new wireless set, Bronwyn picked up the newspaper.

She hadn't meant to read it. Since that day when she read about the fire, and the death of the youngest Benedict son, she hadn't once touched the *Times*. She read the *Leader*, and the fashion magazines, and she read library books. The *Times* she avoided as if the newspaper itself had been responsible for the tragedy that had left her bereft, grieving her lost love.

But on this day, before she realized what it was, it was in her hand. It was already, for some reason, folded to the society page. She couldn't help seeing the headline.

The type had been set in the florid font used for the society pages, with lavish curlicues and sweeping capitals. It practically shouted "The Benedict Wedding" at her. Bronwyn's heart lurched when she saw it.

She should have stopped then. She should have thrown the paper into the breakfast room fireplace, but she didn't. Perhaps resisting temptation was not an aspect of her character.

Standing beside the walnut sideboard with its array of coffee cups on their copper hooks, she gazed down on the photograph of a tall, willowy bride standing beside her dashing groom. They were smiling, the dark-haired bride looking up at her new husband, the husband's arm snug around her narrow waist. Even in black and white, Bronwyn could see that everything was perfect. The flowers, the bride's beaded dress, even the shine of the polished banister where she rested her white-gloved hand were so beautiful that Bronwyn forgot herself in a wave of sorrow. She groaned aloud, and pressed her palm to her chest, where her heart contracted as if squeezed by a pitiless hand.

Her mother had come running from the kitchen, where she and Mrs. Andrew were having one of their awkward conversations, the ones in which Iris tried to order menus while Mrs. Andrew announced what would actually appear on the table. Iris burst into the breakfast room, crying, "Bronwyn! What is it, dear?"

Bronwyn dropped her hand, and drew a shaky breath as she turned hurriedly away. She thrust the paper beneath her arm so the photographs didn't show. "It's nothing, Mother. I'm sorry. I just—I stubbed my toe."

It had been two years since the disaster, but still her mother worried about her. Worried so, in fact, that her doctor had prescribed laudanum, and warned against the strain on her nerves. It was another reason to feel remorseful, and Bronwyn did that in abundance.

She managed to give her mother a weak smile before she hurried out of the breakfast room and up the stairs, the paper burning beneath her arm as if it were on fire.

After all she had been through, it was foolish to torment herself, but she couldn't help it. It was like chewing on a fingernail that was already ruined, even though you knew it was going to bleed. She spread the newspaper on her bed, so the pictures and the headline blazed up at her.

Properly, the headline should have read "The Benedict-Parrish Wedding," but the groom, it seemed, wasn't from an important family. His nuptials would no doubt have passed unnoticed were it not for his bride. It was the only daughter of Dickson Benedict Senior and his wife, Edith, who was newsworthy.

Bronwyn read every word, and matched the descriptions to the photographs.

> The bride, Margot Benedict, a physician at Seattle General Hospital with an additional practice in her private clinic on Post Street, descended the formal oaken staircase of Benedict Hall in an ankle-length dress of white satin with hand-beaded bodice, net sleeves, and a dropped waist. A pearl-encrusted headband encircled her head. She wore white *peau de soie* pumps and white silk gloves with lace edging at the wrists.
>
> The groom, Major Frank Parrish, wore his British Army dress uniform. Mrs. Ramona Parrish attended the bride as Matron of Honor. Mr. Dickson Parrish Junior served as groomsman. The couple exchanged their vows before a backdrop of winter roses and carnations in a stunning framework of sword ferns.
>
> The newlywed couple will take their honey-

moon trip south to California, where the groom,
an engineer with the Boeing Airplane Company,
will inspect several airplanes at the behest of Mr.
William Boeing, who was also in attendance at
the ceremony. Upon their return, the Parrishes
will make their home at Benedict Hall.

There was more, a list of the most prominent guests, and a description of the refreshments. Bronwyn read the whole thing twice through. She pored over the photographs, taking in every detail of Benedict Hall, trying to guess which guest was which. Most of the men were in cutaway coats and vests. The women wore the latest in hats, with furs draped around their shoulders.

It was all very much as she had imagined it should be, except of course she had pictured herself and Preston as the wedding couple. She ran her finger over the photograph of Margot Benedict in her wedding dress. Her own gown was to have been quite different. For one thing, she would have worn a veil, a nice long one, secured with a coronet of flowers. There would have been a train, wide enough to drape across the staircase in shimmering folds. Preston might have worn his uniform, the way Major Parrish did, and Bronwyn would have had Clara as her maid of honor, and Bessie as a bridesmaid. And for a wedding journey, Preston would surely have taken her to Paris, or at the very least, New York.

But Preston was dead; their child was gone. There was nothing left to dream of.

It was a funny thing about innocence, she thought. While a girl possessed it, she wasn't aware of it. Losing it was a shock made worse by not having known it was there in the first place. You paid a bitter price for something you had never truly enjoyed. Her girlish dreams, herself as the dancing princess, as the beautiful bride, as a *Benedict,* mocked her now. Her fairy tale had turned into a grimmer reality than any she could have imagined.

She went to her dressing table for the pair of sewing scissors she kept in the drawer, and came back to cut the two columns of the article from the page. She folded the clipping into a flat square, and slipped it beneath a stack of lingerie in the bottom drawer of her wardrobe before she crumpled the rest of the newspaper and threw it into the fireplace. She stood for a long time, watching it burn, wondering how long grief could last.

CHAPTER 5

There were evenings at Benedict Hall that seemed interminable to Frank. He wanted to take Margot's hand and pull her away from the formal dinner, the after-dinner ritual of listening to the radio, the polite talk. He wanted to rush her up the stairs to their own rooms, where their intimacy had become so easy, and so tender, that sometimes thinking of it during his workday made his belly tighten with longing.

It was Wagner tonight, broadcast from the Metropolitan Opera House in New York, and Frank didn't care for it much. Dick and Ramona had said good night to their daughter, and Louisa had insisted on toddling up the stairs on her own unsteady legs, with Nurse close behind her. The family was finishing their after-dinner coffee now. Frank was settled on the short divan with Margot beside him, her head propped against his shoulder. Her eyes were closed, but he could feel her awareness of the music, and her contentment at the quiet moment. Dickson was drowsing in his usual armchair, his cigar forgotten and cold in its ashtray. Edith sat staring into space, an unreadable expression in her eyes. Frank stole a glance at her once or twice, remembering with a pang the pretty woman he had first met, who welcomed him as Preston's army friend and eagerly pressed him for details of what she believed to be Preston's heroism.

Frank watched her from beneath his lowered eyelids as she breathed a small sigh and shifted in her chair, her gaze blank and distant. Her hair was no longer fair, but a yellowish gray. He hadn't heard her laugh in a long time, and only rarely seen her smile. She was as different from his own mother as any woman could be.

Jenny Baker Parrish, daughter of a rancher, wife of a rancher, had known nothing but hard work all her life. She had borne three children, two of whom hadn't survived their infancy. She had worked steadily through her pregnancies. She milked cows and branded calves. She cooked three meals a day for the ranch crew and tended her hens and her goats in between. She wore stained straw hats and rough leather gloves, and her skin was lined and worn by weather. Her hair, the last time he had seen it, was still mostly dark like his own—in fact, he had more silver in his hair than she did. But her eyes, which had been the same dark blue as her son's, had faded over the years from sun and wind and unrelenting work. She was, he supposed, about Edith Benedict's age, but she looked a decade older.

Jenny Baker Parrish would understand Edith's grief. She would never, though, countenance Edith's preference for Preston over her other children. Jenny, Frank thought, the woman who had buried two babies and mourned her son's war injury, would have taken Edith's hand and chided her for not facing the truth about her youngest son, and for neglecting her other children,

The music came to an end with a crash of brass and timpani. Margot startled, bumping her cheek against Frank's shoulder. "Oh," she murmured. "I'm sorry. I fell asleep."

"Don't worry," he said. He stood and offered her his hand to help her up. "Long day." She had told him, as they dressed for dinner, of the stream of patients in the accident room. There had been a fire in one of the broken-down cottages in the Tenderloin, and several of the crib girls were hurt, though none seriously. He knew well that if anyone had been badly burned, or had a life-threatening injury, Margot wouldn't have come home at all.

She smiled up at him as she gave him her hand, and when she stood, he put his arm around her waist. The touch of her never failed to stir him, even after a year of married life. He tried to moderate his eager smile as they said good night to the family. Together, they left the small parlor and turned up the wide staircase. The servants had gone to bed, and the big house was dim and quiet. The murmur of voices followed them as they climbed to the second floor and made their way to the back, toward their own rooms, and the restfulness of being alone together.

"I'll draw you a bath," Frank said as they reached their doorway.

"Oh, no," she said, yawning. "I'm much too sleepy. I don't have anything tomorrow. A day off! I'll bathe in the morning."

They undressed, side by side, and got into their nightclothes. Margot refused to even consider a lady's maid, saying she was perfectly capable of managing her own clothes. Hattie was the one to help Edith with her hair and her baths, insisting she didn't mind in the least. Dickson said he was just as glad. "Don't like servants sitting up at all hours waiting for the family to finish whatever they're doing," he explained. Frank thought this was eminently wise.

He pulled the bedclothes back for Margot, and folded her into bed. She smiled at him drowsily, and was asleep almost before he completed his good-night kiss. He turned off her bedside lamp, leaving just his small reading light burning on the other side, and stood for a moment, looking down at her.

In the dimness, with her face relaxed, she looked like a young girl. Her short dark hair fanned on the white pillow like the wing of a bird, and her lips were slightly apart as she breathed.

"The great Dr. Benedict," he whispered, brushing a strand of hair from her cheek. "Carrying the world on your shoulders." Though she wouldn't know it, he bent and kissed her again, breathing in the scents of soap and shampoo, savoring the smoothness of her skin.

He had a book he meant to read, Rickenbacker's memoir. He

was hoping there would be something useful in it. The drive to develop airplanes that could carry more weight ruled them all at the Boeing Airplane Company just now, and every insight, every clue, was useful. The Sand Point Aviation Field was being developed to test army pursuit planes, but Bill Boeing was still focused on the problem of weight in non-military craft. Frank wanted to keep his hand in that research, even as he worked on the Model 21, the navy trainer.

He crossed to the window to draw the curtains. He liked looking out at the starlight, but as summer approached, dawn came earlier and earlier, and he didn't want the rising light to wake Margot. She hadn't had a full night's sleep in several days. His father-in-law had been right when he warned his new son-in-law: Marriage to a doctor meant phone calls at all hours. Margot kept the candlestick telephone close beside the bed, within easy reach of her hand. When it rang, she often lifted the bell to her ear while she was still half asleep. He could hear the voice on the other end, "Dr. Benedict? Seattle General." That always brought her fully awake.

As he drew the curtains he glanced to his right, where Blake had his apartment over the converted carriage house. A faint light gleamed from the corner, no doubt meaning Blake was reading in bed, just as Frank meant to do. Frank turned to the bed with a yawn of his own, and was about to untie his dressing gown when the bedroom door creaked, and opened six inches.

A small plump hand crept around the door like a pale starfish inching along a dark beach. Grinning, Frank moved to the end of the bed and squatted, waiting.

A tiny fair head followed the hand, peeking from the dim hallway.

"Escape artist!" Frank whispered. "Does Nurse know you're out of bed?"

Now he could see her merry smile, her eyes sparkling like blue crystals in the lamplight. "Fa!" she gurgled.

"Yes, Fa," Frank murmured. "Uncle Fa. But don't wake your Auntie Margot!"

Louisa toddled forward into the room, her short arms outstretched toward him, her rosy lips pursed in concentration as she
put one foot before the other. Frank waited, his own arms out
and ready to catch her. She looked up at him once or twice from
beneath her tumbled hair, then back to her shapeless little feet,
her stubby toes splayed like pink pearls against the carpet.

When she was two steps away from him, she tripped, and
pitched forward, laughing, into his waiting hands. Behind him
Margot stirred, and muttered something, but didn't wake. Frank
swept Louisa up in his arms, putting a warning finger to her lips.
She grabbed the finger in a fierce grip, and said in a fake whisper,
"Fa! Shhhhh!"

"Yes, shhh," he murmured in her ear. With her cradled against
him, he backed out of the bedroom and pulled the door closed
with his bare foot. "You, Miss Louisa Benedict," he said, when
the door was shut, "are a rascal. You're supposed to be in bed!"

She wriggled in his grasp. "Fa!"

"I hope you don't call me Fa forever, young lady," he told her,
as he turned toward the nursery. "I'll never live it down."

She kicked and giggled, warm and soft in his arms. It wasn't
the first time she'd climbed out of her crib and gone exploring,
although it was later than usual for baby excursions. There had
been very few children in Frank's life, and he loved having this
one. He pressed his nose to her hair to inhale the ineffable baby
essence of powder and lotion and thoroughly bleached diapers.
She relaxed against him, both arms around his neck, her short
legs dangling. "Fa," she sighed.

He kissed the top of her head. "Uncle Fa," he said again.
"Louisa is Uncle Fa's favorite girl, isn't she?"

"Fa," she breathed again, and was suddenly, soundly asleep.

Frank edged the door of the nursery open with his foot. Nurse
was also asleep, mouth open, beaky nose pointed at the ceiling.
Frank carried Louisa to her crib, an elaborate affair in ivory
enamel, with cloth-covered springs and satiny quilts. It had a
drop side, but the side was still in its upright position. Athlete,
Frank thought. She won't stay in it if she doesn't want to!

He laid her down without making a sound, and pulled one of the quilts over her. He stood for a moment, listening to Nurse's raspy breathing, and watching the rosy baby sleep. She was enchanting, and he felt a tug of love for her, liberally mixed with fear. It was the nature of love, he supposed, that such a pure emotion should be tainted by nameless anxieties.

As he padded out of the nursery, and made sure the door latched behind him, he thought of his mother for the second time that night. How had she borne losing two infants? Louisa wasn't even his own daughter, and he couldn't bear the thought of anything happening to her. Yet Jenny Parrish had persevered. Endured.

He took off his prosthesis and laid it ready on the bureau, then turned out his reading light. The book could wait until another time. As he slipped into bed beside his sleeping wife, he reflected that his mother was made of far sterner stuff than Margot's mother. She was more courageous. More resilient. And, at least in his estimation, vastly wiser.

Perhaps Edith's upbringing had made her vulnerable. She had been born to wealth, had always been cared for by servants, had never had to worry about bills or food. Jenny Parrish had known damned few of the comforts Edith had always taken for granted. At the wedding the year before, his mother had been wide-eyed and wary at the opulence of Benedict Hall, the formality of the ceremony, the morning coats of the men and the furs of the women. Frank had been grateful to Ramona, who had exerted herself to make Jenny Parrish feel comfortable.

Frank lay on his side, close to Margot, but careful not to disturb her. His eyelids sagged deliciously, and he relaxed. His last thought, before sliding into sleep, was that Edith's easy upbringing was no excuse for favoritism. He didn't think she had caused Preston's madness, but she had perpetuated it. Ignored it. And hurt Margot deeply in the process.

Margot woke to watery sunshine filtering through the drawn curtains. Frank had gone, slipping out without waking her. She was sorry to miss him, but it was glorious to sleep her fill. It seemed like weeks since she had felt fully rested.

She threw back her blankets, and rang for a maid. She would have her coffee here, she decided, something she rarely did. Perhaps she would even take her breakfast on a tray. The morning felt like a holiday.

Leona came in, bobbing her usual curtsy. Margot asked for coffee and toast, and for a bath to be run. Leona curtsied again and tripped away, and Margot, in her dressing gown, sat down in the window seat, gazing out at the garden. The roses dripped with rain, but the sky was beginning to clear. It would be, Margot thought, one of those delicate spring days, the air bright and clean, but with a sense of fragility, the awareness that it wouldn't last. Margot leaned against the casement, savoring her moment of leisure.

By the time she was bathed and dressed, most of the family was off to their pursuits. She caught a glimpse of Allison on her way out, a satchel full of books slung over her shoulder. The girl grinned and waved as she dashed down the stairs and out the front door to make a run for the streetcar. Late again, Margot supposed. Allison never went out without her hair and clothes in perfect order, and that, apparently, took precedence over punctuality. Margot's own ablutions took barely any time at all. As a general rule a pass with her comb, a splash of water on her face, and clean teeth were all she required to go out into the world.

Smiling over this, she went down the staircase with a medical journal in her hand and a long cardigan over her shoulders. She would dry off one of the Westport chairs on the porch and sit there, where she could breathe the freshly washed air and enjoy the perfume of Blake's roses until Frank returned for lunch.

She heard the maids and Hattie talking in the kitchen, so she used the front door, and made her way around to the side porch, where the morning sun glistened on the damp pillars and brought clouds of evaporation from the shrubs and grass. She turned the chair cushion to the dry side, then settled herself into it. Blake, returned from driving the men to their offices, crossed the lawn from the garage on his way to the kitchen door. He nodded to Margot. She lifted a lazy hand, and they exchanged a smile. A patter of treble voices, like the chittering of birds, poured out of the kitchen as he opened the door, then faded when he closed it again, leaving Margot in a silence broken only by the drip of raindrops from the eaves.

She riffled the pages of the journal, and began to read a piece on infections of the ear, but a moment later she closed it again. Someone opened a window above her head, and Leona's and Loena's voices flitted out. Thelma had more or less taken on Dick and Ramona's rooms, except for the nursery, while the twins did hers and Frank's, and all three worked on Dickson and Edith's. Nurse—who had a name, Mary Everson, though no one used it—was fiercely protective of her small territory, handled everything to do with the nursery, and only showed her sharp nose beyond its door for meals, or when she brought Louisa for her regular visit to the family after dinner. It was a system that seemed to be working, and left Hattie free to assist Edith when she needed it.

Margot had ordered Blake to avoid climbing stairs unless it was necessary, but she knew he still climbed the staircase every day to supervise. He also had the gardeners and the handymen under his direction, to say nothing of the serving of meals and his duties as chauffeur, but he seemed to manage all of it effortlessly, almost invisibly. It was a marvel, the way he had returned to full service. Only the lion-headed cane, never far from his hand, betrayed the disability he had suffered.

Margot let her head drop back, and though she had barely been out of bed an hour, her eyelids grew heavy once again. She was more tired than she had realized. She should take more free days, perhaps, but her clinic had a steady stream of patients now, and her hospital duties demanded her almost daily presence. The Women and Infants Clinic filled an entire afternoon every week, and tomorrow she was due to return to the Ryther Child Home with Sarah to examine and vaccinate the rest of the children. There was an asthma case there, and she had to convince

Mrs. Ryther to stop using asthma cigarettes and accept a nebulizer for epinephrine treatments. She was reasonably confident she could do it. Government money, it turned out, was a decisive factor for Olive Ryther.

Behind Margot, in the kitchen, Hattie raised her rich, tremulous voice in one of the hymns she loved. Margot allowed her eyes to close, letting the swirl of household activity soothe her. She pulled her cardigan a little tighter, and with a sigh, she drowsed.

She barely heard the series of thumps when they came, muffled as they were by closed doors. She was more aware of the abrupt breaking off of Hattie's singing, and the sudden cry of alarm. It was Nurse, her usual calm shattered, crying out for help. A heartbeat later, before Margot had even pushed herself up from her chair, she heard Ramona screaming, and shouts of alarm from Hattie and from one of the maids. Piercing all of it was the shrill wailing of a one-year-old.

Margot, acting on instinct, was halfway through the kitchen before she was fully awake, striding toward the hall where the noise was. Preparations for luncheon were underway, with a board full of chopped vegetables on the counter, the scent of something roasting in the oven, and trays of flatware and crystal laid out. Margot hurried past all of it and pushed through the swinging door into the hall.

She found a knot of women around Ramona, who was seated on the bottom stair with a red-faced Louisa shrieking on her lap. Ramona was clutching the baby so hard Margot thought it was no wonder the child was screaming. Nurse's craggy face was a study in horror, and Hattie was kneeling beside Ramona, tears streaming down her plump cheeks. The twins stood back, pale-faced, their freckles standing out in dotted swiss patterns. Thelma, the third maid, gaped from the top of the stairs. If she made a sound, Margot couldn't tell. The sheer volume of voices, echoing in the big hall, was confounding.

Ramona caught sight of her. "Oh, Margot! She fell! Louisa fell down the stairs!"

Leona said, "Miss Margot, she just did three somersaults, right from the top! I thought she musta broke her neck doing it!"

Her twin elbowed her, and she covered her mouth with a freckled hand, as Ramona burst into frightened tears.

Margot assessed the baby with a glance. Her face was scarlet, mouth open to show six pearly milk teeth. All four limbs milled with fury as she heaved a breath to squall again. Margot pushed past the twins to sit beside Ramona on the stair. Gently, she extricated the toddler from her mother's grasp, and drew her into her own lap. At the same moment Blake arrived, his cane loose in his hand, his face furrowed with concern.

"Mr. Blake!" Leona hissed. "Baby fell down the stairs!" Blake's eyes met Margot's, and a dark, painful memory passed swiftly between them before she turned her attention back to Louisa.

Margot cradled the little girl in her arms, passing her hand over the child's forehead, shushing her under her breath while the other women gasped and wept. "Louisa," Margot said, in a low, firm tone. "Louisa. Listen to Auntie Margot."

Margot could feel the small, hot body tense for another wail. "Louisa, shush. You're all right. You did a somersault!"

The wail came out as a whimper, and then a sniffle. Loena leaned forward, and offered Margot a handkerchief. Margot used it to wipe the child's nose, though Louisa tried to wriggle away from it. Surreptitiously, while her niece wrestled with the handkerchief, Margot felt each of her arms and legs, and ran her fingers up her back. She pressed on Louisa's slender neck, and ran her fingertips through her shock of fair hair. There were no bumps or lumps on her scalp, and already her sobs were subsiding into shudders.

Margot lifted her to her shoulder, and patted her back. "Ramona, she's fine," she said. "Babies are flexible, thank goodness. But look, no bruises, not even a scratch."

"She just—I turned my back for a moment, and she was out of her crib!" Nurse said in a wretched tone. She sounded close to tears herself. "I'm so sorry, Mrs. Benedict, but—"

Ramona, who was wiping her own face with a lace-edged handkerchief, dropped it, and turned blazing eyes to the hapless woman. "It's your *job!*" she cried. "What were you doing?"

Margot felt the child quiver anew in her arms. "Ramona, you'll set her off again. Louisa isn't hurt, but she knows you're upset."

"Of course I'm upset!" Ramona said. "She—she could have—"

"Yes," Margot said quietly. "But she didn't. She's all right, and we'll keep a closer eye on her now, right? She's an active little thing."

"I will, Dr. Benedict," Nurse assured her. "I will! I do, really, but this time—"

"I understand. It can happen in a flash." Margot stood up, Louisa still in her arms. Hattie straightened, and wiped her cheeks with the hem of her apron. The twins drew back into the kitchen, though Margot sensed their intent listening as if they had ear horns extending into the hall. Ramona, weeping openly, rose to her feet, and the nurse stepped forward to take Louisa.

"I'll just keep her for a bit, Nurse," Margot said. "Why don't you go and rinse your face, Ramona? Nurse, you take a moment, too. I'll take Louisa out into the garden for a few minutes and let her calm down."

It took a bit of persuasion, but soon Margot was able to carry her niece out through the kitchen, where Louisa reached for a wooden spoon lying on the counter. Hattie, chuckling and sniffling at the same time, wiped the spoon with a dishcloth and handed it over to her. Margot carried the toddler out to the porch and down to the damp grass that stretched between the garage and the house. She set the child down, and Louisa, though her face was still red and her eyes swollen from crying, began batting at a sodden dandelion with the wooden spoon.

Margot crouched beside her in the thin sunshine, watching, and remembering.

She had been older, of course. Ten years old, and not as resilient as a one-year-old. Preston had pushed her, and she had careened down the stairs, banging her head, bruising both knees, wrenching her back. It wasn't the first time her brother had hurt her, but she had been really frightened that day, trembling and crying. Blake had swept her up into his strong arms and carried her up to her bedroom. She saw, on his face, that he understood how dangerous it could have been. Blake was frightened, too, and deeply angry, but he was as powerless as Margot herself.

Her younger brother had been a constant shadow over her childhood. In her adulthood, just the year before, he had tried and almost succeeded in killing her. For this offense he would spend his life in confinement.

Little Louisa Benedict, with her pale hair and ice-blue eyes, looked so much like Preston had as a child that it made Margot's heart ache with remembered misery.

Louisa glanced up at that moment, and smiled at her aunt. It was such a comical expression, at odds with her puffy eyes and tearstained cheeks, that Margot laughed, and put out her hand to caress the child's towhead. "Darling girl," she murmured. "Auntie Margot loves you. And so does Uncle Frank."

"Fa!" the child proclaimed.

"Yes, Fa," Margot agreed. She pulled her skirt up over her knees so she could settle cross-legged onto the grass to savor the sunshine, the scent of roses, and the company of pure innocence. Her skirt would be wet, but she didn't care. "What will you call me, I wonder, when you get around to it?"

"Fa!" Louisa announced again.

Margot rested her elbows on her knees, and her chin on her hands. It was lovely to be doing nothing but watch a child trying to dig a dandelion out of the lawn. "Louisa," Margot said.

The child looked up, her eyes as merry now as if nothing untoward had taken place. "Sa!" she agreed. She held up the wooden spoon. "Poon! Sa, poon!"

Margot chuckled. "Close enough, darling. Before you know it you'll be ordering us all about, I imagine, and we'll yearn for the days when your vocabulary consisted of ten words."

She felt, rather than heard, Blake's approach. He stood a short distance away, not speaking, until she said, without looking away from the child, "Has everything settled down in there?"

"Yes, Dr. Margot, I think so," he said, a smile in his voice. "But Nurse is terribly worried."

"For Louisa, or for her job?"

"I feel confident it's for the baby. In my observation, she seems devoted to the little one."

"That's good. I gather the maids aren't fond of Nurse."

"No, she's not a friendly sort. She keeps mostly to the nursery, but that's her job, isn't it? And it's why she's so upset now."

"You can reassure her. Louisa's in perfect health." She sighed, and pushed herself up to stand. "As you can see!"

Louisa, her face intent, had reversed the spoon to try working on the dandelion with its handle. Blake said, "Miss Louisa, the roses need weeding, if you're in the mood."

The little girl looked up at him, and said, very seriously, "Bake."

"Yes, miss," he answered gravely, only the twitch of his lips giving away his amusement. "Bake." He bowed from the waist. "At your service."

She nodded, accepting this, and went back to her task. Blake said, "You used to call me Bake, Dr. Margot. Until you were about three, I think. Once you realized there was a missing letter, you never did that again." He twinkled at her. "I miss that."

She smiled. "So now you have another child to fuss over."

"A great blessing," he said. "But children always are."

"Oh, Blake," Margot said, shaking her head. "I wish that were true."

"You're thinking of the Ryther Home."

"All those orphans and abandoned children! It's unthinkable."

"Mrs. Ryther is an astonishing woman."

"Yes, she is," Margot said fervently. "Difficult, and cantankerous, but astonishing."

She watched Louisa push herself up, first sticking her diapered bottom in the air, then coming unsteadily to her feet. Her plump hands grasped Margot's skirt, and she felt the waistband stretch until she feared the button would pop off. She bent to pick up the child, and as she settled her on one hip, she thought she understood now why mothers did that. Frank held Louisa differently, high on his chest, cradling her with his prosthetic arm.

Louisa grasped a strand of her hair, and tugged on it as if she didn't know it was attached. Wincing, Margot laughed. "I think this little rascal could come inside now."

"I'll let Nurse know." Blake turned, and preceded them up onto the porch and through the back door into the kitchen. Margot, following, noticed how little weight he was putting on his cane. Perhaps, she thought, he could lay it aside soon. The thought of his full recovery, when he had been so terribly ill, filled her with pride. He had saved her so many times. He had been her rock through adversity. It was deeply satisfying to have helped him in return.

Margot stood at the bottom of the stairs to watch the nurse, still pale with worry, carry Louisa off. Louisa peeked over the nurse's shoulder, her blue eyes full of light and life, and Margot gave her a farewell wave. When the two of them reached the landing and disappeared down the corridor, Margot stood a moment longer, gazing into empty space. She had just remembered the little boy at the Ryther Home.

Impatiently, she shook her head. The child's resemblance to Louisa—and thus to Preston—was purely coincidental. It had to be.

CHAPTER 6

Bronwyn dreamed, as she so often had in the past three years, of Preston, and of the magical summer night she had met him in the garden behind Morgan House. The gentle lapping of the waves on the beach and the chittering of invisible night birds created the perfect accompaniment for their assignation. It had all felt preordained. Natural. Inevitable.

In her dreams she was sixteen again, melting with desire. Preston was golden, his eyes luminous in the starlight. She had sneaked out of her bedroom in haste, wearing only her nightdress and dressing gown, summoned by a dash of pebbles against her window. In a pair of soft slippers, she crept through the sleeping house. The kitchen door creaked once, but it was the only betraying sound, and no one roused.

Preston was waiting for her on the stone bench beneath the climbing rose, and when she appeared, he rose, and gazed at her for a long moment. She stood very still, aware of starlight on her cheeks and her freshly brushed hair lifting in the salt-scented breeze. Her heartbeat fluttered in her throat, and her breathing was quick and shallow.

She imagined this was the moment he would step forward, take her hand, and drop to one knee. He would beg her to be his bride, and then, when she gave tearful assent, he would rise and kiss her, embrace her tenderly, carefully, as if she were almost too fragile to touch.

It hadn't been like that, of course. He had certainly taken her hand. He had drawn her to him and kissed her, his mouth firm and warm on hers. He hadn't knelt, nor had he spoken a single word. He pulled her tight against him, surprising her with the pressure of his body against hers. He kissed her throat, and pulled her nightdress aside to kiss her shoulder, and then, his mouth more demanding at every moment, her breast.

Bronwyn had trembled with longing, though she didn't know what it was she longed for. When he drew her down to the damp grass, and ran his hands oh-so-gently beneath her nightdress, touching parts of her body she had never exposed to anyone in her life, she gasped in surprise and confusion.

She didn't understand what was happening, but whatever it was, it was exquisite. Intoxicating. Her flesh was eager, unresisting. She had never been kissed beyond a peck on the cheek. She had never seen—much less felt—a man's unclothed body. It was both awful and wonderful, terrifying and irresistible. She was shocked, and at the same time overwhelmed by the sweetness, the luxuriousness of indulging her body's wishes.

The one moment of pain, a sharp tearing within her body, was quickly lost in other sensations, all of them new, all of them compelling. She couldn't have stopped if she had wanted to. Her body was in control, urging her on. This, she thought, was love, and it stunned her with its power. Every moment was a new discovery, an unexpected delight, and the culmination swept her up in its perfect sense of completion.

It was no wonder no one spoke of this great mystery. It must be natural to guard a secret so profound, a pleasure so vast and splendid. When it was over, she lay in Preston's embrace, tears of release on her cheeks. Her hair tangled in the grass, and as her breathing slowed and eased, she gazed up into a meadow of stars, and thought that no night could be more perfect than this enchanted one.

In her dreams, Bronwyn relived that night in aching detail, right up until the moment of fulfillment. That was when she invariably woke, frustrated, burning with hunger for something now denied to her forever.

She lay staring out past her lacy curtains at the marine layer building above the Sound. Why did she dream so often of a single night? Why didn't she have nightmares about all that followed?

She had been certain, after that night in the summer darkness, that Preston would come to speak to her father. Surely no one could share such moments, bare themselves so completely to each other, without being truly in love. She pictured her suitor on the doorstep with roses in his hands. She fantasized about showing off her engagement ring to her friends, the first of their circle to be betrothed. She waited for Preston all the next day, and then the next. She turned to the window a thousand times, watching the street for his black motorcar.

A week passed, and when he didn't come, she bought issues of the *Seattle Daily Times*, searching for clues in "Seattle Razz." She learned only that he was busy, going to parties and teas and fashion shows at Frederick & Nelson, reporting on styles, gossip, society events.

Her engagement hadn't materialized. The week turned into two, then three. She wrestled with herself, wondering if he had somehow forgotten where she lived. Perhaps he didn't know she had a telephone in her house. If he were ill, would the paper report it?

It wasn't possible that he didn't long to see her as she longed to see him. It was beyond her comprehension, after what had passed between them, that she should be forgotten.

She agonized over everything that had happened, turning over the details in her mind, struggling to understand. Had she done something wrong, something that disappointed him? She couldn't talk to Bessie or Clara, because they didn't know any more than she did about such matters. She couldn't talk to her mother, because Iris would only scold her for slipping out to meet her young man without a chaperone.

Bronwyn took to walking endlessly along the beach below her house, yearning across the waters of the Sound, where the steamships chugged majestically toward Seattle. Somewhere, there, Preston lived in Benedict Hall, the finest mansion on Millionaire's Row. She pictured it as a castle, with turrets and towers and a great hall. There, across the water, he was being driven around by his Negro chauffeur, going to the newspaper offices to write his witty pieces, being served tea and cakes in the parlors of elegant women.

As the weeks wore away, Bronwyn felt her dream fading into the distance, the way the steamships grew smaller and smaller until they disappeared over the horizon. Nothing gave her joy, neither her dance classes nor her friends' company, neither shopping outings with her mother, nor the copies of *Vogue* and *Harper's Bazaar* that arrived in the mail. When she started being sick in the mornings, she thought it must be heartbreak that made her stomach churn. She hid her morning bouts of vomiting from her mother as best she could. The maid, Betty Jones, eyed her oddly, but Bronwyn ordered her out of her room, and told no one anything.

When her breasts began to swell and grow tender, she thought she must be really ill. It wasn't until she realized she hadn't had her curse in three months that she began to suspect. Bronwyn was ignorant, but she wasn't stupid. Such symptoms meant something.

On a hot September morning, as she was dressing before her mirror, she froze, gazing in horror at her midsection. Her tummy was no longer flat. It curved outward, as if she had swallowed something enormous. It reminded her of a picture she had seen once of a python that had swallowed a rat, thin along its whole length except for the place the rat was stuck. She knew very little about how bodies worked, but she had seen pregnant women. Was that what the sweetness was about? Was it because of this swelling of the belly, and the dreadful outcome, that it was kept secret?

She had never gone to a doctor on her own. Her mother always took her, and stayed beside her during the examination. Her mother answered the doctor's questions for her, and accepted medicine on her behalf. It was no different for Bessie and Clara. None of them had ever questioned it. If she tried to go on her own, now, the doctor would only insist on talking to her parents.

What was she to do? She pulled on her chemise to cover the swelling of her belly, and dressed herself in a loose cotton frock and her lightest stockings. She didn't feel sick this morning, but hungry, ravenously hungry, hungry enough to put aside, for the moment, the anxiety that made her heart race. She felt as if a battle were going on in her body, her stomach and her heart at odds, a battle she was going to lose no matter what she did. She took up a hat and a pair of summer-weight gloves, and set off down the stairs for breakfast. Whatever it was that had taken over her stomach would have it no other way.

Cook had made a summer meal of soft-boiled eggs, fresh rolls, and a huge bowl of blackberries. Even looking at the blackberries made Bronwyn's mouth water. She felt as if she couldn't get enough of them, refilling her cut-glass bowl twice before she was done.

"Goodness, dear," her mother said. "Be careful of too much fruit. You know what it does to you."

"Yes, Mother," Bronwyn said. She pushed the bowl aside, and replaced it with her eggcup.

Her mother eyed the gloves and hat waiting on the sideboard. "Are you going somewhere, dear?"

Bronwyn, as she cracked the eggshell with her spoon, said, "Yes. The library."

Iris nodded approval. "Excellent idea. It's going to be so hot today, and it's always cool in the library."

To forestall her mother's deciding to come along, Bronwyn said, "Bessie and Clara are going to meet me there."

"Oh, good. That sounds very nice, dear. Let me give you some money, and you girls can go to the soda fountain afterward."

Bronwyn felt a quiver of compunction at her mother's generosity, but it was nothing to the fear that gripped her anew now that her hunger was appeased. She accepted fifty cents, and dropped it into her little cloth handbag before she gathered up her gloves and hat, kissed her mother's cheek, and set off down the hill.

It was terribly hot already, though it was only midmorning. The blackberries settled, heavy and cold, deep into her belly, but her head felt light and far above the rest of her body, as if it might disengage from her shoulders and go floating off into the blazing blue sky. She walked slowly, reluctance dragging at her steps. She trudged up the stone stairs of the Carnegie Library and pulled open the heavy door.

She moved gingerly through the shadowed stacks, passing the fiction sections she was accustomed to, peering at the titles in aisles she had never visited before. The shelves were packed with dusty tomes in forbidding colors of brown and burgundy and rusty black. Their titles made little sense to her, long names with words she barely recognized.

She didn't dare ask the librarian for assistance. Miss Claymore kept a critical eye on the selections Bronwyn and her friends made, and refused to check out anything she deemed inappropriate. Any book that explained the mystery Bronwyn was trying to solve was certain not to meet with Miss Claymore's approval.

Bronwyn understood that the Dewey decimal system organized books by topic, but she wasn't sure how to refine her search. Wandering, frowning up at the shelves, she stumbled upon a section that appeared to contain medical texts. For twenty minutes she browsed in that area, pulling down a text here and there to try to make sense of the table of contents, but without success. At the end of one shelf was a stack of yellowing pamphlets, and she leafed through them, reading titles like *Social Hygiene* and *Path to Purity, a Handbook for Young People.* She opened one or two, encouraged by their covers, but the language inside was so oblique that they told her very little.

She tidied the stack, and replaced it. She felt bleary from breathing dust, and after feeling heated by the walk up Lawrence Street, she now felt as chilled as if she had walked into Aldrich's meat locker. She stood for a moment, one trembling hand pressed to her swelling stomach, and told herself it didn't matter. Books weren't going to help her. Though she was mystified by exactly how it had happened, she was In Trouble.

It was the way they spoke of it, she and Bessie and Clara, and their mothers, too. Being In Trouble meant that a girl would disappear for a time, always with a lame excuse of visiting family or going abroad, explanations no one believed. It meant older women whispering behind their hands, falling silent when young girls came into the room. Once Bronwyn had asked her mother about it, and Iris Morgan had said firmly, "Nice girls don't need to know about such things."

"Wasn't Patricia a nice girl?"

"I thought so once," Iris had said primly. "Not anymore."

Patricia was the eldest daughter of the baker in Port Townsend, someone who had often served Bronwyn and her mother from behind the counter. Bronwyn had admired her masses of black hair and her plump cheeks, always rosy from the ovens. One day Patricia had mysteriously vanished from the town, and Bronwyn had been forbidden to ask about her when she and her mother stopped to buy cinnamon rolls.

Bronwyn never learned what changed Patricia from a Nice Girl to one who was In Trouble, but Clara whispered that she was sent away because she was going to have a baby. The two of them had wondered how that could come about, since Patricia wasn't married. Neither of them knew the answer, and they had no one they could ask.

Bronwyn realized, on that burning September day, that it was she who was no longer a Nice Girl. Her dreams were not coming true after all. Rather, the opposite had happened. She was ruined.

The mystery now, almost three years later, was why she didn't dream of all of that. She remembered it clearly enough. There were those awful moments of understanding, of confession, of her mother's stunned tears and her father's outrage. She had thought she might die of misery when her father ruled that she would not be allowed—not even after it was all over—to study dance at the Cornish School. She was allowed to write a single letter to Preston Benedict. She received no reply.

Reading of Preston's death, in the fire that destroyed his sister's medical clinic, was a waking nightmare. She couldn't bear to read the tragic reports in the *Times*, although her mother did, and told her all about them. She spent most of her pregnancy in a Vancouver hotel, facing her mother's disappointment every single day. She suffered a long, difficult delivery, and when it was over, nothing was left to her.

She would have liked to dream of her baby, but those dreams never came. She had only the memory of him, of holding him in her arms for a precious five minutes before he was whisked away.

Bronwyn dreamed instead, always and only, of those lost moments in the garden. Her dreams betrayed her. They tormented her with what could have been. What she had believed would be.

Now, after her night in the Cellar, she woke slowly, dry-mouthed and miserable. Hot June sunshine poured generously through her window, and glittered on the dancing waters beyond the glass, but the glorious weather held no joy. The taste of last night's Fallen Angels was sour on her tongue, and her head throbbed with the aftermath of homemade gin. She could barely stand the brightness of sun in her eyes. She kept them half shut as she pushed aside her blankets and staggered into her bathroom. She splashed water on her face and ran her damp hands through her tangled hair. When she could open her eyes fully, she stared at herself in the mirror.

It hardly seemed possible three years could make such a difference in a person. Bruise-dark shadows dragged at her eyes, and her cheeks were hollow and pale. Her belly was marked with puckered lines where the baby had grown, the baby that was gone. Even her hair seemed to droop, to have lost the luster she and her mother had been so proud of. She should do something about all of it, she supposed. She hardly cared enough to try.

She walked back into her bedroom and opened her wardrobe. For long moments she gazed at the dresses hanging there, all neatly pressed and arranged by Betty. She would have to put something on. She would have to comb her hair, and go downstairs to endure her mother's worried face. She would have to think of something to do to fill the long empty hours of the day.

The morning mail, waiting on the sideboard in the breakfast room, brought a card from Clara. Iris, her face bright with forced hopefulness, laid it beside Bronwyn's plate. "Look," she said. "Something from Clara! Isn't that nice?"

Bessie had stopped speaking to Bronwyn when she and her family learned of her pregnancy, but Clara, it turned out, was a more faithful friend. She had written to Bronwyn every week during her exile. She had been waiting at the ferry dock when Iris and Bronwyn returned home, disdaining the whispers and shaken heads that followed them. Clara was married now, with her own tidy brick home just off Lawrence. Bronwyn was always welcome there, so long as Clara's straitlaced husband wasn't present. He knew, of course, about the Cellar, and the Fallen Angels, and all the rest of it. All of Port Townsend did, Bronwyn supposed. She told herself—and Clara—that she didn't care, but it wasn't true. She couldn't help caring. She was nineteen years old, and the empty years of her life stretched ahead like a desert.

She picked up the small blue envelope with Clara's familiar handwriting, and slit it open with the silver paper knife. "She's having a tea," she told her mother. "Next week."

"You're invited," Iris said. She gave her daughter a brave, hopeful smile. "How nice!"

"We're both invited, Mother, but . . ."

Iris gave a little, girlish clap of her hands. "Oh, dear Clara! Like old times! We'll need new dresses, don't you think?"

"Oh, Mother, I won't be going," Bronwyn said as she laid the card aside.

"But, dear heart, why not? It would be good for you to get out a bit."

"It won't be like old times, Mother."

"Bronwyn, you need to see people. You should make some friends."

"I have friends," Bronwyn said. She kept her eyes down, avoiding her mother's gaze.

"You never see them," Iris said in a plaintive voice. Bronwyn didn't answer, but slid the card back into its envelope.

There was a silence at the table, broken only by the maid carrying in a platter of toast and a coffeepot. Neither of them spoke again until she had backed out of the breakfast room, leaving the coffeepot on the sideboard. Bronwyn said then, for the dozenth time, "I need to leave Port Townsend, Mother."

And for the dozenth time, Iris answered, "Oh, no, Bronwyn! Please don't say that. You just have to be patient. Everything will settle down. Everything will be fine."

Bronwyn, filled with sorrow for herself and her mother both, gave up the argument.

In the hospital in Vancouver there had been a doctor, a middle-aged, pleasant-looking man, who examined Bronwyn, spoke with her mother, then ushered Iris out so he could speak to Bronwyn alone.

Bronwyn felt a wave of panic as she watched her mother leave. The doctor, whose name was something difficult, Hargreave or Harcourt, closed the door firmly behind Iris and turned to Bronwyn with his arms folded over his white cloth coat, his eyes suddenly gone hard behind his thick spectacles.

"Do you understand what's happened to you, Miss Morgan?" he said.

Bronwyn had to swallow to moisten her dry throat before she found her voice. "I—I think—yes. I'm in trouble."

"In trouble." Dr. Hargreave, or whatever his name was, scowled. "That, Miss Morgan, is a euphemism."

"I know," she whispered, dropping her gaze to her lap. She

was covered with a white sheet, but the doctor had looked under that sheet, probed her belly and her private parts while she scrunched her eyes tight in an agony of embarrassment. "I know what a euphemism is," she said.

"What does it stand for, in this case?"

She stole a glance at his face from beneath the fringe of her hair. He looked tired. He also looked angry, but she didn't think he was angry with her, which was a change. Everyone else in the world seemed to be angry with her. She looked down at her lap again, and wished she could put her clothes back on. "It means a baby," she said, in a voice barely audible even to her own ears.

"That's right. You're going to have a baby."

"I didn't mean for it to happen," she murmured. "I—I didn't know."

The doctor sighed, and there was a rustle of clothes and the whisper of his shoes on the tiled floor. Bronwyn said, "I'm sorry."

"Of course," he answered quietly. She lifted her gaze, and saw that he had turned his back to her. He had crossed to the window, and was staring out as he stripped the rubber gloves from his hands. "I don't suppose there's any question of the father meeting his responsibility?"

Her throat ached suddenly. "He died," she said. That wasn't the whole story, but it was the part that mattered. The part that left her without hope.

"Died." The doctor sighed again, and Bronwyn thought he must be very tired indeed. When he turned, he didn't look so much angry as he did sorrowful. "You didn't understand you could get pregnant, I suppose, Miss Morgan."

Bronwyn looked into his dark eyes, glistening and large through his round spectacles. "I thought he loved me. I didn't really know—I thought he was courting me."

"Do you know how babies get started?"

She shook her head.

"Well." He sighed again, and threw the rubber gloves into a basin on the counter. "I've heard the same story from far too many young women like yourself." He moved to the sink, where he turned on a tap and began to wash his hands, over and over, as if once wasn't good enough. "It troubles me." He stopped soaping his hands at last, rinsed them, and turned off the tap. As he took up a white towel, he said, "I'm going to tell you as much as I can about what happens when you have a baby, and I also want you—before you leave my hospital—to understand how a baby is conceived. And—" He finished drying his hands, and dropped the towel into a basket. "I'm going to make certain you know how to prevent it, if that's what you want."

"My mother . . ." Bronwyn began, but then stopped. She bit her lip. She didn't want to be disloyal to her mother, but she was beginning to understand.

The weary look came over the doctor's face again. "Yes, your mother. Most mothers, in fact, in your social class. She didn't want to tell you, because she thought ignorance would keep you safe. Would keep you chaste."

"Ignorance?"

"It's an ancient concept, and it has never been effective, but it persists just the same." He pushed his thick glasses up to the top of his head, pushed his chair closer to the examination bed, and sat down. As he began to talk, using plain words and sometimes gestures, Bronwyn's cheeks burned with shame.

The things the doctor told her had nothing to do with the moments of sweetness she had shared with Preston. The words, body parts and reactions and fluids, were coldly scientific. Impersonal. It was like hearing her father talk about bolts and screws and railroad ties. The doctor's lecture had nothing to do with the love she had felt. He spoke of sponges and spermicides and condoms. He pointed to her belly, and discussed due dates and labor pains and forceps. She tried to listen, but her head began to ache and her mind to spin. None of it seemed real. None of it seemed to apply to *her*.

The feeling of unreality didn't last. When her labor started, it was all too real, and very, very personal. Dr. Holcomb, which she knew by then was his name, was calm and reassuring, and stayed with her throughout the hours of agony, but it was still a wrenching experience.

And it was all for nothing. She heard her baby cry, and held him in her arms for only moments before he was gone, disappeared, as if he had never been. Her mother hugged her and promised that now they could all go back to normal. That they would forget all about it.

But Bronwyn knew better. Even then, despite her mother's assurances, she knew it couldn't be true. There would be no normal, not for her. And there would certainly be no forgetting.

CHAPTER 7

Preston dreamed, too, but not of Bronwyn Morgan, though he had taken such pleasure in seducing her in her own back garden, right under the noses of her parents. She had been by no means his only seduction, that summer of 1920, but she had been particularly luscious, with such young, sweet-smelling flesh and beguiling innocence. It had been abundantly clear that she knew nothing whatever of men or sex, yet she had quivered beneath him, crying out in ecstasy. If Port Townsend had not been such a long journey from Seattle he might have visited her again, but he hardly needed to go so far afield for his pleasures. Of course, he was wearing the sapphire around his neck in those days, and he was all but invincible.

It would have been nice to dream of such things as an assignation in a garden above the waters of Puget Sound. It would have been even better to dream of Roxelana, the long-dead sultana, the slave girl who had become a queen. He loved Roxelana, though he had never known her. He loved the idea of her, a woman who was both beautiful and ruthless, powerless and yet all-powerful, because she let nothing stand between her and what she wanted. He had taken possession of her sapphire, that ancient and mysterious stone, and taken upon himself all of Roxelana's strength and determination. Once he had the jewel, all of his abilities, all of his talents, found their focus.

Yes, it would have been good to dream of Roxelana, but the mind was a strange thing. At least, *his* mind was a strange thing. The thought made him bark with hoarse, self-mocking laughter. In sleep, when he was trying to escape the grim reality of his waking life, his mind served up all the things he wanted most to forget.

There was the fire, and that awful moment when he heard the bursting of the oxygen bottles in the storage room of Margot's filthy clinic. The fire had accelerated, flared out of control, and the consequences had been worse than he could have imagined.

There was the ghastly period of recuperation in a remote country hospital, where no one knew him, or cared about him, and where they were so stingy with the morphine sulphate prescribed for his pain that he was tempted, once he was released, to set fire to that place, too. Only the fear that some savvy policeman might connect the two events had stopped him.

There was the side trip to Port Townsend, all impulse and no thought. He knew there had been a baby, and he hadn't cared, not when he received the girl's letter. But now—now that there would never be women in his life, now that any woman who saw his monstrous scars averted her eyes—somehow he needed to know the baby had been born, had survived. In those days he clung to anything that might have meant life would go on. Really, people were shockingly easy to manipulate. That cook—Andrew, her name was, as sour an old puss as he'd ever encountered— handed over everything he wanted to know. He crossed her palm with a few dollars, and she spouted all of it—that the baby had been born, was a boy, and had been shipped off to Seattle. The boy might be living in comfort and security with some good family, but in his dreams he was lost and alone, perpetually wandering in a wide world of danger.

Those dreams were bad, worthy of being called nightmares,

but they weren't the worst. His worst dreams, the ones that made him wake shivering with misery, were dreams of his mother.

It was ridiculous. He was a grown man, a decorated war veteran, a noted columnist. He was also, he reflected with neither irony nor regret, a criminal. An arsonist. A murderer. It was laughable that such a person should dream about his mother.

He would certainly have laughed at any other man fitting that description, but there was no disputing its truth. Preston Benedict was incapable of empathy, as a general rule. It was something he had known about himself since childhood, something that had been useful to him in his efforts to get his sister out of his way. His father, and his brother, worshiped Margot as if she weren't quite human. Only Edith, his mother, had truly cared about him.

It wasn't that she saw through Margot, not the way he did, though she wasn't as foolishly enthusiastic over Margot's scholarship and achievement as Father and Dick. They behaved as if no woman before Margot had ever managed to get through medical school. Edith had put her youngest son first in her affections. She loved Preston for himself, and celebrated his special gifts. She didn't want him to go into the family business, or to be a doctor, or a lawyer, or any of those things the pater so valued. Edith wanted Preston to be happy.

And despite everything that had happened, despite his crimes and his incarceration, despite his hideous disfigurement, she still did.

No one was calling the Walla Walla Sanitarium a prison, at least not out loud, but that's what it was. They all knew it: his father; his brother, Dick; and especially—probably reveling in the fact—Margot. Here, they spoke of him as a guest rather than as a patient. His medicines were administered by a pretty nurse in a long apron and starched cap, and a cook sent menus to his room for his approval. It was all charmingly deceptive, but no one was fooled, least of all Preston himself. It was as well-appointed a prison as anyone could expect, but it was still a prison. The pretty nurse never showed up without the burly orderly known as Oscar. Oscar even escorted Dr. Dunlap, or his wife, Nurse Dunlap. The cook never came at all, sending his trays up in Oscar's hairy and brutish hands.

The Walla Walla Sanitarium was a hell of a lot more comfortable than the city jail, and infinitely less unpleasant than the state hospital had been, but it was a jail, nonetheless.

Preston's dreams were of his mother weeping as she gazed out her bedroom window in Benedict Hall. His mother alone in the dark, crying for her favorite son. And he, Preston Benedict, as cold-hearted a bastard as was ever born, felt sorry for her. He even *grieved* for her.

It was ludicrous.

In the year Frank had lived in Benedict Hall, he had never seen the door standing open to the big bedroom at the front of the house, just across from the one Margot had occupied before their wedding. It mystified him at first, an airy front bedroom with all that space, an attached bath, two tall windows facing the park, all of it sitting empty.

His own boyhood home, the ranch house where his parents still lived, had only three bedrooms on its cramped second floor. Until he went to college, he and his parents and the ranch hand had used an outhouse set thirty yards from the back porch. The building of an attached bathroom hadn't taken place until the summer after his freshman year. It occasioned a lot of talk and laughter in the community, but after a few neighbors tried it out, imitators sprang up everywhere in the Bitterroot Valley.

His and Margot's rooms at the back of Benedict Hall were luxurious by contrast. From their windows they had a full view of the garden. Often, when the clouds parted, the shimmering silhouette of Mount Rainier hovered on the horizon in white-shouldered glory. There was a private bath, a sitting room that was almost as big as the small parlor on the main floor, and an enormous bed of black cherry, shipped around the Cape in the previous century. Before he and Margot returned from their wedding journey, someone had covered it with a wedding ring quilt and smooth, new, white sheets.

Benedict Hall was a lively place. The servants lived on the third floor. The family occupied the second floor. Margot's old room was kept ready for guests, dusted and cleaned, the windows opened frequently, the bedding aired often. Only that one bedroom at the front of the house remained always empty, its door closed. Edith Benedict forbade anyone to go into it except the maids, and then only under her supervision, and he knew Margot worried over that symptom of her mother's obsession.

"He's never coming home, Frank," she had said, the night she explained about the closed bedroom. "But everything in that room is just the way he left it. Once a month or so it gets dusted and swept, but Mother watches the maids as they do it so that everything is put back where he wanted it."

"Have you talked to her about it?" They had been relaxing in their sitting room, Frank with the *Times* spread out on the small coffee table, Margot with a medical journal in her lap.

She closed the journal, and idly smoothed its cover with her fingers. "No. I'm not the right person." She gazed out toward the dark garden and the glimmer of light from Blake's apartment above the garage. "Mother can't talk to me about Preston."

"She must know about him by now. What he's done. What he *is*."

"You would think so. I'm sure Father has tried to make her understand. I'm not sure if she listens."

"What about Dick?"

Margot's lips tightened at the corners. "It was always different with Dick. I'm sure Mother cared for him well enough, and he's always done what was expected. He wasn't a girl, obviously, so Mother didn't need him to be—well, feminine.

"She wanted something different from me, some interest in clothes, hairstyles. I passed up a debutante year in favor of getting myself into the University as early as possible. I was a terrible disappointment, I'm afraid. Dick tried to help, but—when a

parent has a favorite, I suppose sometimes there's nothing anyone can do." Her shoulders hunched in a way he recognized, a
gesture that appeared when something hurt her. He closed the
newspaper, ready to go to her, to soothe the pain, but she drew a
deliberate breath and straightened. She gave him a quiet smile.
"It was all a long time ago," she said. "I should be over it by now."

Frank said stoutly, "So should she."

Margot's smile widened. "Fair enough. So should she." She
leaned forward to put her long-fingered hand on his. He turned
his hand over to hold hers as tightly as he dared. The flicker of
the small fire in the grate set reflections dancing in her dark eyes.
"She can't help it, Frank. Poor Mother. She just can't."

That conversation had taken place during the winter. Preston
had just been moved from Western State Hospital, leaving Edith
deprived of her weekly visits to him. It was too far, over snow-
blocked and poorly maintained roads, to drive. The train journey
was an arduous one, south to Portland, east to a tiny place called
Wallula, then across the Columbia River. Dickson had forbidden
his wife to make the trip in winter. In fact, Margot said her father
had forbidden her mother to make the journey with just a maid,
as she proposed to do. He would take her himself, he promised,
when his schedule allowed.

That hadn't happened yet, and Edith, though she wrote regu-
larly to Preston, had begun to mope again, to stay in her room,
sometimes for days on end. Frank didn't know if Preston wrote
back to his mother, but there were always packages going off to
the sanitarium, Hattie sending tins of cookies, Edith collecting
books and magazines and toiletries.

Once, when a brown paper package, neatly tied with white
twine, was waiting on the hall table for the mailman, Frank had
seen one of the twins spit on it. She didn't know he was watching, and he stepped back quickly into the dining room so she
wouldn't see him. When he told Margot later, she said, "Oh, that
must have been Leona. She's never forgiven Preston for what he
did to her sister."

He had seduced her, Frank remembered. Impregnated her,

and then arranged an abortion that nearly caused her death. "I didn't say anything," he confessed. "Didn't think a little spit would hurt him."

"No," Margot said wryly. "And it probably made her feel better."

Edith was another matter. On a sunny June afternoon, Frank came home early, having caught the streetcar rather than telephone for Blake. He meant to go out to the Sand Point Airfield and meet one of the Boeing pilots. Tyndall had been testing the Model 15, the first Boeing-designed fighter airplane, and Frank was going to go up with him, see how the new arc-welding process was working. He hadn't flown in months, and he was as excited as a boy. When Bill Boeing gave him the assignment he had to school his face to hide the thrill it gave him.

He let himself into the hall through the front door. He would have preferred to use the back, and to climb the back staircase, but too often he encountered the maids there, and they embarrassed him by curtsying and stepping hastily out of his way. He would never, he thought, get used to having servants. They were just not the same as the hired hands he had grown up with. Frank and his father worked side by side with those hands, haying, plowing, rounding up cattle, branding. There was very little difference in their social standing.

He hooked his Stetson onto the coatrack and started up the front staircase with his briefcase under his arm. The house was quiet, but not silent. He heard Hattie humming in the kitchen, and the chirping voices of the twins coming from the dining room, with the lower, rougher voice of the maid Thelma answering. He supposed Louisa was napping, with Nurse watching beside the crib. Often Edith rested in the afternoons, too, rousing only to change for dinner, coming down to preside, in her somnolent way, over drinks in the small parlor and the family gathering for dinner.

On this day, something was different. Frank saw, as he reached the landing, that the door to Preston's bedroom stood half open, the afternoon sun slanting through it to cast wedges of light on the patterned carpet. He heard a sound from within, a sibilant murmur, the rustle of fabric, the click and slide of drawers being opened.

It was, of course, none of his affair. He and Preston had never been friends. When Frank first arrived in Seattle, Preston had pretended they were, but that had been for the sake of having a larger audience. Once Preston knew Margot cared about Frank, all pretense evaporated. The tension between them had turned into naked hatred. Frank had no sympathy left for Preston. He knew him to be without remorse. He doubted he possessed any human feelings at all.

But Edith Benedict would never be convinced, and Edith was now his mother-in-law. If he couldn't hold her in the same regard he held his own mother, she was still the only mother Margot had, and Margot worried over her. If something was wrong—or if someone was disturbing the room she kept guard over as if some-day her son would return to it—perhaps that should concern him. Quietly, he set his briefcase down, bracing it against the newel post, and walked along the corridor toward the bedroom.

The murmuring grew clearer as he approached the open door. Once or twice a little gasp punctuated its flow, as if someone had been surprised. Or was weeping.

He eased the door open with his fingertips. It was Edith in Preston's bedroom, whispering to herself as she opened and closed drawers in the bureau that stood opposite the window. The gasps were tiny, muffled sobs, which seemed to escape without her knowing it. Small tears lay on her cheeks, their flow obstructed by a thin layer of face powder. Her mouth, pale and trembling, was a little swollen, as if she had been crying for some time.

Frank spoke with all the gentleness he could muster. "Mother Benedict? Is everything all right?"

She looked up, her pale blue eyes widening and her cheeks flushing beneath her cosmetics. Her hand flew to her throat as if she had been caught doing something shameful. "Oh!" she said. "Oh! Major!"

Frank stepped into the room, but slowly. He felt as if she might startle and flee, like a doe caught nibbling rose hips in the garden. "Surely," he said, "you could call me Frank now? I'd like that."

"Oh!" she said again. Her eyes were unfocused, as if she had been someplace else entirely. She gazed at him as if she couldn't quite place him or understand what he was saying.

Frank took in the small piles of clothes on the neatly made bed, and a brocade traveling bag lying beside them. "You must be sending some things to the sanitarium," he said.

"Taking," she said in a voice both faint and insistent. "I'm taking them."

Frank couldn't think what to say to her. He hadn't heard anything of a trip, though the Sunset Highway across Snoqualmie Pass had been clear of snow for some weeks now. He said, awkwardly, "When are you going, Mother Benedict?"

"Soon," she said. "I'm going very soon."

"Will Blake be driving you?"

Her eyes, wide and blue, came up to his. "Blake? Oh, no. I don't want to go with Blake." Frank gave a little shake of his head, not understanding. She said, "Train. I'm going by train. Preston needs—" She gestured toward the suitcase. "He needs clothes. Brushes. Some things to make him more comfortable."

"I see." Frank thought it probably wasn't his place to argue with her. In a way, it was good to see her with a bit of energy. He decided the best thing was to tell Margot, or even to speak to his father-in-law. "Do you need help?"

"Oh, no, dear, thank you." She didn't look up again, but opened another drawer. She took out a stack of linen collars, something Frank was sure Preston would have no use for where he was. Edith laid them on the bed beside the valise, and Frank, following her movements, saw the antique sapphire glimmering from the dark lining of the case.

He hadn't seen it since the day he watched Margot bury it in the wet concrete of the footings of her clinic. He knew Preston had dug it out, taking a chunk of concrete with it. Preston had used it to send Margot the message that had almost gotten her killed.

Frank's nerves jumped at the memory. Involuntarily, he glanced down at his left hand, the Carnes hand, where the scoring from the straight razor still showed in the hard fiber of the palm. He could have replaced the hand for an unmarked one, but he didn't want to. He had said to Margot that bodies bear the scars of their experiences, and this hand—rubber and leather and metal—was part of his body now. It was part of his life.

He hadn't seen the sapphire again, not then, nor in the year he had lived in Benedict Hall. He pointed to the valise, forgetting to speak gently to his mother-in-law. "Mother Benedict, you don't want to take that thing to Preston. It's better if he never sees it again."

She was just turning back to the bureau, but she stopped. Her hands were empty, and they hung beside her as if she had forgotten what she meant to do. "That thing?" she whispered.

Frank took two long strides forward, and plucked the fist-sized scrap of cement out of the valise. The sapphire, half buried in its jagged surface, glowed in the afternoon light. "This," Frank said tightly, "should be disposed of. Someplace where no one has to see it again."

"Oh, no, dear," Edith said faintly. "We can't do that. Preston asked for it particularly."

"Mother Benedict." Frank drew a steadying breath, and forced himself to speak more quietly. "This isn't good for Preston. He imagines it has—well, that it has—" He couldn't think how to express it, though he knew well enough. Preston believed the sapphire—the *damned* sapphire, as Frank thought of it—had power. Magic, or something like it. It was part of his delusion, one of the symptoms of his derangement. Frank wished he had known the sapphire was here, in Preston's bedroom. He would have happily stolen it, smashed it, made it disappear forever.

Edith lifted her gaze to Frank's face. "He needs it. He says it helps him, and I promised."

"Why would he need it? Have you told Margot?"

Her eyes narrowed, and he saw determination in the set of her delicate chin, in the drawing together of her painted eyebrows. "Of course I haven't told Margot. She opposes anything Preston wants." She glanced away then, as if recalling to whom she was speaking. "They never got along," she murmured, "not even as children. I tried to help, but it was no good."

Frank could see she was attempting to be diplomatic. He did his best to respond in kind. "Yes. It's in the past now, though. I wish we could just get rid of this thing. I don't think it's any help to anyone."

She moved to the bureau, keeping her face averted. She ran her slender fingers across the things arranged on its top, Preston's things, kept in perfect order, just as he had left them. "I don't know why it helps him, Major, but if he thinks so, then . . ."

"It's just a stone, Mother Benedict. An old, old jewel."

"Yes. He told me the story."

"Story?" Frank hadn't heard a story, and he didn't think Margot had, either.

"The sapphire belonged to a queen, hundreds of years ago. Someone Preston studied, I think. She was a slave who became the wife of the sultan. Preston said the sapphire was her power, and he believes it kept him safe through the war." She glanced at him over her shoulder, her chin slightly dropped, looking up from beneath her brows in a way that made her look sly. "You know what the war was like, Frank."

"I do." He was careful to speak without inflection, but even thinking of it made the stump of his arm throb.

"For Preston, it was terrible. He's always been sensitive."

Frank tried to keep the disbelief from his face. Preston had never been sensitive, except perhaps in the case of his mother. He was—there was only one word in Frank's vocabulary to describe Preston Benedict—a monster.

His mother-in-law sniffed once, dismissively. "I don't expect you to understand. I may be the only person in his whole life who understands him."

Obliquely, not sure what else he could say, Frank said, "I'm sorry."

"Yes." She opened another drawer, scanned it, and closed it again. "Yes, I'm sorry, too."

At a loss, Frank moved back to the door, and stood a moment watching as Edith began packing things neatly into the leather valise, smoothing and folding and tucking. She appeared to have forgotten all about him, and not knowing what else he could do, he left her to it.

Frank hadn't made the trip to Walla Walla when Preston was transferred there from Steilacoom. Margot had gone, and her father. Margot reported the place was quite respectable, clean, even attractive. It wasn't meant to be a mental hospital, much less a prison, but Dickson brooked no arguments about it. He had declared that he couldn't live with the idea of his son spending the rest of his life in a state asylum. He paid a staggering price to ensure that Preston was kept safe, never allowed out of his room without a guard, never permitted to mingle with other patients.

Edith, evidently, didn't see Preston's confinement as a punishment. As Frank retreated down the corridor, he heard her whispered monologue resume, about dressing for dinner, about cuff links and tiepins, about handkerchiefs. He heard a single sob as he went into his own rooms. He paused, and glanced back, but he couldn't think of anything he could do that would help her.

The only good thing about Edith knowing where Preston was, he thought, was that it had stopped her visiting the cemetery. In the year she had believed her son was dead, she had made regular trips to kneel on Preston's empty grave, to lay flowers before the headstone engraved with his name.

It was like something out of Poe. Imagining the scene made Frank shudder. He was happier than ever to be headed out to Sand Point to fly an airplane.

CHAPTER 8

Iris presented Bronwyn with a new dress, ordered in secret from Frederick & Nelson in Seattle. It was prêt-à-porter, but Bronwyn was so slender now—at least five pounds lighter than she had been when she first met Preston—that it fit like a glove. It was a pretty peach organdy over a cream silk slip, with a white taffeta sash that skimmed her narrow hips. The bodice was loose, with transparent puff sleeves, and Iris had ordered peach cotton gloves to match. There was a cream straw hat with a drooping brim and one small, elegant, peach-colored rosette on the band. Iris was so delighted with the whole ensemble, and so eager to see Bronwyn wear it, that Bronwyn couldn't refuse her. She accepted Clara's invitation despite her misgivings.

Clara's little house was nearly invisible behind huge rhododendrons and sprawling hydrangeas. Bronwyn and her mother knocked on the blue-painted door, and were admitted by the maid, Clara's only servant.

"I like it that way," Clara had told Bronwyn, after she was first married. "I can trust Lola not to tell Robert every single thing that happens." Lola curtsied as she admitted the two Morgan ladies into the small, airy hallway, and gestured toward the back of the house, where the tea was taking place on the narrow brick patio.

Clara was sitting at a round table covered with a white linen cloth, with a plate of finger sandwiches and a pitcher of lemonade in the center. She was pouring tea from a silver pot, but she jumped up when she saw them, nearly upsetting the tea service. "Bronwyn! Mrs. Morgan!" she cried. "I'm so glad you could come!"

As if nothing had ever changed, as if they were still equals, Clara flew across the patio in a flutter of champagne lace, one hand on her wide-brimmed hat to keep it from falling off. She shook Iris's hand, then embraced Bronwyn, and kissed her cheek. Bronwyn smiled at her, and blinked away the sting of tears at her friend's show of loyalty. Clara took her hand as she led them both toward the table, where several other Port Townsend matrons were seated. They wore pastel dresses and straw hats in every shape and color, and against the backdrop of green shrubbery they looked like flowers arranged to catch the sun.

"Look, everyone!" Clara exclaimed, drawing Bronwyn forward. "You remember Mrs. Iris Morgan, don't you? She has that marvelous house on Monroe, the one at the top of the hill. And her daughter, Bronwyn, one of my oldest friends."

Two of the young women had begun to smile, and lift their gloved hands in greeting, but when Clara spoke Bronwyn's name, their smiles faded. Their hands dropped hastily to their laps like fluttering birds. An older woman, perhaps Iris's age, made a noise in her throat, and turned her head away. Bessie and her mother were present, but neither gave any greeting, nor did Bessie show in any way that she recognized her old chum.

It was every bit as bad as Bronwyn had feared. None of the women spoke. They stared at them, both Iris and Bronwyn, as if they were aliens. As if poor Clara, with the best of intentions, had invited two of the soiled doves who worked the alleys of Water Street to sit down to tea.

Bronwyn's stomach clenched beneath her taffeta sash. She felt her mother stiffen beside her, and she wanted to seize her arm and drag her away, but Clara was not giving in. She pulled out chairs for them, sent Lola to fetch more plates, brightly pressed them to have tea or lemonade, and commenced a stream of chatter, doing her heroic best to disguise the unfriendly atmosphere.

Bronwyn's embarrassment transformed, in the face of her friend's efforts, to cold anger. Perhaps she deserved this treatment, but her mother didn't, nor did Clara. It was unfair. It was rude. Every woman at this table had been brought up to be courteous, no matter what. She knew that, because her own upbringing had taught her the same.

Bronwyn fixed Bessie with an icy stare. She said, when Clara paused for breath in her brave monologue, "Bessie. Clara tells me you and Frederick are engaged. Congratulations."

There was little Bessie could do when addressed so directly. She said, "Thank you."

Bronwyn persisted. "Have you set the wedding date? Chosen your dress?"

"No."

A chill silence settled over the gathering, at odds with the brilliant sunshine, the cheerful birdsong from the surrounding trees, the bright gleam of the water in the distance. Lola came back with a fresh pitcher of lemonade, and spent a few moments refilling glasses. An older woman spoke to another woman, but their conversation lagged, and soon it was quiet again.

Bronwyn's heart began to pound as if she had run all the way from Monroe Street. She pressed her hand to her chest, where she could feel the racing of her heartbeat beneath her fingers. She said, very clearly, "Clara, it was kind of you to invite us. I've missed you." She rose, lifting her chair from the back so it wouldn't catch on the bricks of the patio. Iris, her face bleak with shame, stood up as well. Her lips trembled, and she pressed one gloved hand over her mouth.

Clara jumped up. "Oh, Bronwyn—Mrs. Morgan—don't go yet, please! Surely . . ." Her voice trailed off, and her cheeks flared scarlet. "I wish . . ." she tried, but again, the words wouldn't come.

Bronwyn embraced her. "Never mind, darling," she said. She spoke lightly, but in a voice meant to carry. "You can't be responsible for other people's behavior."

As Clara hugged her back, Bronwyn reflected that her words could be interpreted in different ways. No doubt some of the ladies present would think it was her own behavior she was apologizing for. She put her hand under her mother's arm. Side by side, they crossed the patio to the back door. Lola met them, holding the door open for them to pass through, frowning in confusion at their early departure.

From the shadow of the hallway, Bronwyn turned, and blew a kiss to Clara as if she hadn't a care in the world. Not until she and her mother were safely away, walking through the hot sunshine toward the haven of their own home, did she let her tears fall. Her mother's did, too, and the two of them arrived home weeping helplessly into their handkerchiefs.

"You see how it is, Mother," Bronwyn said tiredly.

"It will pass," Iris said, but even her dogged hopefulness was beginning to fade. "They'll forget, and things can go back—"

"Mother!" Bronwyn leaned forward to cover her mother's hand with hers. They had changed places, Bronwyn reflected. Her mother was now the child and she, Bronwyn, the adult. She was the one who could no longer deny the harsh ways of the world. Her mother still clung to the illusions created by her wealth and her position. She maintained her faith in the rules of society, no matter how dismally they had failed her.

They were alone in their own garden now, safe behind a hedge of rhododendrons. The blooms were spent, but the boughs were thick and dark, with glossy green leaves. Snapdragons and fuchsias crowded a border at the edge of the garden, and hummingbirds, gay and industrious, flashed in and out of their blossoms. Bronwyn watched the tiny birds, but she was oblivious to their charm. "Mother, things will never go back. You have to know that by now."

"Oh, Bronwyn. Sweetheart." Fresh tears, the tears Bronwyn thought were past for the day, darkened Iris's eyes, muddying their flecks of gold. "I just can't bear it!" she sobbed.

"You've been wonderful," Bronwyn said. She pressed her hand over her mother's. "No daughter could have hoped for a better mother through all of this."

Iris cried, "I still don't understand! I thought he was a *gentleman*."

"A gentleman would have answered my letter. And whatever he might have intended, he's gone now."

Iris sniffled, and wiped her eyes. "I still think, if the Benedicts knew—if they understood that there was going to be—"

"A baby. You might as well say it. There was a baby."

"Yes. A baby." She blew her nose delicately. "Your father had decided he should write to them himself, but then we read about the fire. There seemed to be no point."

"It doesn't matter now," Bronwyn said.

"I wanted to keep him," Iris said, so softly Bronwyn wasn't sure she had heard properly.

"What?" Iris shook her head, but Bronwyn pressed her. "Mother? What did you say?"

Iris looked away, and for long moments she was silent. Then, as if giving in to an impulse, she blurted, "I wanted to keep the baby."

"You did? *My* baby?"

Her mother nodded, still not meeting her gaze. "I thought we could say he was mine."

"You never told me this!"

"I mentioned it to Chesley once. He was so angry I thought he might actually—well, he probably wouldn't have, but I . . ." She broke off, shaking her head, dabbing again at her eyes.

Bronwyn sagged back against the scrolled iron bench, so that a trailing branch of rhododendron caught at her hair. She brushed it away, and closed her eyes. "I know what Daddy's like when he's angry."

"Yes. But he knows best, of course."

"Does he, Mother?"

"Of course he does, Bronwyn! You'll understand that when you have a husband of your own, a family—"

"Why should the husband make all the decisions? It's not fair. It's not even logical!"

"It's just the way it is, dear. And so I had to—that is, we had to—let him go."

"He might have been with us all this time. Growing. Happy!"

"Chesley said people would never believe he was ours. That they would know."

"They know anyway! So what good did that do?"

Iris tried to stifle the sob that rose in her throat. In a choking voice, she said, "I did the best I could, Bronwyn. I was raised to respect my husband's wishes, and so I always have."

Bronwyn knew she should let it go, that it did no good to hurt her mother any more, but she couldn't help herself. She opened her eyes, and gazed sorrowfully at the bright water below the hill. "Poor little baby. Out there in the world, and we have no idea what became of him."

"Oh, we do. At least I think we do."

Bronwyn started, and turned to stare at her mother. "We do? *You* do?"

Iris was plucking at a rhododendron leaf, tearing it into shreds and flicking the bits from her lap. "He's my grandson, Bronwyn," she said softly. "I couldn't bear sending him off without some—some accommodation for his welfare."

"Accommodation?"

Iris lifted her eyes, and Bronwyn nearly gasped at the pain in her face. "I knew there was a good orphanage in Seattle. Run by this wonderful woman; everyone knows about her. Your father made a big contribution to their new building—buying bricks, they called it, but really, it's part of the building fund—in exchange for their promise to take the baby in."

There was a click as Mrs. Andrew opened the kitchen window above their heads, but Bronwyn paid no attention. She was gazing in breathless shock at her mother's pained expression. "Mother! My baby's in Seattle?"

"Well, he was. As an infant, at least."

"Why didn't you tell me?"

"Chesley said you didn't need to know. That it was better if you didn't."

"But all this time—I've worried and worried . . ."

"I don't think you have to worry," Iris said, but doubtfully. "Mrs. Ryther is supposed to be very good about placing children in loving homes."

"Who's Mrs. Ryther?"

"She runs the orphanage."

"In Seattle."

Iris crumbled the remains of the leaf, and let them drop from her fingers. "Yes. The baby might not be there anymore, though. He's probably been adopted by a wonderful family."

"Or an awful one," Bronwyn said.

Iris shuddered. "Don't say that, Bronwyn. Oh, please, please don't say that. I have to think the best."

Bronwyn didn't answer. From the open kitchen window came a clatter of china bowls being carelessly stacked. Bronwyn tipped her head back to look up and caught sight of Mrs. Andrew's dour face peeking out at the two of them. "She's listening to us, Mother," she said. "Mrs. Andrew. Snooping again."

"It doesn't matter, Bronwyn. She knows all about it."

Bronwyn brought her gaze back to her mother's face. "Why? Why should she know?"

"There were letters. Telephone calls. It was just easier to tell her."

"She bullies you."

Iris breathed a long sigh, and her eyes reddened again. "I know."

"So does Daddy."

Iris, pressing her lips together to hold back a fresh sob, just shrugged.

Bronwyn looked away, down to the green, restless waters of the Sound. An idea was forming in her mind. It was the first clear idea, the only real desire, she had had in a very long time, but she couldn't share it with her mother. She didn't dare.

The railroad meant to connect Port Townsend with Olympia, and thereby Portland and Seattle, had progressed no more than a mile before the funds ran out. That failure left the city at the mercy of the private boats known as the Mosquito Fleet. The bigger ones, especially those that carried automobiles, offered regular service three days a week. Smaller ones mostly showed up at the docks when it pleased them, unless someone of importance booked passage. When Bronwyn went to Seattle with her mother to shop, they rode in comfort on one of the big boats. Now she would have to take one of the little ones, but they frightened her.

She lived in a seacoast town, and she had been listening to tales of sea disasters since she was a tiny girl. Steamers sank, wood-fueled boilers caused fires, the new diesel engines exploded. Only a few years before, the Colman Dock in Seattle had collapsed, plunging ferry passengers into Elliott Bay. A child and a woman had drowned.

Bronwyn told herself drowning could hardly be worse than childbirth, and laid her plans.

She pulled her old valise down from the top of her wardrobe. A musty smell emanated from its stained interior, and she found a handkerchief and a shawl she had left there from her trip to Vancouver. It stunned her to think she had gone nowhere since then, not taken a single journey that required her to pack a bag. While she rummaged in her bureau for the things she would need, she set the valise beneath the open window to air.

It didn't take long to fold some lingerie, two pairs of stockings, two shirtwaists and a skirt, a nightdress, and a coat. She wedged these into the valise, which smelled significantly better for having sat open to the breeze. She added a hairbrush and some toiletries, and she was done.

A much harder task, one that required twice as much time, was writing the letter to her parents. In truth, she thought of it as a letter to her mother. She was certain her father would be so angry he would no longer care what became of her, but she would address it to both of them out of respect. Her stationery set, engraved with her name, waited for her at the small, girlish desk she had used all through school. She sat down on the matching chair, and drew a page of her stationery onto the blotter. She dipped her pen into the inkwell, but it took her so long to think of what she could say that the ink dried, and she had to dip it again.

Finally, her throat aching with sorrow, she wrote:

> Dear Mother and Daddy:
>
> I don't want to hurt you any more than I already have. You know I love you, but I can't stay here. I'm not a little girl anymore, and people in Port Townsend will never forget what I've done.
>
> I'll write to you as soon as I can. I'm going to find a job, and a place to live. Mother, try not to worry. Daddy, I'm sorry for everything. I wish I could fix it, but I can't turn back the clock.
>
> I hope you'll understand that there's no future for me here. I can't go on living this way with no friends and nothing to do. Please, please forgive me.
>
> Your loving daughter,
>
> Bronwyn Chesley Morgan

Bronwyn reread what she'd written while she waited for the ink to dry. The words brought fresh tears to her eyes, but she blinked them away. It was too late now for tears.

She folded the note in half and slid it into an envelope. She wrote their names on it, and laid it on her pillow where Betty would find it, and carry it to her mother. It would be kinder if they knew she had really gone. Kinder, too, if she didn't mention she was going in search of her lost child. Daddy would be furious if he knew what Mother had told her, and Mother would be sad enough without cringing before one of Daddy's tempers.

She slid the packed valise under her bed before she went down to dinner. During the meal, she did her best to behave as usual, although she could hardly remember, now, what usual was. Her mother sighed once or twice, and spoke little. Her father tried to spark a conversation, but with the women both withdrawn, by the time Mrs. Andrew sent in dishes of blueberries in thick cream, he gave up. They ate their dessert in silence, and Iris and Chesley rose to carry their coffee out to the garden. Bronwyn surprised her mother by catching her arm, and leaning close to kiss her cheek.

"Bronwyn?" Iris said. "You're not—going out?" Her voice cracked a little on the sentence. Bronwyn knew her mother hated and feared her nightlife. Iris never asked where she went at night, and Bronwyn understood it was because she didn't want to know.

Well. After today, she wouldn't have to fear it anymore. Bronwyn responded, "No. I just—just wanted to say good night. I'm going to turn in early." She felt her father's scowl prickling her neck as she went up the stairs. He had made no secret of his displeasure with her, and she supposed he would never forgive her now. She had stolen his respectability. Shattered the family honor. He should be relieved when she disappeared. He might be able to restore his good name without his fallen angel around to remind everyone of the family's embarrassment.

CHAPTER 9

Blake was unusually quiet as he drove the shining green Cadillac down Aloha to Broadway, and onto East Madison. At first Margot didn't take notice of his silence. It was going to be a long day, and she was riffling through a pile of forms, double-checking for errors or omissions. The papers were due at the governor's office to secure the funds she had promised Olive Ryther. Margot wished she could hire someone to handle the paperwork.

She clicked her tongue as she closed the file. "This," she said with disgust, "is not what I trained for."

Usually, Blake would chuckle at such a remark, and ask her for details. This morning, though, he didn't respond, and she lifted her head to eye him in the rearview mirror. He looked much as usual, his cap settled firmly on his head, his driving gloves and jacket spotless as always. Margot set the file on the seat beside her so she could lean forward. "Blake? Is everything all right?"

There was a touch of the South in his pronunciation when he answered, and she knew what that meant. "I think," he began. *Ah think.* "I think Nurse Church is going to be upset."

"Sarah? Why? Has something happened?"

"Something is going to happen, Dr. Margot. Next month. It doesn't directly affect me, but for Sarah—this is a hard moment."

"Do you want to tell me?"

Blake's gloved fingers tapped an irritated rhythm on the broad steering wheel. "I don't know, Dr. Margot. I don't want to upset you, too, especially when there's nothing you can do to help."

"I can listen, Blake," she said. "Anything that affects Sarah— or you, even indirectly—matters to me. I think you know that."

Still he hesitated. She let the moment stretch, turning her head toward the small, square houses of the neighborhood they were just passing. The Women and Infants Clinic was, by design, located in the Negro district. The homes were often shabby, in need of paint and repairs, but in the yards, hydrangeas and sunflowers and even a few roses bloomed in the June sun. Margot had made calls to a number of such houses, and she knew how hard it was for the people who lived in them to pay their rent and feed their families. Planting flowers was a gesture of courage and hope. It touched her, and she admired the housewives for doing it.

They reached the turning for the road south out of the city, and she looked ahead again, still waiting for Blake to speak.

He cleared his throat. "The Klan is having a meeting next month," he said in a deep, hard voice. "In Renton."

"You mean the Ku Klux Klan? Here?"

"Yes."

She heard his effort to keep his voice even, but the anger that underlay it startled her. "They can't touch you, Blake. Father would never allow that."

"I know," he said. "It's Nurse Church I'm worried about."

"Sarah! Why?"

"Dr. Margot, I'm allowed to live on Capitol Hill because of my position at Benedict Hall. But for Sarah—and her family—she hasn't said anything, but I'm worried."

"Because of the Klan?"

He flashed her a look in the mirror, and his eyes were as hard as his voice. It was so rare to see Blake angry, with fierce lines drawn around his mouth, that it stopped her breath for a moment. He said tightly, "I found a pamphlet on the porch. I didn't show it to anyone, because—well. There seemed no point."

"What did it say?"

"It was put out by the Klan, and describes how they have been 'assisting'—that's the word they use—neighborhoods to rewrite their covenants. The Church family has a home near the Sound, a modest one, but they own it. This pamphlet proposes rewriting neighborhood covenants to exclude anyone not of the Aryan race."

"No!" Margot leaned forward to speak over the edge of the seat. "Blake, they can't do that! It's not legal—it can't be!"

The muscles of his jaw bunched, then released. "They can do it," he said heavily. "They just haven't done it yet."

Margot leaned back, blowing out a breath, and folded her arms tight around herself. "That's revolting," she muttered. "Have we made no progress since the war?"

"Which war would that be, Dr. Margot?"

She gave a sour chuckle. "Excellent point. There are far too many to choose from."

"I have to agree with that."

"Maybe nothing will happen, Blake," she said thoughtfully. "This is Seattle, after all. This is an immigrant community, and we have citizens from all over."

"Perhaps you're right, Dr. Margot," he said, but he didn't sound convinced.

"If you come across another of those pamphlets, save it for me. I'll show it to Father. He might want a word with the mayor about something like that."

The fingers beat on the wheel again, then straightened. Margot could just see, by the curve of Blake's cheek, that he was smiling now, and the atmosphere in the motorcar lightened. He said, "I thank you, Dr. Margot. I'm sure if you add your voice, Mr. Dickson will listen."

She relaxed her arms, and tilted her head so he could see her answering smile in the mirror. "I'm fairly certain, Blake, that my father listens to everything you say, whether you know it or not."

"Well," he said. "If that's so, I'm honored."

They drove on in silence, and Margot gathered up her forms to go through them one last time. It hadn't been easy to persuade Olive Ryther to let her and Sarah vaccinate and examine every one of her children, but now that it was done, she felt an obligation to secure the funds she had promised. The only problem she could foresee was Mrs. Ryther's poor record keeping. She and Sarah both had spoken to her about it, but Mrs. Ryther dismissed their concerns.

"God will take care of my little ones," she had said. "He leads them to me, and He protects them when they leave. Where they came from, where they go, those aren't my worries."

Sarah said, "What if someone is looking for a particular child? Sometimes families get separated."

"People should watch over their children more carefully," Mrs. Ryther said. When Sarah and Margot exchanged a frowning glance, she added, "Let go, let God. That's my motto."

Later, on their way back to the Women and Infants Clinic, Margot said, "She sounds like Hattie sometimes. 'Let go, let God' is one of Hattie's favorites."

"I like it better from Hattie," Sarah said, and Margot and Blake had both laughed.

The day trip took even longer than Margot and Blake had expected. By the time they returned to Benedict Hall, the dinner hour was already past. Hattie had been watching from the kitchen window for the Cadillac, and she bustled out to open the front door for Margot.

"Land's sake, Miss Margot, you must be worn out!" she said. She took Margot's hat and coat, and hung them on the rack. Margot submitted to this assistance meekly. She was, in fact, exhausted.

It was just as well, she thought, that Frank was away tonight. He had flown to Spokane with one of the Boeing pilots to have a look at an airplane under development by the Ford Motor Company. They would spend the night at a hotel near the airfield, he said, and be back the next day. The house seemed empty without him, but his absence meant she could go straight to bed and to sleep.

"You get yourself into the dining room now, Miss Margot, and I'll bring you your supper. I bin keepin' it warm in the oven."

"Hattie, why not just let me have it in the kitchen with Blake? That will save you a few steps."

"Now, Miss Margot, that's just not right. Blake won't like it. I've got Thelma here, and she'll serve you."

Margot, too tired to argue, did as she was told. Her place setting had been left, but the rest of the table was empty. The candles in their elaborate silver holders had been snuffed out, and all that was left of the dinner service was a silver butter dish and a cut-glass saltcellar. Margot sat down as Thelma came in with a small bowl of tomato soup and a single roll on a saucer. Margot gave the maid a weary nod of thanks. "Thelma, just bring everything at once," she said. "You don't need to keep running in and out just for me."

Thelma, gray-haired and plump, was as silent a woman as the other maids were chatty. She said, "My orders, miss," and turned to leave. Margot could have pointed out that her own orders should take precedence over Hattie's, or Blake's, but it seemed too much trouble. She chuckled to herself as she picked up her soupspoon.

"What's funny?"

Margot glanced up, and found her older brother peeking in through the open door. "Dick," she said, smiling. "Come and sit down. Keep me company."

He grinned at her, and she thought how much he was beginning to look like their father. Like Dickson the elder, Dick was beginning to thicken at the waist, and his dark hair already showed strands of gray. He had his father's prominent jaw, too—but then, she reflected ruefully, so did she.

"You're late tonight," Dick said, pulling out a chair opposite her and settling into it. "Hospital?"

"No, actually," Margot said. "Not today." She tasted the soup. "Gosh. This is good."

"Hattie's getting better, I think," Dick said. "Mother leaves her alone these days, and she can cook the things she's good at."

"How is Mother? I doubt Ramona has time to watch over her the way she did before the baby came."

Dick pushed the butter dish closer to her hand. "I don't know about Mother, Margot. I see her at dinner, like you do. Breakfast. Mostly she stays in her room, I guess. Ramona says she goes days without seeing Louisa at all."

"What a shame. That precious little girl! These days won't come back, when she's so small and so—" She waved her spoon, not sure of the right word.

"*Adorable*, I think, is the word you're looking for," Dick said drily. "I hear it from my wife all the time!"

"Well, Louisa *is* adorable," Margot said. She took another spoonful of soup. She felt better for the food, but she could feel her eyelids growing heavy already. "She's like a puppy, tumbling every which way. Always happy."

"She's more like Coyote," Dick said.

Margot smiled. "You mean the Trickster."

"I do! We can't keep the child corralled for more than an hour at a time. Poor Nurse is run off her feet."

"I wish I had more time to spend with her," Margot said, spooning up the last of the soup.

"Well, it's Nurse's job, isn't it? I'm just glad Ramona doesn't have to chase after the baby all day by herself. I can't imagine how women manage who don't have any help."

"No," Margot said, sobering now. "No, Dick, you probably can't, nor can Ramona. I see lots of them. They're more or less permanently exhausted."

After a moment, Dick said, "So, if you weren't at the hospital, what kept you so late?"

"I had to go to Olympia today, to drop off the Sheppard-Towner forms. For the Ryther Child Home."

"Oh, yes. I knew that, but it slipped my mind. They haven't finished the Capitol yet, I understand."

"You and Father have your fingers in that pie, don't you?"

Dick leaned back, linking his hands across his small paunch, making himself look even more like their father. "We do," he said with satisfaction. "All our fingers. Or I should say, we did. Lots of hullabaloo about costs, but Father saw that coming, and saw to it we were paid on delivery."

"You're not responsible for those pricey spittoons, I hope," Margot said wryly. She split the fresh roll, and the enticing scent of yeast rose from it. "Not much to be proud of, from what I heard."

Dick laughed. "No, we didn't handle the spittoons. Not sure who did, but Hartley's screaming that they charged nearly fifty dollars apiece."

"I heard the same. What did you and Father sell, then?"

"Masonry for the dome, mostly. And we imported some stone and marble, for the floors, columns, that sort of thing."

"The dome's finished, at least. It's impressive."

"We didn't choose the style, but we like it," Dick said. "It's a great design, though, don't you think? The classical look. I was down there when they first started building it a couple of years ago. Glad they didn't move the capital to Yakima, or wherever they were talking about."

Thelma returned with a serving of white fish and asparagus, and set it in front of Margot without a word. When she had gone, Margot said, "Does that woman ever speak to you, Dick?"

"Sometimes."

"I never hear her say a word."

"They're all afraid of you, Margot. The great doctor!"

"That's ridiculous."

He smirked at her. "You are a bit scary," he said. "You go around looking so stern."

With a mouthful of fish, that somehow Hattie had managed to keep moist despite the hour, Margot shook her head. When she had swallowed, and touched her lips with her napkin, she said, "I am *not* scary, Dick."

"Not to me," he said. "But I'm used to you. You still scare Ramona a bit, though. Most certainly not Louisa!"

Thinking of the child made her smile. "I don't think Louisa is frightened of anything."

"No," her brother said ruefully. "I'm the one that's frightened, when I hear about her escapades."

They sat in a comfortable silence while Margot finished her meal. Thelma came in with a freshly made cup of tea, which Hattie knew Margot liked at night. Margot said, "Thelma, Dick might like a coffee," but Dick said no, and sent the maid off with the used china.

It wasn't until her tea was half gone that Margot remembered Blake's worry of the morning. "Dick," she said. "I almost forgot. Blake is hoping we can do something to help Sarah Church's family. It doesn't seem possible to me, but evidently the Ku Klux Klan in Seattle is having an influence on certain neighborhood covenants."

"It hardly seems possible we *have* a Ku Klux Klan in Seattle."

"That's what I thought, too, but they're having some sort of rally next month. Down in Renton."

"I don't know that Father can do anything about that, Margot."

"No, not about the rally. What sort of people are attracted by all that white Christian America nonsense?"

"They must not think it's nonsense."

"But it's so—so ignorant!" She stiffened, and glared at him, pushing her teacup aside, leaning forward. "You agree with me, surely? Think about Hattie, and Blake—and Sarah Church!"

He was grinning at her now, and she said, "What?"

"There you are, looking fierce as a thunderstorm, and you wonder why all the servants tremble in their boots when they see you coming!"

Margot subsided, giving a little flick of her fingers as if she could brush the whole subject aside. "The thing is, Dick, there's a Klan office here, and Blake tells me they've agitated to keep

Negroes and Chinese out of certain neighborhoods. The Churches' home is in one of those areas."

"That can't be legal."

"That's what I said. Blake thought it was possible the Churches could be pushed out of their own house, even though they're the owners."

The remnants of Dick's smile faded, and he leaned his elbows on the table. "I've heard of this in other cities, but I thought Seattle—I mean, it's not a new idea. But Sarah Church—she's a professional!"

"So is her mother. And, Dick, lots of Negroes, and Chinese, too, are professionals. Doctors, lawyers, teachers . . . they're no different from us."

"They claim it's about property values, I suppose."

"They can claim what they like," she said. The old sense of frustration she had suffered when she was struggling against bias in her profession made her voice bitter. "It's blatant racism, just the same."

Dick considered for a moment, his brow furrowed, his dark eyes narrowed as he gazed at the darkness beyond the picture window. "I don't know, Margot. There may not be anything we can do."

"We can try, can't we? Talk to the mayor, perhaps?"

He shook his head. "Our business depends on goodwill in the city, Margot. I feel sorry for the Churches, but—maybe they'd be happier living in one of the Negro neighborhoods."

"You can't mean that!"

"It's not fair, of course. I see that."

"Not fair! It's—it's criminal!"

"Evidently not, or the police would stop it. There would be laws—"

"Laws!" Margot spat. "The law lags a hundred years behind, it seems to me!"

Her brother put up his hands and grinned at her. "There you go again, Margot."

She rubbed her eyes with her fingers, drawing a deep breath

behind her palms. When she released the breath and dropped her hands, she tried to speak more calmly. "Dick, you have to understand. Sarah is something special. She could have been a physician if she wanted to." Margot pushed herself up from the table. "Or if she could have afforded medical school."

"Come on, Margot. You're tired. It may not happen, in any case." Dick stood up, too, and came around the table to open the dining room door.

Margot walked past him, and together they turned toward the staircase and started up. "It's just not right, Dick. They don't have the right to do this."

"It's a tough world," Dick said. In an unusual display of affection, he put an arm around her shoulders and gave her a squeeze. "You can't fix the whole world, Margot."

She managed a dry chuckle. "That's exactly what Frank says."

"Listen to your husband, then." He smiled and released her. "Good man, Frank."

"I know." She gave him a grateful look and turned toward her own room. A bath, a book, an early night. A long sleep was just what she needed.

Dick stopped her with a hand on her arm. In a low voice, he said, "Margot, about Mother."

She glanced down the hall at the closed door to her parents' large bedroom. The door to their bath was closed, too. "What, Dick?"

"Ramona tells me she talks endlessly about this child—this other child."

"The one Preston claims, you mean."

"Unfortunately, yes. Ramona says she's obsessed with it. Him."

"Oh, dear," Margot said heavily. "That must hurt Ramona. And you, too."

Dick gave a one-shouldered shrug. "I always knew Mother preferred Preston over the two of us. I'm used to it."

"But your little girl—"

"Fortunately, Louisa has the most devoted mother in the world."

He smiled a little. "I can't imagine Ramona favoring our next child over Louisa!"

"No, of course not." Margot yawned. "Are you planning the next one already, Dick?"

At this he laughed. "No, the next one is yours and Frank's."

"Now you really do sound like my husband!" It felt good to say that, to say the words *my husband*. Even after a year of marriage, it gave her a little thrill of pride, and of happiness, that a man like Frank—handsome, smart, brave—was her husband.

She and her brother smiled at each other as they parted, and moved on toward their separate beds. Margot was still smiling when she turned out her light. She couldn't help imagining, as she laid her head on the pillow, how her own child—and Frank's—might look. Not fair like Louisa, of course. Dark, like the two of them, but surely with Frank's wonderful blue eyes.

In the last moments before she slept, she thought of how terrible it would be if Preston were telling the truth. She wasn't inclined to believe anything he said, ever, but if she believed there really was a Benedict child somewhere in Seattle—a Benedict child without the protection and love of this fierce and loyal family—it would break her heart.

CHAPTER 10

In the chill half-darkness that preceded the summer dawn, Bronwyn dressed in a green linen traveling suit and printed cotton shirtwaist. She slipped out of her bedroom and tiptoed down the stairs in her stocking feet. She had her valise in one hand, and her sturdiest shoes, a pair of Mary Janes with brass buckles, in the other. She wore a wide-brimmed straw hat with a green hatband, and she carried a small handbag, with all the money she possessed and a scrap of paper with an address on it.

Holding her breath, she unlocked the front door and eased it open. When she closed it she waited, head tilted, to be certain no one had heard her. In the suspended silence of the small hours, when even the birds still seemed to be sleeping, she picked her way carefully over the brick path to the street. She had to set her things down to buckle on her shoes, then resumed her burdens and started down the hill toward the ferry dock.

By the time she crossed Water Street to reach the dew-slicked boardwalk, the sky was brightening, and workmen in coveralls and flat canvas caps were calling to one another as they moved to and fro, their shoulders bent beneath coils of thick rope or wooden toolboxes hung on wide leather straps. They cast side-ways glances at the well-dressed young woman coming among them in the chill dawn, but no one spoke to her. The air smelled of salt and fish and the greasy tang of diesel oil. The breeze rip-pled Bronwyn's hat brim and cut through the cloth of her jacket, making her shiver. Men shouted back and forth, their voices competing with the strident calls of the seagulls that swarmed above the docks as the light began to rise.

Three boats bobbed in the dark water beside the dock, two on one side and the third on the opposite. It was huge, three hun-dred feet at least, with a curved railing running all the way around a high passenger deck, and a wide ramp for automobiles to be loaded into the lower deck. A man in a smart uniform and cap stood with his hands in his pockets, supervising the loading of wooden crates tied up with brown rope. He was giving orders to two laborers, but when he saw Bronwyn he turned away from them. He pulled his hands out of his pockets and started down the little gangway, sliding his hands along the rope railings. He looked familiar, and when she saw that the name of his ship was *The City of Olympia*, she remembered. She and her mother had taken it to Vancouver, and this man had been solicitous of her pregnant state. He might remember her. He might even stop her from boarding.

She spun away from his sharp gaze, and walked purposefully toward the other two boats, trying to act as if she knew what she was doing. Her valise bumped awkwardly against her leg, and she had to hold her hat with her other hand. She wished she had thought to use a hatpin, although since she had cut her hair, it wasn't as effective as it had once been.

The morning light rose swiftly. She could make out the details of the two smaller boats, and her heart sank. One was clearly cargo only, its decks crowded with barrels and boxes. A bearded man with a large stomach beneath a canvas jacket was already unwrapping the mooring rope from its bollard.

The second boat couldn't have been more than thirty feet long, dwarfed by the ship opposite it. There was no upper deck, and certainly no space for even a single automobile. Bronwyn gazed in dismay at its splintered wooden sides, the dents in its bow, and the angry hissing of its boiler, which she could hear even from the dock. All her fears about disasters at sea came rushing back. She bit her lip, wondering if she should take her chances with the big ferry. If that man refused her, though, if he sent her back home, would she have another chance? If her parents had found her note, if they knew what she planned, she would lose what little freedom she had left.

As she hesitated, a man came around from the starboard side of the little boat, and when he saw her, dashed down the gangway. She sucked in a startled breath, and began to back away, but he rushed toward her, saying, "Miss! Miss! Wait!"

His appearance didn't inspire confidence. He was scrawny and slight, half a head shorter than she, and dressed in a pair of stained coveralls and a shirt with a frayed collar. As he approached, she saw that he was young, very likely no older than she was. His very eagerness frightened her, as if he were desperate for custom, and she was the only prospect in sight.

He skidded to a stop directly in front of her. "Miss, are you wanting to travel? To go somewhere? I'll take you—Edmonds, Kingston, Olympia—where is it you're wanting to be?" He gestured back at his poor little boat with its splintered hull and noisy engine. "This is the *Sadie Ann*, named for my mother, and I'm her captain. I know she don't look like much, but I promise you, she's just as reliable as my mama is! She'll get you where you want to go!" As Bronwyn still hesitated, the young man said, his bony face full of hope, "Got any money, miss?"

Bronwyn was on the point of saying that no, she had no money at all, but a loud voice from the boardwalk made her flinch. "Hey, Bronwyn! Bronwyn Morgan! Hang on a minute!"

It was Johnnie Johnson, and he looked as if he hadn't been to bed at all. His face was puffy, his steps angry as he stamped toward her. His shoes echoed on the wooden boards. "Hey!" he shouted again. "Whatcha think you're doin'? I'm thinkin' you owe me!"

Bronwyn whirled to face the unprepossessing young boatman. "Yes!" she said hastily. "Yes, I have money! Can you take me to Seattle?" Before he could answer, she picked up her valise, clutched her hat onto her head with her free hand, and started up the gangway. It swayed under her weight, and the cleats were slippery with morning dew. She thought for one terrible moment she might slip, and fall into the greasy-looking water as those poor people had done on the Colman Dock, but the scrawny young man caught her by the shoulders with surprisingly gentle hands, and steadied her until she set her feet safely on the deck.

He was, she soon understood, more capable than he looked. He pulled up the gangway in a matter of seconds, so that by the time Johnnie reached the *Sadie Ann,* there was no way for him to board her. Johnnie stood on the dock for a moment, shouting imprecations at Bronwyn, but the young captain took her arm and escorted her, with an elegance more suited to a tearoom than the deck of a dilapidated boat, around to the far side of the pilothouse, where its bulk blocked Johnnie's view. There were two deck chairs and a long bench, all empty. At the stern, she saw a pile of wood, chopped into lengths for burning and neatly tied down. The pilothouse, lit by an oil lamp, seemed to be empty.

Bronwyn quavered, "Don't you have a crew?"

Her captain grinned, showing a gap between his two front teeth, but making his brown eyes dance. "Don't need one!" he said.

"Am I the only passenger?"

"Sure! That's the best way—no side trips." He patted one of the chair backs, indicating she should sit. "Now don't you worry about a thing, miss. I'll have you in Seattle by dinnertime!"

Bronwyn took the deck chair the captain had indicated, and clung to it as the boiler's hissing grew louder. The engine of the *Sadie Ann* clanked and gurgled. The skinny young boatman scrambled here and there, casting off, tossing chunks of wood into the furnace, then scampering into the pilothouse. Moments later, the *Sadie Ann* chugged smoothly away from the dock. As they headed toward open water, Bronwyn glanced back. Johnnie still fumed on the dock, standing with his thick hands on his hips and his hat pushed back on his head.

Bronwyn jumped up from her chair and crossed the narrow deck. She clung to the wet rail with one hand, soaking her cotton glove. With the other hand, she pulled off her hat and waved it at Johnnie. She was too far away to see precisely, but she was confident his face would be purple with anger, and the thought made her laugh into the wind. She felt daring and independent, and she also felt alone as she had never been in her life. She was frightened, but she was exhilarated. She had done it! She had made her escape, and whatever was to become of her now would be all her own doing.

Her young captain's name, she soon learned, was Albert. Beneath his grimy cap he had a thatch of dirty blond hair, and his upper lip was barely disguised by a wispy yellow mustache. He told her his surname, but it was something Scandinavian and complicated, and she didn't catch it. It didn't seem to matter. Albert guided his little vessel past Point Hudson and out into the Strait, where passenger ships and ferries and freighters carved their way through the whitecaps. The wind stung Bronwyn's ears and nipped at her hat brim until she gave up and took it off. Albert pointed the bow of the *Sadie Ann* south and east, and ran back and forth between the boiler and the pilothouse every few minutes. As the *Sadie Ann* picked up speed, Bronwyn's eyes began to stream, and she sniffled indelicately, her handkerchief soon sodden.

Albert noticed, and came to pull her to her feet. "Miss Morgan! Come into the pilothouse, out of the wind. Nothin' fancy, mind."

She accepted this graceful invitation with alacrity. He was correct, of course, that there was nothing fancy about the inside of the pilothouse. It was piled with oily ropes and cans and boxes of every description, and it smelled strongly of fish, but it was such a relief to be away from the bite of the wind that she didn't care.

"No proper chair," Albert said, as he produced a three-legged stool for her to sit on.

"That doesn't matter," she said. "This is perfect." She mopped her eyes with the damp handkerchief, and blew her nose one more time, then settled her hat back on her head.

Albert went to stand before the large wooden wheel, one hand around one of the spokes, the other thrust with self-conscious insouciance into the pocket of his jacket. Bronwyn turned her head to hide her smile, and fixed her gaze on the view of the coastline. They steamed steadily past inlets and coves, hills dark with evergreens, gravelly beaches here and there. An occasional cabin chimney sent spirals of clear gray smoke into the summer air.

At length, when she felt warm again, and her nose had stopped running, Bronwyn stood, straightening her jacket and smoothing back her wind-ruffled hair. She was only a step or two from Albert, and she moved forward to stand at his shoulder, peering ahead to assess their progress.

"I have sandwiches and root beer," he said with pride. "My mother always sends me out with provisions."

"You live at home, then?" Bronwyn said, and added, with a fractional pause, "Captain?"

She knew she had said the right thing as she saw the flush of pride creep up his freckled cheeks. "Oh, yes," he said, with a toss of his head. "Saving money, don'tcha know. For a bigger boat." Then, with a sideways glance, "Not that there's a thing wrong with the *Sadie Ann*!"

"Oh, no, I can see that," Bronwyn murmured. "It's—I mean, she's a fine boat."

"That she is, Miss Morgan. Not like some of these diesel boats, everything slimy and stinking of bunker oil. You wouldn't like standing in the pilothouse of one of those, I can tell you! Turn your stomach, that smell."

"Oh, I wouldn't like that at all," Bronwyn assured him. "It's very pleasant in here."

They sailed on for a time in companionable silence, watching

the great black freighters with their angled stacks steaming toward the Pacific. Waves rippled out from their wakes, and set the
Sadie Ann rocking, but Bronwyn found she wasn't in the least
afraid. Albert was young, but it was obvious he knew his boat,
and knew the channels and passages, too. She folded her arms,
balancing easily on her feet as the boat climbed a steep wave and
then settled again in smooth water.

Albert cast her a sidelong glance. "Found your sea legs already, miss," he said with a smile.

She smiled back at him. "I suppose I have," she said. "I've
never been on a boat so small. I mean, this size."

"My first boat," he said. "Have to start somewhere."

"You have big plans, I gather," Bronwyn said. "Did you always
want to be a boatman?"

"Oh, yes, miss," Albert said with assurance. "My grandfather
was a boatman in Norway, and my father, too. When he came
here, he had to work for somebody else, but I want to be my own
man. Born in the twentieth century, don'tcha know, and times is
different from what they was."

"That's very true," Bronwyn said.

With a small, private sigh, she reflected that it was true for her,
too, or it would be soon. Her parents wanted to believe times had
not changed, but they had. The society they had placed their
faith in, that had worked so well for them, no longer existed.
They believed in ladies and gentlemen, in honor and honesty, in
purity and faith. A wave of sorrow swept over her, as cold and
deep as the ones the *Sadie Ann* rode so bravely.

As if he could hear her thoughts, her young captain said, "So,
Miss Morgan, you haven't said why you're going to Seattle. Not
forced to run away from that bravo on the pier, I hope?"

Bronwyn gurgled with laughter. "Johnnie! Oh, no, not at all!"

"He didn't want you to leave, that was clear."

"He's just angry because I—well, I sort of stood him up."

"Not your fiancé, then."

"Oh, my goodness, no! Not Johnnie." The idea of Johnnie
Johnson as her fiancé gave her a slight shock, and a feeling of dis-

gust—not just for poor Johnnie, but for herself. What had she
been thinking, trying to drown her misery at the Cellar? She
should have taken this step long ago, left Port Townsend the moment she realized she could never regain her standing. She blew
out a breath, and said, "I think you have the right idea, Captain.
Be your own man. Don't take orders from anyone."

"That's it, Miss Morgan," he agreed, nodding. "That's it. A
new world since the Great War. Do whatever we like."

She glanced at him. "Did you fight, Albert?"

He lifted one shoulder. "I wanted to. They said I was too
young."

"I think your mother must have been glad about that."

He laughed. "Oh, yes. Mama's a peach, but she thinks I'm still
a kid. Her little boy."

Bronwyn laughed, too. "Oh, Albert. I know exactly—I know
precisely—how that feels!"

The hours of the voyage passed all too swiftly for Bronwyn,
though her captain thought the speed worth bragging about.
When the sun had risen nearly to its zenith, he produced the
sandwiches and bottles of root beer. Both were delicious, and
Bronwyn found herself eating with surprising appetite.

"Sea air," Captain Albert told her, speaking around a mouthful
of thick white bread and sliced ham and cheese. "Best thing for
making food taste good."

Bronwyn swallowed her own generous bite, and said, "Please
thank your mother for me. This is one of the best luncheons I've
enjoyed in—oh, I don't know, forever!"

He smiled, and offered her another sandwich. They drank the
root beer straight from the bottle, and dabbed at their lips with
worn, but very clean, cloth napkins.

When the skyline of Seattle came into view, Bronwyn's good
mood began to fade. The thirty-eight stories of the Smith Tower
looked enormous from her vantage point in the middle of Elliott
Bay. She had seen the city before, but she couldn't remember
taking it all in at once this way, the skyscrapers, the bridges, the

wide sweep of the Public Market, and ahead of them, the long, low buildings that marked the dock. A chill of anxiety prickled on Bronwyn's neck, and while Albert pointed out the sights to her, she had difficulty responding.

She said farewell to him with real regret. "Miss Morgan," he said, snatching off his cap at the last minute, as if he had almost forgotten. "It's been an honor to serve you. If you need to go somewhere on the water, you just call me!" He dug in his pocket, where he had just dropped the two dollars she had paid him, and produced an actual business card. It was handwritten, and a little dog-eared, with an address in West Seattle. "We don't have the telephone yet," Albert said, "but you can find me at that address. If I'm at sea, my mother will know when I'm gonna be back."

"Thank you, Albert," Bronwyn said. "The voyage was marvelous."

He carried her valise for her, all the way to the street, where she promised him she would find a taxicab. She stood watching as he backed away, twisting his cap in his hands, then turned and strode back down the dock with a jaunty step. Imagine, she thought. He has his own boat. He has a bit of cargo, he has two dollars in his pocket, and the whole world before him.

Resolutely, but with her heart fluttering in her throat, she turned to face the prospect of the bustling city. She had the address of the Ryther Child Home in her handbag. She had a few changes of clothes, and nearly twenty dollars. She had a full stomach for the moment, thanks to Albert's mother. And she was utterly alone. Free.

She had to admit, freedom was scary. But she had made her choice. She couldn't turn back now.

She swallowed, picked up her valise, chose a direction more or less at random, and started to walk.

CHAPTER 11

The smells and sounds of the Ryther Child Home were familiar to Margot now, and probably to Sarah. The two of them walked down a long corridor behind a young woman wearing one of the long aprons the assistants favored. Margot saw Sarah's nostrils flutter at the odors of wet diapers, Fels-Naptha, and spilled milk gone sour on the carpet. Her own nerves itched at the incessant sounds of children crying, others shouting, and the admonishing voices of adults trying to restore order.

The young woman who had opened the door and was guiding them to the sickroom was someone new to them. Her hair was a light brown, worn in shingled curls, and she had unusual eyes. The word for their color, Margot thought, was *hazel*, but they were distinguished by flecks of gold that caught the light when she glanced back at them. She looked young, but she carried herself with the dignity of a much older woman.

She also spoke in a cultured accent, something Margot hadn't heard at Mrs. Ryther's establishment before, the unmistakable sign of an upper-class background. "Mother Ryther told us to isolate him," she said over her shoulder. "Until we know what's wrong."

Olive Ryther had called the Women and Infants Clinic very early this morning, and Sarah, hearing the details of the baby's illness, had called Margot immediately.

The telephone had rung early, when the sky was just beginning to brighten. Margot had managed to get seven hours of uninterrupted sleep. There would be, of course, no money for this visit unless the Sheppard-Towner funds covered it, but she spared no thought for that now. She was worried. "How long has the baby been ill?" she asked.

The starry hazel eyes turned up to her. The girl's curls drooped, as if she hadn't washed her hair in some time. "His fever started yesterday morning," she said. "I'm new here, so I asked Mother Ryther what to do. She said lots of times babies run fevers, and it doesn't hurt them, but it kept rising all day, and it seemed to me he had trouble breathing. By midnight he was so hot I was worried."

Sarah said, "Have you been up with him all night, miss?"

The girl nodded. "I thought he would feel better if I stayed with him."

"Did you sponge him?"

"Yes," was the answer. "Vinegar and water, I was told. The water was too cold, though, and it gave him shivers. That didn't seem right."

"That's correct," Sarah said. "The water should be room temperature, or you can bring on a seizure."

The girl, who had been composed until that moment, pressed her fingers to her mouth, and her eyes filled with weary tears. "I didn't know that. No one told me that."

"Don't worry," Sarah said calmly. "It didn't happen, did it? Next time you'll know."

As they reached a door at the end of the corridor, Margot said, "What's your name, miss?"

The girl avoided Margot's eyes as she reached for the doorknob. "Betty. Betty, um, Jones."

Sarah and Margot glanced at each other, and Margot raised a skeptical eyebrow.

They followed Betty Jones into a small, dim room with a crib at one side and a table holding a basin and ewer at the other. The room smelled of sickness, and the air was stifling. Sarah moved swiftly to the crib. By the time Margot had opened the single window and pushed the curtains aside to admit the fresh summer air, Sarah was already stripping a wet diaper and sweat-sodden singlet from an infant of about ten months. As Margot reached her, she glanced up. "He's very hot. And this rash . . ."

"I see it." Margot opened her medical bag and took out her stethoscope and a pair of rubber gloves.

"Is it bad?" Betty whispered. "Should I have done something else?"

Margot answered, "You did everything you could, Miss Jones. Please don't leave the room, though. If this is diphtheria, we'll need to administer a Schick test for you, to know whether you need to be vaccinated."

"D-diphtheria?" The young woman's voice faltered. "Oh, the poor baby! We should have called you first thing, but Mother Ryther—"

"We're here now," Sarah said with her customary calm. "We'll do all we can."

Margot and Sarah bent over the child, who lay limply on the cotton sheet of the crib. He was dark-skinned, perhaps Indian, so it was hard to judge the extent of the cyanosis, but the sound of his rasping struggle for air was alarming. When Sarah touched the base of his neck, he gave a slight, small gasp at the touch of her cool fingers, but didn't open his eyes. "Swollen," Sarah said shortly.

Margot set the bell of her stethoscope to the hot little chest, and listened for several seconds. She said resignedly, "I don't think there's any doubt."

"No. I'm afraid not."

The danger, as they both knew, was immediate. "We'll swab

the fauces," Margot said quietly, "but we won't wait for the results. I don't think we dare."

Margot stepped back while Sarah opened the baby's mouth with one gentle finger so she could touch the back of his throat with a cotton swab. He gagged briefly, then struggled to cough again. Margot bent over him, stroking his arms, steadying the quivering of his legs while Sarah secured the result of her swab in a glass tube.

"I have antitoxin in my bag, in the upper compartment," Margot said. "Give him two thousand units."

While Betty Jones stood to one side, her hands clasped and her eyes glistening, Sarah gave the little boy the intramuscular injection. Even at this, he didn't cry, though he gave a slight, choking moan.

Margot found the bowl of vinegar water on the table, and carried it to the crib. She tested the temperature with her fingers, and then bathed the child's chest and belly with a soaked cloth. "We'd better transport this little one to the hospital. I don't want to try a tracheotomy here, and I'm afraid he's going to need one. Better we do it in the operating theater, and I don't think we can wait for an ambulance. Tell Blake, would you? Then if you don't mind, we'll leave you here to test Miss Jones and make arrangements for her to be quarantined."

"Yes, Doctor."

Sarah went to the basin and washed her hands with care before she hurried out. Betty took a hesitant step forward. "Can't I go with him?"

Margot, her hands busy as she laved the feverish boy with cool vinegar water, looked across the bars of the crib at the young woman. "First, I want you to have the Schick test. Then, a good night's sleep."

"I don't know what a Schick test is."

"Have you been vaccinated against diphtheria?"

"I don't think so."

"The test will tell us whether you've been exposed, and are immune, or whether you also need the antitoxin. A few weeks ago we vaccinated everyone in the Child Home, but I haven't seen you before."

"No." The girl closed her eyes, and wavered a little on her feet.

Margot said, "Sit down, now. It won't help the baby if you faint." Betty obeyed, sinking onto a straight chair beside the head of the crib. Margot folded a light blanket over the wheezing child, and went to wash her own hands. "Does he have a name?" she asked over her shoulder.

"No," Betty said faintly. "Someone left him in the yard. Just lifted him over the fence and left him there."

"Where's Mrs. Ryther now?"

"I don't know. I'm sorry. I've only been here three days, and I don't know her routine."

"I hope you don't object to having the vaccination, if you react to the test," Margot said. "You've been exposed now, and it's the best way to prevent your developing the illness yourself."

Betty shrugged. "I suppose it's safe," she said, giving Margot the unmistakable impression that she didn't much care either way.

"As safe as we can make it," Margot said. She crossed to the crib again, and crouched beside Betty's chair to look into her eyes and touch her wrist. "There have been a few problems, but most were not as serious as coming down with the disease." She passed her hand over Betty's forehead. "Well, you don't have a fever, at least. You feel all right, other than needing some rest?"

"Yes. I'm fine."

"Do you have a room to yourself?"

"No. I share with two other girls."

"We'll need to make some other arrangement about that."

"Oh!" Betty pressed her palms together, as if in supplication. "Oh, that will be such a bother, and Mother Ryther was so kind to take me in. . . ."

"Nurse Church will speak to her."

Sarah returned at that moment. "Blake is at the door," she said.

"Good. I'll carry the baby. Sarah, would you pack up a few

things, those diapers over there, a change of the baby's clothes? Hand them to Blake. It's best if he doesn't come in. Miss Jones, Nurse Church will administer your test. The test only takes a moment, but she'll need to wait to read your reaction. Sarah, could you speak to Mrs. Ryther afterward? Miss Jones will need to be in a private room for at least two days."

As she was speaking, Margot was bundling the baby into a light blanket and lifting him to her shoulder. Sarah had found a basket and tossed in the baby's things. She opened the door for her, and Margot saw Blake waiting in the hall, his back to the doorway.

Sarah said, "Dr. Benedict? Your bag."

Margot freed one hand to take it. She was halfway through the doorway when she heard an odd sound, one that didn't come from the infant in her arms. She glanced back, and saw Betty staring at her, one hand gripping the railing of the crib, the other pressed to her mouth. Margot paused midstride. "Are you all right, Miss Jones?"

"D-Dr. Benedict?"

"Yes?"

Sarah had drawn up the Schick serum into a syringe, and put her hand on the girl's arm to turn it for the injection. Betty hardly seemed to notice. "You're Dr. Benedict?" she breathed.

"That's right. Didn't I say?" The girl didn't respond, and Margot said, more harshly than she intended, "I'm sorry, but we really need to hurry. If you have questions, put them to Nurse Church." She walked out, holding the baby close to her chest, to join Blake in the hallway. Blake shut the door to the room, leaving Sarah and Betty Jones alone inside.

It wasn't the first time Blake had served as an ambulance driver. He tended to be stoic in such cases, keeping his eyes on the road, watching for other automobiles or the occasional cart or wagon trundling over the uneven streets. This was, though, the first time the patient had been an infant, and Margot saw the tension in his face.

There was little she could say to reassure him. The child was very ill indeed. She had feared diphtheria because of an outbreak on the Tulalip Reservation. Now, as Blake drove as swiftly as he dared down Stone Way and across the Fremont Bridge, she held the feverish baby close as if she could keep his spirit in his body with the pressure of her hands.

Margot dreaded losing any patient, but children were the hardest. The children's ward at Seattle General was her favorite place in the hospital as a rule, but it was also the ward that caused her the most anxiety. Infants, in particular, were worrisome, because they couldn't tell her what was wrong. She had to rely on her ears and her eyes, her nose and her fingers, and, finally, on her instinct.

Her instinct was good. She had come to trust it, that intuition that led her to make diagnoses before she had every fact laid out before her. Matron Cardwell had it, and she was fairly certain Sarah Church had it, too. Dr. Creedy, the Benedict family physician, had it. There were plenty of physicians who didn't, and no blame accrued to them for the lack, but they were sometimes obstructive when she felt certain of a diagnosis, confident of her conclusions.

With babies, her gift for diagnosis could be lifesaving, but in the case of this little one, she feared there was little she could do.

Blake said, "We'll be there in ten minutes, Dr. Margot."

"Thanks." She let her cheek brush the top of the baby's head. His breathing had grown even more tortured, and he was so hot she felt as if his skin could burn through the thin blanket. The antitoxin would need twelve hours to take effect, and it would be, she understood, a miracle if this baby survived that long. His fingernails, the palest spot on his body, were already showing blue.

"Are you all right back there?" Blake asked. She could see by the set of his jaw that he understood all too well. His intuition wasn't bad, either. He knew this was serious, knew because she had hurried, and she almost never hurried.

"Yes," she said. "So far."

Blake nodded, a brief acknowledgment.

Straight to the operating theater, she thought. Call for assistance, someone to watch the baby while she scrubbed, prep his tiny throat. A tracheotomy, so the little one could breathe, and then alcohol baths to bring his temperature down. A nurse around the clock, and a consult from the hospital's pediatric specialist.

She would fight for this baby. She would do everything she knew how to do. But she was terribly afraid it wouldn't be enough.

Frank stepped outside the front doors of the Red Barn in the company of two other engineers, all of them with their jackets off and their sleeves rolled up. The dahlias in the flower beds drooped in the summer heat, and the waters of the bay shimmered like shards of glass under the lowering sun. The Olympic Mountains raised their whitecapped peaks against a sky of a perfect cerulean blue, and Frank paused on the sidewalk to admire them.

"Come out with us, Frank," one of the other engineers said. "We're going to stop at the Merchants Café and have a cuppa joe."

Frank grinned at him. "Cuppa joe, is it?"

Harry smiled back. "Of course! That's all we're allowed these days, don't you know."

"I'll have to say no, thanks," Frank said. He put his Stetson on at a cheerful angle. "My wife's expecting me for dinner. Looks like I'll need to catch the streetcar."

"Oh, ho," Harry said. "No fancy motorcar tonight? You in the doghouse?"

Frank laughed. "Don't think so. Just busy, I expect."

The others waved, and made their way across the dry field toward their own automobiles, a Model T and an open saloon car that had seen better days. Frank turned the other way to walk to the streetcar stop. He had assured Blake he was not to worry if he was too busy at the end of the day to make it to the Red Barn, but despite that, it was rare for the Cadillac not to be waiting when Frank emerged in the evening. Somehow Blake had worked it out so he could pick up all three of the working Benedicts and still meet Frank to drive him home.

Frank didn't mind the stroll through the warm evening, and he recognized a number of people who also rode the streetcar. It was a pleasant trip home, though it took so much longer than it would have in the Cadillac. He was whistling, his jacket slung over his shoulder and his briefcase in his left hand, as he walked up Aloha to Fourteenth Avenue. The sunshine, which had poured through the tall glass windows of the drafting room and made all the men fold back their sleeves, was fading now into a warm blue evening. Bees whirred in the rosebushes around Benedict Hall, and a hummingbird flashed past Frank's head on its way to sup on a fuchsia hanging just outside Hattie's kitchen window. Frank paused on the porch to appreciate these summer pleasures.

Summers in the Bitterroot Valley were hotter, dryer, more intense than the gentle summer of the Pacific Northwest. His mother would be picking huckleberries to preserve, bringing in ears of sweet corn to steam, cooking huge meals every day for the haying crew. His father would come in at night, sunburned and smelling of sweat and horses and sunshine. Frank's memories of Montana summers were filled with sun. Here in Seattle, every sunny day was a special pleasure, all the sweeter because clouds could gather at any time, and the rain could return.

Frank had just opened the door of Benedict Hall when he heard the rumble of the Cadillac's motor coming up the hill to the house. He stopped, looking out to the street.

Blake was at the wheel, sitting very straight in his driving jacket and cap. He stopped at the sidewalk, and got out to open the back door. Margot, with her medical bag in her hand, swung her legs out and stood up. She saw Frank on the porch, and lifted a gloved hand in a halfhearted wave. Blake said something to her, and she nodded. The two of them stood close, gazing into each other's faces, though they didn't speak again. They didn't touch, of course, or make any gesture to indicate a relationship beyond that of mistress and servant, but Frank knew them, and he understood. Something was wrong, and Blake was trying to comfort Margot.

They finished speaking, and Margot straightened her hunched shoulders. As Blake climbed back into the Cadillac, she turned stiffly, like a soldier on parade, and started up the walk. Frank stepped to the edge of the porch and waited for her. The setting sun framed her lean figure as she walked toward him, so he could see only her silhouette, her face obscured at first by the brilliance dazzling his eyes. Not until she stepped into the shadow of the porch did he see her face, and understand the degree of her unhappiness.

He was accustomed to seeing his wife tired from a long day, spent, even irritable after hours of dealing with patients, or more likely, hospital administration. Occasionally, he himself was worn out at the end of a day, disinclined to talk, and Margot sensed his mood, and adapted to it. He tried to do the same for her, assessing the tension in her face, the weariness in her eyes. Tonight, though, she looked—*stricken* was the word that came to his mind. Her lips were pale and set, and her dark eyes seemed oddly opaque, as if she was trying to hide her feelings from him—and perhaps from herself.

Frank moved to meet her without speaking. He took her hand, tucked it under his elbow, and guided her across the porch and into the coolness of the hall.

Once inside she bent to set down her medical bag. She pulled off her gloves with deliberate movements, almost as if her hands hurt. She removed her hat and hung it with exaggerated care on the coatrack. Thelma emerged from the kitchen, a tray in her hands, and passed the two of them with a nod on her way to the small parlor. Margot ran her hands through her hair, ruffling it over her ears.

Frank had his own coat off, and his hat on the rack next to Margot's. He said, "A drink, maybe, sweetheart."

"Yes," she said in a voice pulled tight with tension. "Please."

He guided her down the hall to the small parlor with his good hand circling her waist. Thelma, tray delivered, passed them again on her way back to the kitchen. Frank was glad to find the small parlor empty. Blake had no doubt gone to pick up the Benedict men from their office, and Ramona and Edith had not yet come down. He led Margot to the small divan before he crossed to the tray of chipped ice and glasses laid ready beside the decanter of whisky. He poured two fingers of liquor into one of the heavy cut-glass tumblers, and dropped three ice chips into it. He made a similar drink for himself, but with more ice and less whisky, and carried the two glasses back to the divan.

He sat down, and handed her drink to her. She took it with steady fingers, but she avoided his eyes. "Drink," he said. "Come on, Margot. It will help."

She did, swallowing half the contents of her glass in a single gulp. She let her head drop back, and her eyes closed. Frank took in the butterfly sweep of her dark lashes against her too-pale cheeks, and the complete lack of color in her lips. Her pulse was visible in her long, smooth throat, and its beat seemed quick to him, restless and unhappy.

He said now, "Sweetheart. Tell me about it if you want to."

She drew a slow, whistling breath. "Sometimes I wonder if I can keep it up, Frank."

"Perfectly natural." He sipped his own drink, and settled himself closer, willing his strength into her.

Her eyes opened, and she stared at the molded ceiling, where the chandelier moved slightly in a faint gust of air, carved crystals twinkling with the evening light. "I don't know if it's fair to share this one."

"Up to you," Frank said. He let his arm press against hers, and he leaned back so their shoulders touched. "If it would help."

"It was just ghastly, from beginning to end," she said. "Thank God I wasn't on my own."

"You were at the hospital."

"Yes." She sighed. "We lost a baby. I did everything I could think of—I should say, we did, Dr. Clegg and I—he's the pediatric specialist. It wasn't enough. We don't *know* enough."

"Can't blame yourself, Margot."

"I know." Her lips trembled, and she lifted her free hand to press a finger to them. "Poor little boy," she said in a whisper. "He never had a chance."

"Parents?"

Without moving her head, she transferred her gaze to his face. "Oh, Frank," she said, even more softly. "This little one, not even a year old . . . Someone left him in the yard at the Child Home. Just lifted him over the fence and deposited him there, like—like he was an unwanted puppy. He came down with diphtheria."

"Poor little guy."

"Yes. We did a tracheotomy, but it was too late. He—expired—a few minutes later."

"I'm so sorry. For him, for you . . . it's terrible."

"It is. I hated having to call Mrs. Ryther to tell her. And there's a young lady there who will take this hard."

"Diphtheria. I thought we had gotten ahead of that."

"We're trying, but there's an outbreak on the Tulalip Reservation."

"Anything to be done about that?"

She moved one shoulder, and blew out her breath. "Quarantine," she said shortly, "until it's over. Vaccinations, but a lot of people don't trust them. At least the other Ryther children were vaccinated. Thank God for that." She drained the rest of her drink. Frank took the empty glass to refill it, but she said, "No, thanks, Frank. No more. I'll go up and have a bath. Go to bed early."

"I'll have someone bring up a tray."

She hesitated, as if she were about to refuse, but then nodded. "That would be nice." She started to push herself up from the divan. "We could both have our dinner upstairs. Together. I'm sure no one would mind, this once."

He found her hand and squeezed it. "I'm sure they wouldn't."

"I'll speak to Blake—"

"No, I'll do that. You go up. Run a bath, get comfortable."

He was rewarded by seeing a little color rise in her cheeks, and though he suspected, from the brightness of her eyes, that she would shed a few tears when she was alone, that seemed like a good thing. They stood together, and he kissed her cheek. She clung to him for a moment, and Frank held her, pressing his cheek against her hair, before they walked out of the small parlor, parting at the bottom of the stairs.

The rest of the family began to gather, the men coming in from work, Allison dashing through the front door with her tennis racket, the ladies descending the stairs even as she raced up them. Frank greeted everyone, and explained that he and Margot would have their meal upstairs. He waited where he was for Blake to come in, just putting on his serving coat.

Blake frowned when he saw Frank. "Is Dr. Margot all right?"

"She will be, Blake. Could you organize a tray for the two of us? She doesn't feel much like company." Frank gave a wry smile. "Other than mine, I guess."

"That's the best thing for her," Blake said. "She's had an awful day."

"She told me."

"I'll take care of it, Major."

"Thanks." Frank was about to start up the stairs himself, but he saw that Blake was leaning more heavily on his cane than usual, and there were pale lines graven around his mouth. He stopped. "You're taking it hard, too," he said.

Blake cleared his throat. "Well," he said, his voice rumbling through the hall, "that was just a baby. It's a sad thing, and Dr. Margot worked so hard to save him."

"Can't save them all, Blake."

"No. No, indeed. You remind Dr. Margot of that, Major."

"I will. Thank you, Blake. I will."

Blake said, "It's not my place to say so, sir, but I'm very glad Dr. Margot has you to support her."

Frank regarded him gravely. "She has both of us."

Blake nodded acknowledgment, and limped on toward the kitchen.

CHAPTER 12

Bronwyn was alone in the tiny single room Mother Ryther had arranged for her. She had watched the site for the test Nurse Church had administered, a stinging injection just beneath the skin, and when it flared into a hot, itchy circle of scarlet, that meant she was susceptible. The nurse injected her other arm with the antitoxin, and said there would be two more injections, a week apart.

"No contact with the children for at least three days, Miss Jones," the nurse said. "We think they've all been vaccinated, but Mrs. Ryther's record keeping is not the best. We could have missed someone."

Nurse Church was the first Negress Bronwyn had ever met. She was very pretty, with full lips and what looked like a dimple in one cheek, though she hadn't had occasion to smile that day. The dimple lay quiescent in her satiny skin, a hint of something that might show itself in happier times. She patted Bronwyn's arm, and handed her a glass of water. "Drink this, please, and several more today and tomorrow. I'll explain to Mrs. Ryther, but what Dr. Benedict wants you to do now is rest. Your meals should be brought up to you."

Bronwyn was installed in a cramped, windowless bedroom, hardly more than a closet, furnished with nothing but a cot with a thin mattress and dingy sheets. Nurse Church returned in the late afternoon, and knocked on her door. When Bronwyn opened it, she recognized the sorrow in the nurse's face, and a sudden pain wrenched her heart.

"I'm sorry, Miss Jones," Nurse Church said, and it was clear by the misery in her eyes and vibrating in her voice that she truly was. "The little boy passed away at the hospital. Dr. Benedict thought you should know, and she wants to make certain you understand there was nothing you could have done."

Bronwyn leaned against the doorjamb, suddenly so weary she could hardly stand. She passed her hand over her eyes, not daring to speak in case she sobbed. The little nurse said, in a voice as gentle as the touch of a silk scarf, "Miss Jones. Go to bed now. You'll feel better after you've slept."

It was the only thing Nurse Church had said that wasn't true. Bronwyn didn't feel better. She cried for hours, once she was alone, and she lay awake far into the night, only falling into a thick sleep when the sky began to lighten. Even then she was haunted by nightmares.

She felt infinitely worse when she awoke. She lay on the narrow cot and cried again, thinking of the baby. Alone. He had died all alone. No one had wanted him, and no one had been with him at the end but doctors and nurses. Strangers. The cruelty of it stunned her, and the idea that her own baby, hers and Preston's, could have suffered the same fate filled her with desperate anxiety.

She had presented herself at the Ryther Home as a young woman in need of work and a place to live, fabricating a complicated story of dead parents, vanished siblings, nowhere to turn. She didn't dare use her own name, lest someone decide to search for her. She had borrowed her maid's name instead, the first that came to mind, and Olive Ryther had taken her in without hesitation. Mother Ryther's only question had been whether Bronwyn was pregnant, but even that would not, evidently, have meant a rejection. Mother Ryther, it seemed, was prepared to deal with whatever baggage she might be carrying.

Bronwyn knew nothing of caring for children. She couldn't boil an egg or make toast. She had no idea how laundry was done, or how a floor should be mopped. Every time she was asked to perform some task, someone had to show her how to do it. It was a wonder, she thought, that they didn't turn her right out of the house.

Her one great talent, she had discovered, was lying. She lied about her name, and she lied about her reason for coming to the Ryther Home, but it had been in vain. As nearly as she could tell, her own baby wasn't here.

There were plenty of others, though, and when the nameless little one fell ill, she felt as if she had a purpose at last. She wasn't much good at the other kinds of work that needed to be done, but she could sit beside the bed of a sick child. She had held him, sung to him, changed his sweat-soaked clothes, coaxed him to take sips of water. She had sat with him for hours, while around them the life of the house went on.

He had died anyway. She had failed even at nursing a sick baby.

It didn't help that his doctor had been the very same woman in the clipping from the *Seattle Daily Times*. Preston's sister, the bride in her gauzy dress with the long net sleeves and the pearl-encrusted headband, posed on the staircase of Benedict Hall. This tall, sharp-eyed woman with the long fingers and direct, almost masculine way of speaking—she was Preston's sister. She looked very different from her wedding photograph, but this was Margot Benedict, and to her, Bronwyn was nobody at all.

When she could shed no more tears, Bronwyn stared at the unadorned ceiling with burning eyes, and wondered what she was to do with the rest of her life.

*   *   *

Margot found respite from her sadness in a full day of seeing patients. The waiting room in her clinic was full from midmorning till late in the afternoon. Angela barely had time to step into the storeroom to eat the sandwich she had brought from home, and Margot didn't eat at all. She was grateful, as the day wore on and her stomach started to grumble, that Hattie had risen early to give her scrambled eggs and one of her baking-powder biscuits before she went to do her hospital rounds.

Her last patient was a giant of a man, broad-shouldered and big-bellied, who had to stoop to pass under the lintel when he came back to the examining room. He wore the coveralls and heavy boots of a laborer. He dropped the suspender of his coveralls and rolled up his shirtsleeve to present a badly infected arm, and explained he had been clearing blackberry vines from a building site.

Margot made him take off his shirt, but she allowed him, seeing his embarrassment, to keep his undershirt on. She cleaned his arm herself, to take a good look at the depth of the scratches and the extent of the infection. She washed the arm thoroughly with Dakin fluid, then instructed Angela to apply a layer of sulphur ointment, and cover it all with a thick bandage. She was confident there would be no complications, but she told the man to return in two days so she could reexamine the area. She scolded him in what she hoped was a mild way, reminding him that carelessness was the way a minor irritation became a serious crisis.

He hung his head and said, "Yes, Doctor. Yes, Doctor," with such contrition that her lips twitched, and she almost smiled.

Not until the man had left did she remember the lost baby, and her sadness of the night before. As she walked up Post Street to the waiting Cadillac, smoothing on her gloves, she reminded herself that she was supposed to be objective. She couldn't grieve for every patient she lost, or she would be worn to nothing. The day a physician could prevent every untimely death would be a day of miracles, and she didn't expect that day to come in her lifetime.

She sighed as she slid into the backseat of the motorcar, setting her bag beside her. "Good evening, Blake."

"Good evening, Dr. Margot. I trust you had a good day." Blake glanced at her in the rearview mirror.

"I did. A busy day."

"Your clinic is well established now." He started the engine, and steered carefully toward Madison, braking to let a horse cart cross ahead of him. "That must be satisfying," he finished, when the maneuver had been accomplished.

"Yes, indeed," she said. "A good day's work."

She told herself to take comfort in that. It was awful losing a patient, and nearly unbearable when it was a baby. But today—and many other days in the past months—her work had made a difference to the people who found their way to her clinic. The laborer who had waited too long, and come in with an infection that could have harmed him, would recover. There were others, as well: a young mother who had burned her hand on an iron, an elderly woman with anaemia, an ironworker with a badly cut finger, which required seven stitches. Some patients could pay, and some couldn't, but Margot treated them all the same, and made sure Angela did, too. She would remember the baby, as she remembered every child she treated, but she couldn't have done anything more for him. She knew that.

It was best, as Matron Cardwell had reminded her, to save her energies for the living.

She remembered, then, who it was Olive Ryther reminded her of. It was Matron Cardwell, matter-of-fact, disciplined, demanding, and good-hearted.

"Is Frank already at home?" Often Blake picked up Frank at the Red Barn before coming to Post Street.

"He is," Blake said. "When I came to meet you he was giving Nurse a break. Playing quite a serious game of red rubber ball with Miss Louisa, I believe."

The image of this made Margot smile in spite of her somber thoughts. "Oh, good. I may just join them."

"An excellent idea, Dr. Margot. I gather Miss Louisa is winning with ease."

Margot chuckled. "I'm not in the least surprised."

The ball game, however, had concluded by the time they reached Benedict Hall. Margot walked up onto the porch, and found Frank, in his shirtsleeves, seated in one of the Westport chairs, enjoying the painted sunset. Margot dropped her bag beside the door, and went to sit beside him, pulling off her hat and gloves and letting them fall. Frank kissed her, and encircled her with his arm.

"I hear Louisa bested you at red rubber ball," she said.

"Yup. Uncle Fa had to concede the match."

"You spoil her."

"I know," he said, and pulled her closer. "You look better tonight."

"I feel a bit better, thanks to you," she said. "A quiet evening was what I needed, but I wouldn't have thought of it on my own."

He put his head back, and they sat together in peaceful silence, watching the layers of pink and gold fade bit by bit beyond the Olympics. Margot said, finally, "How was your day, Frank? Did you see Mr. Boeing?"

"I did." He moved a little, and she had the idea he had been waiting for the right time to say something. "I have a surprise for you, Margot."

She straightened. "A surprise? Good, or—or not?"

He leaned forward to kiss her cheek again. "Depends."

"Frank!"

"You said you'd like to fly again."

"Am I going to?"

"You are if you can take a bit of time off. Mr. Boeing wants me to go back to Spokane, and this time I'm going to fly one of our airplanes. I asked him about taking a few extra days, to see my folks. . . ."

"You're going to fly to Missoula? Is there an airfield?"

"Hale Field." He drew a finger down her cheek and under her chin. "Come with me, Margot. My parents would be so glad to see you. I want to show you the ranch."

"Oh, my, Frank. Fly all that way? That's—that's a bit daunting, don't you think?"

He laughed. "Nope." He tapped her chin with his finger. "I'm going to fly the Model 21, the navy airplane. The one that's too easy to fly."

"How can an airplane be too easy to fly?"

"It's technical, but essentially, they can't spin it. It's a trainer, and if the pilots can't spin it, they can't learn from it."

"Well, the clinic is awfully busy. . . ."

"Think about it, sweetheart. You haven't had a holiday since our honeymoon."

"True." Margot leaned against his shoulder, and let her cheek drop against the smooth linen of his shirt. He felt amazingly solid to her. She knew the muscle of his arm, the bone of his shoulder, could picture the way they worked together, knew how the Carnes arm attached, how it worked with the remains of his arm. The feeling of solidity was much more than that, though. It was the man behind the arm, the sort of man who was a strong, uncompromising, unshakable presence. "Frank, I'd love to go with you. I'll figure something out."

"Good." He said it in an offhand manner, dropping a kiss on the top of her head, but she heard the deep satisfaction in his voice. The grief of the day before retreated into its proper place, parceled away where she could recognize it, revisit it if she needed to, but not carry it with her as a burden never to be laid down.

Blake came to call them to dinner, and smiled to see them curled together in the fading daylight.

CHAPTER 13

Bronwyn obediently stayed in her closet of a bedroom, waiting for the three days of her quarantine to pass. One of the other girls brought trays to her at mealtimes, and a basin for washing. She could use the bathroom, but only when no one else was there, which was almost never. She felt feverish and headachy and as restive as a cat in a cage.

Mother Ryther came to see her on the afternoon of the third day, frowning at her over her spectacles.

"It's the vaccination, Betty," she pronounced, after pressing her cool, wrinkled fingers to Bronwyn's forehead. "We saw it with the children. Everyone was itchy and weepy for days."

"I'm sorry to be a bother," Bronwyn said.

"You're not," Mother Ryther said. "We're grateful for your care of the baby." She didn't sound grateful. She didn't sound like anything, really. Her voice was always matter-of-fact, even in the case of a baby who died.

"His mother will never know," Bronwyn said. Her own voice trembled with misery. She was sitting on the cot. Mother Ryther perched next to her, a pile of mended clothes on her lap.

"No. She'll never know. She probably doesn't want to know. The poor tyke was just dumped here, wasn't he? Thrown away." Mother Ryther pushed herself up with some difficulty. She was always in motion, it seemed, carrying, bending, tidying, as if her gray hair and wrinkled skin meant nothing. Bronwyn wondered how she bore the weight of so many people depending on her.

Maybe, she thought, it was by not feeling things. Bronwyn wished she could do the same.

"You mustn't worry, now," Mother Ryther said. "Tomorrow you can rejoin the family."

It was a kind thing to say, but Bronwyn couldn't think of anyone in the Child Home as family. She missed Port Townsend. She longed for her own airy, sunlit bedroom. She wondered how Clara had managed her guests after they snubbed her. She supposed Johnnie would be telling tales about her, and everyone would believe him. She worried about her mother, who must be terribly unhappy, and who had no one to step between her and the people who frightened her—her husband, her cook, the people in town.

When Mother Ryther left, Bronwyn lay back on the cot, but her muscles jumped and quivered. She felt as if the walls of the tiny room were closing in, compressing the air until it was too heavy to breathe. She got up, and went to the door to peek out into the empty corridor. Everything looked hazy and somehow unreal, as if the same fever that burned in her chest and face was affecting her eyes.

Or perhaps it was her brain. She couldn't think what she was doing here, in this cramped, windowless room. Her mind was as restless as her body, flitting vainly from one thought to another, none of them making much sense.

I need air, she thought. Just a breath of fresh air to clear my mind.

Voices swirled from every corner of the house, as they always seemed to do, but the corridor remained empty. She slipped out, closing the door of the little room behind her. She wandered down the hallway, and found herself in her original room, the one she shared with two other girls. Her coat and hat and handbag were in the closet. She snatched them up, and made her furtive way to the back stairs.

She couldn't think why she felt she had to sneak away. No one appeared in the least concerned about where she was going or why. Two of the older children dashed past her on the cramped staircase, racing to the bottom. Others were in the garden with hoes and baskets, weeding and watering rows of vegetables. The sun had begun its slow descent past the mountains to the west, but the day remained hot and sticky, with no breeze to ease the July heat.

Bronwyn walked through the backyard and out through the swinging metal gate. She went around the outer edge of the garden to the street, and turned down Stone Way, feeling some relief in movement. She had no particular intention other than being out-of-doors, in the clear air. She hadn't really meant to leave the Ryther Home, but now that she was walking, she didn't want to stop. Her muscles still ached in a vague way, but were no worse for the exertion. Her coat hung over her arm, and her hat and handbag swung, half-forgotten, from her other hand.

She was startled to find herself, after perhaps ten minutes of walking, at the streetcar stop. She blinked and looked around. Two or three passersby nodded to her, and one man touched his cap. She realized she hadn't put her own hat on, and the afternoon sun burned on her feverish cheeks. As she pulled it on, the streetcar clicked up the road toward her.

She had nickels in her handbag, and a few dollars left from the twenty she had started with. When the streetcar stopped in front of her, and the operator opened the doors, she stepped inside. She dropped a nickel into the fare box and automatically took a seat, without having really decided to do it.

Blake climbed the stairs, taking satisfaction in leaving his cane behind him, propped beneath the hook in the kitchen where he hung his driving coat. His leg felt a bit sluggish, but it did as he asked it to do, and that was a minor triumph.

Hattie had noticed, of course. "What do you think Miss Margot would say, she sees you walkin' without your cane, Blake?"

He had smiled at her, and said with conviction, "I think this is what Dr. Margot has been hoping for, bless her."

Hattie shook her head, making her frizz of hair quiver. She had been baking all morning, despite the heat of the day, and rivulets of perspiration streaked her wide cheeks. "I don't know 'bout that, Blake." She waved the dough-studded wooden spoon in her hand. "I just don't know."

"Don't fuss, Hattie. I'll be careful."

"You do that. You take good care, Blake." She went back to her baking, and he left the kitchen, careful to minimize the limp still left to him. By the time he reached the stairs, he heard Hattie start humming, and smiled to himself.

Dr. Margot and the major had left this morning for Spokane. Blake had driven them to Camp Lewis early, when the last stars of the night were still flickering through the gloom. Mr. Dickson and Mr. Dick had promised they could take the streetcar this one time so Blake could stay to watch the airplane take off. It was a prototype of the Model 21, Major Parrish said, an aircraft meant to be a military trainer. Mr. Dickson had pressed the major on its safety, but the major assured him that the military thought it was so easy to fly that their pilots couldn't learn enough from it. Part of his current assignment was to suggest ways to make the aircraft more demanding.

Blake stood beside the grassy strip, watching with a mix of anxiety and affection as Dr. Margot donned a leather helmet and worked her arms into the sleeves of a borrowed jacket that was far too big for her.

She wore trousers, too. He couldn't think where she had gotten them. Of course, there was a quite famous aviatrix, a Miss Earhart, who was setting records and appearing in newsreels. Miss Earhart wore trousers all the time, so he supposed there was precedent.

He watched as the major and Dr. Margot climbed up into the dual cockpits and stowed their tiny valises. Dr. Margot would have to wear the same clothes over and over, due to weight concerns, but she wouldn't mind that. She never cared about her clothes. They both waved to him before they settled into their seats.

The motor started, sounding alarmingly small compared to the deep grumble of the Cadillac. The propeller began to turn, slowly at first, then faster and faster until Blake could no longer see the blades. He kept his face impassive as the little airplane bumped out onto the grass. It paused there, as if gathering itself, then began its run down the strip. When it lifted into the air it appeared to leap from the ground like a horse in a steeplechase. Blake's heart lifted, too, but it thudded unsteadily, and he took a slow breath to quiet it.

He had watched the major take off once before, from the Sand Point Airfield. That had been exciting. But that time, Dr. Margot had not been in the second seat. As Blake watched the airplane's painted fuselage dwindle into the pale blue of the morning sky, he set his jaw, resisting his fear for Dr. Margot's safety. He stood where he was until the white speck of the Model 21 disappeared from his view. Only then did he turn back to the Cadillac, to make the long drive alone back to Seattle.

He tried not to think too often of the two of them winging their way across the Cascades in that tiny contraption of wood and metal and wire. He kept himself occupied through the day with tasks that had been awaiting a good moment. He had aired the rooms Dr. Margot and the major were using, and directed the twins as they turned the mattress and took down the curtains to be washed. He collected shoes that needed cleaning and eyed the major's wardrobe for clothes that could use a press. By the time these chores were finished, the day was far gone, and he found his anxiety considerably lessened.

He was just closing the door on the Parrishes' sitting room when he heard a hoarse cry from the other side of the house, where Mrs. Ramona and Mr. Dick had their rooms, with Louisa and her nurse just next door. It was Nurse's voice, he was sure, followed immediately by a cry in the high, fragile tones of Mrs.

Ramona. Blake started, and spun to his left, forgetting his weak leg. It sagged under his weight, and he stumbled, nearly falling. As he caught himself, he saw Mrs. Ramona dashing toward him, her hands out, her hair tumbled over her forehead.

She had been sleeping, he thought. Her cheek was creased and flushed from her pillow, and she was wearing a dressing gown. Her feet were bare, and her eyes wide and frightened. Nurse was running behind her, her apron flapping around her black-stockinged legs.

Mrs. Ramona clutched Blake's arm so hard he nearly stumbled again. "Blake! Have you seen her? Louisa?"

Nurse said, her voice tight with anxiety, "She was napping with Mrs. Benedict! She was right there beside her, sound asleep. I saw her myself! I was just folding—I was—the sheets—" She broke off, gesturing pointlessly back at the nursery, then smoothing her apron, over and over.

"We have to find her," Mrs. Ramona moaned. "Blake?"

"Yes, ma'am," he said. "Yes, ma'am, we'll find her." He hobbled toward the back staircase, supporting himself with one hand on the wall. He called, in a voice that echoed down the stairwell, "Leona! Loena! Leave what you're doing. I need you."

In half an hour the entire staff had turned out. They searched all four floors of the house, and the basement, which held nothing but the Eden washing machine and the mangle. They fanned out to look behind the chairs on the porch, to peek under the porch itself, where Thelma reported that the spiders were the size of baseballs. Ramona, weeping now, stood in the front door, calling her daughter's name. Leona, with hurried permission from Blake, dashed across to the garage, where she searched the Cadillac thoroughly and then ran up the stairs to check in Blake's apartment. When there was still no sign of the little girl, they started on the neighbors' gardens, and Blake, leaning on his cane, went to their front doors to explain what was happening.

By the time Louisa had been missing an hour, Blake felt the icy beginnings of real fear stir in his belly. He telephoned to Mr.

Dickson's office and explained that the men would have to come home by taxicab, or on the streetcar. He ended the call with an abruptness he would have to apologize for later, but Ramona was beginning to panic, and he thought it best to send Hattie up to her.

"See if you can get Mrs. Ramona to dress," he said in an undertone, as Hattie began her lumbering ascent up the back staircase. "We may have to call in the police."

"Oh, my Lord," Hattie was murmuring as she climbed the stairs. "Oh, my sweet Lord, in Your mercy, help the poor little thing." It wasn't clear whether she meant Louisa or her mother, but Blake thought it didn't really matter. Hattie hadn't said a word about dinner, and Blake supposed it would be ruined. They hadn't had a glimpse of Edith, either, but he spared no energy for that. He wouldn't be surprised if Mrs. Edith slept throughout the whole thing.

He made his way to the front door again, and down the sidewalk to the gate. He stood there, uncertain which way to turn, longing to see a fair, curly head pop out from behind one of the rhododendrons or perhaps a tree trunk where she had been hiding.

So small, he kept thinking. She's so small. A motorcar might not see her. A horse cart, with its iron wheels, could . . .

He forced himself to stop. There was nothing to be gained by allowing such thoughts. Hattie had the right idea, combining prayer and action.

He tried to think what would appeal to him, if he were fifteen months old. Louisa had been giddy at her mastery of the fine art of walking, and had advanced to running soon after. She loved the wide space of the back lawn, where she could run and fall without hurting herself. She loved riding in the motorcar, but Leona swore she wasn't in the garage. She loved being outside, and crowed with glee over birds and flowers and even strangers who went by.

Strangers. Oh, dear God. Blake thought of the strangers Louisa had smiled at, men who couldn't resist smiling back, some who removed their hats and bowed to the little lady in her ribbons and lacy pinafores. It couldn't be. It just couldn't be.

The Benedicts had suffered such torments over the past two years, tragedies that would have broken another family—a lesser family—into pieces. They wouldn't survive another.

He let himself out the gate, and started across the street. In a stentorian voice, one he almost never used, Blake shouted, "Miss Louisa! Miss Louisa! Come back to your mama this minute!" He strode toward the park, which was crowded with summer visitors, children and adults playing on the grass, walking along the reservoir, preparing to climb up the water tower. He peered into the crowd, wondering if it were even possible to find a toddler among all those people.

The evening air was warm, even stifling, but Blake's heart felt as if it were encased in ice.

A friendly streetcar operator explained to Bronwyn all about how to get to Millionaire's Row. "Gotta change downtown, miss," he said. "It's easy, though. Signs everywhere. Then you go up Madison, and change again for the Broadway line. You can't miss it."

"Thank you," she said. She settled onto the bench seat closest to the driver, to make certain she knew where to change. The streetcar stopped often, and men with briefcases climbed on, or women with bags of shopping edged past her to get off. To pass the time, she gazed out at the traffic, and tried to name the automobiles. They were mostly Fords, all of them black. There were a few fancier ones, in different colors. She spotted an Essex, and what she thought was a DeSoto, though she wasn't sure. They had to stop and wait as the streetcar clanked past. Twice the streetcar had to stop for a horse and cart to go by. Bronwyn shrugged into her coat, feeling chilled now despite the heat of the afternoon. It was the fever, she supposed. It didn't help that she had eaten so little, only a cup of broth and a bit of bread and butter. She had been careful about water, though, because Dr. Benedict had ordered it.

Meeting Dr. Benedict had put the idea of seeing Benedict

Hall into her head. Once she was on the streetcar, it seemed the most natural thing to simply travel all the way to Millionaire's Row, to have a glimpse of the house she had once dreamed of living in.

She could hardly believe she had encountered the woman from the wedding photograph. Margot Benedict was taller than she had expected. She wasn't stylish in the least, but her bobbed hair was smooth and shiny, and her eyes were a clear, dark brown. She had an air of command that Bronwyn envied. She gave orders, and people followed them. She wasn't anything like Preston had been. Something about her made Bronwyn want to see her again, curious to understand how this dark, assured woman could be Preston Benedict's sister.

The driver, as he stopped the streetcar for two ladies in flowered straw hats to get down, leaned out of his chair to speak to her. "You didn't say, miss, why you want to see Millionaire's Row." He grinned, showing several gaps in his teeth. "Hoping to meet one of them millionaires? Now, that would be a thing, right?"

Bronwyn started to draw herself up, to say something to put a stop to his overfamiliarity, but then she remembered. She wasn't Bronwyn Morgan of Uptown anymore. She was just a girl on her own. Her hair needed washing and her dress was stained. She had no real explanation for what she was doing. She was certainly of less consequence than this middle-aged man with his home-style haircut and stubbly chin.

She sighed, and sagged back against the slats of the seat. "No," she said. "No, I don't expect to meet a millionaire."

"I guess that's where they keep 'em!" he teased, as he started up the car again. "Pretty girl like you might get lucky."

"No," she said. "I just want—I mean, I would just like to see them. The mansions, I mean, not the millionaires."

"Never saw 'em, myself," he said. He stepped on the brake, honked his horn at a knot of pedestrians blocking his way, then shifted gears to drive forward again when the tracks were clear. "I hear they're big as hotels. Bigger than some, even."

"I'll let you know," Bronwyn said with a faint smile.

He nodded and winked at her. "You do that, little lady," he said cheerfully. "You just come back on my car and do that."

When Bronwyn stepped down from the streetcar at Broadway, she cast about for the Aloha Street sign. Instead, she spotted a small, neatly painted sign that read THE CORNISH SCHOOL, with an arrow pointing toward a side street.

A rush of memory flooded her mind, arresting her movement. She had come with her mother, carrying a valise with her dance clothes, brand-new ballet shoes, and a wide white ribbon to tie around her hair. They had taken a taxicab from the hotel, and climbed the shadowy stairwell of a tall brick building. At the top, the doors had opened onto a dance studio brilliant with light from a wall of windows. The polished floor and the long ballet barre along one side shone with sunshine. Bronwyn, nervous but excited, had taken her place with the other dancers, with the sunshine glinting on her hair and dazzling her eyes.

She had been so young, she thought now, and so naive. Her dress of white lace and silk swirled around her ankles as she danced the required patterns to the accompaniment of a grand piano. There had been a dozen girls in hopes of a place at the school, girls whose fathers were ready to pay the tuition, whose mothers were poised to assemble wardrobes and dancing shoes and anything else that would be needed. Nellie Cornish herself had been there, flanked by two dance instructors who looked to Bronwyn like goddesses, long-necked as swans, graceful as birds in flight.

It all seemed very long ago now. Her feet, which had felt so light that day of her audition, seemed leaden and clumsy as she crossed the road. Following the arrow's direction, she trudged the long block to the school.

It wasn't the same building. This one was new, all white, with a brass sign over the entrance. She stood under one of the cotton-wood trees that lined the street, and gazed up from its shade at the building, which seemed as fantastic and distant as a fairy-tale castle. The upper windows were open to the summer air, and music trickled from them. Tidy shrubs lined the walkway leading to the front door. As Bronwyn watched, several mothers with tiny girls in wide tulle skirts emerged from the double wooden doors into the sunshine. The girls were laughing and chattering together, and one of them pirouetted ahead of her mother as if the music were still playing.

Bronwyn had been no different, lighthearted, confident, happy. But now—now she stood in shadow, anonymous and insignificant, a rather grimy girl peering at the school she had been meant to attend. All her plans had come to nothing. Those little dancing princesses had no idea how quickly their dreams could crumble away.

She tore herself away from the pretty scene, but as she walked painfully back toward Broadway she sent a wish toward the little girls that they would be luckier than she had been, and perhaps wiser.

She had to climb steep Aloha Street to reach Fourteenth Avenue. The afternoon was wearing away, the sun slanting through the trees and burning the lawns and shrubberies that lined the street. Perspiration ran down her cheeks from beneath her hat, and her skirt clung to her white stockings. By the time she reached the hill's crest, and turned toward its crown of elegant houses, she was nearly at the end of her strength. She felt headachy and confused, and her mouth and throat were terribly dry.

There was no doubt she had found Millionaire's Row. She gazed up at mansion after mansion, with soaring columns, wide entries, broad, elegant porches, and manicured lawns. The scent of roses hung on the heavy air.

She would always, she thought, think of the perfume of roses when she thought of the neighborhood where Preston had been born. Where their baby, their little fair-haired, blue-eyed boy, should have grown up. She could so easily imagine him tumbling across one of these emerald lawns that it was almost as if such a thing had actually happened. She looked up and down the street, and in her fevered mind, it seemed possible that if she just found the right house, if she just peeked into the right garden, he would be there.

She stumbled along the sidewalk, feeling sticky and thirsty and slow. She didn't know which of these towering, sprawling homes was Benedict Hall. The photograph she had pored over so often was an indoor view, with a wide, polished staircase and tall vases of flowers. Any one of these houses, these magnificent creations of wood and brick, wrought-iron fences and balustrades, cupolas and dormers, could be the one. In her mind, Benedict Hall had been a palace, sitting in solitary splendor at the top of the hill, but this was a row of such palaces, facing one another across a single street, as if—just as the streetcar operator had said—Seattle had gathered its millionaires together and told them where they could live.

She blinked against the perspiration dripping into her eyes, and found herself at the end of the street, crossing it, walking blindly on into a sort of park, where a brick tower soared above carefully planted gardens, and the glass walls of a strange building glittered in the late afternoon light.

Bronwyn wasn't sure where she was, or how she had gotten there. She felt light-headed, disconnected from the increasing discomfort in her body. She was thirstier than she could ever remember being, and the need for water drove everything else out of her mind. The park was enormous, with long curving sidewalks, a great shining reservoir to her left, and spreading lawns where children were playing, rolling balls back and forth or wading in a pool.

The pool drew Bronwyn to it. A half-dozen children stood knee-deep in blue water, stretching out their hands to the center fountain and its cooling spray. Bronwyn's mouth had gotten so dry she could barely swallow. Her thoughts were so jumbled she couldn't organize them. Some part of her knew she should find a cleaner source of water, but desperation drove her. She reached the pool, and sank to her knees beside its rim of pale stone. Distantly, she was aware of several adults watching her curiously as she scooped water in her palm and drank. No one spoke to her, but they stared and whispered. The water was warm and stale, but she didn't care. It was wet, and it soothed her parched tongue and throat.

She could have drunk more, but when her first intense thirst was slaked, the taste made her stop. She put both her hands into the pool, and stroked her hot cheeks with water. She drew a few rather shaky breaths, blinking in the glare of the lowering sun.

After a time she felt a bit better, and began to be embarrassed by the curious gazes turned her way. She came stiffly to her feet. This had been a bad idea. She could see that now. She hadn't been thinking clearly at all. She should find her way back to Mother Ryther's, slip up the stairs to the cramped bedroom, and sleep until she was herself again.

She was gathering her coat and her handbag, adjusting her hat, when she saw the child.

Except for the fact that this child was a girl, in a pinafore and ruffled dress, the child could have been the one Bronwyn had imagined a half hour before. She was rosy from the heat, and the sun shone through her halo of pale curls. Her eyes were a light, clear blue, the same blue that had so enchanted Bronwyn when she first encountered it. The little girl stood waist-deep in the water, and her round face was just crumpling in preparation for tears.

Bronwyn, with a hand to her throat, gazed around the pool, but no one seemed to be watching this particular child. She looked back just as the little girl tried to take a step forward, stumbled, and fell sideways into the water. It was no more than ten or twelve inches deep, but the child was soaked now to her chest, and she emitted a sudden wail of fury at the feeling of it.

Again Bronwyn looked around, but she found the other adults were doing the same thing, searching one another's faces, looking for the person responsible for the little girl. No one moved. Other children turned to gape at the screaming toddler.

Bronwyn pressed her fingers to her temples as she tried to make sense of the scene. The heat and the glitter of light from the water, her worsening headache, the noise of the child's wails and the other children playing in the field beyond, all combined to create a sense of unreality. She was trying to sort the details into some sort of rational picture when the little girl suddenly thrashed with her arms, and fell backward into the shallow water. It closed over her head, stopping her wails and leaving a sudden, terrifying silence.

Bronwyn kicked off her pumps, dropped her handbag, and stepped over the rim of the pool. She waded through the water, oblivious of her wet hem and stockings, and lifted the child, choking and gasping, out of the water and into her arms.

As she turned to wade back out of the water, a woman stood in front of her, hands on her hips. "You should watch your daughter more closely, young woman! You want to see your little girl drown?"

It was Bronwyn's turn to gape, her mouth open and working, but wordless. Her thoughts churned like muddy waves, and she couldn't find the words to explain that this wasn't her child.

The other woman stalked away, leaving Bronwyn holding a wet, furious little girl.

She *could* have been mine, was the thought that surfaced out of the turmoil of Bronwyn's thoughts. She's a little younger, but she's blond, and blue-eyed. She *could* have been my baby. Mine, and Preston's.

Energized now, with a purpose, Bronwyn bent to pick up her handbag and her coat from the grass. She shoved her feet into her pumps, cuddled the now-sobbing child close against her, and walked out of the park with determined steps.

Surely this baby was hers now. She had a place to take her, a place where she would be safe. Surely, if she explained, Mother Ryther would allow it. It was no different from leaving a child in the yard, was it?

The woman in the park was right. So was Mother Ryther. People should watch their children more closely.

CHAPTER 14

Blake resisted an impulse to run into the park, to beg people to look for a little blond girl in a ruffled pinafore. It wouldn't help the family, he reminded himself, for him to have another bout with his heart. He forced himself to use his cane, to walk with steady steps across the road, up onto the sidewalk, on past the brick tower. He looked right and left, searching the crowd. The late afternoon light had a lucent quality he always associated with summer, and in his agitated state, it seemed to him that every man, woman, and child who came into his view was illuminated with particular clarity, like those Renaissance paintings with saints haloed in gold.

There were so many people! It was an ocean of humanity, surging this way and that, blocking his view of the lawn that spilled down toward the reservoir, and of the glass walls of the conservatory, where the iron framework glistened above the heads of the crowd. He reached the point where the sidewalk curved down the hill, and his steps slowed, then stopped. He cast about for some idea, some hint as to which way he should go. It was possible Louisa wasn't here at all. It was a long way for a toddler to come, although Louisa was, as they were learning, no ordinary toddler.

He felt uncomfortable among so many strangers. There were too many suspicious looks, even wary ones. He supposed he made an unusual sight in this place, a tall Negro in a black suit, wearing neither hat nor gloves, leaning on an ancient marble-headed cane.

He tried not to look into individual faces, but to scan the scene at the level of their knees, hoping against hope to see Louisa's curly head, the flash of her blue eyes.

The sobbing of a child drew his attention, piercing the noise of the crowd. He would have said, at any other time, that one child's cry was very like another, but this one didn't seem that way. It sounded familiar. It sounded like the cry he had been hearing for more than a year from the nursery in Benedict Hall.

It could be wishful thinking. It might not mean anything. Just the same, he threw up his head, and cast about for the source.

Coming across the lawn was a slender young woman carrying a coat over her arm and wearing a dilapidated straw hat. She had a handbag pressed awkwardly under her arm, and she was carrying a child who clung to her, wailing and kicking. Both woman and child were dripping wet.

Blake couldn't move for several seconds, struck nerveless by the wave of relief that swept up from his belly to his throat. When he could make himself speak, he cried, "Louisa! Miss Louisa, what—what's happened?"

It was obvious the child couldn't hear him over the sound of her own weeping, and the girl carrying her didn't respond. Blake had to step forward, into their path. Cautiously, hoping not to frighten the young woman, he put up his free hand. "Excuse me," he said. "Miss, please excuse me, but—I've been searching for this child."

The girl carrying Louisa stopped walking. She stared up at Blake with red-rimmed hazel eyes, and her hat fell off, revealing light brown hair that was matted and tangled. She blinked at him, and stammered, "I—why, I *know* you!"

At the same moment, Louisa twisted in her grasp. When she caught sight of Blake she launched herself out of the girl's arms and into his. He dropped his cane, throwing up his hands just in time to catch her. She squalled, "Bake, Bake, Bake!" and buried her face against his chest.

He held her tightly, with arms that trembled. He pressed his cheek to her wet hair, though he knew people were staring at the strange sight they made, the tall Negro and the tiny blond child. He said, "Miss, thank you! How can we ever thank you? This little rascal is Louisa Benedict, and she—oh, my goodness. There are no words. What happened?"

The young woman was bending to pick up her hat, and as she straightened, she said, "We've met, sir. I'm Bronwyn Morgan, of Port Townsend."

Blake narrowed his eyes in concentration. "Miss—Morgan, is it?"

"Yes. I'm sorry I can't recall your name, but you're—that is, you were—Preston Benedict's driver. He dined at Morgan House, and you . . ." She broke off.

At her words, the memory came back to Blake, all at once, as if someone had switched on a light. He recalled the long, narrow kitchen with its view of Puget Sound. There had been a sour-faced cook who reluctantly served him a meal, but didn't speak to him. There was a maid, a nondescript sort of woman who stared at him when she thought he wasn't looking. Morgan House, that was it. When Mr. Preston was still at the newspaper.

"Miss Morgan!" he said, even as Louisa broke into fresh sobs against his lapels. "I do remember! That was quite some time ago, wasn't—"

He didn't get to finish his thought. A short man wearing a straw boater and a white linen jacket stalked into his view, and demanded, "What's going on here? Miss, is this fellow bothering you?"

The girl started, and turned to face the inquisitor. "What?" she said.

Blake recalled her well now, remembering a bright, loquacious sixteen-year-old and her youthful, shy mother. Their eyes had struck him, hazel flecked with gold, and he remembered worrying about Preston's behavior toward them. It seemed, though, at least on that night, that Preston had acted in a gentlemanly fashion. Blake felt reasonably certain that had he not, Mr. Morgan would have intervened. They had driven back to Seattle the next morning, and nothing had seemed amiss.

The girl had changed more dramatically than just the passage of three years would explain. She looked worn and thin and perhaps not very well. Worse, she couldn't seem to think of what to say to the man in the boater.

The stranger said again, "Bothering you, miss? This darkie?"

Blake stiffened. "Sir," he began. "I'm the—" but Miss Morgan interrupted.

She lifted her head to glare at the interloper. "This is Mr. Benedict's chauffeur," she said, with a haughtiness Edith Benedict, in her better days, would have been proud of. "We're acquainted, thank you, sir."

The man eyed her doubtfully, and gave Blake the same scrutiny. It was no wonder, either. Miss Morgan was wet to the thighs, and her hat was crumpled. Little Louisa was soaked from head to toe, while Blake, his cane at his feet, was dressed in his usual service coat, with carefully shined shoes and neatly pressed trousers.

Miss Morgan said again, "Thank you for your concern, sir, but there is no need." Blake thought she might even have sniffed, once, as if irritated at having to repeat herself.

The man in the boater touched his fingers to his hat. "Glad to hear it, miss," he said, though he didn't sound convinced. He nodded to her, and walked away without another glance at Blake.

Miss Morgan appeared to wilt again, as if she had pulled herself together just for the necessity of the moment. Her shoulders sagged, and she held her bedraggled straw hat in her two hands as if it didn't belong to her.

"It's Blake, miss," Blake said gently. He was patting Louisa on her back. Her sobs had subsided to an occasional shudder. She clung to him like an oyster to a rope, arms around his neck, legs scrabbling for purchase around his waist. He held her under his chin, and regarded Miss Morgan above her dripping curls. "My name is Blake. I remember you very well, but I certainly didn't expect to meet you here."

"I—I was just—" Miss Morgan made a helpless gesture with the ruined hat. "She fell in the wading pool!" she finished, which hardly explained anything, but was borne out by the evidence.

"Will you follow me, miss? The family is in a terrible state. This is Miss Louisa, and she's been missing for quite some time. Her mother is frightened half to death."

Bronwyn, filled with misgiving, plodded after Blake's tall figure. She had told him her name. She hadn't meant to tell anyone her name. She had handed over the little girl, realizing in a flash how foolish it was to have thought she could pretend the child was hers. She had stood there, her dress dripping and her hat bent nearly beyond recognition, and defended the poor chauffeur as if she were still someone of consequence.

Now, she supposed they were on their way to Benedict Hall. She would get that glimpse she had hoped for, but they—the residents, perhaps even Dr. Benedict, which would be humiliating—would see her at her worst. She considered dropping back, letting herself be lost in the crowd, but as she began to slow her steps, the tall Negro looked over his shoulder.

"Oh, do please come to Benedict Hall, miss," he said in his deep, elegant voice. "Mrs. Ramona will want to thank you. Perhaps help you with your frock."

Bronwyn walked faster, until she was side by side with Blake as they crossed the street. "No one was watching her," she said, a little defensively. It was silly, of course. Blake couldn't know—nor could anyone else—that she had entertained, even for a moment, the idea of taking the little girl with her.

"She slipped away when everyone thought she was asleep," Blake said. They had reached a scrolled iron gate in a fence surrounding a large white house, four stories at least, with a broad porch and cupolas everywhere. It was three times the size of her own house, Bronwyn thought, tipping up her head to try to take it all in. There was a garage behind it, too, painted white, and broad green lawns edged by rosebushes. An enormous camellia towered at the front, all the way to the top floor.

The child was quiet now, emitting only a faint, occasional hiccup. With the little girl in his arms, Blake led the way up several steps and across the wide porch to the front door. He opened this, and stood aside for Bronwyn to precede him. When she hesitated he said, "You must come in, Miss Morgan, or Mrs. Benedict will never forgive me."

Whether this was true or not, she would never know. At the sound of the door, a pretty, disheveled woman came flying from somewhere at the back of the house. She screeched when she saw the child, and seized her from Blake to hug her and smother her with kisses. She wept and scolded through all of this, and had no eyes for Bronwyn at all. A middle-aged woman in a dark dress and dark stockings came behind her, a little more slowly, and she was weeping, too, though she didn't scold. She stood beside the younger woman, wearing a look of such remorse on her craggy face that it made Bronwyn avert her gaze.

Blake stepped away, disappearing down the broad hallway to pass through a swinging door. Bronwyn stood uncertainly where she was, waiting for someone to look up and demand to know who she was and what she was doing there. Before this could happen, the swinging door opened again, and a plump Negress appeared, twisting her apron in her broad hands and crying out, "Oh, thank the Lord! Thank the sweet Lord! Miss Louisa's home safe!"

Behind her trailed two girls, a matched set of freckled redheads, grinning and adding their voices to the tumult. The child began to cry again in response to the racket around her, and her mother and the middle-aged woman turned toward the wide staircase.

Bronwyn, watching them, realized that this was the site of the photograph she had pored over so often. It was the image she had dreamed of, picturing herself on the staircase instead of Margot Benedict, and Preston beside her in place of Frank Parrish. The carved newel posts gleamed in the light from the open front door. A strip of thick carpet ran over the polished wooden steps, and the bottom of the staircase widened as it dropped to the floor of the hall. Preston's sister had stood just there, with her handsome groom beside her. There had been vases of flowers on the stairs, and glimpses of garlands.

That had been Margot Benedict. Dr. Benedict. This was her home, and if she found Bronwyn here . . .

Dr. Benedict thought she was Betty Jones, while Blake knew her to be Bronwyn Morgan of the Port Townsend Morgans. How could she ever explain?

Clutching her hat and her handbag, with her coat trailing from her arm, Bronwyn edged toward the front door. The women with the little girl climbed the stairs away from her, and the others— the Negress and the two redheaded girls—clustered around Blake, peppering him with questions. No one noticed Bronwyn slipping away, ducking out the open door into the warm evening light. She crossed the porch and descended the steps, hurrying now. If she got away before Blake could stop her, if she hurried back down the hill to the streetcar, he would forget all about her. He would surely forget her name, and not be tempted to try to discover where she was staying, or if her parents knew.

Bronwyn lifted the sun-warmed latch on the wrought-iron gate and started to pull it open. She gasped when a cold hand gripped her arm. It was a small hand, but surprisingly strong. Bronwyn stared at it for a heartbeat, then lifted her gaze to the face of the woman who had stopped her.

It was the second time that day she had seen the hair and eyes that reminded her so much of Preston, but this woman's hair was mixed with gray, and her eyes were faded to a wintry blue. Her fingernails were manicured and her hair dressed, but though she wore a well-pressed linen afternoon frock, there was something oddly unkempt in her appearance, as if all the pieces of her didn't quite fit together.

The woman said in an urgent whisper, "Did you find him?"

A chill ran through Bronwyn. Could this woman, whoever she was, have looked into her mind? How could she have known her reason for being in Seattle, for going to the Ryther Home. . . .

Bronwyn took a breath, banishing the notion. Of course the woman meant the little girl. She had simply misspoken. Bronwyn gently lifted her arm away from the woman's grasp. "You must mean little Louisa," she said, in what she hoped was a soothing tone. "She's in the house now. She's fine, ma'am."

The woman stood where she was, searching Bronwyn's face with her pale gaze. Her hand was still extended, the fingers curved, as if she didn't realize Bronwyn had removed her arm from beneath it. "Not Louisa," she said, blinking. "The little boy. My grandson."

Bronwyn's chill returned in force. She shivered with it, and wondered vaguely if her fever was rising again. She said, haltingly, "Ma'am? I don't know what—"

The older woman slowly dropped her hand, and Bronwyn saw that she was carrying something in her other hand, what looked at first glance like a rock. It was rough-edged and uneven, a weathered-looking gray, and it took a moment for Bronwyn to understand that it was a piece of concrete.

The woman lifted it, and held it up on her two palms. "I hate this thing," she said, as if Bronwyn should understand what it was she was showing her. "I saw you from my window, you see."

Bronwyn couldn't see how the two were related, and she suspected the woman wasn't quite sane. She didn't want to be rude, but she really did want to get away before Margot Benedict appeared and exposed her deception. She put her hand on the gate again. "If you'll excuse me, ma'am," she began, "I really must be . . ."

In the middle of her sentence, the older woman turned the chunk of concrete over in her palms, and Bronwyn saw the stone embedded in it. Her throat dried, and she stood, wordless, staring at it.

She had seen that stone before. It was a sapphire. He had worn it around his neck, under his shirt. He told her he never took it off, that it had belonged to a Turkish queen, long ago. Even when he—when they were in the garden together—the jewel was around his neck. It had pressed against her, caught between Preston's body and her own. Its heavy silver chain had been cool against her bare skin. Later, as she had undressed in her half-dreaming state, the imprint of the sapphire was still there, marked into the soft skin of her breast.

"It's so strange, don't you think?" the woman said, turning the stone so it glowed in the evening light. "I don't really believe in such—that is, it never made sense to me, but—Preston likes it." She gazed at Bronwyn's face. "Is it you, dear?"

"Is it me?" Bronwyn stammered. "What do you mean?" This woman had to be Preston's mother. This was Benedict Hall. It was perfectly logical to meet her here, but the circumstances were so strange. Bronwyn raised one hand to her temple and rubbed it, wishing she could understand what was happening. One of them was making no sense, and she wasn't entirely certain it was the other woman.

"I think it must be you. Preston described you to me, and when I heard all the noise, and looked out of my window, I thought you might be the girl. It's your eyes, you know. So distinctive."

"He—Preston described me?" Bronwyn found herself gaping in confusion, and forced herself to close her mouth.

"Oh, yes. Yes."

"What are you doing with that?" Bronwyn asked, pointing one finger at the chunk of concrete with its buried jewel.

"Oh, the stone! He wants me to bring it to him. I'm going to do that."

"B-bring it to him? Do you mean, to the cemetery?"

At this artless question, Mrs. Benedict emitted a sudden, incongruous ripple of laughter. "Oh, no, dear! No. That was all a foolish mistake."

"I don't understand at all," Bronwyn said. She dropped her hand from the latch of the gate, and leaned weakly against the cold scrolled iron. "Mrs. Benedict, I know Preston is dead. I read it in the *Times*, all about the funeral and everything. I cried for days."

The older woman put a hand under her arm, and turned her about. "You look terrible, young lady. Come in. Let our cook make you a cup of tea."

"Oh, no, I can't. I—" Bronwyn made a feeble attempt to pull away, but what was left of her strength drained away, all at once, as if someone had pulled the stopper in a tub full of water. The frail hand of Mrs. Benedict wasn't strong enough to hold her, and she sagged to her knees on the brick path. Her vision blurred, and she put out her hands, searching for support.

The hands that met hers weren't the cold ones of Mrs. Benedict. They were large and warm and very strong. "If you'll permit me, miss," came the deep rumble of Blake's voice. One of his hands gripped her left hand, and the other slipped under her right arm. He lifted her from the path as if she weighed nothing. She leaned on him, because she had no choice. He felt as solid as a mountain. With uncertain steps, she made her way back up the path, submitted to him assisting her up onto the porch, over the doorsill, into the coolness of the hall.

She heard Mrs. Benedict fluttering alongside, speaking words Bronwyn couldn't make out. She longed to lie down for a few minutes, to close her eyes, to stop trying to comprehend this bizarre day.

She wasn't sure how much time passed after that. She opened her eyes to find herself in a room that was dim and cool and quiet. Her shoes had been removed, and her wet dress. She was covered by the lightest of blankets, and the curtains were drawn against what remained of the daylight. As she turned her head on the pillow, a voice said, "Oh, there you are, miss! You've had a nice lie-down, now, haven't you? Just be still one more moment while I fetch Mrs. Ramona."

Bronwyn wasn't sure she could have moved even if she had wanted to. She no longer felt feverish, but she was thirsty again, parched. Her body felt somehow empty, and her skin was dry

and tender. She knew she should get away, leave this place before she was discovered, but she couldn't summon the energy to
do it.

The door to the bedroom opened, and the young woman she
had met in the hallway appeared. She had a glass in her hand,
and as she crossed to the bed, she gave Bronwyn a sweet smile.
"Oh, my dear," she exclaimed in a fluting voice. "How can I *ever*
thank you for finding my little girl? What you must think of us!"

She settled onto the side of the bed, and with a gentle hand,
helped Bronwyn to sit up. The glass held orange juice, and Bronwyn, though a little embarrassed at her greediness, drank it
straight down before she said a word. She felt better immediately.

"So kind," she murmured, as the woman set the glass on the
bedside table. She was lovely, with finger-waved hair and round
pink cheeks. "I don't know what happened."

"You fainted," the woman said. "I think you were just exhausted. You'll have to explain who you are and what you were
doing in the park, but please, please take your time! I'm Ramona
Benedict, and I was so frantic about my daughter, I can't even
tell you! It was terrible, just *ghastly*. You're our savior!"

"Oh, no," Bronwyn said automatically.

"Oh, yes," Ramona Benedict insisted. "Blake tells me she fell
in the wading pool. She loves that pool, but I never thought she
could find her way there all alone! And no one stopped her! It's
just too *devastating* to think about what might have happened.
I'm so grateful to you, my dear."

"Not at all," Bronwyn said politely. Surely she had never contemplated taking the little girl away with her. She couldn't have.
Like this pretty woman, she was a lady. She had been raised
properly, and she would never . . .

But she almost had. And then she had met Mrs. Benedict in
the garden. This memory made her sit up straighter, and put a
hand to her head. "Oh!" she breathed. "Mrs. Benedict! It was
so odd."

Ramona patted her arm. "I know. Mother Benedict can be—

well. Sometimes she says strange things. She's very sweet, though." She smoothed the blanket over Bronwyn's legs. "Would you like some supper brought up? Or better yet, let's run you a bath, and then you can join us all for dinner if you feel up to it. It's very late, of course, but Hattie was helping search for Louisa. I can find you a fresh frock to put on. Yours was soaked. One of the twins—that is, one of our maids—will put it right for you, but it will take a little time." As Bronwyn hesitated, Ramona said with a laugh, "And you *must* tell me your name! I can't just keep calling you 'my dear,' now, can I?"

CHAPTER 15

Hattie, flustered and perspiring, was struggling with a roast of halibut that had been delivered that afternoon. "It shoulda been marinating all this time," she lamented. "It's gonna be ruined, and here we are with company and all."

"Never mind, Hattie," Blake said equably. He had put on one of Hattie's aprons, and was sorting flatware onto a tray. "Dinner will be late. Under the circumstances, I'm sure Mr. Dickson and Mr. Dick will understand."

There was no one else to help Hattie at the moment. At Mrs. Ramona's insistence, their unexpected visitor would be staying the night. Thelma had been dispatched, with Loena, to air out a room for her. Leona had gone up to assist Mrs. Edith in dressing for dinner, because Ramona wouldn't leave little Louisa's side. The nurse was weeping in the nursery, swearing she didn't know how it had happened, offering her resignation every five minutes until even Mrs. Ramona, who never lost her temper, snapped at her that if she wanted her resignation, she would ask for it.

The two men had found their own way home from the office, and now were huddled with their evening cocktails in the small parlor, with the door firmly closed against the feminine ructions above stairs. Blake envied them—not the cocktails, but the ability to shut out the commotion. It had taken some time to calm Louisa down after her adventure, and though Mrs. Ramona had been white with fear for her daughter, it was Nurse who had, in the end, required several whiffs of sal volatile to prevent a bout of nervous hysterics. Blake had overseen all of this, then been called to the front garden to assist the young woman who had found Louisa.

All in all, he admitted to himself, it had been a wearing afternoon, and if Dr. Margot had been here she would probably have ordered him to go to his own rooms and rest.

She wasn't here, however, and he could hardly leave poor Hattie alone to try to keep order in the house. He placed glasses and salad plates on the tray, and, leaving his cane leaning beneath the rack with his serving coat, he carried everything into the dining room. After he had laid the table, he brought the empty tray back to the kitchen. Hattie glanced up as he backed through the swinging door.

"I guess you givin' up that cane for good, Blake."

"You know, Hattie," Blake said, smiling at her, "I seem to have made a full recovery."

"Hmmm. Hope you ain't rushing things," Hattie said, and went back to chopping sprigs of dill for the fish.

"No, ma'am," Blake said, chuckling, but he left the cane where it was. It was nice not to have to maneuver it around furniture. It was wonderful to have both hands free. He promised himself he would make a conscious effort to walk without limping. He wondered if it was habit rather than necessity that made him favor the leg. "What else can I do to help?"

"That salad needs tossing, and the butter dishes need filling. Good thing I done snapped those beans before Miss Louisa took it into her curly little head to go explorin'!"

Blake took up the salad tongs as Hattie went on muttering to herself. To distract her, he said, "Tell me, Hattie. Have you heard anything from Miss Allison?"

"She sent me a postcard with a picture of a cable car, which looks like some sort of streetcar. She didn't say too much, though. I hope being with her parents hasn't made her unhappy again. That poor chile! Her mother's home now from that sanitarium, and she's probably pestering Miss Allison all over again."

"Maybe not. Maybe the treatments did her some good."

Hattie threw him a dark look, and shook her knife in the air. "You can't do good for some people, Blake, and that's the Lord's truth. Some people just can't be helped."

"Well," he said, wishing he'd chosen a different topic, "Miss Allison isn't one of them."

"No, no," Hattie said, resuming her chopping, shaking her frizzy curls. "No, Miss Allison is a sweet chile, that's for sure. Such a sweet chile. Gonna be a fine nurse one day!"

"I'm certain of that," Blake said as he turned to the icebox for the butter crock.

"Seems to me," Hattie said, laying down her knife and scooping up the dill to sprinkle over the halibut. "Seems to me every chile out of this house is gonna be fine. All except the one." She bent to slide the roasting pan into the oven, and straightened with a little *whoof*, one hand on the counter and one on her back. "That's a sad thing, but that can't be helped, neither."

"No," Blake said with sympathy. He watched as Hattie moved a little stiffly back to her counter. "No, there's no help for him, I'm afraid."

Hattie clucked, and shook her head again as she ran water into a kettle for the beans. "Such a pretty little boy, he was. I don't think I'll ever get over it."

"No." There was nothing to add to this. Hattie had clung to her belief in Preston's good nature for a long time. She had passionately grieved his supposed death. When they learned he was alive, Blake had feared for her, but Hattie had met that turn of events with an inner strength that sustained her through everything that followed.

Mrs. Edith had not. Even now, more than a year after Preston had been confined, Mrs. Edith behaved as if he were merely in a hospital, as if he, like the other patients there, suffered from a lung ailment or some other treatable condition. She spoke as if one day he would return to Benedict Hall, and she kept his bedroom untouched and his place set at the table, all in readiness. No one argued with her about any of it.

Blake thought that might not be the healthiest thing, but it wasn't his place to have an opinion.

Bronwyn found herself, without having actually agreed to it, facing an enormous claw-foot tub filled with lilac-scented water. There was a maid to help her, a middle-aged, gray-haired woman in a black skirt and white apron. They hadn't had nearly so much staff at Morgan House. It hadn't been part of Betty's duties to help Bronwyn dress or run her bath for her. This woman—who had introduced herself as "Thelma, miss," with a shallow curtsy— held up a wide bath towel and averted her eyes.

Behind the modesty of the towel, Bronwyn stripped off her underclothes and stepped into the tub. The warm water gave her a wave of nostalgia for her own pink-tiled bathroom and towels washed by Betty and dried in the sunshine. She had bathed at the Ryther Home, but in tepid water that rose only to her hips, and she had felt as if she might drown when she tried to wash her hair.

Now, she sank into water over her head, and gratefully used the shampoo left in the tray beside the tub. She scrubbed and scrubbed, and then, reluctant to leave the water, she lay soaking and thinking and wondering what the older Mrs. Benedict had been talking about, and why the sapphire that had once hung around Preston's neck on an antique silver chain now was embedded in broken concrete. Mrs. Benedict had said, "No, no. That was all a foolish mistake." Whatever could that mean?

When a soft knock sounded on the door to the bathroom, Bronwyn started in surprise. She didn't know how long she had reclined in the water, but her hair had started to dry and the water had grown cool. She called swiftly, "Just a moment, please!"

It was Ramona's high voice that answered. "Of course, Miss

Morgan. Take your time. I have a dress for you, and some other things. I'll meet you in the bedroom when you're ready."

Bronwyn hurried to dry herself, to towel her hair and run her fingers through it, and to wrap herself in the borrowed bathrobe Thelma had provided. She let herself out of the bathroom and into the adjoining bedroom.

Ramona was waiting there, seated at the dressing table and fussing with her own hair. She caught sight of Bronwyn in the mirror and gave her a delighted smile. "Oh, you look as if you feel *so* much better, Miss Morgan! Isn't a bath just the most *marvelously* restoring thing?"

"Yes, thank you, Mrs. Benedict," Bronwyn said. "This is so kind of you, but—"

"Oh, don't say it!" Ramona cried. She jumped up from the stool, and stroked the fabric of a dinner dress she had laid out on the bed. It was a green georgette with a low waist and handkerchief hem, and the high neck of the bodice was trimmed in matching satin ribbon. "I know your coloring is different from mine, but I think this will look well on you." She made a dismissive gesture with her hand, skimming her own figure. "I haven't quite been able to wear it since I had Louisa, I'm afraid. But you're so slender, it should be perfect!"

She lifted a little pile of folded things from the dressing table. "Now, here is a bit of lingerie, and a pair of stockings. Borrowed, of course, but all clean, I promise you!"

"Oh, you shouldn't have," Bronwyn said.

Ramona set the pile beside the dress, and patted it with her palm before she straightened, and turned a suddenly grave face to Bronwyn. "I can never repay you, Miss Morgan," she said. "My little Louisa—oh, I can't bear to think what might have happened if you hadn't been there. My daughter means *everything* to me."

The simple statement struck Bronwyn to her heart. She wanted to protest that she hadn't been the heroine they thought. She wanted to confess to this woman, who was being so kind to her, that she had been ready to carry her child away in place of the one she had lost. She opened her mouth, but no words would come.

Ramona gave herself a little shake, and then laughed. "Everything's all right, though, isn't it? Nothing bad happened, thanks to you. No point in dwelling on it!" She started for the door. "Now I'll go and dress for dinner, and you do the same. I have a hundred questions to ask you, and I know my husband will want to hear them, too. He'll be so grateful! And you must call me Ramona, all right? If I may call you by your Christian name, too?"

She was gone a moment later, smiling, pulling the door gently shut behind her. Bronwyn was left alone in the bedroom, staring at herself in the dressing-table mirror and wondering, now that she had managed to get herself into Benedict Hall, what she could do to extricate herself before someone found her out.

Thelma and Leona had come down at last, and were helping Hattie to plate the salads and fill the silver baskets with rolls. Blake exchanged his apron for his serving jacket and white gloves, and was on his way to check the dining room's readiness when Loena came flying down the hall from the back staircase. Her red hair was falling out of its pins to trail on her collar, and her apron was twisted halfway around.

Blake stopped and gazed at her in consternation. "Loena," he said, frowning. "Is Mrs. Edith all right?"

Loena skidded to a stop in front of him. "Mr. Blake, I was looking for you! I didn't know what to do when she showed it to me, but I don't think Mr. Dickson would like—" She broke off, out of breath, and pressed a hand to her chest.

"Who showed you? And what?"

"Mrs. Edith! She has that—that awful stone, the one Mr. Preston . . ." She dropped her hand, and seeming to realize the disarray of her appearance, began straightening her apron. "She's been keeping it in her room all this time, looks like!"

"That damned sapphire," Blake muttered, winning a look of shock from the maid. She had never heard him swear. In fact, he couldn't remember the last time he had uttered a curse word, and certainly not in front of the staff. Just the same, if there were any circumstance that deserved hard words, this had to be one.

"I hope you'll pardon me, Loena," he said. "You surprised me. I was under the impression that stone was out of the house for good."

"She's been hiding it in a drawer," Loena said. Her eyes were wide with excitement, and her freckled cheeks were flushed. "But now it's on her bureau, with all that concrete around it. I saw it when I was dressing her, and she said she's takin' it to Mr. Preston. Is she going to see Mr. Preston? I thought Mr. Dickson said—"

"That's enough, Loena," Blake said firmly. "We do not talk about the family that way, as you know very well."

"Yes, sir." Loena dropped her gaze to the floor.

"Now," Blake said. "Please tidy your hair, then go into the dining room to help Thelma set out the salad plates."

"Yes, sir." Loena fumbled with her hairpins, but she glanced up from beneath her sandy eyelashes. "Are you going to tell Mr. Dickson?"

"Never you mind, Loena," he answered dismissively. "This is not something for you to worry about. Go, now. We have a guest, and Hattie's trying to hurry dinner along. She needs you."

"Yes, Mr. Blake." Loena spoke demurely, but there was another inquisitive flash of blue eyes before she smoothed the last wisp of hair underneath a pin, and tripped off to the kitchen.

Blake, despite his concern, felt a smile tug at his lips. Loena had suffered at Mr. Preston's hands, but she had made a full recovery in both body and spirit. He tried to be firm with the twins, but he—and Hattie, too—were awfully fond of them. They would one day marry and leave Benedict Hall, he supposed, but he would miss their quick steps on the stairs and their light voices, chattering together as they went about their work.

He sighed, and drew himself up. He would have to speak to Mr. Dickson after dinner. He wished he had taken charge of the sapphire himself, and disposed of it properly. It was all delusion, of course, part of Mr. Preston's illness, but it had haunted the Benedicts since he brought it home from the war. All that was required for an object to have power, he supposed, was for someone to place their faith in it. It was irrational, but Mr. Preston had not been rational for a very long time.

Mrs. Edith's delusion was proving to be every bit as persistent as Mr. Preston's. Blake hated to burden Mr. Dickson with this latest evidence, but he couldn't see a way to avoid it.

The dining room of Benedict Hall was everything Bronwyn had imagined it would be, and more. The table was twice as long as the one her family used. A silver candelabra stretched down the middle, fitted with slender white candles. A vase of white roses mixed with cut ferns rested on a sideboard. There was a large chandelier, but the electricity was off, and the curtains partly drawn so the room remained cool. Still, the silver sparkled, and the pale flowers and candles gave a sense of lightness to the scene, augmented by the white linen tablecloth and snowy napkins. It made the dining room of Morgan House seem darkly Victorian by contrast.

As Ramona ushered her to a chair, Bronwyn remembered, with a wave of embarrassment, her childish fantasies. The reality shamed her, even though none of these people would ever know that she had once imagined herself becoming mistress of their house.

Two men came in, and were introduced to her as Dickson Benedict and his son, Dick. The elder Mrs. Benedict drifted in after them, looking vague and a little lost. There was an empty chair at her right, with a full place setting of china and silver. Bronwyn watched it anxiously, expecting Margot Benedict to come in at any minute, and exclaim, "Miss Jones! Whatever are you doing here? You're supposed to be in quarantine!"

Dr. Benedict didn't appear, however. A crisp salad of greens and yellow tomatoes was served, followed by baked fish and asparagus. Still there was no Margot Benedict. Bronwyn could hardly eat for the nervous expectation that rumbled in her stomach, but dinner progressed with no sign of the doctor. The conversation turned to the events of the afternoon, and Bronwyn found herself the reluctant object of everyone's attention.

Ramona began by describing everything that had happened, and how relieved she was when Blake and Bronwyn had shown up with the wanderer safe and sound. There were murmured exclamations over the adventure, and expressions of gratitude, as well as criticisms of the child's nurse, and a brief discussion of whether she should be sent packing.

When the rush of comments subsided, the younger Mr. Benedict, called Dick, said, "How did you come to be in Volunteer Park, Miss Morgan? Are you visiting friends in Seattle?"

"I—well, yes, in a way." Bronwyn lowered her gaze to her half-eaten dinner, hating to lie to these nice people.

"Oh," Ramona said. "If you're staying with friends, they might be expecting you. Will they be worried, Bronwyn, dear? We could telephone to them."

"Oh, no," Bronwyn said. "That's not necessary. The thing is, I—"

"You're one of the Port Townsend Morgans, I think." This came from the elder Mrs. Benedict, who had so far not spoken more than three words altogether. It seemed a surprise to everyone at the table. Every head turned in her direction, and there was a suspended moment, empty of conversation.

It was Ramona who broke the silence, with the courtesy that seemed to be her special gift. "Oh, are you, Bronwyn? How delightful. I was in Port Townsend once, when I was just a girl. Where is your house?"

"It's at the top of Monroe Street, facing east."

"Oh, I think I remember it! It looks out over the water."

"It does."

"And it's that lovely peach color."

"Father says it's the color of raw fish," Bronwyn said, attempting a smile.

"How amusing!" Ramona said. "You could call it a salmon color, I suppose. That sounds ever so much nicer. In any case"—she reached to pat Bronwyn's hand—"it's a stunning house."

"Thank you, Mrs.—that is, Ramona." Bronwyn glanced around the elegant dining room. "Of course, it's much smaller than Benedict Hall. And a good bit older."

"I don't believe I know your family," Dickson Benedict said in a gravelly voice. "What's your father's name, Miss Morgan? What business is he in?"

"His name is Chesley Morgan," she answered. "Morgan Shipping and Supply."

"Oh, yes," said the younger Mr. Benedict. "You know them, Father. There was the railroad line they started, and Morgan Shipping was involved with delivering the tracks and managing the labor."

"Only laid a mile of that railroad, didn't they?" his father said. "Before it went bust?"

Dick Benedict made some reply, and the conversation, to Bronwyn's relief, shifted to matters of commerce. The maids came in to set crystal bowls of pink sherbet in place of the dinner plates. It was chilled and slightly tart, and Bronwyn ate every spoonful.

Ramona said, "Isn't this nice on a hot day, Bronwyn? Our cook makes good use of raspberries. It's my favorite."

Bronwyn said, "Yes, it's lovely."

"Preston loves it," Edith Benedict said, with one of those interjections that seemed to startle everyone. An embarrassed silence followed, but Mrs. Benedict turned to Bronwyn as if the statement had been meant for her.

"Excuse me?" Bronwyn stammered, wondering if she'd missed something.

"Preston. My son." Mrs. Benedict pushed away her own barely touched dish. Her breathy voice cracked, and she took an unladylike sniff. "Poor Preston," she said, and pulled a handkerchief from her sleeve. "Preston loves sherbet. He just loves it."

Bronwyn froze. "Mrs. Benedict, I don't—that is, I thought—"

Dickson Benedict cleared his throat, with a rumble like thunder. "Now, now, Edith," he said. "I'm sure they have sherbet in Walla Walla."

Bronwyn, at a loss, turned to Ramona, but the younger Mrs. Benedict gave a subtle shake of the head, and changed the subject. "So, Miss Morgan," she said, with deliberate cheerfulness. "What friends are you visiting? Will you be staying long in Seattle?"

CHAPTER 16

Blake waited until the family started toward the small parlor with the intent of listening to a wireless concert. Mrs. Ramona gathered everyone together, like a hen marshalling her chicks. Their young guest followed. In her borrowed frock, she looked a bit like a child playing dress-up, but her manners were impeccable. She clearly knew how to behave, including what flatware to use for which course, and how to sustain a polite conversation.

It had been a strange dinner, with Mrs. Edith bursting out with odd comments now and again, but the young lady had managed quite well in the face of such confusion. The only truly awkward moment had come as Blake stood in the doorway to announce that coffee would be served in the small parlor. He heard Mrs. Ramona asking about Miss Morgan's Seattle friends, and the painful pause that followed.

The girl had said, haltingly, "Actually, I—I've come to—to do some shopping. I understand the fall line is at Frederick & Nelson now, and I . . ."

Mrs. Ramona exclaimed, "Shopping! How lovely. Perhaps you'll let me accompany you. I haven't shopped for a *thing* for the autumn, and we have a dinner-dance coming up, don't we, Dick? What fun! We can have luncheon in the Tea Room. I haven't done that for just *ages*."

The moment passed as easily as that, but Blake felt young Miss Morgan's tension as she moved by him. Though he had never been a parent, he had a sense for young people. He was sure the young lady was troubled by something.

Mr. Dickson was the last to leave the dining room. Blake, standing at the door, cleared his throat as he walked by, and Mr. Dickson looked up. "I know that sound, Blake."

"Yes, sir," Blake said impassively.

"You need to speak to me." It was not a question.

"I do, sir. Perhaps in your study?"

"Very well. I think I can miss the first portion of this concert. Not my cuppa joe, as the longshoremen say."

Blake inclined his head, and followed his employer down the length of the hall to the door that led to his private room, the book-lined study to which he retreated when he had had enough, he often said, of women and children. His son teased him from time to time about "going to ground," but Mr. Dickson always shook his head and said, "You'll learn, son. You'll learn. Wait till that minx Louisa is a little older!"

The study was quiet now, and dark, its single window open to the night breeze. As Dickson took a cigar from the enormous box beside his padded armchair, Blake bent to turn on a lamp.

Dickson settled into his chair, and snipped the end of the cigar with a small pair of silver scissors. "Problem, Blake?"

Blake took up his usual position, standing beside the bookcase with his hands in the pockets of his serving coat. He waited until Dickson set a flame to the end of his cigar and puffed on it until it caught. He said then, "I'm not sure if it's a problem or not, sir, but I thought you should know."

Dickson merely raised his eyebrows, gazing at Blake above the length of the cigar between his teeth.

Blake shifted a little, and cleared his throat again. "Sir, it's the stone. That sapphire, the one Mr. Preston brought back from Jerusalem."

Dickson took the cigar from his mouth, and gazed at it as if there were answers hidden in its layers of cured tobacco. "You've seen it," he said dourly.

"Not I," Blake said carefully. "But Loena. She has—ahem—occasion to recognize it. She came to report to me when she realized that Mrs. Edith has the stone in her room."

"I thought we got rid of the goddamned thing," Dickson growled.

"I did, too," Blake said. He remembered with painful clarity the shock Dr. Margot had received when she found the sapphire, in its casing of broken concrete, lying on her bed. Left there as a message from her brother, who was supposed to be dead. Mrs. Edith had found it after the crisis, stowed in a drawer, and had known instantly what it meant. "I suppose each of us thought someone else had disposed of it."

Dickson didn't speak for some time. He chewed unhappily on his cigar, exhaling intermittent gouts of smoke. At last he said, "It's hard to understand. A Christian woman like Edith, indulging in such foolish superstition. It's just a stone."

"Perhaps it's a symbol for her, Mr. Dickson," Blake said gently.

Dickson flashed him a look from beneath his thick gray eyebrows. "You're being kind to Edith, Blake."

"She's suffered, sir. I suppose she takes comfort where she can."

"Could we get rid of the thing somehow?"

"I am loath to take it from her room without her knowledge, Mr. Dickson. She would be terribly upset, I'm afraid."

"That makes it my job, I guess." Dickson puffed on his cigar, letting his head drop back against the armchair.

"She told Loena she was going to take the stone to Mr. Preston. I thought you should know. I'm not aware of a planned visit."

"Creedy says she shouldn't go. That she's too fragile."

"So I understand." Dr. Creedy had been a regular presence

throughout the past year. "Mrs. Edith has seemed a bit better, it seems to me."

"I believed she was," Dickson said heavily. "Now I'm not so certain."

"I'm very sorry, sir. I thought you should know."

"Quite right, Blake. I'll have to think about this. Thank you."

"Thank you, sir. Will you join the others now?"

"No. Make my excuses, will you? And if Edith—well. There's nothing to be done right now."

"No. No, I think not. I'll say good night, then, sir."

Blake withdrew, leaving Dickson puffing on his cigar and staring at the ceiling. As Blake walked past the small parlor, he could hear the music and voices from the wireless, and the laughter of the family. He wanted to feel relief at having passed his burden on, but he was troubled by a hunch that this was not going to be easily resolved. It felt like the leading edge of a storm. He wished he knew how to prepare.

Bronwyn learned, as they were waiting for the radio program to begin, that Margot Benedict was to be away from home for two weeks. Relief over that enabled her to relax somewhat, to smile with the others, to drink a demitasse of coffee and enjoy the cookies served with it. She didn't know how to escape from the proposed shopping expedition, but she supposed she could manage that somehow. It would have been fun at any other time, but of course she had no money with her, and she hardly dared show herself at Frederick & Nelson, where one of the saleswomen was bound to recognize her. She and her mother made twice-yearly trips to Seattle to buy their clothes, and Frederick & Nelson was always their first stop.

An urgent message, she thought. She would pretend to telephone to her imaginary hotel and receive a pressing message calling her home. Her skills as a liar were already proven.

When the evening was over, Ramona insisted on lending her a nightdress and a dressing gown, as well as a pair of knitted slippers. "And do sleep as long as you like," Ramona said, as they parted at the bedroom door. "Louisa has her breakfast in the nursery, and I often sit with her. I doubt Nurse will let either of us out of her sight, but I'll try to join you. Just go downstairs when you're ready—we have breakfast in the same room where we had our dinner. We have a breakfast room, but it's small, and we find the dining room more convenient."

Bronwyn said, "Thank you so much. I'll be perfectly comfortable."

Ramona pointed down the hall. "My room is right there if you're not. And the thanks are still mine. I'll never be able to thank you enough."

The events of the day now seemed remote to Bronwyn. She felt stronger than she had in some time, her head clearer than it had been since the baby fell ill at the Ryther Home. She must have been stupid with fever when she walked into the park and came upon Louisa in the wading pool. The whole incident had taken on the aspect of a dream, in which the sequence of actions and reactions had become confused. She washed her face, and brushed her hair with the brush laid out for her use, then gazed for some moments at her reflection. What on earth was she doing here? What had she thought she could accomplish?

Poor Mother Ryther! Someone would go to that little room on the second floor and discover Betty Jones had vanished without a word to anyone. It was shameful, after they had all been so kind.

She should give up. Go back to Port Townsend. She still had Captain Albert's card in her handbag. She should search him out, board the *Sadie Ann* again, and go home. At least that would make her mother happy, even if she herself had to go on being miserable.

Blake learned all too soon that his hunch had been right. There was more trouble to come, and for once it had nothing at all to do with Preston.

He had settled the family in the small parlor, everyone with coffee or tea or, in Mrs. Ramona's case, a cup of cocoa. Mr. Dick tuned the wireless to the station, and as the music began, Blake withdrew, and went to the kitchen to take off his serving coat and see that the maids and Hattie were finished with their work for the day.

He found the three maids sitting around the enamel-topped table with cups in front of them. Hattie was lifting cookies out of the fat pottery jar on the counter. She arranged them on a plate, and brought them to the table. She gave a slight groan as she settled her weight into a chair.

"Tired, Hattie?" Blake said.

"No, no, Blake," she said. "Just good to get off these feet. Goodness, what a day! Miss Louisa going missing, an unexpected guest—I hardly knew which way to turn!"

"Yes," he agreed. "It was a demanding day." He went to the peg rack to hang up his coat.

Hattie was pushing herself up again. "Oh, Blake, you ain't had your coffee. Do you want—"

He put up his hand to stop her. "I'll get it," he said. "Sit down, Hattie. Rest yourself."

She nodded, and sank back into her chair. The maids had been chattering about something, and they took their conversation up again as he crossed to the percolator. He was just reaching for a mug from the upper cupboard when a knock sounded on the back door, the one that led to the porch.

Hattie frowned. "Who's that, do you think? Don't usually get deliveries at night."

"I don't know," Blake said. "I'll go and see." He hesitated just a moment, wondering if he should put on his coat before answering the door. It was the back, though, which meant a deliveryman or some other servant. He decided he didn't need to take that precaution. With an unhurried step, he went out through the kitchen door to the porch, where a screen door led to the back garden.

He could see her through the zinc screen before he reached it. The summer evening light lasted a long time, until almost ten, and the white of her nurse's cap glowed through the gloom. Once he realized who it was, he hurried, crossing the porch in two strides, unlatching the screen door and opening it wide.

"Nurse Church!" he exclaimed. "Why, whatever are you doing here?"

She stepped over the sill and into the wedge of light falling through the open kitchen door. He saw that her face was drawn, her full lips trembling and a little swollen, as if she had been crying. There was no sign of her dimple.

"Mr. Blake," she said, with a catch in her voice. "I'm so sorry to trouble you, but—but I didn't know where to turn!"

"Come in," he said. "No need to apologize. Come in, and let Hattie give you coffee. Have you eaten?"

"I couldn't," she said, a little obscurely, but she followed him out of the cool shadows and into the warm light of the kitchen.

Leona was speaking to the other maids, but as Sarah Church appeared, she broke off. All three of them stared, open-mouthed, at the petite Negress in her nurse's cape and cap. Only Hattie seemed to collect herself in time to be polite.

"Why, Blake," she said, coming to her feet. "Why, this is your nurse, isn't it? Nurse Church, I recall? Come in, come in, miss, and set yourself down. Old Hattie will get you something to drink. Are you hungry?"

This torrent of kind words brought a tremulous smile to Sarah's lips, though she shook her head. "No, thank you," she said. "I'm not hungry. I just needed to speak to Mr. Blake. I need—we need help, Mr. Blake, my family and I."

"Do sit down," he said, and held a chair for her. "Let Hattie get you a cup of tea, at least. You seem to be upset."

She was carrying a large black bag with round handles. She set it on the floor, and accepted the chair from Blake. She slipped out of her cape, and draped it behind her. Hattie bustled to set the kettle to boil and took down a teacup and saucer. Blake said, "Nurse Church, this is the staff of Benedict Hall. Leona and Loena, and Thelma, the third maid. Hattie is our cook."

Sarah nodded to the assembly. Loena said, "Hello," in a half whisper. Neither of the other maids spoke, but their faces were lively with curiosity. As Hattie scooped tea from a canister, Blake said, "You three can go on to bed. Hattie and I will take care of our visitor."

He pretended not to notice the disappointment on their faces. They rose, though with reluctance, and trudged out of the kitchen, casting backward glances at Sarah Church. When Loena dragged her feet, Hattie clucked at her. The girl wrinkled her freckled nose, but she followed her sister and Thelma out into the corridor, and let the door swing shut behind her.

"Now, Sarah," Blake said. He took the chair nearest Sarah, and leaned on his elbows to look into her face. Hattie set the teacup close to her hand, and settled into a chair on the other side of the table. "Tell us what's wrong. You can speak in front of Hattie. She's an old friend."

Sarah put up her hands to unpin her cap. She removed it, and folded it between her hands. "It's our house," she said. "My family's home." She bent to open the bag at her feet, and drew out a folded sheet of paper, closely printed. She smoothed it open, and slid it across the table to Blake. "Some men brought this. They made my mother read it, and then they told her we can't live there anymore. This company is going to build on the empty land behind ours, and they said they will have restrictions. They told my mother our presence ruins the value of the homes they want to build."

"Can they do that?" Hattie asked. "Blake, can they—"

"I don't know, Hattie. I don't see how they can turn a family out of the home they've bought and paid for."

"They told Mother they could block our driveway, or cut off our sewer and water service. They said the new neighbors wouldn't like her being there, and that they couldn't be responsible for any damage that might be done—or any violence. Mother was terrified. My father was so angry when he found out—I was afraid he was going to do something foolish. Dangerous."

Blake took the paper, and bent over it. The letterhead proclaimed it to be the work of the Goodwin Company, a land developer he had heard Mr. Dickson mention more than once. His stomach contracted as he read the cruel words:

> Said lot or lots shall not be sold, conveyed, or rented nor leased, in whole or in part, to any person not of the White race; nor shall any person not of the White race be permitted to occupy any portion of said lot or lots or of any building thereon, except a domestic servant legally employed by a White occupant of such building.

For a long moment, Blake couldn't speak past the tightness of his jaw. He thrust the paper across the table to Hattie, who took it and read it slowly, her lips working as she puzzled out some of the words. Blake pressed his hand to his chest, where anger rose like a fountain.

When he could trust his voice, he spoke with deliberation. Echoes of the South broadened his vowels and softened his consonants. "I am the child of slaves, Sarah," he said. "I am proud to be a servant in this house, because I had little preparation for any better career. But you—" He paused, and lifted his head to look into her troubled eyes. "You are an educated woman. A professional. I can only imagine how hard your family worked to give you that opportunity. This is—" He shook his head, and swallowed the angry words that threatened to pour forth. He settled for, "This is shocking."

"My parents are so proud of that house," Sarah said. "My mother's garden is the nicest in the whole neighborhood, and my father—well. He's the first in his family to own his own home, and he's just—he's—" Her lower lip trembled, and she pressed her fingers to it.

Hattie refolded the paper, and gingerly handed it back to Sarah, as if it were dirty. "I'm so sorry, Miss Church," she murmured. "It ain't fair. It ain't fair at all."

"No," Sarah said. She cleared her throat, and folded her hands. "Mr. Blake, I don't mean to take advantage of our friendship."

He put out his big hand to cover her smaller ones. "Don't be modest, Sarah. I wouldn't be walking around as I do if it hadn't been for your care."

She gave him a tremulous smile, and he saw the ghost of a dimple flash in her cheek. "You give me too much credit. It's good to see you walking unaided, though."

He patted her linked hands, and released them. "Tell me what I can do."

"I thought perhaps Dr. Benedict's father could help. Since Dr. Benedict isn't here."

"I think that's a good idea."

"I don't like taking advantage of our connection," Sarah answered. "But since Margot won't be back before . . ." Her lip trembled again, and she caught it between her teeth, shaking her head.

"Before the covenants go into effect," Blake said.

Sarah nodded and took a breath that whistled through her tight throat. "The men who came told my mother they—we—have to go now. That they'll force us out if we don't."

Hattie drew a sharp breath. "My sweet Lord, they can't do that! They can't do that, can they, Blake?"

She turned her beseeching gaze to him, and he looked unhappily from one woman to the other. "I don't know, Hattie. I don't know if they can do it or not."

Sarah stared down at her hands, curled on the white enamel tabletop. "They said we have to move before the Klan meeting on the twenty-third. There will be hundreds of Klansmen down in Renton. These people told my father the Klan would send some of their members to turn us out."

"But that's only a week away!" Blake said.

"Yes. A week. To find a place to live, to move our belongings, to sell our house." She covered one of her hands with the other in a grip that tightened the skin over her knuckles. "They frightened my mother. She cried all afternoon."

"Blake," Hattie said. "You have to speak to Mr. Dickson. We have to do something!"

Hattie didn't know the trouble Mr. Dickson was already facing, but she was right, just the same. Something had to be done. Dr. Margot would wish it. Blake wished it himself, and he was sure Mr. Dickson would agree, when he knew.

Blake said, "I'll speak to him in the morning."

This time it was Sarah who reached out, seizing his hand in hers. "Thank you, Mr. Blake. I'll be so grateful. Any help at all— it's just that there's no time!"

Blake cleared his throat and stood. "I'm sure Mr. Benedict will want to help, Sarah. He's a fine man. Now, I'm going to get the motorcar out of the garage and drive you to your home."

"That's not necessary," she said hastily. She stood, too, picking up her bag and retrieving her cape. "I came on the streetcar. It's only two changes."

"I won't hear of it," he said. "And it's no good arguing. I'm a stubborn man."

Hattie said, "That he is, Nurse Church. When Blake sets his mind on something, it's as good as done."

"I learned that for myself," Sarah said, and her dimple flashed again, more convincingly this time. "A less stubborn man than Mr. Blake might never have walked again."

"I'll pull up beside the porch," Blake said. "You just wait for me there."

"Thank you," Sarah said simply. "I'm in your debt, Mr. Blake."

"Well, not yet. But let me see what I can do. Are you on the telephone?"

She nodded. "I'll write down the number."

"Good. I will speak to Mr. Benedict after breakfast, and then I will telephone to you." He collected his driving coat, his cap and gloves, and began putting them on. "There's one more thing, Nurse Sarah Church," he said. He took the liberty of waggling his forefinger in her direction. "You are not a servant. When you visit Benedict Hall, you enter through the front door like the professional woman you are. Remember that."

Meekly, but with a sparkle in her eye at last, Sarah said, "Yes, sir, Mr. Blake. I promise. I will remember."

Bronwyn was exhausted from the long, confusing day, and the bed was soft, with cool sheets and a feather-light comforter. One of the maids had opened the window to a rose-scented breeze, and the night was dark and peaceful. Despite her shame, Bronwyn slept more soundly than she had since leaving Port Townsend. When a hand fell on her shoulder, and shook it, she swam up from the peaceful depths of a dream with reluctance, mumbling protests all the way.

"Shhh," someone said. "Miss Morgan, we need to be quiet. They'll try to stop us."

Bronwyn forced her eyelids to open. In the half-light of what felt like the middle of the night, she saw who was bending over her, and gasped. Fully awake now, she wriggled upright, clutching the comforter to her chest. "Mrs. Benedict!" she hissed. "What—what is it you want?"

Edith Benedict was a pale ghost in the dimness, her gray hair in a cloud around her thin face, her lips and cheeks all but invisible. Only her eyes, with their light, luminous blue, held any color, and they seemed sharper and more focused than they had at dinner. "You want to see him, don't you?" she breathed. She leaned forward, a little too close, enveloping Bronwyn in the scent of lavender water.

Bronwyn couldn't help shrinking back. There was something odd about Mrs. Benedict and more than a little scary. She was a small woman, but she seemed tightly wound, like a watch stem twisted so far it was about to break. The hand on Bronwyn's shoulder was insistent.

"Mrs. Benedict," Bronwyn said. Her throat and mouth were dry, and she swallowed. "Mrs. Benedict, I don't know whom you mean."

"Preston!" Mrs. Benedict said. She smiled, as if this were the most natural thing in the world, as if she hadn't just invaded Bronwyn's bedroom in the small hours and woken her from a sound sleep. "You want to see Preston, don't you?"

"What?" Bronwyn stiffened, staring at the older woman. "Mrs. Benedict, you know that can't be. Preston's—"

Mrs. Benedict moved her hand to cover Bronwyn's mouth. Her hand was cool and dry, and smelled of powder. "Shhh," she said again. "I'll explain everything, but not now! If they hear us, we won't get away. Come, get up and get dressed. Clean your teeth and brush your hair. If we hurry, we can catch the five o'clock train."

The thought flashed through Bronwyn's mind that she might still be dreaming. She dreamed so often of Preston and their night in the garden. This could be an extension of the dream, a sort of wish fulfillment brought on by days of fever and a bizarre day of strange adventures and new people. It was cruel, in a way, when she had made such an effort to relegate it to the land of dreams where it belonged.

She drew a long breath, trying to convince herself of this, but Edith Benedict seized her wrist with her hard little hand, and tugged on it. "Get up, Miss Morgan," she hissed. "You must hurry! We don't have much time!"

There could be no more doubt. She was awake, and this was Preston's mother, who wanted her to do something, to go somewhere. A small enamel clock on the bedside stand read four a.m.

The chill of the hardwood floor was cold beneath her bare feet. The water in the basin, as she splashed her face and cleaned her teeth, was also cold. Bronwyn, shivering, turned to find Mrs. Benedict holding out a day frock in crisp dotted swiss, still on its hanger from whatever wardrobe she had taken it.

Bronwyn stepped into the dress, and did up the buttons in the back with trembling fingers. Mrs. Benedict, smiling as if it were all a great lark, draped a long sweater over her shoulders without comment, pressed her handbag and her hat into her hands, then opened the bedroom door. Bronwyn tried to speak, to ask again what they were doing, to press Mrs. Benedict about where they were going, but Edith gave a girlish giggle, and put a finger to her lips. Bewildered, Bronwyn followed her down the staircase to the hall.

Benedict Hall slumbered around them. Bronwyn heard only the faint sounds of a big house creaking, curtains swishing in the currents of air from open windows, eaves vibrating in the pre-dawn breeze. Mrs. Benedict's swift breathing was louder than any of these, and growing louder by the moment. She seized Bronwyn's arm and held it as she unlocked the heavy front door and pulled it open. They slipped through, and Mrs. Benedict closed it with a click that seemed to pierce the darkness.

She giggled again, giving Bronwyn the strangest feeling that they were two girls sneaking away from their parents in search of mischief. Her hand was firm as she guided Bronwyn down the walk and out through the scrolled iron gate to the street.

Mrs. Benedict said, "We'll have to take the streetcar. I didn't dare call for a taxicab." She set off down Fourteenth Avenue at a brisk pace.

Bronwyn hurried after her. It didn't seem right to let a woman of Mrs. Benedict's age—and in her doubtful mental condition—go off alone in the half darkness. It occurred to her, as they stepped up into the streetcar and Mrs. Benedict dropped two nickels into the fare box, that she had become the Benedicts' un-witting and unintentional savior in the past twenty-four hours. She hoped Ramona would see it that way, and forgive her this headlong flight into the dim streets of Seattle.

She saw now that Mrs. Benedict carried a small brocade travel-ing bag that she set beside her on the bench seat of the streetcar. Mrs. Benedict, following her glance, smiled as if this were all the most natural activity in the world, setting off in secrecy, pattering down Aloha to the streetcar, where the uniformed driver gave them an odd look, and touched two fingers to his cap, but said nothing.

"It's in here," Mrs. Benedict said in an undertone. She patted the brocade bag with her hand. "He's going to be so glad."

"What's in there, Mrs. Benedict?" Bronwyn said, in the same

low voice, as if there were anyone to hear their secrets. There were no other passengers.

"The sapphire!" Mrs. Benedict whispered, raising her eyebrows as if surprised Bronwyn hadn't already known. "Preston asked for it particularly."

"Mrs. Benedict—" Bronwyn bit her lip, searching for a way to ask the important question. She wondered if the older woman would fly into a fit if she said the wrong thing. "Mrs. Benedict," she began again, speaking as gently as she could. "I know Preston died. We read it in the *Times*. My father brought the paper home and we all—we know about the fire. It was three years ago. There was a funeral."

"Oh, no," the older woman said, with a dismissive flick of her fingers. "I told you. I thought so, too, for a long time, but I was wrong. It was all a mistake."

"Wh-what was a mistake? There was a fire, wasn't there? There were pictures in the newspaper—awful pictures."

"Oh, yes, dear, there was a fire. It was terrible. My daughter's clinic was destroyed. My son tried to save it."

"But—" Bronwyn's words trailed off into silence. Mrs. Benedict clearly believed she was speaking the truth.

"Oh, yes," Mrs. Benedict said. "Preston was away for a long time, and we all thought we had lost him. Then, a year ago, he came back." She folded her gloved hands in her lap, nodding primly as if it were the most natural thing in the world. "I know I shouldn't have favorites," she said in a confiding way. "But Preston is different from the other children. He's fragile. He always has been. Margot and Dick—they're strong, like their father. Preston is like me."

She stopped talking, and turned her delicate profile to the darkness outside the window. She looked wistful for a moment, her mouth trembling, her eyelids fluttering as if she were blinking back tears. After a moment, she took a shuddering breath, and as she faced forward again, she fixed a smile on her lips, as if it were her duty. As if this were a formal tea, and she was entertaining a guest.

Bronwyn's head spun. She wished she knew the best thing to do. She could drag the older woman back to Benedict Hall, she supposed. She was taller, stronger, younger. But what if Mrs. Benedict was right?

No. That couldn't be. There were the newspaper reports—

But what if it *was* true? What if Preston had been in a hospital all this time, and no one knew how to let her know?

She searched Mrs. Benedict's face, but found only innocence and anticipation. Haltingly, Bronwyn said, "Mrs. Benedict, are you quite certain—?"

Edith Benedict was smoothing on a pair of fine kid gloves. She nodded peacefully. "Oh, yes, dear. You'll see when we get there. My prayers were answered. My son came back to me."

CHAPTER 17

It pleased the management of the Walla Walla Sanitarium to call the cramped space allotted to Preston a "suite." No doubt the bills sent to Dickson referred to it that way, with commensurate surcharges on a price that was already inflated. It was, of course, nothing of the sort. Preston paced it through the hours of darkness, counting the steps to keep himself from screaming with frustration. Six steps from the wall to the door, with its tiny screened window. Eight from there to the narrow doorway into the bathroom, which featured an elegant lidless toilet, a basin with a single tap that ran mostly cold water, and a tin tub with no sharp edges and neither soap dish, glass, or towel rack, or anything else that could conceivably be turned into a weapon. He was allowed a ewer and a basin beside his bed, but they were also tin, painted white, trimmed with peeling bands of red. They were dented and bent. He loathed them, but they were all he had for decoration.

It was a cell. No civilized man would call it anything else. He lived like an infant in a playpen, all dangerous objects out of reach, every movement observed, each bite of food or dose of medicine supervised. There was no outer window, and the only excitement was in peering through the little window to watch people get out of the elevator, or go back into it. It was, in fact, not living at all, and he didn't intend to continue this way.

There was nothing Preston hated more than being controlled, than being told what to do or not to do. It had been the earliest sticking point between him and Margot, the older sister, the smarter sibling, his father's favorite. It should have been obvious to her that she could avoid all the—*unpleasantness,* was perhaps a good word, though it caused a sour chuckle when he thought of it—she could have avoided it if she had simply stepped out of his way. Given him room to be himself. But she had been, always, unbearably egotistic, and her disdain for him had been evident from an early age.

One of the troubles with the non-life he was now stuck in was having too much time to think. He had been a man of action. A decisive man, even a bold one, at least after acquiring the sapphire. Now, as he paced, the insults and injuries he had suffered came back to him, revolving in his mind like a child's carousel, in which all the creatures were demons. The book Margot had snatched from him when he was four, claiming he had torn the page. Her superior smile when she won special honors in school subjects he could barely master. His father's look of disappointment when he announced he would be writing a society column. Blake's cool disdain as he lifted his marble-headed cane.

Of course, he had taken care of Blake. Blake had meant to kill him, and Preston had instead nearly killed Blake. Not that anyone knew that. It seemed Blake had decided to keep the truth to himself, but that made sense. No doubt the old man was too cowardly to tell his employer what he had tried to do to his youngest son!

Not that the pater would care. If he did, would he have consigned him to this living death? No. He was perfectly happy, with his precious Margot and her crippled cowboy living under his roof.

Preston reached the wall again, and spun to pace back toward the door. He kept his eyes down when he reached it. The dark hall made the window a mirror, and he didn't need to be reminded what he looked like.

He was a monster. There was no other word for it. The fire had caught him, and ruined him forever. It was the one and only time the sapphire had failed him.

He needed it back. He needed it to take this final step, but first—the child had to be found. His child. Then, every time Margot looked into that boy's face, she would know her brother was still with her.

It was hard on Mother, of course. She would have to explain the brat's existence, somehow, but she could do it. She would manage. She would be happy, no doubt, to have something of her youngest son with her.

Poor Mother. It had been hardest on her, all along. It wasn't fair, especially as she was the only one who had always understood him, always been faithful. As far as Preston was concerned, it was another sin to place at Margot's door.

It shouldn't have been this way. He had made mistakes; there was no doubt. He could admit that. Now, though, there was nothing left in his arsenal, no remaining weapon he could use to make certain the great Margot never forgot.

Except the boy. Once the brat was found, and all the mighty Benedicts were forced to acknowledge him, he could bring all of this to an end.

God, what a relief that would be.

King Street Station was almost deserted when Bronwyn and Mrs. Benedict passed under the huge tower with its four clock faces. Two idle porters called to each other, their voices echoing against the coffered ceiling. Mrs. Benedict marched to the ticket counter, her little heels clicking loudly on the empty marble floor. Bronwyn listened as the clerk described what was necessary to reach Walla Walla.

"Nothing direct," he said. "You'll have to go to Portland, ma'am, and from there . . ."

Bronwyn looked away, feeling anxious and out of place. There was a policeman stationed beside the door, and she wondered if she should run to him, beg him to call Benedict Hall, send someone to collect them. Bronwyn knew how it was to cling to illusions in the midst of despair. No one else in Benedict Hall, not a single other person, had mentioned Preston's name. All of this could be a delusion Mrs. Benedict had concocted to relieve her grief.

But what if it were true? What if he lived?

She was tempted to revisit her old dreams, Preston at her side, a wedding in Benedict Hall, her fairy-tale life restored. What if these past three years had been nothing but a horrid nightmare?

She closed her eyes, sick with confusion. She imagined Preston—golden, blue-eyed, charming—folding her into his arms, begging her forgiveness. She thought of the two of them searching together for their lost baby. She pictured Mrs. Benedict smiling a welcome at her new daughter-in-law, welcoming her to Benedict Hall.

Mrs. Benedict startled her out of this reverie by seizing her hand. Bronwyn's eyes flew open, and she found the older woman's face very close to hers, her eyes glittering in the glare of the station's lights. She spoke with one of her odd flashes of clarity. "You think I'm crazy." She lifted one thin shoulder in a resigned gesture. "Preston lives, Miss Morgan. I know it's a surprise, and you don't believe me, but you're going to see. I'm going to take you to him. The two of you have things to talk about."

In a state of perplexity, Bronwyn allowed herself to be led to the train, to be helped up the metal steps into a first-class compartment by a porter, to be guided to a seat in a Pullman car. The porter appeared again, bringing a tray with a small porcelain pot of coffee, a plate of toast, and a cut-glass dish of butter. The train started up, chugging slowly at first and then faster. The porter folded out the small table that fitted between their plush seats, and supplied them each with the morning edition of the *Seattle Daily Times*. As he withdrew, Bronwyn gazed after him, bemused at finding herself on a train, clicking farther and farther away from home, in the company of her dead lover's mother.

"You see," Mrs. Benedict said now, pouring out the coffee with a steady hand. "My son was in a rural hospital, and no one knew who he was." She spoke in the most matter-of-fact way, as if nothing she was describing was remarkable. "Everyone assumed he died in the fire, and since there was absolutely nothing left of it, no one could argue." She offered Bronwyn a cup, and Bronwyn accepted it. "But I knew," Mrs. Benedict said simply. "I could feel it. I knew my boy was alive."

Bronwyn sipped the coffee, and thought that Mrs. Benedict had as rich an imagination as her own.

"It's been more than a year since he came back," Mrs. Benedict said. She held her cup between her two small hands, hands that looked deceptively fragile. "You're thinking, quite naturally, that Preston should have contacted you, once he returned."

Bronwyn turned her gaze to her right, letting the early morning brilliance of Puget Sound sting her eyes. She recalled her bewildered hurt as she waited for a telephone call or a letter from Preston. She remembered the despair that swept her when she read of his death, and her misery when she understood there would be no engagement, no society wedding, only the loneliness of a husbandless girl expecting a baby. She said in a low voice, "If Preston had wanted to, Mrs. Benedict, he could have. He knew where to find me."

"With your parents. Quite proper." Mrs. Benedict spoke in a conversational tone, as if they were merely discussing some society event.

"I wrote to Preston when I found out I was pregnant," Bronwyn said, still staring at the breeze-rippled water. "He didn't answer."

"I scolded him severely for that," Mrs. Benedict said. "Boys can be so thoughtless."

Bronwyn was glad, when she turned her gaze back to Mrs. Benedict, that her eyes were sun-dazzled. She couldn't quite see the expression on the other woman's face, and she thought that was probably for the best. She tried to keep her own features smooth and still, giving nothing away, but there was ice in her voice. "I don't think of Preston as a boy."

"Oh, of course not!" Mrs. Benedict's laugh was like crystals clinking together. "That's just a mother's way, you know!"

Bronwyn pressed her lips together to stop herself from retorting that, of course, she did *not* know, because her baby had been taken away from her.

Her companion didn't notice her silence. "He did try to trace the baby, though," Mrs. Benedict said. "He knew there was a child, and he feels responsible." Bronwyn felt a choking sensation in her throat, but again, Mrs. Benedict didn't notice. "He has been telling me," she said in a confiding way, "that we should find the baby. The little boy. Truly, if the baby's mother had been anyone less—well, less fitting—I should have told him to leave well enough alone. But you, Miss Morgan, come from such a good family."

Bronwyn raised her eyebrows. Her eyes had adjusted now, and she could see that Mrs. Benedict looked quite sincere. There was no irony in her expression.

Mrs. Benedict smiled. "Oh, yes! Preston has told me all about you. The Port Townsend Morgans, he said. With a lovely house in Uptown. A charming mother, successful father . . . Naturally, I would have preferred that the two of you were married, but still—quite respectable relations for my first grandchild. We can think about the issue of marriage later."

Bronwyn blinked at the casual mention of marriage, as if it were nothing more than a housekeeping detail. It prompted her to speak bluntly. "Mrs. Benedict," she said. "If Preston were alive, wouldn't he be in Benedict Hall, with you?"

Edith Benedict's smile faded, and her eyelids and lips drooped, changing the outline of her face. She looked away, out into the bright morning. "If only he could come home," she said softly. "I've begged and begged, but my husband—and *Margot*—" She spoke Dr. Benedict's name tightly, as if she had bitten down on a pebble. "They tell me it's impossible."

"Why should that be?"

"Well, you see . . ." Sudden tears sparkled in Mrs. Benedict's eyes, and she paused for a moment, the back of her hand held to her lips. She sniffed once, and said, "Preston was injured, you know. In the fire. He hasn't been the same ever since. Not himself at all."

Bronwyn eyed her doubtfully, and Mrs. Benedict's eyes flashed up to hers and then away, as if she had read her disbelief. "It's a sanitarium." She spoke on a little rush of breath. "He's in the Walla Walla Sanitarium. I haven't seen it, but I understand they have a very good doctor there. Nurses, too. Mr. Benedict insisted on that, of course."

Bronwyn watched Mrs. Benedict's profile, and tried to believe she knew what she was talking about. It would be marvelous if Preston truly was in a sanitarium. She didn't know what a sanitarium was like, but she pictured rooms like those in a fine hotel, bright and clean, with tall windows and white bedspreads, and landscaped grounds to stroll in.

"Margot and Mr. Benedict don't really understand what troubles Preston," Mrs. Benedict said. She dabbed at her eyes with a lace-edged handkerchief. "It was the war, you know. He was a hero," she added defensively, as if Bronwyn might suspect otherwise. "But war changes a man. There's this sapphire—It's not like Preston to care about a jewel, but I always thought, if it mattered to him . . ." Her sentence died half-spoken.

"He wore it around his neck," Bronwyn said, then felt heat staining her cheeks. She couldn't think why she had said that. She had never discussed any of these details with anyone, not her mother, not her friends.

Mrs. Benedict, evidently, saw nothing unusual in her comment. "Yes, he did. He thought it helped him. Made him stronger." She sighed. "Margot calls it a delusion. I don't understand why she can't allow her brother his comforts."

Bronwyn breathed a small sigh of her own. The delusion was all on the part of Mrs. Benedict, obviously. She wished she had refused to come. She should have made a scene, woken Ramona, stopped this strange journey before it started.

But if it was true—if Preston were alive after all, and he truly wanted to find their baby—

She turned her gaze back to the bright water. She knew better. Entertaining such thoughts would make her as deluded as Mrs. Benedict.

Blake rose, as he usually did, earlier than anyone else in Benedict Hall. Hattie had left the electric percolator filled and ready for him. He plugged it in, and collected the bottle of cream from the icebox while the percolator gurgled and dripped. When the coffee was ready, he poured a mug full, stirred in cream, and carried the mug to the back porch. He sat there for a time, savoring the cool peace of the early morning, and planning his appeal to Mr. Dickson on behalf of the Church family.

It would all have been easy if Dr. Margot were here. Dr. Margot and her father would argue about the issue. Dickson would say it was not their business to interfere, while Dr. Margot would argue that it was a matter of conscience, that honorable people could not stand by and watch a blameless family thrown out of their home. Mr. Dickson would grumble, but that was mostly for show. He and Dr. Margot were far more alike than either of them realized.

But the major and Dr. Margot weren't due back for ten days. The Churches didn't have ten days.

Blake couldn't argue with Mr. Dickson the way Dr. Margot could. It wouldn't be proper. He meant to present his case as objectively as he could, politely reminding his employer that the credit for his own return to health, after nearly a year of recuperation, owed a great deal to Nurse Sarah Church. Of course, Mr. Dickson's generosity had made that possible. Blake's savings would never have covered a year in a rest home.

The whole situation was delicate. Blake watched the yellow cream swirl in the surface of his coffee, and pondered what he could say. He would wait until Mr. Dickson had breakfasted, and had read his paper. It would be best, perhaps, to speak to him as they drove to the office, with only Mr. Dick to listen. If he made a good case, Mr. Dickson could telephone to the mayor this morning. There was no time to waste.

Poor Sarah! She had been too quiet as he drove her to her home the night before. Following her directions, he had steered the Cadillac into a tidy neighborhood of two-story brick homes, each with a patch of lawn in front and a garden in back. Her family's home had a garage, which set it apart from its neighbors, and a well-aged but clean Ford parked inside. When he pulled the motorcar up to the curb, and climbed out to hold her door, her mother appeared in the lighted doorway, wearing a printed apron and a worried expression. He bowed to her, and touched his cap. Mrs. Church lifted one hand in an uncertain gesture.

Sarah had said, "I'm sure my mother would love to give you a cup of tea, Mr. Blake."

"Thank you, no. It's late, and I know you have to be at the clinic in the morning."

"I expect you're tired, too. I'll explain to her. Thank you for driving me."

He touched his cap again. "I'm always at your service, Nurse Church." He had stood watching until she was safely through the door, then remained a moment longer, eyeing the surrounding neighborhood, and wondering who the men were who had insulted this family.

He was, he thought now, as he pushed himself up and walked toward the kitchen, reasonably tolerant when it came to himself. His dear little Sarah was another matter entirely.

Hattie was already at the stove, cracking eggs into a wide cast-iron skillet. In another pan, slices of ham were frying, filling the kitchen with smoky fragrance. Loena was setting flatware on a tray, and Leona was filling the toaster with thick slices of the bread Hattie had baked the day before. Thelma was arranging small plates on a tray for the nursery.

Blake tied a big cotton dishtowel around his waist, and picked up a spatula to help Hattie at the stove.

The knock at the swinging door that led from the hall made everyone pause, and automatically turn to Blake for a response. He said, "I'll go," and crossed the kitchen. Before he opened the door, he remembered to pull off the dishtowel and drape it across a chair.

He found Mr. Dickson standing in the hall, his heavy features drawn. "Sir?" Blake said, surprised. "Coffee will be—"

"Is Mrs. Edith in the kitchen?" Mr. Dickson blurted.

Foolishly, Blake glanced over his shoulder, although he knew perfectly well Mrs. Edith wasn't there. Every face was turned toward the doorway, the maids with wide eyes, Hattie lifting her dripping spatula from the scrambled eggs.

Hattie dropped her spatula, and bustled across the kitchen. "Mr. Dickson, is something wrong? Mrs. Edith maybe needs me upstairs—"

"She's not there," Dickson said harshly. "I thought she might be with you." He rarely spoke to the servants in such a tone, and Blake and Hattie exchanged a glance.

Blake said carefully, "Mr. Dickson, I don't believe any of the staff have seen her yet this morning. Would you like me to come—"

Dickson, in another unusual gesture, turned his back before Blake finished his sentence. "Goddammit," he muttered. "She's gone. Slipped away while I was asleep."

Blake, with a movement of his head, indicated to Hattie and the rest of the staff that they should go on about their business. He stepped out into the hall, and let the door swing shut behind him. "Mr. Dickson, I'll come up and check the rooms. She could be in Mr. Preston's bedroom."

"I've looked," Dickson growled. "She's not there, and she's not with Ramona, or in the nursery. Or in the Parrishes' rooms. If she's not in the kitchen, she's not in the house. And—" He had started toward the front door, but he stopped, and faced Blake with his hands on his hips. His chin jutted, and his eyes were flinty. "Her handbag is gone, Blake. And her valise, the little brocade one the children gave her. That young woman who was with us at dinner last night has also vanished. Her bedroom door is open, and the bed is rumpled up, but it's empty. I have to surmise they left together."

"I think we should ask Loena where the sapphire was," Blake said. "You'll remember—"

"Oh, goddammit. You're right. She spoke of taking it to Preston, didn't she?" He groaned, and Blake felt a stab of sympathy. Dickson rubbed his eyes with his fingertips, and said, with an air of resignation, "Send Loena out to me, will you? I'll have her check, since she was the one who saw it. Then you'd better get the car out. Pack a bag, too, Blake. And better ask Hattie to fix sandwiches or something. We're in for a long drive."

CHAPTER 18

Margot rose at a shockingly late hour in the narrow bedroom under the eaves of the Parrish ranch house. There were three bedrooms in the rickety, sun-faded building, but only one bathroom. Frank had teased her she should be thankful it was indoors, and she assured him she was. The elder Parrishes were out of their beds by the time the first sunlight glistened on the fields of the Bitterroot Valley, so although Margot wasn't used to sleeping in, she stayed in bed, listening to the house wrens chattering under the eaves. Only after she heard the older Parrishes descend the steep staircase to the first floor did she throw back the quilt and slide her feet into a pair of borrowed slippers. Even her dressing gown was on loan.

Her mother-in-law had clicked her tongue over the paucity of luggage her son and his wife had been able to bring with them. Jenny and Robert Parrish had driven their battered Model T out to Fort Missoula, where there was enough open space to land the airplane. The propeller had barely stopped spinning before they started eagerly across the field. Margot and Frank climbed down to meet them. Robert shook Frank's hand and kissed Margot's cheek, his lips dry and leathery against her skin. Jenny, too, kissed Margot, then folded her son into a long embrace that made Margot's eyes sting with sympathy. They brought down their modest valises and Margot's medical bag, and crossed the uneven grass of the field. Jenny clung to Frank's good arm as if she couldn't bear to let him go.

Once they reached the ranch house, Jenny showed Margot up the stairs to the bedroom she and Frank would use. It was at the front, facing west. The slanted roof cut the space nearly in half, but the window, tucked under the eaves, gave a beautiful view of the valley and the bulk of the mountains beyond.

When Margot had set down her valise, her mother-in-law took her to her own bedroom, where she opened her closet with an apologetic air. "Not much call for nice clothes, here in the country," she said. "I'm a mite smaller than you, too, Doctor, but I hope you'll help yourself."

"Please call me Margot, won't you?" Margot said.

"Of course. If you like," the older woman said, but Margot noticed she didn't do it. She just didn't call her anything.

The wardrobe held the simplest of clothes. There were a few dresses, the nicest of which Margot remembered her mother-in-law had worn to their wedding in Seattle. There were a couple of thick jackets that looked as if they were meant for snow. Everything else looked like clothes any workingman could have worn, and Margot hesitated, unsure what to do and not wanting to offend.

She said, "You know, Mother Parrish, I'm sure I could get by."

"In those trousers?"

Margot glanced down at her flying clothes, and laughed. "Well, no. But I brought a skirt and two shirtwaists."

Jenny Parrish shook her head. "Oh, no, dear, you don't want to ruin your nice city clothes. Here now, here's a dressing gown I hardly ever wear. It's clean," she added.

"I can see that. Thank you," Margot said, feeling helpless.

Jenny dug out a pair of worn but comfortable leather slippers from the bottom of the wardrobe, and from a drawer she pulled a pair of faded denim trousers. The fabric was a lighter weight than the canvas ones Margot had worn for the airplane. Margot chuckled. "I've always wanted to wear these," she confided, and Jenny laughed.

"Best thing for mucking out barns," she said. "Of course, that's about the least ladylike thing you could possibly do."

"Oh, no," Margot had said. "I've done far less ladylike things at the hospital, I'm afraid."

She wished, a moment later, that she hadn't referred to her profession, but her mother-in-law appeared unaffected. Unlike Ramona, Jenny Baker Parrish was well acquainted with the gritty side of life, and would have been, Margot suspected, impatient with Ramona's squeamishness. Jenny only nodded, saying, "Such important work you do." They smiled at each other then, and Margot's awkwardness began to ease.

It had been an auspicious beginning to what was turning out to be a wonderfully successful visit. That first day, Frank showed Margot the beloved places of his boyhood, meadows and lofts and streams where he and his friends had fished. The next morning, the two of them tramped through the hot July fields, following Robert as he supervised the haying crews. Robert was tall and lean, like his son. His face was deeply seamed by the sun and wind, and he had more silver in his hair than Frank, but no one seeing them side by side could have mistaken their relationship.

Frank and his father fell into a discussion of the hay crop, the weather, and what price beef on the hoof would bring in the coming winter. Margot lost interest. She sniffed, savoring the sweet smell of freshly cut hay. She listened to the men calling to one another through the dry air. She lifted her head into the wind that blew up the valley, and took off her hat to let it ruffle her hair, and she waded through the thigh-high hay, happy for the protection of the denim trousers. They were surprisingly comfortable, and afforded her a freedom of movement her skirts never did. She wondered if she dared buy a pair to take home.

She was in awe of the great draft horses that pulled the hay wagon. There had been a carriage horse at home, when she was a girl, but the two gray Percherons were nothing like that slim-legged, bad-tempered bay. The Percherons had magnificent feathers draping their wide feet. Their heads were broad, and their eyes large and deep and thickly lashed. They smelled of sun and straw, and their hides shone like silver in the brittle sunlight. She soon discovered they were the gentlest of creatures, careful of where they stepped, tolerant of her cautious attempts to stroke them. The men went in at midday for their dinner, and Frank led the horses into the shade of the barn so they could cool off. He gave Margot a couple of wrinkled apples from the root cellar, and she offered them to the big horses. Their thick, velvety lips tickled her palm as they accepted the treat, making her giggle like a child.

Jenny Parrish's work-worn hands and sunburned cheeks gave testament to the never-ending labor that was her life. Margot never saw her idle. She was either cooking, or weeding her garden, or, at night when she and Robert settled down in their back room to listen to the wireless, working on a pile of mending.

Margot was no cook or seamstress, and she ruefully explained to Jenny that she couldn't tell a weed from a vegetable. Jenny had waved that off, saying she hadn't expected her to come to do chores. Margot learned there was a shopping list, though, and suggested she and Frank drive into Missoula to get what was needed. On a breathless day, with heat shimmering in transparent waves over the hay fields, the two of them piled into the Model T and drove the dusty, rutted road into town.

Missoula was nothing like Seattle, but the setting was beautiful. It lay in a circle of blue, distant mountains. The Blackfoot River threaded right through the town, edged with blackberry bushes and willows with branches that drooped right to the water. Fishermen stood in the shallows near the banks, their fly rods catching the sunlight as they flicked back and forth.

The town boasted a single skyscraper, the Wilma Building. Frank pointed it out as they drove past. The rest of the buildings were one- and two-story structures, some of them unchanged since the previous century. Frank parked the Model T in front of the Mercantile. Its shady interior smelled of grain and coffee and, somehow, hay. In fact, Margot thought, everything in this sun-baked state smelled like hay. She wondered what it smelled like in the wintertime, when the hay crop was stored away and the fields were buried in snow.

Frank wandered the aisles of the Mercantile with Jenny's list in his hand, while Margot took a seat at the soda fountain counter. The soda jerk greeted her, and suggested a root beer. She watched him pour syrup into a tall frosted glass and then fill the glass with soda water until it was crowned with foam. He put a straw in the glass, and served the drink on a napkin, watching as she took her first sip. The bubbles stung her nose, and when she sneezed, the soda jerk grinned at her.

Margot couldn't remember the last time she had been to a soda fountain. In the summers, Blake sometimes made sassafras root beer on the back porch, but his brew wasn't nearly as strong as this one. When Frank joined her, she made him have a root beer himself. Feeling as carefree as a girl on an outing with her young man, Margot drank a second one. It made her burp as they left the store. Frank cast her a surprised look, and both of them were laughing as they climbed back into the Model T.

They drove back late in the day, arriving just as the haying crew was assembling for supper. Margot and Frank ferried the supplies in, cans of Maxwell House Coffee, enormous cans of Monarch Baked Beans, and a big sack of flour. Jenny, her lined face damp with perspiration from laboring over the stove, nodded toward the pantry. "Just put everything in there, will you? Frank knows where things go."

Frank opened the door to a cool, dim room lined with fragrant cedar shelves. Margot, with the flour sack in her arms, followed him in. When she had wriggled the sack onto one of the shelves, she straightened, and gazed around her with a little exclamation of pleasure. "Why, Frank! What is all this?"

He grinned at her, and put an arm around her shoulders. "I meant to show you this. These are my mother's remedies." He pointed to an overhead pole. It ran the length of the room, and was festooned with bundles of dried herbs. "Let's see, that's mustard, I think. That's coneflower, and there's a bunch of marigolds. These dry all summer, and then in the winter she makes ointments and things. 'Simples,' she calls them, like her grandmother did."

Margot ran a finger over a row of jars filled with preparations of various colors. They were clearly labeled in Jenny's small handwriting—*lemon balm tea, eucalyptus powder, chamomile, mint leaves.* There was a dark glass jar with a warning cross on its label. It read *Foxglove.*

"Foxglove—that's digitalis," Margot marveled. "It looks as if she understands the risks."

"She has a book she refers to all the time," Frank said. "Doctor can't always get out here, so people come to her for help."

"I'd love to have a look at that book."

"I'm sure she'd be happy to show you. The pages are all stuck full of cards and papers with recipes collected by her mother, her grandmother, a few friends. Even some she got from the Flatheads."

"Those are the Indians?"

He nodded. "There's a bark they use, if I recall. And bear fat, but it smells so awful Pop and I won't let her bring it into the house."

Margot smiled, and turned to go back to the kitchen. "I'm no cook, but I can at least help your mother serve," she said. "Maybe after supper she'll show me the book."

Jenny, she had learned, never sat down when the hired hands were eating. She bustled back and forth, her hands full of bowls and dishes and plates, while her husband, the regular hired hand, and the four extra men of the haying crew ate at the oilcloth-covered table. Margot found an extra apron, and started rinsing the used bowls as they came back from the table. Jenny didn't argue. "That's a big help," she said. "Thanks."

Frank joined Margot at the big double sink. By the time the crew finished, said their good nights, and went off to the bunkhouse, the dishes were done. He and Margot and Jenny went to sit at the table with their own supper while Robert drank coffee and made notes in a ledger with a fountain pen. "Good crop," he said to his wife. "Half again as big as last year."

Jenny said, "Now if we could just have an easy winter, we'll get ahead a bit."

Margot felt Frank shift restlessly beside her, and she cast him a surreptitious glance. He was frowning as he cut his pot roast into slices and drenched them with Jenny's dark gravy. She knew he felt guilty about leaving his parents to work the ranch without him. She had heard Robert comment on how well the Carnes arm worked, and she didn't think she had imagined the longing in his voice, though he gruffly went on to a different subject a moment later.

She started on her own meal, beef from the ranch, sweet corn, a platter of fresh vegetables from Jenny's kitchen garden. She couldn't imagine how her mother-in-law managed it all. She had no help, either inside the house or out. "Mother Parrish," she said warmly, "this is the best pot roast I've ever had."

"Now, now," Jenny said, smiling. "I'm sure that cook of yours—Hattie, isn't it?—I'm sure her pot roast is wonderful."

Frank laughed. "No, unfortunately. It's not."

Margot said, "Frank's right, I'm afraid. We love Hattie, but—"

"She's getting better," Frank said loyally. "You have to admit that."

Margot touched his hand. "That's because you like simple food. It's what she's best at."

"I know. Margot's right, though, Mother. Wonderful supper."

"Well, I'm sure you two are just real hungry. I'm always worn out after a drive up to the city."

Margot hadn't really thought of Missoula as a city. There had been none of the hurry and bustle of Seattle. Frank had pointed out to her, as they flew over the mountains and dropped down toward the valley, the other towns lying along the course of the Bitterroot River. They were far smaller even than Missoula, hardly more than villages. It was no wonder, she thought, that the Parrishes and their neighbors had to be self-sufficient. She could only imagine how hard it all must have been without an automobile. The trip into town with a horse and wagon must have taken hours each way.

In fact, the remoteness of the Parrish ranch, and their distance from the others, surprised her. This visit was her first experience of rural life. She loved the great silence of the nights, the wide spaces that met her eyes when she stepped outside. She didn't know if she could tolerate the isolation for any great length of time, but it was a pleasure for the moment.

As Jenny sliced thick pieces of apple pie and served them, Margot said, "Mother Parrish, Frank tells me you're the woman people turn to when there's no doctor available. Your pantry is full of wonderful things. Did you collect them all yourself?"

Jenny smiled across the table. "Most," she said, a little shyly. "They probably seem primitive to you, but—"

"Quite the opposite! One of my favorite professors emphasized the roots of contemporary medicines in folk remedies. I expect you know far more about those than I do, but the foxglove you have, for example—"

"Oh, yes," Jenny said, with more confidence. "Digitalis is made from foxglove."

"I know that one. I don't know the uses for a lot of what you have, though. I'd love to learn."

Jenny made a small gesture with her sunburned hand. "Oh, I'm sure you don't want to put up with a lecture from someone like me," she said.

Frank swallowed a huge bite of pie. "Trust me, Ma. If she says it, she means it."

"Well." Jenny smiled again, looking pleased and embarrassed at the same time. "If you really are interested, I'll just do up these dishes, and we can—"

"Pop and I will do them," Frank said. He made a shooing motion with his right hand. "You ladies run and play."

So it was that Margot found herself again in the dim pantry, breathing the fragrance of drying herbs and flowers, and following her mother-in-law's pointing finger as she explained the uses for the herbs and powders and tinctures. She had made every one of them in her own kitchen and stored them against a time they might be necessary.

"Those are marigolds. I dry the flowers and add them to mustard plasters. Worked well on Robert when he had the pneumonia. Also good for bee stings, without the mustard. There's dandelion, and fennel, and over there is burdock. Good in an infusion of bitters, though it needs ginger, and I haven't been able to grow that. The old recipe calls for angelica, as well, but I leave it out. Bad for pregnant women, and bitters are what I give them for stomach upset."

She turned, gesturing toward the labeled jars, listing the contents and their usage without hesitation. Margot listened with increasing respect. When Jenny fell silent, she said, "Frank tells me you inherited a book."

"Oh, yes, from my grandmother. It's old, but the advice is still good. Based on Culpeper, but updated, of course. A little hard to read now. I could use a new edition."

"I'll write down the title. Maybe I can find you one."

Jenny glanced up at her. "Mighty kind of you," she said. "Of course, it's not like I've been to medical school. But what I do can only help. I take care to never hurt anyone."

" 'First, do no harm,' " Margot quoted. "That's the first dictum we learn, but there are lots of doctors who can't make the same claim."

"I'll show you the book," Jenny said. She led the way out through the kitchen, where the dishes were dried and put away, and the pots were clean, resting on the top of the wood stove to dry. She went into the front room, which was small and rather dark, curtains drawn against the sun. A thick book with a cover gone brown with age rested on an old-fashioned bookstand, the kind meant for a family Bible. When Jenny began to turn the pages, she did so with the same reverence another woman might have used for a holy book, and when it was Margot's turn, she was careful to do the same. The pages were yellowing and the typeface was archaic, but she could see they held a treasury of information.

"Who comes to you, then, Mother Parrish?" Margot asked, as she traced a drawing of eucalyptus leaves with her finger. Beneath the drawing were instructions for making a tea.

Jenny, shy again, shrugged. "Not a lot, you know. Folks who don't want to have to drive into Missoula, or can't afford to. Mostly women with female troubles."

Margot glanced up at her. "Like what?" She had spoken more sharply than she intended, but it was something that deeply interested her.

Jenny didn't flinch. "Pregnancy sickness. Pain with their monthlies. Things they don't want to talk to a man about."

"There's no woman doctor?"

"No. We've been asking, writing to some of the medical schools. There aren't enough of you to go around."

Margot sighed, and turned back to the book. "It's not easy, being a woman physician. And it's harder than ever for a woman to get into one of those schools."

"Why?"

"Have you heard of the Flexner Report?" She turned a page, and then another.

Jenny said, "No. I don't know what that is."

"It was an assessment of American medical schools that came out in 1910." Margot carefully pulled out one of the loose sheets that bristled from the pages of the book. She held it to the light in order to see it better. "Flexner concluded there were too many medical colleges, and they weren't rigid enough. The consequence was that about half the schools either closed or merged, and reduced the number of students accordingly. First to go were the women." She carefully replaced the handwritten sheet. "There's a hospital in Missoula, though, isn't there?"

"St. Patrick's, yes. Some can't go because they don't have the money. Others are too embarrassed. They'll talk to me, but they won't tell a male doctor what troubles them."

"I know how that is." It was the reason for Margot's devotion to the Women and Infants Clinic, the same reason Sarah Church labored so hard in it, every day and many nights as well.

Jenny's eyes were a lighter color than Frank's, and made rheumy by years of working in rough weather, but glowed with both wisdom and sorrow, in equal measure. In fact, Margot thought, looking into them was like looking into her own eyes as they might be thirty years hence, though their color was so different. She said, as they gazed at each other in understanding, "I wish I could help."

Jenny broke the moment, turning away, beginning to untie the apron she'd worn all day. "I wish you could, too, dear. Not your problem, of course."

"It is, though," Margot said softly. "Mine as much as yours."

Over her shoulder, Jenny cast her a sympathetic glance. "We can't heal everyone."

"No."

Jenny reached around the kitchen door to hang her apron on a peg, and turned back to Margot with her arms folded. "You would think, with airplanes and X-rays and telephones and so forth, that we might be able to do more for people. For women." She blew out a breath. "My lands, I'm out on my feet. Didn't mean to turn gloomy. I'll say good night now."

"Good night. If it's all right with you, I'll just spend a bit more time with your book."

"Be my guest. Put out the lamp when you're done, will you?"

"I will. Good night, Mother Parrish."

The older woman hesitated a moment. "I'd be happier if you called me Jenny, dear. I'm used to it."

Margot smiled in return. "Of course. But you have to call me Margot."

Jenny smiled. "It's a bargain. Good night, then, Margot." A twinkle appeared in her tired eyes, and she added, "Dear." Margot chuckled.

She watched Jenny walk upstairs, and a moment later, Robert followed her. Frank appeared from the back room, and crossed to stand beside her over the bookstand. "Interesting?" he asked.

"Fascinating." Margot turned a page, and another. She took

out another of the handwritten sheets, and held it close to the lamp. "Look at this, Frank. This is about honey as a treatment for allergies."

"Hard to read." He bent to squint at the page in the poor light. "This has always been Ma's little sideline, people showing up once in a while asking her for help. I never thought much about it."

"There's a wealth of information here."

He straightened, shaking his head. "Just country remedies, things folks use when they don't have a doctor."

"The thing is, Frank, many of our medicines are based on these same plants." She smoothed the loose sheet and replaced it in the book. "That's a recipe for making a tincture from eucalyptus leaves, for someone with asthma. We don't have a good drug-based therapy for asthma, but we do use something called eucalyptol for bronchitis. I wish I could observe that remedy in actual practice. It might be helpful."

"Ask Ma."

She nodded. "I will."

"Are you finished for now?" He put an arm around her waist, and pulled her close. His body was warm and firm against her, and she smiled up at him.

"You're trying to get me into bed."

"Ah ha. Just can't fool you."

She laughed, but she bent to put out the lamp, and walked with him to the staircase. It was one of the great pleasures of this time in his old home, going to bed when she wasn't exhausted, making love with the window open to the night breeze, waking only when she was ready, in a place where there was no telephone to command her. A woman of leisure.

She was pulling her nightdress over her head when she remembered. "Your mother tells me they've been asking for a woman physician."

Frank had already removed his prosthesis and laid it ready on the bureau. He was sitting up in the bed, propped with pillows against the headboard. "Never been one around here that I know of."

"The women—and the girls—there are things they don't want to talk about with a man."

"Not surprising, I guess."

"Not at all." She took a moment to run a brush through her hair, and to dash water on her face from the basin on the washstand, then went to sit on the edge of the bed beside him. He stroked her hair with his right hand. "It's worrisome, though, Frank. Young women might not get the help they need. Some illnesses only get worse if they're not treated."

"You're taking the world on your shoulders again," he said softly. He reached out to extinguish the bedside lamp. "Come to bed, Mrs. Parrish. You can take on the problems of the world tomorrow."

Margot sighed, but she knew he was right. She rose, and walked around to her side of the bed. She slipped under the comforter, and nestled close to him. He turned to kiss her, and she put the matter out of her mind.

When she woke later in the night, though, it was the first thing she thought of. She lay watching the undimmed stars wheel above the Bitterroot Valley, pondering the surprise that was Jenny Parrish, and wondering what she could do to help her.

CHAPTER 19

Union Station in Portland hummed with trains coming in and out, crowds of people surging this way and that, and porters and conductors shouting commands over the hubbub. Bronwyn felt shaky with fatigue and anxiety, but Mrs. Benedict seemed charged with energy over their mission. "This way!" she exclaimed as they stepped down from the train. "We have to change lines, but we have time for a sandwich. I'm starved, aren't you, dear?"

Bronwyn stumbled after her as she led the way across the busy concourse. The high-ceilinged lobby had a curved wall at the front, where shelves of a newsstand stretched from one side to the other. Through the two tiers of windows she saw a circular drive filled with touring cars and sedans and an occasional horse and buggy. She had been here before, with her mother and father, but that time she had been rested, unworried, comfortable under her parents' protection. At this moment she felt less secure than she had dashing home late at night from the Cellar, with Johnnie's angry shouts following her.

Everything about Edith Benedict seemed unreliable. She had been silent to the point of rudeness at dinner the night before, and so still that if her eyes had not been open, Bronwyn could have believed she had fallen asleep at the table. Today she was talkative, restless in her movements, fixated on her purpose. She glanced over her shoulder repeatedly to see that Bronwyn was following, and each time she flashed her an eager smile.

She trailed after Mrs. Benedict into the small café at the far side of the lobby. She had no choice, now, but to see this through.

Her parents must know, by now, what had happened and what she had done. When they learned at Benedict Hall that she and Mrs. Benedict had both disappeared in the night, they would surely telephone to Morgan House, but Bronwyn was too exhausted to think about that. She had trouble keeping her thoughts consecutive. Her mind flitted from one thing to another, as random as a foraging bird.

She didn't hear Mrs. Benedict ordering food. She blinked, and roused herself to see that someone had served her a ham-and-cheese sandwich on a china plate, with an enormous pickle at one side. "Coffee?" Mrs. Benedict asked cheerfully.

"Yes, please," Bronwyn said. She hoped coffee would help to clear her muddled brain.

"Do eat something now, dear," Mrs. Benedict said in motherly fashion. "We still have quite a long journey in front of us." She picked up her own sandwich, and took a delicate bite.

Bronwyn did the same, and discovered all at once that she was ravenous. The ham was rich and savory, and the bread was fresh, spread with sweet butter and tart mustard. Her sandwich was half gone by the time the coffee arrived.

She did, in fact, feel better as they left the café. She would watch over Mrs. Benedict until she had achieved her goal—whatever that might be—and see her safely returned to Seattle. Then she would go home.

Her attempt at independence was at an end. She had surely lost her place with Mother Ryther, and she could hardly stay on in Benedict Hall. Mrs. Benedict might forgive her indiscretion. No one else would, once they knew of her connection to Preston. And Dr. Benedict knew her as Betty Jones.

She was a fallen angel, and she was a liar. When they found her out, it would all be over.

Dickson withdrew to his cramped study to make hasty notes for his son to take to the office. "An hour, Blake," he said gruffly. "Do you think Mrs. Ramona and Hattie can hold things together here? We'll be gone at least three days. There's no help for it."

"I will discuss it with them," Blake said. "Since needs must, I'm sure they can manage."

Blake knew the drive would be long and sometimes arduous. It hadn't been so many years since it took a team of horses to pull an automobile over the mountain pass. Even now, the journey to Walla Walla meant a rough ride on the graded gravel of the Sunset Highway, the motor roaring on the steepest climbs. It would run more smoothly on the descent. They would drive south through the Yakima Valley, then east to the farthest corner of the state. In many places the roads had no pavement. In others they were rutted and broken by weather. Filling stations could be hard to find, and sometimes when they did come upon one, there was no motor fuel for sale. Against that eventuality, Blake stocked the Cadillac with cans of gasoline, but they made him uneasy, rattling and banging together when the road was rough. He had advised Mr. Dickson long ago that there should be no cigars in a motorcar, and received no argument.

Blake hastily packed a valise, and stowed it in the back of the Cadillac along with the two gasoline cans. He spoke to Hattie, and she assured him she could manage the maids, and that she and Mrs. Ramona would see that Mr. Dick had what he needed.

Blake was already putting on his driving coat when he suddenly remembered Sarah. A chill ran through him, and he stopped with one arm in a sleeve and the other still out. The disappearance of Mrs. Edith, and the urgency of preparing for the drive across the state, had driven the Churches' crisis right out of his mind.

He had promised Sarah. And he knew what Dr. Margot would want.

He stood in the hallway, frozen with horror. He could hardly speak to Mr. Dickson about it now. He was too upset about Mrs. Edith to take on anyone else's problems, and he would only growl impatiently that it would have to wait.

Blake glanced at the big clock in the corner, and saw that he had perhaps fifteen minutes until their departure. An idea formed in his mind, slowly, the parts of it falling into place like jigsaw pieces. It wasn't a good idea, nor even an ethical one, but it was all he had. The risk of his being caught out was high. He could lose his position—if his idea even worked—but it would buy the Churches some time until someone had a better plan.

He pulled his arm out of the sleeve of his coat, and hung it on the coatrack in the hall. Smoothing his shirtsleeves, he started up the stairs, and when he reached the second floor he turned to the back of the house, where Dr. Margot and Major Parrish had their apartment. He heard Louisa's piping voice from the nursery, and the answers from Mrs. Ramona and Nurse. Downstairs, Hattie and the twins were working in the kitchen. He hoped he wouldn't find Thelma in one of the upstairs rooms. At least the Parrishes' apartment wasn't due to be cleaned until just before they returned.

He opened the door, and found their small sitting area empty. The bedroom beyond looked orderly. He closed the door to the hall before he went to make certain. The bedroom was also empty. He had the apartment to himself for the moment, and very little time to accomplish his goal.

He turned back to the sitting room, where Dr. Margot's private telephone rested on a small table under an oval mirror. As he picked up the receiver and held the handset to his ear, he caught sight of himself in the mirror, his brow furrowed with anxiety, his lips pressed so tight they had gone pale. He didn't often look in a mirror, other than to shave, and catching sight of his face this way was a bit of a shock. His hair had gone white almost without his noticing it. He didn't feel particularly old, as a rule, but this glimpse of his worried features, when he wasn't prepared to see them, reminded him how far in the past were the days of his youth.

Blake straightened, and turned his back to the mirror. He cleared his throat in preparation. His voice and Mr. Dickson's weren't all that different, though he would never have presumed to share such a thought with anyone else. He remembered Mayor Brown's last visit to Benedict Hall quite clearly. Mr. Dickson addressed His Honor in a familiar way, as if they were great friends. He recalled the mayor's pleasant, rather youthful demeanor, his thick dark hair, the round glasses that gave him the air of a schoolboy.

Mayor Brown was, at least, a Democrat. He might be sympathetic.

Blake lifted the handset from the receiver, and waited for the operator. He asked for the mayor's office, and when he was connected, he told the secretary who answered that he was calling from Benedict Hall. He didn't say who was speaking, but the secretary made an assumption, and put him through immediately.

"Dickson!" the mayor exclaimed. "Good of you to call." This, Blake understood, was what substantial political donations earned for their donors. Access. Courtesy.

Power.

"Ed," he said, with what he hoped and prayed was Mr. Dickson's usual growl. "Good to talk to you."

"Any time, Dickson. You know you can reach me any time."

Blake blew out a breath in relief. He tried to imagine himself as Mr. Dickson, a cigar jutting from his mouth, his feet propped up on his desk. He said, in a gravelly tone he could only pray was convincing, "Good, good to hear. Need a favor, Mr. Mayor."

By the time the two Benedict men emerged from Dickson's study, Blake was properly attired in his driving coat, black gloves, and cap. The Cadillac, with its motor running, waited at the end of the walk. Hattie had come out onto the porch with a hamper of sandwiches and several Blue Bottles with various liquids to sustain them through the long drive. Blake got out of the car to come and meet her.

"Now, you listen to me, Blake," Hattie said as she handed over the hamper. Her eyes were red, and he was sure she had been weeping in the kitchen. He heard the aftermath in her voice. "You drive careful. Won't help nobody if you go and crash that motorcar because you hurryin'."

"I know, Hattie. I promise." He stood with the hamper in his hands. Hattie had packed enough to sustain an army.

"When you find her—poor Mrs. Edith, I mean—" Hattie broke off, and twisted her hands in her apron. More tears rose in her eyes, glistening in the morning light.

Blake said as gently as he could, "Don't worry, Hattie. We'll find Mrs. Edith. We'll bring her safely home."

"She can't help it, you know, Blake. You explain that to Mr. Dickson. Mrs. Edith just can't help it. She loves her boy, and whatever he tells her, she figures it's God's honest truth."

"I know that." He tried to give her a reassuring smile as he turned to go down the walk. He opened the passenger door of the automobile, and secured the hamper in the front seat. Through the open door he heard Mr. Dickson's step in the hall. Mr. Dick shook his father's hand, nodded to Blake, and set off for the streetcar. Mr. Dickson climbed into the backseat, and Blake into the front. A moment later they were on their way.

The mayor, to Blake's relief, had promised to intervene in the matter of the Churches' home. He had said he couldn't do anything about neighbors being unpleasant, but he had leverage in the matter of the developers. If the Goodwin Company wanted to go on acquiring permits for excavation, plumbing, and building, it couldn't afford to ignore a direct request from the mayoral office. Blake had thanked him, but tersely, the way he thought Mr. Dickson would. He had kept the conversation short, agreed that the two men should dine together soon, and broken the connection with a brief good-bye.

In for a penny, in for a pound, Blake supposed. He picked up the telephone once again and spoke briefly to Sarah.

When he had hung the earpiece back on the receiver, he stared at it for a moment, marveling at his own daring. It was a good thing, he thought, that he had no time to worry about what fate this act of deception might bring about.

As he negotiated the turn down Aloha, then south on Broadway, Blake estimated how long their trip would take, and how long—assuming they found Mrs. Edith with ease and smoothed things over at the sanitarium, if necessary—it would take for them to return. By the time those things were done, and if Mayor Brown was as good as his word, the Klan meeting should be over, and the Church home should be safe. He couldn't guess how long it would be before his trick was exposed.

It was even possible, he told himself, as he turned the Cadillac onto Rainier Avenue toward Renton, that Mr. Dickson would never know. He hoped that would be the case. Regardless, it was done now. He would confess everything to Dr. Margot, and she could rule on whether Mr. Dickson should be told.

He tried to put it out of his mind. It was a bridge to be crossed in its own time. He faced bridges aplenty already.

In the backseat, Mr. Dickson leaned back with his hat brim turned far down against the hot sun. Blake glanced at the oil and fuel gauge to reassure himself, adjusted his own cap to shade his eyes from the glare, and settled in for the grueling drive.

CHAPTER 20

When Mrs. Benedict asked for tickets for the last leg of their journey, the agent informed her, in disinterested fashion, that there was no Pullman on the route. "Second class only," he said. He was, apparently, unimpressed by Mrs. Benedict's fine clothes and expensive hat.

She frowned, and asked again. When he assured her the information was correct, she said, in a tone of real confusion, "Do you mean we have to sleep sitting up?"

"That's it, ma'am," he said brusquely. "You and every other passenger. This is a second-class train."

"I don't understand. Why is there no Pullman?"

"Ma'am," he said, scowling. "There ain't no Pullman on this route. Do you want the tickets or not? If not, move out of the way. I got other people waiting."

Mrs. Benedict glanced over her shoulder at the short line behind her, and said, "Well, yes. Two, please. The best you have."

"I told you," he growled. "All the same on this train."

"Very well." She sniffed, and opened her handbag. "Near the dining car, then."

"Seats not assigned," the agent responded wearily. "You have to change trains at Wallula, mind. Don't sleep through or you'll end up in Spokane."

Bronwyn gave him a small, surreptitious smile, and he surprised her with a wink, even as he unceremoniously shoved the two tickets under the partition of his cubicle.

The car they stepped up into wasn't unpleasant at all. It was rather new, the velvet upholstery only a little shiny in places, and rows of small electric lights glowing overhead. They settled side by side into wide seats with worked metal armrests. Mrs. Benedict stowed the valise beneath her feet, and Bronwyn took off her hat so she could rest her head. She gazed through the window as they chugged out of the Portland train yard onto the tracks running alongside the massive Columbia River.

They soon learned the train had to stop at any station with its flag up. In places like Cooke and Goldendale, towns so small Bronwyn could hardly believe they had names, the train ground to a grudging halt before exposed wooden platforms. After taking on passengers or cargo, the train jolted forward again, wheels and rails whining together as it picked up speed. The pattern repeated every hour or so.

At first Bronwyn watched the river. It was so wide that in the gathering darkness she could hardly see the far bank. When she could no longer see the ebb and flow of the water, she turned her head the other way. Here and there lights glimmered in the distance, houses scattered on hilltops or nestled in valleys. Farms, she supposed. She wondered about the people there, living so far from any city or town. Perhaps they would be sitting down to supper. Perhaps they had spent the day laboring in the sun, and now, tired and hungry, they gathered around their tables, satisfied with the day's work. Such a life, so different from the one she knew, seemed idyllic to her, purposeful and cozy and safe.

It had been a long, strange day after a long, strange week. She had slept little the night before. Her eyelids drooped, and she yawned. Soon she drowsed, and despite sitting up, and the frequent disruptions of tiny stations, she dreamed.

Her dream was, as it so often was, of Preston. But this time—
perhaps because of the clanging of bells and blowing of steam
whistles, or just the constant jostling—this time she didn't dream
of the magical night in the garden. In this dream, Preston was not
the charming sophisticate who had so enchanted her. He was
angry, cursing at her, his eyes dark with fury. He shook her with
hard hands, so that in her dream she cried out and tried to get
away from him. He seemed a monster, not the lover of her imagination. He frightened her, and she struggled to free herself.

She startled awake to find herself being shaken by Mrs. Benedict.

"Wallula," Mrs. Benedict whispered in her ear.

Bronwyn blinked, and glanced around. Other passengers slept,
some braced against the glass windows, others nodding over their
folded arms. It was chilly in the car, and it was still dark outside.
It seemed cruel to have her sleep interrupted yet again. She
couldn't remember the last time she had slept, undisturbed,
through the night.

"We have to change," Mrs. Benedict said. She bent to pull her
valise out from beneath the seat, and clutched it close in her arms
as she led the way out of the car and onto an uncovered platform
beside the tracks. The station was a small wooden building with
a single sleepy ticket agent dozing behind his window. Mrs.
Benedict took a seat on a wooden bench, her coat tucked around
her. Bronwyn pulled the collar of her sweater up to her chin, but
she was still cold, and she paced back and forth in an effort to
warm herself. As the sky began to brighten, the ticket agent
came out to lower the flag to signal to the train. Five minutes
later, the train to Walla Walla appeared, blowing an earsplitting
blast on its whistle.

Bronwyn turned to Mrs. Benedict. She half expected her, at
any moment, to come to her senses. She thought she might gasp,
shiver suddenly, and press her hands to her cheeks as she realized where she was. She would blush, and apologize, and explain
that since her son's death she had been subject to such turns,

times when she convinced herself Preston was alive, that he needed her.

Bronwyn meant, in that circumstance, to be kind and understanding. She would say soothing things, and promise to accompany the older woman back to her home, to help explain everything to her family.

None of this happened. The new train pulled in to the station, and Mrs. Benedict set out across the platform with a determined step. Bronwyn, yawning in the pre-dawn air, followed her. They settled on the first seats they could find, and Mrs. Benedict brought out sandwiches she must have bought at Union Station in Portland. She said brightly, "Breakfast!"

Mrs. Benedict showed no evidence of second thoughts when the conductor announced their arrival at Walla Walla. On the contrary, she glowed with excitement as they stepped down from the train into a hot, sunny morning. The station was newer than the big stations of Seattle and Portland, but far more modest, built of brick, with just one story. There was a ladies' lounge off the simple lobby, and the two of them stopped in it to freshen up.

Bronwyn gazed at herself in the mirror, dismayed by the flaws in her appearance. Her borrowed dress was creased, and inevitably stained by two days of travel. She fluffed her hair with her fingers as best she could. She had natural curls, but they were pressed flat at the back of her head. She resolved to keep her hat on.

Mrs. Benedict, however, had brought a change of clothes in the brocade valise, and she was resplendent now in a summer frock and opaque white stockings. She wore an enormous gold brooch in the shape of a spray of flowers, studded with tiny rubies and emeralds. She took out a compact, and powdered her cheeks. Bronwyn splashed water on her face, but didn't bother with anything else. In the clear daylight, the whole escapade seemed even more preposterous than it had the day before.

Three taxicabs waited outside the station. Mrs. Benedict chose the newest-looking vehicle, an enclosed sedan. The driver was polishing his windshield, but when she signaled to him with an imperious wave of her gloved hand, he hurried to jump into the driver's seat. He started his motor and pulled out of the line to come up to the curb where the two of them waited. He jumped out with a jaunty tip of his hat and an eager "Good morning, ladies, good morning!" He took Mrs. Benedict's valise, and held the door of his automobile for them to get in.

Mrs. Benedict bestowed a sunny smile on Bronwyn. "Almost there!" she said. And to the driver, "The Walla Walla Sanitarium, please. In College Place."

Mrs. Benedict appeared utterly confident, sure of herself and her destination. Bronwyn's heart fluttered uneasily beneath the dotted swiss bodice of her dress. She took off her hat, eyeing its bent brim with misgivings. She worked it with her fingers, trying to restore its shape, and trying not to think about what would happen when they arrived. Would it fall to her to explain Mrs. Benedict's odd behavior? Would the people at this sanitarium perhaps hold her responsible?

The taxicab driver said cheerily, "Yes, ma'am. Walla Walla Sanitarium. My pleasure." He touched his hat brim again, climbed into the driver's seat, and they were off on the final stage of their improbable journey.

Bronwyn put her hat back on, and hugged herself as they drove. She felt the dryness of this place in her throat, as if she had swallowed dust. Her skin itched. The sun was punishing, burning the shrubberies and browning the lawns they passed. The images of the bad dream didn't fade, as nightmares usually did, but stayed with her. She couldn't shake off a sense of impending disaster.

Mrs. Benedict clearly felt no such sense of doom. She glanced in her compact two or three times, smiling at herself, tucking in a strand of hair. She said, in a confiding tone, "Preston wants me to color my hair. It's gone gray now, but once I was a true blonde, just like he is—well, was."

The change in verb tense startled Bronwyn. "Was—?" she

ventured. Perhaps this was the moment when Mrs. Benedict would realize—

But Mrs. Benedict waved one white-gloved hand in a negligent gesture. "Oh, well, I mean when he was a boy, you know." She smoothed her chignon with the palm of her glove. "He thinks I should do something about the gray, but I don't see why it matters. I'm a grandmother, after all!" Her little laugh was like the shaking of tiny bells, incongruously girlish. Her eyes were brilliant in the glare of the sun.

None of it felt right, or natural. Mrs. Benedict's gaiety was as brittle as glass. The taxicab bearing them to their destination had been too easy to command, as if the driver had just been waiting for two unescorted women to appear so he could carry them off to a place of his own choosing.

Bronwyn turned to the window, gazing blindly at sunbaked fields and weathered farmhouses, horses and cattle switching their tails against flies. She was still looking out when the sanitarium rose into her view.

The building was reassuringly solid, rising against the pale summer sky, three pillared stories surrounded by landscaped gardens and graveled paths. It looked much as Bronwyn had imagined a sanitarium should look, and it had a large sign proclaiming it THE WALLA WALLA SANITARIUM, in florid script. The taxicab swept up to the front steps without hesitation, and the driver smiled at them both in his mirror. Bronwyn's feeling of dread began to seem foolish.

Whatever was to come, it was clear they were actually going to go inside this elegant place. She took her own compact out of her small handbag.

Mrs. Benedict swept her with a sly glance. "That's right, dear," she said softly. "You'll want to look your best. You never know—you and Preston might work things out after all."

The floor nurse came to tell him he was about to have visitors. She said the Dunlaps were bringing his mother up to see him, and she reminded him that it was a special privilege. "Not a visiting day," she said sternly.

Preston barked a sour laugh at that. Special privileges came with the hefty fee the pater was paying every month to keep him here. Old Dunlap never failed to remind him of that. They treated him well, Dr. and Mrs. Dunlap, but Preston understood perfectly that their respect was due to the pater's dollars, and not his own charming person.

He hadn't, however, been expecting his mother. Her letters assured him she was trying, but that his father couldn't spare Blake for the long drive. Something must have changed. He hoped she had brought the stone. Once he had it in his hands again, he would feel he could do anything. He would have the courage he needed.

He hurried to put on a fresh shirt and a pair of the good trousers his mother had sent to him. He wasn't allowed cuff links, of course, or a tie, or even a belt. He folded back his shirt cuffs, though that made him look like a day laborer. There was nothing he could do about the belt. At least his shoes had a nice shine, since he had had plenty of time to polish them, though he had nothing much to polish them with. An orderly had shaved him just this morning, and of course he had no need of a barber. His hair—wasn't. Completely burned away. He was as ready as he could make himself.

Odd that in the current circumstance, it was only for his mother that he would make such an effort. It wasn't like him, but he felt sympathy for her. She had suffered a great deal, believing him dead. That was hardly his fault, but he had tried, in the few small ways he had at his disposal, to make it up to her. He had almost none of the feelings other people wasted their energy on, yet he clung to this shred of filial devotion. It made him feel virtuous.

Poor Mater. She was going to suffer again, and soon. She deserved better, but it couldn't be helped.

He pressed his forehead to the tiny window in his door, peer-

ing down the corridor to watch his mother step out of the elevator. The Dunlaps were with her, and they were followed in their
turn by a slender young woman with brown curls and a hesitant air.

He knew her instantly. Unlike himself, she had hardly changed
at all. She looked a bit older, of course, but the difference between sixteen and nineteen wasn't a significant one. She was
wearing a dotted swiss frock that was a style unsuited to her,
slightly too big and too long. It was as if she had lost weight, or
made a bad purchase.

That didn't seem like her. He remembered being impressed
by her good clothes and her natural *chic*, though she had been so
young. Deliciously young. Soft, in that unformed way young girls
had. She had even been rather sweet, if a little silly, like her girlish mother.

He wondered if Bronwyn was still silly. She should have ac-
quired a bit of seasoning, considering what had happened. He remembered thinking, three years ago, that the girl had potential,
if she could avoid turning into her mother. It would be interesting to know if her potential had ever been realized. More likely,
she had just given in, like other girls in her social class, followed
the rules, found a husband, given up.

He couldn't see her eyes yet, but he remembered them. He
had never seen eyes like that, hazel dusted with gold flecks that
gleamed in the sunlight, and were even faintly visible by moon-
light. In most other ways, she was ordinary, but those eyes, and
the soft brown curls that went with them . . .

Yes. Bronwyn Morgan was a very pretty girl. And of course she
had adored him, which was gratifying.

None of it signified now. But it was nice to think that his son
had an attractive mother. The boy should be good-looking. Well
bred.

But what the hell was the girl doing here? How had Mother
found her?

Edith was carrying a smallish valise, the brocade one they had all given her for a birthday eons ago. He hoped it was in there. He hoped she had remembered. Sometimes, these days, Mother didn't seem to be precisely clear in her mind.

But it *must* be in there. That was how she had found Bronwyn Morgan! Great things happened to those who possessed Roxelana's sapphire. And here it was, nearly within his grasp. Its power would be restored to him. Nothing would hold him back.

Poor Mother. When she realized, she would break her heart anew. It was regrettable, really it was.

It had been clear from the moment they climbed the neatly painted steps and went into the bright tiled lobby of the sanitarium that the management was eager to please Mrs. Edith Benedict, once they understood who she was. There were some startled comments about her visit being unexpected, but these were hastily amended to words of welcome, assurances that all was well, offers of tea and a comfortable place to sit while the patient was informed of her presence.

No one spoke Preston's name, though, and Bronwyn was assailed by a fresh wave of anxiety. She wished she could speak to one of the staff privately, ask them what this was all about.

A Dr. Dunlap was called, and he came hurrying out of an inner office to bow over Mrs. Benedict's hand and inquire after her husband and the rest of the family. Mrs. Benedict introduced Bronwyn as "my young friend, Miss Morgan."

Dr. Dunlap was a silver-haired man with a dark mustache and thin dark eyebrows. He took Bronwyn's hand in his large, smooth one, and raised an eyebrow at the uniformed nurse who had come to fetch him.

"Call Mrs. Dunlap," he said. She nodded, and hurried off with a rustle of her starched apron.

The doctor turned back to Mrs. Benedict. "Were you planning to take Miss Morgan—er—up with you, Mrs. Benedict?" he said, with an air of delicacy.

"Of course," Mrs. Benedict said. "They're old friends."

The doctor's mouth pursed beneath his mustache. "Don't you think that might be—er—just a little too much for your son?"

Bronwyn's knees suddenly trembled. Your son.

He had said it, this doctor, this man who was obviously in charge here, and that meant it was true. Preston lived. The newspapers had been wrong. He hadn't burned up in the fire after all, but was here, a patient in this sanitarium. The fact of it, the import of the realization, made Bronwyn's head spin as if someone had struck her. She reached for something to steady herself, and her groping hand found the wall. It was a flocked pattern, and she focused on the feel of the flocking under her palm, something to keep her from fainting.

The doctor said other things, and Mrs. Benedict answered. Mrs. Dunlap appeared, a woman on the verge of old age, with gray hair and a thick waist. She wore a nurse's uniform with heavy black stockings, but no apron. She joined in the conversation, but Bronwyn heard nothing that any of them said. The tumble of her own thoughts drowned out every word.

She hardly knew how they all made their way to the elevator, or what was said as it bore them up two floors, to the top of the building. The doors of the elevator parted to show a hallway drenched in sunlight from dormer windows set into the outer wall. Opposite the windows were several single doors, all closed. Bronwyn barely noticed any of it.

He was alive. Mrs. Benedict wasn't deluded. She hadn't brought Bronwyn all the way across the state on a fool's errand.

Preston was alive. He hadn't abandoned her after all. He had been ill. Injured in that terrible fire.

Stunned by the implications, she stumbled as they left the elevator, and Mrs. Dunlap turned to look at her. "Are you all right, Miss Morgan?"

"Yes," Bronwyn said. Her voice sounded faint in the tiled corridor.

"Are you sure? Are you prepared for this?"

Bronwyn frowned at the question. The spinning of her mind

slowed, and she focused on Mrs. Dunlap's kindly face. "Prepared?" she asked.

"You know about Mr. Benedict's condition, I hope," the nurse said. They were still walking, following Mrs. Benedict, who led the way with eager steps, the valise bouncing against her knee. Dr. Dunlap hurried to stay beside her, a solicitous hand hovering behind her thin back. Bronwyn and Mrs. Dunlap trailed behind them.

Bronwyn said, "His condition?"

Mrs. Dunlap put a hand on Bronwyn's arm, slowing her progress. Mrs. Benedict and Dr. Dunlap were already far down the corridor. Bronwyn glanced to her left, to one of the closed doors. Through its small, screened window, she could see that the room beyond it was bare and empty.

Mrs. Dunlap followed her glance. "There's only one patient on this floor," she said. "It's that room at the end, the one facing us." Her hand was still on Bronwyn's arm, and she brought her to a stop with a gentle pressure. "Miss Morgan," she began. "It would be best, before you visit Mr. Benedict, that you understand—"

Mrs. Benedict interrupted her. She looked back down the hallway, and called, "Miss Morgan! Oh, do come along! He's waiting for us!" She had come to a stop before the last door at the end of the hall, and was shifting from foot to foot with eagerness as she waited for Dr. Dunlap to find the right key on a large ring.

Bronwyn started toward her, suddenly eager. It was simply marvelous, that after all this time—all the heartbreak and misery and loneliness—she would see him again. He was alive!

He would be changed, of course. He had been ill, after all. Still, her heart lifted in anticipation.

"Miss Morgan, wait," Mrs. Dunlap said. She caught her arm again, and held it. "I'm afraid it's going to be something of a shock—"

"Oh, no, Mrs. Dunlap," Bronwyn said. "He knows me. I can't think it will be a shock to him to see me."

"Not for him," Mrs. Dunlap said. Later, Bronwyn would think of this, and remember the grimness in the nurse's face, but for now, impatience drove her. She tugged her arm free of Mrs. Dunlap's hand, and hurried down the corridor.

She came to a stop just short of the room. In her haste, her hat had slipped askew. She put a hand up to straighten it, then dropped the hand to her throat to smooth the collar of her dress. After all this time, his first sight of her should be perfect. At least, as perfect as she could make it under the circumstances.

She found she was holding her breath. She released it, and took a fresh one, preparing herself.

The door opened, and Mrs. Benedict rushed past Dr. Dunlap into the room. Bronwyn heard Mrs. Benedict's light voice, then a deeper, rougher one. A man's voice. It didn't sound familiar to her, but it must be Preston. Mrs. Dunlap reached her side, but she didn't speak again. She stood just outside the door, gazing at Bronwyn with resignation.

The moment had come, the moment she had despaired of for so long. Bronwyn fluffed her hair a bit with her fingertips, fixed her most charming smile on her lips, and stepped forward.

CHAPTER 21

As the old-fashioned skeleton key rattled in the lock—it was laughable, really, to see the faith old Dunlap placed in his antiquated locking system—Preston adopted a nonchalant pose, leaning against the wall, his scarred hands thrust into his pockets. When the lock clicked and the door opened, his mother fairly burst into the room, pushing past the doctor. She glowed with pleasure. She dropped the valise to the floor and crossed to Preston with her hands out.

"Preston, darling!"

"Mater," he said, straightening, reaching with his own arms to accept her embrace, and return it. "How lovely of you to come all this way." His voice was better than it had been, a little smoother, a bit more resonant. Oddly enough, though Dunlap was practically an antique himself, his hydrotherapy approach had helped a good bit with the scarring of Preston's throat and lungs. The air here in Walla Walla was devilishly dry, but the steam of the hydrotherapy room was soothing, when he was allowed to go there.

"Darling, I have a surprise for you!" Edith withdrew from his arms, and looked up into his face with a coquettish air. She put up her hand, and stroked his scarred cheek as if it were still the fine-skinned surface it had once been.

"Oh, do tell, Mother," Preston said with a smile. "I'm absolutely agog."

Edith stepped aside, and indicated the doorway with a flourish of her arm.

Preston turned toward the open door just in time to see Bronwyn Morgan step into view. The sunlight from the dormer window behind her made a halo around her slight form. Her golden brown curls glowed with it, and the dotted swiss turned to gauze under the harsh light. She wore a smile on her pretty mouth, and those gold-flecked eyes were wide and eager.

She lifted one foot to step over the sill, then froze. One hand gripped the doorjamb. The color drained from her rosy cheeks until she was as white as the iron frame on his bed. Her smile faded, bit by bit, her lips parting, mouth open. The greeting she had been about to speak caught in her throat, supplanted by a single, wordless sound.

The mater took no notice. She said brightly, "It's Bronwyn Morgan, dear! The girl you told me about, the one who—well, you know, don't you! She's come to see you."

Preston pushed away from the wall, and walked with deliberate steps toward the door. "Bronwyn," he said. "Time has been much kinder to you than to me."

The girl's pupils flared in those lovely eyes, nearly swallowing the irises. She pulled back her foot, then her hand, as if she were shrinking into herself. Mrs. Dunlap stepped up behind her, hands out in support, a look of fury on her face.

Nice woman, Mrs. Dunlap. Nice, but stupid. She should have known Mother wouldn't warn the poor girl. Mother didn't see his scars. She managed, in some magical way, to see her golden boy the way he had been, instead of perceiving the ruin he had become. It was perfectly understandable if Mother believed little Bronwyn Morgan would do the same. The Dunlaps should have known.

Bronwyn managed to close her mouth, at least. Her nostrils flared as she drew a long, noisy breath, and then another. Beads of perspiration appeared on her temples, and Mrs. Dunlap put a steadying arm around her waist.

Preston grinned, knowing how horrible the expression looked on his scarred lips. He said, "Pretty, ain't I? So sorry to surprise you."

The girl swallowed, and drew herself up with obvious effort. Mrs. Dunlap released her, but stayed close. Probably thought the poor kid was going to faint. "I knew there was a fire," Bronwyn said in a frail voice. "I didn't know you were so—so badly burned."

"No. Bit of a surprise, isn't it? I do think someone might have warned you."

She lifted her little pointed chin in a gesture that was oddly courageous. "Yes," she said. "That would have been good. But your mother thought we—that we should—" Her words trailed off into silence, and her face bore the look he had come to dread and hate. He would rather have seen her swoon, right there in the corridor, than have to see her look like that.

"Mother thought we should," he snapped in his roughest tone, "and now you pity me. Not what you expected, was it?"

"No." Her voice steadied, and the color returned to her cheeks. She stood as tall as she could, and didn't look away, though she must have wished she could. Gutsy little thing, really. She said, "Of course I pity you, Preston."

"Don't."

"Those are terrible scars. You would pity me, if I had suffered such injuries."

He laughed with a grating sound that made her flinch. "No," he said. "I wouldn't." He swayed toward her, without his volition. His hands were clenched, the scarred flesh aching as his fingers pulled on it. "Explain to her, Dunlap. Mother, *you* tell her, for God's sake. Tell her the way I am. Make her understand."

"Understand what, dear? I don't know what you—"

"Oh, for Christ's sake!" he shouted, directly into Bronwyn's face. "Can't you see it for yourself?"

Old Dunlap took a step toward him, saying in a warning tone, "Mr. Benedict—"

It happened fast, faster than he would have expected, so fast he had no control over it.

The old anger rose in his belly, burned in his lungs until he couldn't breathe, blurred his thoughts. It was familiar to him, that anger, blazing up like a bonfire, flames and smoke and heat, all demanding an outlet. He had tried, all his life, to manage it in his mother's presence, but there was nothing he hated more than that look of sympathy, that look of empty, meaningless sorrow for him. The great Margot wore that look all too often. He loathed seeing it on this girl's face, this girl who had loved him, who thought he was a hero, her shining knight.

He couldn't bear it. It made him shudder with fury.

"Listen to me, you little fool!" He staggered forward, a single step, wary of Dunlap's interference. He had to get that look off her face or he would explode. "I wouldn't pity you! I wouldn't give a damn what happened to you! I *didn't* give a damn, don't you get that?"

"That can't be true, Preston," she said steadily. Her face still wore that sad expression—for him. Why should she be sad for him? It should be grief for herself. She was the one who had to carry the brat, after all. She was the one whose life path was altered, whose childish dreams were shattered. Why the hell should she feel sorry for *him?* What in damnation was the matter with her?

"Listen!" he cried. "You think I didn't read your silly letter?"

Her smooth brow wrinkled. "My letter? You mean you received it? You read it? But you never answered me."

"Why should I answer?" he snarled. "So you were pregnant!" Dunlap drew breath to protest, but Preston threw up a hand to silence him. "What did you expect me to do about it? You expected me to take on your brat?"

Mrs. Dunlap said, "Mr. Benedict—"

Bronwyn cried, "Naturally, I thought you would—when you knew, you would—"

"What?" he said, his voice rising, thinning. "What? You thought I would care?" He staggered forward, and was rewarded by seeing her fall back a step, into the corridor. "You thought," he shrieked, "I would *marry* you? Christ, don't parents teach their daughters *anything?*"

"Preston!" his mother cried. "Darling, there's no need to be cruel! She couldn't have known—"

But he couldn't hear her anymore, nor could he see her. Rage blinded him, turned his vision scarlet, made his scarred flesh burn with agony, as if he had been plunged anew into the flames. He threw himself toward the door. He seized the girl, feeling the tender flesh of her arms give beneath his hard, burned hands, and he heard her cry out in pain. He shook her. He had to wipe that look of pity from her face. He had to force her to understand, to comprehend that he would never, *never* have had anything further to do with her, no matter—

Oscar burst into the room, a large, hairy tornado blocking his path, seizing him in thick, unsympathetic arms, tearing him away from Bronwyn. She fell back, and Preston gasped out a final curse.

He had lost all control. He hadn't intended to harm her, only shake sense into her, but he wouldn't bother explaining that. He regretted having such an outburst where his mother could see him, but it was done now. Like so many things, it couldn't be changed. Couldn't be reversed.

Oscar hauled him backward, away from Bronwyn, and well out of range of his mother's reaching hands. A syringe appeared in Dunlap's fist, and before Preston could draw another breath, the steel needle pierced his skin, sending the cold syrup of a sedative into the muscle of his arm.

His mother was weeping, of course. "Goddammit," he muttered, as the drug began to quench the fire, to calm the tremors of his fury. "Goddammit, Mother. So sorry! I just—it's all so—"

How many times had he persuaded her, with his heartfelt explanations, his clever justifications? How often had he heard her trying to explain to other people that he was just sensitive, that he felt things more deeply than anyone else?

How many excuses could there be?

He sagged against Oscar's broad chest, the drug sapping all the strength from his muscles. His eyelids grew heavy, and the light in the room seemed to dim. He said again, "Goddammit," but weakly.

Oscar lowered him to the bed, and he felt the humiliating pressure of straps being buckled around his arms, around his ankles. He heard, distantly, his mother's sobs, her pleas to Oscar to be careful, not to hurt him.

He heard the patter of Bronwyn Morgan's feet as she retreated down the corridor, and the heavier tread of Mrs. Dunlap going after her.

Dunlap was trying to persuade Edith out of the room, assuring her Oscar had everything in hand, that it would be all right, that they would give the patient a bit of time, let the sedative do its work. Preston, over the slowing thud of his heartbeat, heard all of that. He heard his mother's cries escalate, heard her screeching his name from the corridor, heard her begging to be allowed back into the room, to talk to her son, to plead with him.

What he didn't hear was his mother making excuses for him. He wondered if, at last, her supply was exhausted.

He turned his scarred face to the door to watch Dunlap leave, closing the door firmly behind him. Preston heard the heavy click of the key in the lock.

But on the floor, forgotten in the melée, was Edith's small brocade valise. And inside it, if there was any justice at all, was his sapphire.

Bronwyn fled the commotion without a backward look. It had taken all her strength to conceal her horror at Preston's appearance. There was almost nothing left of his face! He had been so handsome, with such silken skin and finely cut features! Now his golden hair was gone, his lips distorted, his cheeks drawn with scars. Only his eyes, those icy blue eyes, told her it was really he, and those had been filled with such anger, such—such *hate*—

She had done her best. She had swallowed her shock, tried to speak to him with kindness, and he had lashed out at her, raised his fists, said those awful things. She had never been witness to such an ugly scene. Could being hurt change a person so much? Could his disfigurement have altered his true nature?

If not, then he was not at all the person she had believed him to be. Not the man she had mourned, and had yearned for all this time.

She reached the end of the hallway on flying feet, pursued by shouts and screams and sobs. She didn't bother with the elevator, but pushed through a heavy door leading to a stairway, and dashed headlong down the steps. She tripped on the first landing she came to, but caught herself on the wooden banister, and plunged onward. The door at the bottom of the stairwell opened onto a blank corridor, the sort used by servants and tradesmen. She raced on, not choosing a direction, simply moving, escaping.

As she ran, the last fragments of illusion fell away. She felt as if she were crushing each and every one beneath her feet. Mrs. Benedict was wrong. There could be no reunion between herself and Preston Benedict, and not because his looks had been destroyed. The man she thought she loved didn't exist. Perhaps he never had. She couldn't understand what he was, but she would never, ever, want to see him again.

She came upon a door and pushed it open. It led into a kitchen, where women in white aprons were working at long wooden counters. Bronwyn froze just inside the door, then spun back, searching for an exit.

One of the cooks, a girl hardly older than herself, stepped forward, saying politely, "Miss? Are you looking for Reception?"

Bronwyn's mouth opened, but she couldn't speak. She shook her head, and the young woman looked concerned. She put down the spoon she was using, and started toward Bronwyn, but before she reached her, Bronwyn gulped an awkward apology, backed out into the corridor, and ran the other way.

She burst through a set of double doors, and found herself on a loading platform. A truck was just backing up, its driver peering over his shoulder as he worked the gears. He spotted her, and braked with a squeal of metal and rubber. Bronwyn whirled, and crossed the platform to jump down from the far side. She dashed around the side of the building toward the gravel drive where their taxicab had dropped them. Bronwyn hardly knew where she was, or where she was going, but she raced down the drive, out to the packed dirt of the road, and on.

CHAPTER 22

The temperature was well into the eighties as the elder and younger Parrishes, along with Tim, their hired hand, piled into the Model T and drove down the valley to a neighboring ranch. Several other automobiles and two or three trucks were already parked along the packed dirt lane leading to the ranch house. The barn was a weathered two-story structure with an enormous weather vane in the shape of a running horse. Two carriages waited near it, their shafts resting on the ground, the horses that had pulled them stabled in the shade. Long cloth-covered tables had been set up in the yard, and at least twenty people were standing around them. The women wore broad-brimmed hats and printed cotton dresses. The men were in their usual boots and denim trousers.

Everyone turned to wave as Robert and Jenny stepped out onto the running board of the dusty Model T. Tim followed, and then Frank. When Margot appeared, the easy smiles turned to open stares of curiosity, making her glad of the drooping brim of her borrowed hat. She wore a white shirtwaist and a trim linen skirt, and she saw, before she climbed down to the ground, that her skirt was shorter by six inches than any other in the gathering. She was the only one wearing gloves, as well. She found herself wishing Ramona were here to reassure her.

Frank helped her down. He tucked her hand under his arm as they followed his parents toward the group of their friends and neighbors, and he gave her fingers a reassuring squeeze.

He had told her when they went to bed the night before that Elizabeth would probably be present at the picnic. "Everyone comes to these things," he said. "Old folks, kids, ranch hands—everyone."

"I understand," she said. "It's wonderful, really. Community."

"They'll like you," he added, unnecessarily.

She laughed, and nestled close to him under the age-softened quilt. "For your sake, maybe, Frank," she said softly. "I'm not much good at social events."

"Doesn't matter," he said.

That made her laugh again. "I suppose not. But I warned you."

He laid his book aside, and reached to put out the lamp. As was their habit, she slept on his right side, so he could encircle her with his good arm as they fell asleep. She laid her head against his shoulder, and sighed with contentment.

He startled her, a good five minutes later, by saying, "Margot, I think you might be surprised by these folks."

She had been half asleep, but her eyes opened to the starlit darkness, and she glanced up at him. She could just see the lean plane of his jaw, the gleam of silver in his hair. "In what way, Frank?"

"They're not social the way—say, the way Ramona is. Or Allison."

"What do you mean?"

She felt the lift of his shoulder beneath her cheek as he shrugged. "Oh, they gossip, of course. Talk about what everyone's up to. But to me they seem more—more real, I guess."

"Real?"

"We're so close to the ground here," he said, which might

have been obscure, but somehow wasn't. He didn't speak again, and she didn't say anything more.

Soon she heard his breathing slow and soften, and she lay listening to it, and listening to the faint night sounds from beyond the open window. She thought about what he had said, applying it to Jenny and Robert, to Tim. Close to the ground. The phrase made sense. They worked hard to care for the land, the animals, to put food on the table. There was nothing artificial in their lives, because there was no room for it.

Before she fell asleep, she couldn't help comparing Jenny Parrish to Edith Benedict, which was probably unfair. Her mother was a product of her background, and Jenny was no doubt the same. But if Jenny had had a son like Preston, he might have turned out a different man.

Margot thrust the thought aside. Speculating was a waste of time. She turned on her side, and plumped her pillow, and reminded herself that the part of her life with her younger brother, as awful as it had been, was over and done with. Preston was safely stowed, and though her mother longed for him, that couldn't be helped. She would put it out of her mind, and enjoy the few days of vacation left to her.

She intended to enjoy this picnic, too. She walked beside Frank, and as the introductions began she pulled off her gloves, and shook every hand that was offered to her. She did her best to listen to the flurry of names, each one inevitably followed by a description of where their ranch was in relation to the Parrish place. She met women of Jenny's age, and younger women with babies braced on their hips. She met older men, a few young husbands, a young man in a wicker wheelchair, several girls and boys in their teens.

Their hostess was a plump, red-cheeked woman well into her fifties. Everyone, it seemed, called her Grandma. She wore a bib apron just like one of Hattie's, and was busily supervising the food. Every family had brought something. Jenny had been up early frying two of her fattest hens. There were bowls of potato salad, loaves of fresh bread, a large platter of cucumbers in vinegar, and an array of pies. Grandma greeted Margot and Frank over her shoulder, and said, "So glad to meet Frank's young lady at last. Hope you came hungry!"

Margot eyed the bounty with appreciation. She wished she could take a photograph to send to Hattie. She said, "It all looks wonderful."

She turned from the table, and found Frank shaking the hand of a pretty, rather soft-looking young woman in a white cotton dress and a matching hat. She was smiling, looking up into Frank's face and holding his hand with both of hers. He took a step back, releasing her, and reached for Margot to draw her forward.

The young woman's smile faded as he said, "Margot, this is Elizabeth. Elizabeth—my wife. Margot."

Margot extended her hand, and Elizabeth, after a fraction of a second, took it. Her hand was hot and dry, and her cheeks were pink with heat beneath the white straw. Margot said, "I've heard so much about you. It's good to meet you at last."

There was a moment's pause, not long enough to be truly awkward, but distinct. Elizabeth pulled her hand back and said bluntly, "I don't know what to call you. Since you're a doctor, I mean." Her eyes were a soft blue, but there was strength in her mouth, and despite the feminine dress, with its layers of lace and ruffles, she looked sturdy, as if she was used to physical labor.

Margot found her frankness refreshing. It eased things somehow. She was glad not to have to come up with some artificial courtesy. "Since my husband has known you for so many years, Elizabeth, why don't we go straight to Christian names?"

"Sure." Elizabeth tilted her head up, and gave Margot a measuring look. "Your photograph doesn't do you justice."

Margot blinked. "My photograph?"

"Jenny showed me your wedding pictures."

"Oh." Margot laughed a little. "I'm no good at being photographed. I always look too tall and too bony."

Frank took her hand, and tucked it under his elbow again, pressing it tightly against his side. She glanced at him sideways, and gave him a small smile. It was uncomfortable, meeting Elizabeth, but they had expected that. She could see he didn't know how to ease the situation.

"Well," Elizabeth said unexpectedly, "I have to say you don't look like a lady doctor."

At this Margot laughed aloud. "You must tell me what a lady doctor looks like!"

Elizabeth broke into a grin, and Margot felt an odd sense of relief. She could understand, she thought, why Frank had once cared for this woman. Elizabeth said, "You know. Spectacles. Gray hair, maybe."

"I'm sure I'll have those one day," Margot said easily, feeling comfortable now. "Not yet, thank goodness."

"No, I see that."

Someone hailed Frank, and he waved. Margot said, "Go ahead, Frank. I'm fine here."

Elizabeth said, "We'll get some lemonade, and sit over there in the shade." She indicated a wide-limbed tree of some type Margot didn't recognize. It had wooden chairs beneath it, and a little table that sat crookedly on the bare ground.

"That sounds nice," Margot said. Frank nodded, and walked away across the yard. Margot and Elizabeth poured themselves glasses of lemonade, and carried them to the chairs, settling in the welcome coolness of the tree's shade.

Elizabeth said, "You operated on Frank's arm, Jenny says."

"Yes."

"I saw it before that, when he was in the hospital in Virginia."

"I know you did. Frank told me."

"I'm ashamed of that time," Elizabeth said. "I didn't behave well at all."

Margot was struck again by her lack of dissembling. She couldn't be sorry Elizabeth and Frank had broken off their engagement, but she felt a wave of sympathy. "To someone who's not a medical professional, his amputation must have looked awful," she said gently. "It was disturbing even to me, and I've seen a good many disturbing things."

"I hurt him, and I sure didn't mean to."

"Perhaps you couldn't help it, Elizabeth."

The other woman shrugged, and sipped at her lemonade. "Guess I wouldn't have made him much of a wife, if I couldn't handle that." Her eyes met Margot's over the rim of her glass. "You're the perfect woman for him, it seems."

Margot drank, too, finding the lemonade more tart than Hattie's, and full of lemon pulp. It was perfect for the hot, dry day. The glass was slippery with condensation, and she set it carefully on the rickety table. "If I'm the right woman for Frank," she said carefully, "I hope it's not because I was able to repair his arm. I hope it's because—" She broke off, not sure how to express herself. It didn't seem right to discuss her emotional life with this woman she didn't really know, and who had shared an emotional life with her husband long before they had met.

"Oh, no," Elizabeth said. She didn't seem in the least embarrassed. "That's not it at all. No, Jenny tells me the two of you are a love match." She put her own glass down. "Frank and I weren't, really. Our parents wanted to merge the ranches, and we liked each other well enough."

"You're very plainspoken," Margot said.

Elizabeth made an apologetic gesture with one hand. "Hope I'm not offending you."

"Not at all. Quite the opposite."

Elizabeth's fair eyebrows rose. "Really?"

Margot chuckled. "Really. I have no talent for small talk. I would always prefer just to be able to speak my mind."

"Does that come from being a doctor?"

It was Margot's turn to shrug. "Perhaps. It could be that I don't have the patience to be polite."

"You'd like it out here, then," Elizabeth said with assurance. "We're plainspoken people."

"I can see that. And I do like it out here."

"Good. Good. Jenny and Robert are fine folks, and they miss their son."

Margot had no answer for this. She was saved by Grandma calling, "Come and get it, everyone!" Two other ladies, also in aprons, shooed people toward the laden table, and Margot glanced up to see Frank coming to fetch her. She smiled at Elizabeth, and went to join him.

Darkness crept slowly over the Bitterroot Valley, bringing the welcome coolness of a breeze from the river. Tiny white moths fluttered around the oil lamps someone had set out, and the friends and neighbors sat on into the evening, chatting about children and grandchildren, about the government, about the prices of hay and grain and gasoline. Margot and Frank returned to the chairs beneath the big tree, and sat side by side, not speaking much, but listening to the conversation. Someone had brought a banjo, and plunked quiet melodies from the porch of the ranch house. Stephen Foster, Margot thought. She recognized "Jeanie with the Light Brown Hair" and "Camptown Races." Her mind was peaceful, and her heart was full as she tipped her head back to watch stars flicker to life in the wide sky. Frank's hand found hers in the darkness, and their fingers interlaced as if that were their natural position.

When people began to stir, to find their hats, and look for their emptied bowls and casseroles and baskets, Margot sighed. It had been a marvelous day. She was sorry to see it come to an end. Frank rose, and extended a hand to pull her to her feet. They turned in search of Jenny and Robert, and Margot found Jenny at her side.

"Frank, someone would like to see Margot before we go."

"See me?" Margot said.

"Do you have your bag?"

"It's in the motorcar."

Frank said, "Do you mind, sweetheart? I'll get it for you."

"No, it's fine," Margot said. In truth, she did mind, but she would never let Jenny see that. Or Frank. She had been relaxed, growing drowsy, feeling at ease in the knowledge that she would have a good long sleep, and not rise until she was ready. This sudden summons was jarring.

She didn't speak about any of this. She followed Jenny across the yard and up onto the porch. Inside the ranch house, a lamp burned in the front window. Frank appeared with her medical bag, and handed it to her with a little shrug of apology. She shook her head, took the bag, and went on into the house.

Jenny said, as they passed through the front room and on into a long, low-ceilinged kitchen, "It's Cissie Borders. She's the wife of one of the ranch hands at the Connolly place."

"Where is she?"

"She's in here." Jenny opened a door at the end of the kitchen, and waved Margot through.

Margot found herself in a small bedroom lit only by a candle on a battered-looking bureau. It was the sort of room a cook might have used. Hattie had one like it, though hers was twice the size, well furnished and well lighted. In this one there was a narrow bed with what looked like a handmade quilt on it, and an ancient washstand with a basin and ewer. A young woman—a girl, really—rose from the bed when the door opened. Margot went in, and Jenny came after her, closing the door and standing near it.

Margot felt the shift in herself, the change from relaxed wife and daughter-in-law. She forgot about the interruption of her evening. The girl looked miserable, her eyes too wide in a small face, her skin sallow in the shifting light from the candle. Margot was touched, as always, by the thought that she might be able to ease her unhappiness in some way.

She put out her hand. "Hello, Mrs. Borders," she said. "I'm Dr. Benedict. I understand you wanted to see me."

"Yes," the girl said. Her voice trembled. "I thought you were Dr. Parrish."

"When I'm working, I use my maiden name. I am Margot Parrish, though."

"Jenny said you wouldn't mind if I asked you about—about something. I can't afford to go to Missoula, and I'd rather not talk to a man." She dropped her gaze. "I got woman trouble, Doctor. I don't know what happened."

"Maybe nothing happened," Margot said. "Sometimes we just get sick."

"But I was fine, even after Eldon—that's my husband—even after he came home from France. I know some of the others brought disease with them, but not my Eldon."

"You're thinking of venereal disease?"

"I don't know what that is."

Crisply, to reduce the girl's embarrassment, Margot said, "It's a disease transmitted through sexual intercourse."

The girl's face turned scarlet, a furious blush visible even in the candlelight. "Oh," she mumbled. "I didn't know the right name, I guess. I think that's what's wrong with me, though."

"Let's sit down, Mrs. Borders. Tell me what you're feeling, and then I'd better have a look at you." She glanced back at Jenny, who stood with her hands linked before her, a look on her face of both sympathy and interest. "Jenny, do you think you could find a better light? A lamp, perhaps?"

"I'll do that, Margot. You go ahead."

It didn't take long for Margot to elicit Cissie Borders's symptoms and their duration. It was the sort of thing she had heard a dozen times at the Women and Infants Clinic, young women mystified by what they were feeling, by what was happening in their bodies. Jenny returned with a lamp, and Margot took rubber gloves from her medical bag and put them on. She helped Mrs. Borders to lie back, and covered her with a blanket.

The examination revealed what she had expected. Swelling, the classic yellowish discharge, and a badly infected cervix. The girl was long overdue for treatment. She was in danger of becoming infertile if her infection wasn't reined in swiftly.

As she stripped off her gloves, and washed her hands in the basin Jenny had thought to bring, she said, "You have gonorrhea, Mrs. Borders. It's not unusual for symptoms to appear quite some time after the initial infection."

"Gonorrhea. Is that the—" The girl's voice broke, and she swallowed noisily. "Is that the clap?"

"In the vernacular, yes."

"I was afraid of that. So that means my Eldon . . ." She drew a shaky breath, and Margot steeled herself for tears, but the girl didn't weep. "It was awful over there," the girl said.

"Yes," Margot said. "My husband, Mrs. Parrish's son, was injured in the war. I think it was about as awful as we can imagine."

"I don't blame him," Mrs. Borders said.

Margot sat next to her on the bed. "Then your husband is a lucky man," she said. She pushed back the girl's hair with her hand, and felt her brow. Her eyes were bright, as if with fever, but she felt cool to the touch.

"Can you fix me?" the girl asked. "Will I be okay?"

"I believe so, but it takes time," Margot said. "We have fairly good success with silver solutions. I'll give you a wash that you can use yourself. I should start it for you, to be thorough."

"Will you?"

"Yes, of course. We need to treat the infection in your husband, too."

Cissie Borders's eyes went wide, and she sat bolt upright. "Oh, no! I'm not supposed to be seeing a doctor."

"Why ever not? You're ill, Mrs. Borders. This is a serious infection, and if you don't—"

"You can't tell him! Jenny, you have to explain to her—Eldon won't have it. He'll kill me if he finds out!"

Jenny said, "Cissie, you'd best listen to Dr. Parr—I mean, Benedict."

Margot cast her mother-in-law a swift look, then turned back to Cissie. "I understand this is difficult. I can treat you with Protargol, and leave you enough to go on with the treatment yourself. But you and your husband have to avoid intercourse until you're both well. If you have sexual relations while he's still infected, you'll simply reinfect yourself. The long-term implications are quite grave, Mrs. Borders."

"I can't—I just don't know what to do," Cissie said, her voice rising. "He told me it would go away, that I'd get over it. He had it, he said, and it went away."

"No, it didn't," Margot said wearily. "I know people hope

that's true, but they're wrong. The disease goes dormant, but unfortunately, it doesn't go away. That's why you're ill now."

"But if I—"

Margot said, "Do you plan on a family? Does your husband plan to keep working as a ranch hand? All of these are at risk if you let this illness go untreated."

Cissie slumped forward, her elbows on her knees, her head in her hands. "He'll kill me," she groaned. "He told me not to tell anyone, that they'd think he—that he shouldn't have—"

"Well, he shouldn't," Jenny said flatly. "That's the truth of the matter, Cissie."

Margot said, "I could speak to him for you, Mrs. Borders."

"Oh, no! He wouldn't talk to *you!*"

Margot didn't know whether to laugh or scold at that. When she could trust her voice she said, "He needs to see another physician, then, Mrs. Borders. I have enough Protargol to treat you, for now, though someone will have to acquire more. You'll need to keep up the irrigation until long after your symptoms are gone."

The girl didn't answer.

Margot met Jenny's glance above the girl's head, and shook her head helplessly. Jenny's lips tightened, and after a moment she said, "Cissie. We could ask Mr. Connolly to speak to Eldon, tell him he needs to see a doctor whether he wants to or not. The Connollys don't want the clap in their bunkhouse."

Cissie wiped her nose on her sleeve and chewed on her lip, considering. "He don't like talking about such things."

"That's too bad," Margot said. "But sometimes we have to deal with things we would rather not think about."

Cissie said, "I guess."

"Shall we let Mrs. Parrish handle it, then, with the Connollys?"

Cissie only shrugged. Margot sighed, and reached into her bag for a fresh pair of gloves, and tugged them on. "Well, Mrs. Borders. Lie back again, please. Let's get your treatment started, at least."

* * *

It was midnight before Margot finished with her unexpected patient, and completed the cleanup required, making sure the blankets and sheets on the bed were soaking in Lysoform, cleaning her instruments in the same mixture, wrapping them to be boiled later. Jenny helped her, following her instructions, asking a question now and again.

They started back to the Parrish place under a sky so brilliant with stars the road was almost as clear as it might have been in daylight. Jenny turned around in the front seat to say, "Thank you, Margot dear. I know that was a lot to ask."

"Don't mention it," Margot said. "It's wasted effort if they're not both treated, though."

"I'll drop in on Lettie Connolly tomorrow. I'll be as discreet as I can, but make clear that Eldon needs medical care."

Frank said, "Not the only doughboy to bring a disease home from France."

"No," his mother said. "Definitely not."

"I can send you some pamphlets," Margot said. She was tired now, her eyes scratchy from the dry air. Her face felt dry, too, and a little sunburned. "Seattle General keeps them in the lobby."

"I'll pass them around," Jenny said, "though the church ladies won't like it."

Frank chuckled. "They'd rather have their daughters infected with the clap." Robert laughed, too, and Margot smiled into the darkness. It was a relief to be with people who spoke plainly about things. She felt a rush of affection for her in-laws.

As she and Frank, hand in hand, climbed the narrow staircase to their bedroom, Jenny called after them. "Have a good sleep-in," she said. "No need to get up early."

Margot gave her a grateful smile. Frank said, "Thanks, Mother. 'Night, Pop."

"Good night, son."

Jenny said, "Thank you again, Margot. I can't tell you how much it means to have you here, however briefly. Sleep well."

Margot raised a hand in acknowledgment, and she and Frank went up to bed.

CHAPTER 23

Margot meant to sleep in, as her mother-in-law had suggested, but as the early summer sunshine spilled through the bedroom window, she woke to the rattle of a motor and the answering bark of the bunkhouse collie. Frank slept on, his cheek nestled deep in his pillow and a spill of black-and-silver hair falling across his forehead. Margot lay on her back for a moment, wondering who would drive up the long lane to the ranch house at this early hour.

She heard the door of an automobile open and close with a fearsome screech of metal, then hurried footsteps on the porch. Giving up on sleep, she slipped out of the bedclothes, trying not to disturb Frank, and reached for her dressing gown just as she heard a heavy knock on the kitchen door. She went to the window and looked out into the yard, where a dusty truck was parked just in front of the steps. The visitor must have gone around to the side, familiar with Jenny's habits. Margot left the bedroom quietly, and went into the bathroom, where she could see Jenny and Robert had already taken their turns at the washbasin.

When she felt she was presentable enough, but still in her

dressing gown, she started for the stairs. She met Jenny on her way up, already in her apron, her gray hair pinned into a roll and covered with a kerchief.

"Oh, Margot! I'm so sorry, but—there was a telephone call for you. At the general store in Florence. The manager drove out to tell you. I'm afraid it's your father."

Margot put a hand to her throat. "Father? Is he ill?"

"Oh, no, no, I'm sorry. I said that badly. I meant, it was your father calling, and he needs to speak to you."

"Oh. Do you know anything more?"

"No, I don't, dear. I'm sure if it was something really upsetting, he would have said so."

He wouldn't have made the call, though, Margot knew, unless it was urgent. She hadn't realized he had a way to reach her, but she supposed he and Frank had worked that out together. "What do I need to do? I'll need to drive to Florence, I suppose."

"It's the only telephone in the Valley, unless you go all the way to Hamilton."

"I'll dress."

"Yes. I have coffee ready, and I'll make you some sandwiches. Wake Frank. The two of you can take the Model T."

In less than half an hour, Jenny was standing in the kitchen doorway, looking worried as she waved them on their way. Frank explained to Margot that the surrounding ranches shared the expense and the use of a single telephone. "Your father asked if there would be any way to reach us if he needed to. I told him he could call there, and someone would let us know."

"I appreciate the foresight. This is nerve-racking, though."

Frank took one hand off the wheel to briefly hold hers. "I know, sweetheart. I'm sorry."

"It could be Blake. I worry about his heart."

"Too soon to worry, Margot. Wait until you know."

"You're right. I know that." Still, she found herself jiggling her foot against the floorboards, and clenching and unclenching one hand against her thigh.

"Could you eat a sandwich? There's tomato and cheese, and I think fried egg."

"It's so sweet of your mother, Frank, but I couldn't. Not yet."

They drove on through fields of hay and wheat, and once or twice Frank waved to crews working near the road. "One Horse, they used to call Florence. Funny old name, isn't it?"

"One Horse? What does that mean?" Margot knew he was trying to distract her, but she welcomed it.

"You might think they called it that because it's so small, but in fact, they named it for a creek that runs nearby. Then someone renamed it after his daughter. It's not much more than the general store, a filling station, and a tiny little church."

"The only telephone in all this country?"

"That's it," he said. He braked, and turned into a dusty road that led across a dry, empty field. In the distance, she could just make out a cluster of buildings set against a hillside. "Could be a while before one of the telephone companies decides it's worth it to string wire out here."

"We take so much for granted in the city," Margot said.

"Good to remember that sometimes."

They pulled up in front of the general store, and Margot made herself wait for Frank to turn off the motor, to get out, to hold her door open. She climbed out onto the running board, and straightened her skirt before she took his hand, and stepped down onto the packed dirt of the street. The heat was already rising, but the interior of the store was dim and cool. The air smelled of burlap and coffee and the tang of cigar smoke. Frank led the way to the back, where the telephone was hung on the wall. He spoke to the proprietor, Bill, the same man who had driven all the way out to the Parrish place with the message, and then he nodded to Margot. "Go ahead, sweetheart."

"I'll reverse the charge, Frank."

"That would be easiest. Otherwise, we'll leave some money."

She picked up the receiver, and held it to her ear while she waited for the exchange. She gave the switchboard operator the number of Benedict Hall, and the woman said, "I'll connect you, but it will take a few moments. This is the Missoula exchange, and we'll need Seattle."

"Shall I hang up the receiver?"

"Yes, ma'am. I'll ring you back as soon as I reach your party."

While she waited, Margot paced the aisles of the little store, until Frank came and put an arm around her shoulders. "Take it easy, sweetheart," he said. "I'm sure it's going to be all right."

"I can't help myself," she said.

"Come on, Bill has a coffeepot on. Drink a cup."

Obediently, Margot followed him to the counter, where Bill, with a hand-rolled cigarette hanging from his lower lip, poured coffee into a heavy white pottery mug, and offered her a glass jar of the yellowest cream she'd ever seen. The coffee was strong, but the cream was sweet and rich, and the combination tasted good. She took two or three sips before the telephone emitted a shrill ring. She set down the mug, and strode back to answer.

"Yes," she said into the mouthpiece. She had to bend slightly to speak into it. "Yes, this is Dr. Benedict."

"Margot! Oh, thank goodness."

"Ramona? Is everything all right there? Blake? Louisa?"

"Yes, yes, everyone here is fine. I told Father Benedict I would get a message to you, though. It's hard where he is—"

"Where he is? Isn't he in Seattle?"

"No, he's in Walla Walla."

Margot's heart skipped a beat. She had always thought when people said that, they meant it figuratively, not literally, but in this case, she felt the slight pause of her heart muscle, and the flutter in her chest when it resumed. She had to swallow through a suddenly dry mouth. "Walla Walla," she said. Her voice was steady, but her thoughts raced.

This was a problem that was supposed to be resolved. It was the burden she had carried too long, that had shadowed every part of her life. It had been—presumably—lifted.

She said, "What's Father doing there, Ramona? Is Mother with him?"

"She went alone," Ramona said. "She slipped out in the middle of the night, we think. And she took Miss Morgan with her."

"Miss Morgan? Who's that?"

"It's a long story, I'm afraid. Some friend of Preston's, from before . . ." She didn't finish the sentence, but Margot understood. She knew precisely what she meant by "before."

Margot set her teeth, trying to accept that Preston still had power. That he was still tormenting the family. She drew a tight breath through her nostrils, and said in a hard voice, "What happened, Ramona?"

"I don't know, Margot, I really don't. Mother Benedict disappeared, and your father guessed where she'd gone. Bronwyn—that's Miss Morgan—disappeared at the same time. Blake drove your father to Walla Walla, and apparently Mother Benedict had collapsed by the time they got there."

"Dr. Dunlap is with her, isn't he?"

"Yes, but Father Benedict—he wants *you*, Margot. He says he needs you. He's afraid to attempt the long drive home without you being there to take care of your mother."

"Of course. Can you call him? Is he at the sanitarium?"

"The Dunlaps have put them up there."

"Tell Father I'll be there as soon as I can. Wait just one moment, and I'll ask Frank."

She lowered the earpiece, and turned to find Frank standing close behind her. "Could you hear?" she said.

"Most of it. Walla Walla?"

"Yes. Father needs me."

"We can fly, Margot. There are fairgrounds there. Other pilots have used them."

"How long?"

"We can get away this afternoon. The weather's good. We can be there before it's too dark to land."

She lifted the earpiece again. "Ramona, tell Father we'll be there by tonight. As soon as we can. Tell him we'll land at the fairgrounds."

"I will. Thank you, Margot. And thank Frank for me—for all of us."

"Of course. But, Ramona—what did Preston do? Did he hurt anyone?"

"I don't know. Father Benedict says there was a scene. Your mother had hysterics, and then collapsed."

"A stroke?"

"No one said that, Margot. I just don't know anything further."

"What about this girl? This Miss Morgan? Where is she?"

"I wish I knew. Her parents are here, and they're frantic."

Margot's first flight had been on their honeymoon, when Frank took her up in one of the Jennys he had been studying. Before then, her experience of flight had been limited to treating the injuries of pilots who had crashed, or come to grief in some other way. She had been anxious, that day at March Field, but eager, too. Her heart pounded with excitement as Frank helped her up into the forward seat and adjusted the straps around her. As the propeller began to turn and the Jenny bumped forward along the packed dirt of the airfield, she had felt terror and delight in equal parts. Once they were in the air, her fear was forgotten in the exhilaration of soaring above the green California valley, grinning at the curious birds that dipped and darted around the airplane.

She had enjoyed their flights from Seattle to Spokane, and then on to Missoula. Frank was right that the Model 21 was almost too easy to fly, and when he allowed her to take the controls, the sensation was unlike anything she had ever felt. She loved sailing high above the mountains, flying through clouds, tasting the wind in her teeth. She meant to learn, one day, everything about flying an airplane.

But today, all that mattered was its practicality. By air, the distance was just over two hundred miles. She and Frank would reach Walla Walla in a fraction of the time it would have taken to drive, or to go by train.

Jenny and Robert didn't speak of their disappointment over the abrupt end of their visit. Robert filled the Model T with gasoline while Jenny helped them pack the few things they had brought. They were off again in short order, with Robert at the wheel, to drive back to Missoula, where they had left the airplane. Jenny had to stay behind to cook for the haying crew. She gave each of them a brief, hard hug, and stood on the porch in her apron, the collie at her knee, shading her eyes with her hand as they rattled away down the lane. Margot waved until she couldn't see her anymore.

Frank had arranged in advance to have fuel in the airplane, so once they reached it, they said a quick farewell to Robert, and were in the air soon afterward. Frank had studied the maps as they drove back to Hale Field, and pointed out their route to Margot.

"We'll head straight west at first," he said. "You'll be able to see the confluence of the rivers—the Bitterroot, the Blackfoot, and the Clark Fork. When we're over the mountains, we'll follow the Snake River Canyon, and where the Snake meets the Columbia, we're there."

She could see all of that clearly once they were aloft. The weather was fine, the patchwork of fields below them laid out as if by a talented painter, green and yellow and brown, with an occasional road running between them like a narrow dark ribbon. Frank pointed to one of those, and called, "We could land if we had to. Just so you know."

Margot tried to enjoy the flight, to put off worrying about her mother until she could assess her condition for herself. She gazed down at the ranches and farms beneath them, and felt a stab of nostalgia for the Parrish place, for the friendly, easygoing people she had met, and for her mother-in-law. In her medical bag, she carried a tiny bag of dried herbs, which Jenny said might help to calm Edith. It was a mixture of lavender and skullcap and belladonna, meant to be steeped into a tea. Margot thought it was worth trying. In the year Preston was believed to be dead, her mother had taken enough laudanum to last anyone a lifetime.

Margot feared the excess of laudanum had permanently affected Edith's mind.

They flew through the heat of the day, but the air, once they climbed above the green flanks of the mountains, was pleasantly cool. Margot was glad of the goggles that shielded her eyes from the unfiltered sunshine. Well before the sun began to sink in the west, they spotted the town, nestled among yellowing fields. Ten minutes later they were circling the fairgrounds, searching for the open field where they could land. As Frank guided the airplane to a stop near a cluster of low barns, Margot saw the Cadillac waiting for them in the road beyond. It was so dusty its color was all but obscured. As they climbed down, Blake came across the rough ground to meet them. He had his cane in his hand, but he used it sparingly.

As Frank busied himself securing the airplane, Margot hurried to meet Blake, pulling off her goggles and helmet as she walked. They didn't embrace, but she put out her free hand, and he took it in his strong grip, squeezing her fingers, nodding acknowledgment of the haste of their meeting.

"How is she?" Margot asked.

"We're told Mrs. Edith suffered a long bout of hysterics," he said gruffly. "By the time Mr. Dickson and I arrived, yesterday evening, she had stopped all of that. Now, she just—she just stares. She hasn't spoken."

"Not a word?"

He shook his head.

"Did she sleep?"

"I don't know, Dr. Margot. The Dunlaps very kindly secured me a room behind the kitchens. Mr. Dickson and Mrs. Edith stayed in one of the upper rooms, and I believe Mrs. Dunlap attended Mrs. Edith through the night."

Frank reached them, and he and Blake greeted each other as all three of them started toward the automobile.

Blake opened the rear door, and held it. Margot paused on the running board. "Blake, what about Preston? Did you see him?"

"No. Mr. Dickson did, but only through the window of his room. He was—he was restrained, Mr. Dickson said."

"I see." Margot sat down, and moved over to make room for Frank. "It must have been bad," she said, half to herself.

Blake was climbing into the driver's seat. As he pressed the starter, he spoke over his shoulder. "I think it must have been, Dr. Margot. Mr. Dickson wants to speak with Preston, but he thought it best to wait for you."

"Poor Father. He's had a terrible night."

"Yes." Blake pulled out into the road, and turned away from the fairgrounds. "I have to say, though, if you'll permit me, I'm glad to have you both safe on the ground."

"Fly with me one day, Blake," Frank said. "Then you'll know you shouldn't worry."

Yellow dust billowed around them as they drove, and the Cadillac jounced on the dirt road. Margot thought wistfully of the sweet air she had so recently breathed, and sighed.

Blake said, "There's a Thermos of coffee on the seat, Major. If you and Dr. Margot could share the cup?"

"Thoughtful of you, Blake. Thanks." Frank found the Thermos, and poured coffee into the attached cup. They took turns sipping it.

"Are you hungry?" Blake asked.

"My mother sent us with some sandwiches," Frank said.

"I hope you found your parents well?"

"We did. It was a good visit."

Margot added, "It was marvelous, Blake. A wonderful vacation."

"I know Mr. Dickson was sorry to make you cut it short."

"That's all right," Frank said. "We'll go back again when—when things are settled."

Margot cast him a grateful glance. "I haven't had a chance to say, Frank, but I'm sorry, too. And sorry to miss flying home with you."

"Another time, sweetheart," he said, and patted her hand.

She turned hers over, and wound her fingers through his. "I love it there," she said quietly. "I didn't know I would."

"So glad," he said.

Margot's heart sank when she saw her mother. Edith's face was blank. Her eyes were open, but empty. She was sitting in an upholstered chair, her hands limp in her lap, her chin slightly dropped. Someone had brushed her hair and washed her face. It had been some time since Margot had seen her mother without cosmetics, and the lack of them made her seem somehow exposed. Naked. She wore a linen frock, the material bedraggled and in need of laundering. Her brooch was one of her favorites, emeralds and rubies in a flower spray, one she kept for special occasions. Seeing it made Margot's throat ache with sorrow.

She crouched beside her mother, taking her hand, speaking gently to her. There was no response. She lifted her eyelids, one by one. The pupils looked normal, and Edith's color was adequate. Margot lifted one of her mother's hands to feel her pulse, which was a little bit rapid, but strong enough. When she released it, it fell into its original position as if there were no strength at all in the muscles.

Margot straightened, and found Dr. Dunlap in the doorway. She said, "Just one moment, Doctor." To her father, she said, "There's no immediate danger. I'll speak with Dr. Dunlap, and be right back. Frank, do you mind—"

"I'll be right here, Margot."

Dickson said, "Thank you for coming, daughter. And you, Frank."

Frank said, "No thanks necessary, sir. Glad you could reach us."

Comforted by this exchange, Margot stepped out into the corridor. "Dr. Dunlap. Something happened, I gather."

"Your brother—he was—well, he was agitated. Extremely agitated. It was upsetting to Mrs. Benedict, and I have to say, as I've explained to Mr. Benedict, that we're not really equipped to deal with—with—"

"Mental illness."

"Yes."

"There's no need to be tactful, Doctor. I know my brother's condition very well."

He pushed his spectacles up on his nose. "We deal with issues of general health here, Dr. Benedict. Lung cases, or anaemia. Patients come to us for rest and recuperation."

"We appreciate the special arrangements you've made for Preston."

"Yes. We felt we had to shackle him at first, for which I apologize. Once he was sedated, we fitted him with a restraint jacket. It's a bit more comfortable, I believe, and it keeps him safe."

"I'm sure my father has no complaint."

"The thing is—we didn't expect Mrs. Benedict, and we certainly didn't expect this young woman. It seems the two together were too much for the patient, and he—he simply—well. Of course I knew he had problems, or he wouldn't be here. But I have never seen anyone so angry."

Margot had seen Preston angry many times. She knew what his outbursts could be like. She suspected that now, with all his power gone, they were the only outlet for what troubled him. It seemed pointless to discuss it. She said only, "My mother was frightened? Did she think Preston was going to hurt her?"

"I don't know," he said. "She was hysterical for quite some time, and when neither my wife nor I could calm her, I gave her a sedative I sometimes use for patients who are having trouble sleeping."

"What drug was that?"

"Tincture of valerian. We administered four ccs."

"That's quite a small dose."

"Yes. I don't see how it could account for her present condition."

"What about this young woman you mentioned, Dr. Dunlap?"

"She was introduced as Miss Morgan, and she arrived with Mrs. Benedict. That's all I know about her. It was she who seemed to—to be the cause."

"Of Preston's outburst, you mean."

"Yes, I'm afraid he rather lunged at her. He was shouting, but I couldn't make much sense of what he said. Oscar was present, naturally—he's the orderly who keeps an eye on your brother. No real harm came to the young lady, but she ran off, and we haven't seen her since."

"You haven't medicated my mother since last night, then."

"No. My wife managed to get her to take a bit of water, but no food. She's been sitting very much as you see her now."

Margot pushed her fingers through her hair. "I've seen this reaction before, Doctor. In my residency, we treated a number of soldiers. We called it shell shock, and it sometimes looked just like that. Apathy. Detachment. It usually resolves in a day or so, but I'll keep a close eye on her."

"Naturally, you can stay here as long as you like, Dr. Benedict."

"Thank you, Dr. Dunlap. You and your wife have been very kind." She rubbed her forehead with her fingers for a moment, thinking. "I understand my father wants to speak to Preston. I want to be with him when he does, and I think having the orderly present is a good idea, too."

"We sedated him last night, of course," Dr. Dunlap said. "An injection of potassium bromide, which is all we had on hand. I didn't like to do it against his will, but I couldn't think of any other course."

"You did the right thing. My family doesn't like to think so, particularly my mother, but my brother's illness is quite unmanageable, I'm afraid."

"Would you like another opinion? There are several fine physicians in the town." He put out a hand, and touched her shoulder in a fatherly way. "This has to be painful for you."

Margot gave him a bleak look. "It's an old, old story," she said. "My family has protected Preston for years. I suppose that makes it our fault."

"You shouldn't blame yourself. It's what families do," he said.

"I suppose," she said doubtfully. "I don't think we can do it anymore, though. We can't have this happening again."

"If I may suggest, Dr. Benedict, this isn't the time to make big decisions. Take care of your mother—and yourself, too. We can discuss the next step when the current situation is resolved."

"That's sound advice. Thank you." She glanced back into the room, where her father sat close to Edith, not speaking, but gazing at her as if he might never see her again. Reluctantly, Margot said, "No point in putting this off, I suppose. If Mrs. Dunlap could stay with my mother, you could accompany my father and me. We might as well talk to Preston now."

CHAPTER 24

Bronwyn was jarred out of a heavy slumber by the sound of music. Loud music, in deep, wide chords that erupted out of nowhere, and rattled the floor and the bench beneath her. Her brain was thick with sleep and fatigue, and for a few seconds she couldn't remember where she was, or why.

She was lying on something hard, a bench, or a bare floor. She felt beneath her head with her fingers, and found a book serving as a makeshift pillow. Her legs were curled up beneath her sweater, which was drawn over her like a blanket. The bones of her ankles rubbed against the unforgiving wood, and her uncushioned hip had gone numb. She blinked into wakefulness, and when she remembered, she drew a sharp breath of dusty air that made her cough.

This wasn't a bench. It was a pew. Her pillow wasn't a book. It was a hymnal. And the music—

Another crash of sound came from somewhere above her, the thundering tones of a pipe organ. It surrounded her with an army of notes, prodding her, urging her to get up, to flee.

The events of the day before came back to her in a fearsome

rush, the sight of Preston's disfigurement, his ugly fury, his scarred hands reaching for her. Most disturbing of all had been the sound of Mrs. Benedict's hysterical sobs underlying Preston's shouts and the answering shouts of the doctor and the orderly.

Bronwyn had run as fast and as hard as she could out into the road, and turned blindly toward the town. She had run until she couldn't run anymore, and then she had walked until she staggered. All she could think of was getting away, escaping from the sanitarium, from the twisted perceptions of Mrs. Benedict, and from the creature Preston had become.

The fire had burned away a façade, a false front behind which he had been hiding. That façade had crumbled away, revealing the real man. She had wasted three years dreaming of someone who had never existed in the first place. Where did that leave her?

She coughed again, and again, trying to muffle the sound with her hands. She was desperately thirsty, and she needed a bathroom.

The music stopped suddenly. The high ceiling above her head still resounded with the last notes, but also with the echoes of her coughing. Feet clattered somewhere, growing louder and louder, surely those of someone hurrying down a set of uncarpeted stairs.

Bronwyn, alarmed, pushed herself up. She slid the hymnal back into its slot, gathered up her handbag, and scrabbled under the pew for her shoes. She tried to put them on, but her feet were covered in blisters, and so swollen they wouldn't fit. Wincing, she tried wriggling her toes, then pulling at the heels, but it was no use. She gave it up. Carrying her shoes in her hand, she sidled between the pews in her stocking feet.

Light poured through stained-glass windows, coloring the shafts of sunshine that fell across the polished wood of the pews and the inlaid floor. When she had stumbled in here so tired she could no longer stay upright, the church had been dim. She had seen nothing of its interior. She had felt her way to the nearest pew, collapsed onto the bare wood, and despite the nightmare images whirling through her mind, fallen fast asleep. It seemed she had slept right through the night.

Now she stood in the aisle, the cool marble soothing her aching feet, and tried to orient herself. There were doors on every side, and she had no idea which one she had used when she came in. She turned her back to the altar, where a gold candelabra glittered with colored light, and faced the double doors at the opposite end of the nave. As she started toward them, a small man appeared, a book of music under his arm and a pair of round spectacles shoved up onto his thinning gray hair. His eyes were gray, too, and as round as the lenses of his glasses. He stood in the aisle, blocking her path.

Bronwyn's throat was so dry she could barely speak, but she croaked, "Oh! Oh, I'm sorry! I—I fell asleep on the—the—" She pointed to the pew she had just vacated, but a fresh fit of coughing seized her so she couldn't finish her sentence.

The man lowered his spectacles, peered through them, then shoved them back onto his head. "You slept in a pew?" he said. His voice was high and startled, and his eyes grew even rounder. "All night?"

Bronwyn put a hand to her throat. "I didn't mean to," she said hoarsely. "I was—I was lost," she finished. It was hardly an excuse, though it was true enough. She was fairly certain she had reached Walla Walla, but she didn't know how she had found this church, or even what church it was. For the first time since it had all happened, tears flooded her eyes and closed her throat. Her nose instantly began to run. She swiped at it with her sleeve, coughing and sobbing at the same time.

The little man reached into his breast pocket, and held something out to her. She glanced down, and saw that he was offering her an enormous white handkerchief edged with black embroidery. The kindness of the gesture broke down the last remnants of her control. She burst into a full bout of tears, burying her face in the stranger's handkerchief, her shoulders shaking.

The strange man tutted, and with small, gentle hands, turned her about. He guided her down the aisle between the pews, then on through a door to one side of the altar. Moments later, she was seated at a table in some sort of anteroom. The room was scattered with chairs, and a row of wooden pegs on the wall opposite her held robes and stoles in various colors. The man pressed a glass of water into her hand, and when her sobs had eased enough, she drank it straight down. He refilled it from a fat pottery pitcher, and then, as she drank again and wiped at her eyes, still sniffling with the aftermath of her tears, he filled a kettle and set it on a small electric range. He opened the enamel doors of a cupboard, and brought out a gaily flowered teapot and two matching cups.

He didn't speak again until the kettle had boiled, and the tea was steeping beneath a crocheted cozy. He had laid his book of music on one end of the table, and taken off his black suit coat, leaving him in snowy shirtsleeves and a waistcoat with a satin back. He pointed to a washroom just outside the room, and Bronwyn gratefully went to use it. When she came back, he had set out a creamer and sugar bowl and two silver spoons, and was pouring out the tea. She sat down again, embarrassed at her unshod feet, the state of her reddened nose and swollen eyes, and the dampness of the handkerchief clutched in her hand. She didn't know what to say, but the small man smiled at her as he placed a full teacup on a saucer and set it before her.

"Now, my dear young lady," he said in his high-pitched voice. He took a teacup for himself, and tapped his fingertips neatly on the table, as if calling a meeting to order. "Now," he said again. "I believe I should introduce myself. I am Mr. Bernard. I'm the interim organist here at the First Presbyterian Church—my practice session seems to have woken you, for which I apologize— and I'm also the caretaker. May I have the pleasure of making your acquaintance?"

"Bronwyn Morgan," she said, in a tear-swollen voice. "S-so kind of you, M-Mr. Bernard." She started to put out her hand to shake his, then realized she was still holding his crumpled, tearstained handkerchief. She withdrew her hand with a little gasp, which made her hiccup. Helplessly, she pressed the handkerchief to her mouth again. When she had regained a bit of control, she said, "Oh, gosh. I'm so sorry."

"Now, now, no need for that." He took a delicate sip of tea. His smile was prim and constrained, but his eyes were bright with interest. "You are a damsel in distress, I believe. I must tell you, Miss Morgan, that I am quite enamored of playing the role of knight in shining armor." He gave a light laugh. "We musicians tend to be romantic, I'm afraid. You can see by looking at my modest person that in the general way of things, I am not a romantic figure. Perhaps this is my chance." He gave a small, self-deprecating laugh. "Why not tell me your tale of woe, Miss Morgan? Perhaps I can be of some help."

Bronwyn heaved a shuddering sigh, and picked up her teacup to take a steadying sip. She set it down again with a decisive click, determined to hold on to her composure. "I'm in a bit of trouble, Mr. Bernard," she said.

His eyebrows drew together. "Are you? Aside from being lost?"

"Yes."

He pressed his lips together, and looked stern. It was an expression that didn't sit well on his kindly face. "If that is the case, Miss Morgan, I had better call one of the ladies of the altar committee. One of them would be better suited . . ."

She realized, watching him frown, that he had misunderstood. "Oh, no, Mr. Bernard, not that kind of trouble. I'm not—that is, I—" She picked up her cup again, and stared into its amber depths. "It's not like that," she sighed.

His prim smile returned, and he poured more tea into his cup. "Well, then, that's a very good thing," he said cheerfully. "Surely whatever's wrong can be mended."

"I don't know exactly," she said. He tipped his head to one side, waiting for her to go on. "It's just that I shouldn't be here. It's a long story, and awfully hard to explain. The thing is—I need to go home. I *should* go home. But I have spent the last of my money."

"Parents?"

"Yes. My parents must be terribly worried."

"Well." Mr. Bernard twinkled at her above the rim of his cup. "Let's drink our tea, shall we? Then I believe we can do something about sending you on your way. Where is your home, Miss Morgan? Will a train ticket do?"

Two hours later, Bronwyn boarded the train once again. She carried with her a lunch packed by Mr. Bernard himself, who, it turned out, lived in the manse right next to the church. He had paid for her ticket with a withdrawal from the church's charity box.

"I will repay the cost," she assured him, as they shook hands at the station.

"You mustn't worry about that. It's what the charity fund is for," he said. He released her hand, and nodded toward the train already chugging into the station. "Have a good journey, Miss Morgan. I will take pleasure in thinking how relieved your parents will be when they see you."

She had recovered from her fit of tears, and had managed to restore her hair and her dress to some sort of order. Her feet were still swollen, and her shoes painful, but at least she had managed, with difficulty, to get them on. She promised herself the moment she was in her seat, she would take them off.

As distressing as it had been to cry in front of a perfect stranger, her bout of tears had left her mind and her heart clear for the first time in months, and she welcomed that unexpected side effect. She felt as if a bright new morning had broken after a long, long night of storms and darkness, as if the tears had washed away the fog that had clouded her mind for so long. She knew, now, what she needed to do.

She had said this to Mr. Bernard, her acquaintance of all of two hours, as they walked to the station. "I've been lost for some time," she said. "Not only on this trip, but for much longer. Years."

He had bestowed his little smile on her, and nodded so that his spectacles flashed in the July sunshine. "You are very young,

Miss Morgan. I believe most of us do things when we're young that we regret as we get older. I find this to be true of myself, I assure you."

"I can't imagine you making a mistake," Bronwyn said. "You seem to know just what to say and what to do."

"But I'm quite old," he said. "I have learned some lessons, at least."

"Well," Bronwyn sighed. "It seems that when I make a mistake, it's a big one."

"The thing is," he said, as they stepped inside the station and crossed to the agent's window, "you have plenty of years ahead of you to set things right."

That was what she concentrated on, as she waved farewell to her unlikely champion from the window of the train. She tugged off her shoes with a sigh of relief, and removed her hat to lay it in the empty seat next to her. She tipped her head back against the shiny velvet upholstery, but she didn't mean to sleep, at least not yet. She had things to think about. Mr. Bernard was right. She had time to repair some of the damage her mistakes had wrought.

She wanted to make amends to her parents for the worry and pain she had caused them. She wanted to build a life that was her own, not her mother's, nor even her father's idea of what was proper. She didn't want to live Clara's life, or Bessie's. She wanted to live her own life, in her own way.

All of these things she thought about as the train carried her westward, these and the most important one of all. She would begin, she promised herself, by telling Olive Ryther her real name and her real purpose in coming to the Child Home, and she would ask what had become of her baby. She wanted to assure herself he was safe and cared for. She needed to banish the image of a child abandoned in the yard, sickening and dying all alone.

Once she knew her baby was all right, she could go forward. It was the most important mistake she had to rectify.

As she tipped her head back, and let her eyelids grow heavy, she thought, strangely, of Captain Albert and his brave little boat. She was a bit like that boat herself, more than a little battered, but still strong and capable. If someone like Albert could make his own way, she thought, build a life with only a willingness to work, she could, too. Her mother would hate it, and her father would forbid it, but she would stand up for herself. She must. This was the twentieth century, after all.

CHAPTER 25

Margot approached Preston's room with reluctance. She kept her pace steady, and her grip on her father's arm firm, but that was for his sake. Inwardly, she rebelled at having to revisit a problem that was supposed to be solved.

The big orderly pulled a ring of keys from his pocket, and sorted through at least a dozen of them before he came to the right one. With a clank of the old-fashioned lock, he pulled the door open. He went in first, stood aside for Dickson and Margot and Dr. Dunlap to enter, then closed the door and stood just inside it, his arms folded and his small eyes watchful. Margot had the impression that Oscar would welcome another opportunity to overpower the intractable patient.

The room was crowded with all of them inside. It was cooler here than the rest of the building, as there was no outer window, but it was stuffy, smelling of bleach and sweat and something else, something not easy to define. Despair, Margot thought bleakly. Despair, and no wonder.

When she saw Preston, his arms bound by the long sleeves of a white canvas jacket and his eyelids drooping under the influence of the sedative, she resented the wave of pity that swept over her. He didn't deserve her pity. And most assuredly wouldn't want it.

Preston sat on the narrow cot, his back braced against the outer wall, his chin sagging toward his chest. His eyes were closed, but at the sound of the door, they opened. Without lifting his head, he looked up from beneath his scarred eyelids. His eyes flicked from Dickson to Oscar, and then to Margot. He said sleepily, "A deputation. Oh, joy."

Dickson said, "Preston. You've shocked your mother."

At this, Preston sighed, and turned his head away to stare at the blank wall. He said, "She shocked *me*, Pater, bringing that girl here." He wriggled inside his restraints, and Margot knew they must be painful.

"How long have you been in that thing?" she asked.

"Too goddamned long," he said, without looking at her. "I can't feel my fingers at all."

"Dr. Dunlap," Margot said. "The jacket is tied too tightly. It's cutting off his circulation."

"You can take it off, Doc," Preston said. He turned his pale gaze up to Margot, and she knew he was speaking to her. He had called her "Doc" ever since medical school. He had never meant it as an honorific. "I'm harmless now."

Oscar, at Dr. Dunlap's nod, stepped to the bed, and bent to undo the ties behind Preston's back. Preston groaned as feeling began to return to his hands and arms. He rubbed them, then swung his legs over the edge of the bed. He didn't stand up, but sat folding back the long sleeves of the jacket. His burned face was as unreadable as the face of a cliff. "What now, Pater?"

"I thought I should tell you. I'm not going to let your mother come again unless you can be—dependable," Dickson growled. "I have to protect her."

Preston said, "No more visits. Righty-ho."

"It's not funny," Margot said. "Mother's not well, Preston."

His eyes drifted slowly to hers, and fixed on her face. "Perhaps you haven't noticed, Doc," he said, "but I'm not too well myself."

"No excuse," Dickson said.

What was left of Preston's eyebrows lifted. "No? Well, Pater. That seems a tad bit harsh, but there's no need for you to worry." His eyes were clearer now, and Margot thought the sedative must be nearly worn off. He rubbed his arms again, and shook out his fingers. "It won't happen again. I can assure you of that."

Margot said, "Who is this girl, Preston? Why did Mother bring her?"

Preston rested his hands on his knees, and pushed himself up to stand. Oscar tensed, ready to block him, but Preston waved him off. "Down, Oscar, down. I'm quite tame now."

Dr. Dunlap and Dickson exchanged a glance, but Margot kept her gaze on Preston. "Why should she have set you off, Preston? What is it about this girl—"

"This *girl*," he said mockingly, in imitation of his old insouciance. "She has a name, Doc. She is the charming Bronwyn. Bronwyn Morgan." He waved his hand, and executed a mocking bow. "Of the Port Townsend Morgans, if you must know. Only the best for your little brother."

"I still don't understand why she matters so much, or why Mother brought her here."

"Come now, Doc. It's not like you to be slow."

"What do you mean? I know nothing about this girl."

"Well, you should, sister mine. Bronwyn Morgan is the mother of my bastard."

The stunned silence that followed his pronouncement was most gratifying, Preston thought. Father's jaw thrust forward in his customary bulldog way, and his mouth worked, but evidently he couldn't come up with a comment. Dr. Dunlap stiffened at the rudeness of the word, but of course he wouldn't know anything about the circumstances. Oscar just glowered. Oscar was the glowering sort.

But Margot—now, that was amusing to watch. Satisfying.

Her lips paled, and a muscle quivered in her chin. Her eyes darkened until they were nearly black. He had surprised her. No doubt she had believed he no longer had the power.

But the sapphire was here now, hidden behind the leg of his bed, safely tucked into a hole in the plaster. He had kicked it in there during the night, between sedative doses, and he had felt, despite being tied up like a corpse in a shroud, that she was with him. Roxelana, the laughing one, the slave girl who rose to become a queen. He sensed her spirit in the jewel, as he had the first day he laid eyes on it in the dusty shop of the hapless Turk. He had taken possession of it, and she had bestowed her power upon him. He was the only man worthy of it. And she was the only woman worthy of him.

It was a kind of power the great Margot would never know. He would take it with him. He couldn't bear the thought of someone else having it.

The stupefied silence lasted for at least a minute. When Dickson spoke at last, sorrow vibrated in his voice. "Son. Your mother said there was a child, but . . ."

"A boy. Your grandson, Pater. Good news, no?"

Margot said, "Preston, if you're making this up, it's beyond cruelty. Poor Mother!"

"Poor Mother? Whatever do you mean, Doc? She's thrilled!"

"What's become of this child?" Dickson growled. "Where is he?"

Preston shrugged, and said in the lightest voice he could manage, "No idea, Pater. I've been—*away.*" He gave a hoarse chuckle. "I would guess our little Bronwyn doesn't know, either."

"So that's why Mother brought her here. Because of the child." Margot folded her arms, her hands gripping her elbows until the knuckles turned white. "My God, Preston. There's never an end to it, is there?"

"You're looking for an end?"

"Preston," Dickson said somberly. "This is disturbing news. If there's a Benedict child somewhere, I don't see how we can ignore that."

Preston spread his hands and attempted a grin. He knew the effect was ghoulish, nothing like the old charming smile he had always placed faith in. It was all he had, so he offered it one last time. "Thought you should know, Pater. I guessed you wouldn't believe the mater if she told you."

"I wouldn't believe you now, if it weren't for Miss Morgan," his father said.

"Well, then. There you are. How superbly providential."

There was a knock on the door, and Dr. Dunlap put his head out. When he came back, he said, "Mr. Benedict, your wife has asked for you."

"Good, good. I'll go to her. I think we're done here," Dickson said. He squared his shoulders, and thrust his chin at Preston. "Good-bye, son. I don't know when I'll see you again. It may be a while. I hope you'll reflect on all of this. You should write to your mother. Apologize."

Preston wanted to give a snappy answer to that, but none came to mind. It was the drug, he supposed, slowing his thoughts, thickening his tongue. Old Dunlap had gotten carried away with the dose this time, and the worst of it was that it made him soft. He didn't like being soft.

He made himself raise two fingers to his brow in salute. "See you, Father," he said.

"Son," Dickson said. His lips pursed, as if he might have wished to say something more, but like Preston himself, couldn't think of anything. Perhaps, indeed, there was nothing left to say. As he turned to follow Dunlap, Dickson looked diminished some-how, his shoulders slumping and his head down. He glanced back at Margot. "Coming?"

"In a moment. I'm going to have one more word with Preston," she said.

Preston hated the way Margot spoke, as if she never expected anyone to disagree with her. It was just one of many, many things he abhorred about her, and now there was nothing he could do about it. She gave orders to people, and they usually, madden-ingly, obeyed.

He managed to say, "What about Oscar, Doc?"

She eyed him, obviously considering before she said, "Oscar should stay."

Well, no one could call her stupid. She wasn't likely to forget that he had come within a hair's breadth—a razor blade's breadth, more accurately—of putting her out of both their miseries. And she was right. If he were capable of overcoming the sedative, he would gladly put his hands around her neck and squeeze the life out of her.

Instead, he would have to play his final card in this long, long game the two of them had been engaged in. The last blow. It should be one she would feel for a very long time to come.

Margot watched her father leave, and her heart twisted at the way the events of the past three years had aged him. He was like a granite pillar, once seeming invulnerable and unbreakable, but now worn down, as if by the incessant current of a river. Preston had brought such pain to Benedict Hall that she was sure it would take years to fully measure it.

And for how long, she wondered, turning back to face her brother, could they maintain him here? Too many incidents like the one of the day before might cause the Dunlaps to refuse to keep him. It wasn't their business, after all, however profitable they might find it. It could be, in truth, that he belonged in some other place, some less lenient establishment.

"So, Doc," he said. Only his eyes were the same as they had been, glittering with intelligence, humor, and malice. "What now?"

"I'm not going to see you again, Preston. I thought I should tell you that."

"Gosh," he said. He tilted his head, and grinned. "How will I bear up?"

"I've never understood why you feel the way you do about me, but I think I understand you better now."

"Do you, Doc? You think so?"

"I do." She took a step closer, causing Oscar to move also, staying near her elbow. She looked into Preston's face, searching for the brother she remembered behind his distorted features. "I think, Preston, that you were never capable of living in the world the way everyone else does."

"Oh, that's a bit unfair," he said. His gaze met hers without flinching. "I could live in the world just fine, as long as it was on my own terms."

"What terms, Preston? What would you have changed?"

"I think you know."

"It couldn't all be about me. There are always people we don't like, but we manage to go on with our lives just the same."

"You do. I don't."

"You can't just kill everyone you dislike."

"Sad, isn't it? Because I'd prefer that." He laughed without a trace of humor.

"I know you hate it when I use medical terms, but I think there's one that fits you."

"You're thinking of Birnbaum?" he said, with a flick of his fingers. "Oh, yes, I've read him. I've known all about that for a very long time, of course, but aren't you the clever one to figure it out. Yes, it seems your little brother is a psychopath, if there is such a thing."

"So you know. But you don't care."

"That's the very definition, Doc. I don't care." Preston heaved a long sigh, and sank back down on his narrow bed. He leaned back and crossed his legs, the posture looking incongruous in the untied straitjacket, with the sleeves folded back and the tail hanging loose around his waist. "The thing is, Margot," he said, and she thought for just a moment she saw a flash of the man he could have been. "The thing is, I can't change. This is the way I am."

"People can change, Preston. They do it all the time."

"You would have to want to change, though, wouldn't you?"

"Obviously."

He stopped smiling, and regarded her soberly. "You still don't understand, Margot. I don't feel what other people feel. I especially don't feel what *you* feel."

"Yet you're kind to Mother."

He shrugged. "Mother appreciates me. She's the only one."

"Hattie adored you."

He put up one finger. "Ah. Note the past tense."

"What about this girl? The one you claim bore your child?"

"I didn't claim it. She did it. I went to Port Townsend to make certain. She had the child in Vancouver, a boy, and her parents shipped him to Seattle."

"Do you have any feelings for her at all?"

"Nope. Couldn't care less."

Margot glanced to her left, where the orderly stood staring at the ceiling, then looked back at her brother. A wave of sadness swept over her at the futility of all of it, the waste of life and possibility. "If you could feel what I do, Preston," she said softly, "you would be able to understand how sorry I am for you."

His neck stiffened, and his eyes narrowed. "Don't be sorry for me. I don't need it."

"But I can't help feeling it any more than you can help not feeling it. You're my brother, and I grieve for you."

"Grieve for Mother, if you want to grieve for someone. Leave me out of it."

"I'll try." She nodded to Oscar, who pulled out his key ring and began sorting through it. To Preston, she said, "I don't think there's anything more I can do for you."

"Since when did you ever do anything for me, Doc?"

Margot made a wry face. "I tried, Preston, believe it or not. I did try."

"Waste of energy."

"Yes. Evidently."

Oscar had unlocked the door, and was holding it open for her. She turned her back on Preston and started toward the corridor. She had one foot over the doorsill when Preston called, in a low voice, "Doc."

She looked over her shoulder. "Yes?"

"Find the baby. My son. Your nephew."

For a long, long moment Margot gazed into her brother's eyes. They had gone, as they so often had, guileless. Innocent. She didn't trust those eyes, and didn't trust his expression, but there was something in his voice, the vulnerability in his words, that touched her just the same. "Why?" she finally said.

"For the mater."

"You think that will help her?"

"I think it's the only thing that will."

Margot said wearily, "We'll try, Preston, of course. We'll do everything we can."

"And tell her good-bye."

"Do you want to tell her yourself?"

"No. I'm done." He turned away to face the empty wall. Margot watched him for a moment longer, but he didn't speak again. She turned abruptly to walk away. Behind her, she heard the click of the door, and the clank of the key in the lock. Then there was only silence.

CHAPTER 26

"There was no need to lie to me." Olive Ryther sat behind her cluttered desk, wiping her spectacles on a handkerchief. She replaced the glasses on her nose, and picked up a fountain pen. "It wouldn't have made any difference."

"I was afraid you would write to my parents."

"You're not a child, Miss J—I mean, Miss Morgan. You needed a place to live, I believe. You had no money. Your reasons were not my concern."

"Just the same, I'm sorry, Mother Ryther. You were kind to me, and I—well, I'm not proud of running off that way. I didn't really intend to do it. It just sort of—happened."

"Very well." Mrs. Ryther removed the cap of her pen and opened the thick ledger in front of her. "If you've come to apologize, I accept. I don't think I can take you back into my home, however."

"No. I didn't expect it." Bronwyn shifted in her chair. She could see that Mrs. Ryther was eager to get on with her paperwork, but finding the words for what she had to ask was proving to be difficult. It had been much easier to lie to this woman than it now was to tell the truth.

"Something else?" Mrs. Ryther said with a touch of impatience.

"Y-yes." Bronwyn looked down at the handbag in her lap, which still carried a bit of money from the charity box of Mr. Bernard's church. She had managed to pay for a hotel room, which included a bath and a chance to wash her hair and sponge the stains from the dotted swiss material of her borrowed dress. Though the dress and her hat had seen better days, she had done the best she could. She knew she looked down-at-heel, but at least she was clean. She drew a deep breath, and made herself meet Mrs. Ryther's gaze. "Yes, Mother Ryther. I need to tell you that—the thing is—I had a baby. Three years ago."

Mrs. Ryther showed no surprise. "Yes? Did your parents throw you out, then?"

"N-no."

"You were fortunate. Many girls find themselves out on the street."

"My parents—no. They were angry, of course, especially my father."

"Why are you telling me this?"

"Because they sent my baby here. To you. I came to try to find him."

Mrs. Ryther's expression changed at that. She laid down her pen, and folded her hands across the open pages of the ledger book. "That wasn't your decision, Miss Morgan?"

"No, but—they meant well." As Bronwyn said it, she recognized the home truth of her own words. Her parents had indeed meant well. They had tried to do what they thought was best in what had seemed an impossible situation. What was best for her. "I was only sixteen," she said ruefully. "I was shockingly ignorant."

"You've learned a few things since then, I think." Mrs. Ryther smiled a little, and Bronwyn thought it was the first time in their association that she had seen the old woman show any feeling at all. She dealt in action, not emotions, and that could be hard to understand.

"I want to find my child, Mother Ryther. I need to know he's safe. That someone loves him. That he's not—not like the little boy who was just left in the yard. The one who died."

"Whoever left that child here might have meant well, too," Mrs. Ryther said. "Sometimes people simply can't take care of their children."

Bronwyn thought with a pang of her beautiful bedroom, her closet full of clothes, her mother hovering over her. "It's so sad," she breathed.

"Not when we can do something about it." Mrs. Ryther straightened, and spoke crisply. "I have to tell you, Miss Morgan, that your parents were here looking for you."

"Oh! They came here? Did you tell them?"

"How could I? I thought you were Betty Jones."

"Oh, dear. Were they—are they all right?"

"They're terribly worried, of course. Think about it." She fixed Bronwyn with a hard gaze, made even more daunting by the gleam in her spectacles. "You're worried about what's become of your child. You are your parents' child, and naturally they're fearful for you."

"Do you know where they went? I have to find them!"

Mrs. Ryther hesitated, tapping her lips with the closed fountain pen. "I couldn't say, of course, where they are now. But they mentioned something about Benedict Hall. Something about a clipping they found in your room."

Bronwyn jumped to her feet, and tucked her handbag under her arm. "I'll go there," she said. "I know where it is."

"They also asked about your baby, Miss Morgan. Your mother and father."

Bronwyn put a hand to her throat. "What did you tell them?"

Mrs. Ryther came to her feet, too, laying aside her pen, pushing herself up with an effort. "A child," she said stiffly, "is not a toy to be tossed away and then picked up again when you change your mind."

Bronwyn lifted her chin, and met Mrs. Ryther's stern gaze as best she could. It wasn't easy. The bubble of grief and guilt in her chest swelled until she could hardly speak. "I know, Mother Ryther," she said. "As you've pointed out, I'm no longer a child. I've felt like one—and acted like one—for far too long."

Mrs. Ryther nodded. "Then you'll understand. I don't know where your child is now. I remember a baby who might have been yours, brought in by a nurse from Vancouver. He stayed with us for quite some time before he went to a foster family."

"Surely you have records," Bronwyn said.

"As I told your parents, I'm not even sure it's the child you're looking for."

"But it could be?"

Mrs. Ryther pursed her lips. "It's not possible to keep track of every child who comes through my doors, Miss Morgan. That little boy could be the one. He might not be."

Bronwyn tried to adjust the drooping brim of her hat. "I think, Mother Ryther," she said carefully, "that you know where he is. But you don't want to tell me."

"Because I'm not sure."

"I don't know if I'll ever be sure of anything again." Bronwyn started toward the door. "Thank you for seeing me, and for your kindness. I don't know what I would have done."

Her hand was already on the doorknob when Mrs. Ryther said, "I told your parents, and I'll say it to you as well. I think you should keep the baby in your prayers, but leave him be. Go on with your life."

"I suppose I'll have to." Bronwyn turned the knob.

"Wait, Miss Morgan. Where are you going?"

"Benedict Hall. I should reassure my parents."

"I can telephone to them. They had their motorcar, I believe. I'm sure they'll be happy to come and fetch you."

Bronwyn closed her eyes at the thought. Her mother would be

tearful. Her father would be rigid with fury, but he would come. She had to admit, as tired as she was, as emotionally drained, it would be a great relief to hand herself over to them once again. If only it didn't feel like a step backward.

She pressed her forehead to the rough wood of the door, trying to think. For a long moment, she didn't speak, and didn't move. Mrs. Ryther, with uncharacteristic empathy, waited for her. At last, Bronwyn opened her eyes, put her back to the door, and nodded. "Yes, please. I think that would be best."

Blake, Dr. Margot, and the elder Benedicts had been on the road the better part of two days. Mr. Dickson rode in the front seat, while Dr. Margot stayed in the rear with her mother, keeping her medical bag close at hand.

Mrs. Edith spent the drive gazing blankly out the window. Blake was sure she saw none of the scenery, which was a shame. The mountains were richly forested, layered in shades of green from the lightness of feathery pines to the near-black of ancient spruces. Frequent waterfalls spilled beside the road, fed by snowmelt from the peaks and sparkling like diamonds in the sunshine. Despite the grim circumstances, Blake enjoyed the drive. The Cadillac rolled smoothly on the freshly graded gravel, and the mountain air was cool, a relief after the stifling heat of Walla Walla.

He was also, he admitted to himself, glad to have Dr. Margot safely in his own hands. He trusted the motor and the frame of the Cadillac far more than the frail-looking airplane the major favored. He only wished she didn't look so worried.

She wasn't enjoying the scenery, either. She watched her mother, and though she didn't try to get her to speak, she did coax her to take sips of water, and to drink cups of tea when they stopped for food. Blake had to wait outside, of course, as the Benedicts ate. He assured them he was glad of the chance to stretch his legs. Mr. Dickson always sent out a sandwich or a platter of bacon and eggs, and Blake leaned against the hood of the Cadillac to eat his meal.

At their last stop, the Benedicts went into a small roadhouse in Fall City to use the washroom and order sandwiches to last them the rest of the drive. Traffic had increased steadily as they left the mountains, and the driveway of the roadhouse was crowded with trucks and automobiles. Blake dropped his passengers off in front of the entrance, and parked the Cadillac beneath a tall maple that bent so far to one side its branches trailed in the current of the Snoqualmie River. The sun was high and hot. He got out of the automobile to stretch. He removed his driving coat and cap, and lounged against the trunk of the tree, enjoying the fresh breeze that carried the scent of the river up over its banks.

A family emerged from the roadhouse as he stood there, a man and two tall sons, with a woman in a straw hat and a summer dress. They walked toward their automobile, a battered Dixie Flyer, but as they passed, the boys paused to admire the Cadillac. Their father, a thin man in a pair of worn overalls, glanced across the automobile's hood, and spotted Blake. "Hey, boy," he said. His eyes were narrow, fox-like. "Whatcha doin' there?"

Blake pushed away from the tree, and smoothed his shirtsleeves with deliberate movements. "Are you addressing me, sir?"

"You bet I am," the man said. He strutted toward the Cadillac, his thumbs hooked into the pockets of his overalls. "You gotcher eye on this motorcar?"

Blake felt an old, familiar resentment rise from his belly, a resentment he would have to ignore. "Yes, sir," he said, keeping his tone as neutral as possible. "I drive this automobile."

"Oh, yeah? What's a boy like you doin' with a Cadillac?" The man slapped the shining green hood with a grimy hand, then bent to look through the open window.

Blake drew a slow breath, willing himself to be calm. The man's two sons, grinning now, flanked their father on either side. The woman, who had been waving a paper fan to cool her face, folded it, and stood frowning.

"This motorcar," Blake said, "belongs to my employer. I am his chauffeur."

"Oh, yeah?" one of the boys said. He reached in through the

rear window, and fingered the stamped leather of Dr. Margot's medical bag where it rested on the seat. "What's this, then?"

"Sir, if you please," Blake said, although the boy couldn't have been more than fifteen. "That's a medical bag."

The youth grinned. "Yeah? Good stuff inside, then?"

"Nothing you'd be interested in, I'm sure."

Before he could finish his sentence, the boy hooked his finger through the handles of the bag, and hoisted it out through the window. Blake said again, "Please, sir. The bag belongs to Dr. Benedict. She's in the restaurant, but she'll be back in just a—"

The boy was paying him no attention. He held the bag in one arm, and began to work the catch with his other hand. Blake, his belly tight with tension, cast the parents a pleading glance, but the woman had turned away, and the man was smiling as if it was all a great joke.

The catch clicked, and the bag opened. Blake, his options gone, took one long stride forward, and put out his open hand. "Give me that, young man," he said.

The woman belatedly turned, and in a nasal voice said, "Now, Tommy, don'tcha go—"

Her husband threw a hand up in her face. "Shut up, Dolly," he said. "I'll handle this." He thrust his other hand into the pocket of his overalls, and drew out a small, ugly pistol. He held it barrel up, pointing at the sky, and fixed Blake with an angry look from his narrow eyes. "See this, boy?" he snarled. "You best get away from my son, or I'll—"

Blake hadn't heard the footsteps approaching on the packed dirt of the road. He didn't realize she had returned until Dr. Margot's long-fingered hand closed over the handles of her bag, and tore it away from the boy in a gesture violent enough to make him stumble to one side. The man in the overalls whirled to see who had interfered, and found himself looking up into her face, which was drawn in lines as severe as Blake had ever seen.

Her dark eyes flashed, and her voice was almost as deep as Blake's as she said, "Put that thing away this moment."

The thin man stared at her, the pistol hanging limply now

from his hand. Dr. Margot glared at him with her jaw thrust forward. "Your son was interfering with my private property. Get away from here, or I'll have the police after you for attempted theft."

"Oh, miss, he wasn't gonna—" the woman began, but Margot threw her such a hard look that she let her protest die away.

The man thrust the pistol into the pocket of his overalls, and said, "Come on, Dolly. I just didn't want that Nigra givin' you any trouble." He put his arm around his wife's waist, and strutted across the road to his own dilapidated car. His sons trailed after him, and Blake was gratified to see Tommy glance warily back at the tall woman who had taken such swift command, and whom his father hadn't dared to challenge.

Mr. Dickson and Mrs. Edith appeared a moment later, and when Dr. Margot explained what had happened, Mr. Dickson's face darkened. "I'll just have a word," he said, turning toward the Dixie, but Blake stopped him.

"No, sir," he said in an undertone. "Just let it go, if you would, Mr. Dickson."

"I won't have you treated in such a manner!"

"I appreciate it, sir, but we won't see them again. Those people are likely a bit worked up because they've been to that rally. The one in Renton."

"What rally?" Dr. Margot asked.

Mr. Dickson snorted and turned toward the car. "You're right, Blake. Dick mentioned that to me. The Klan meeting."

Dr. Margot groaned. "I forgot, too."

"Damned fools," Dickson muttered.

"It's unconscionable," she said. "People like that—their children will grow up the same way."

Blake said, "Please don't worry about this now," and both Mr. Dickson and Dr. Margot nodded, though reluctantly.

Throughout all of it, Mrs. Edith stood in silence, staring at her dusty shoes. Nothing showed on her face, no recognition or interest. Dr. Margot, with a sigh, opened the back door of the Cadillac and guided her mother into it. With her medical bag in her hand, she moved around to the other side, and moments later they were on their way.

It was unworthy of him, Blake knew, but he took pleasure in the sight in his rearview mirror as he drove away. The man in the overalls was trying to start the motor in his old Dixie Flyer. His two sons were standing to one side, watching him struggle with the crank. They were both laughing.

When they reached Benedict Hall at last, Dickson went directly to his study while Blake garaged the automobile. The house was quiet, Louisa napping, Ramona out shopping. The twins stood in the hall, wide-eyed, as Margot escorted her mother up the stairs and down the corridor to her bedroom. She drew the curtains, and helped Edith to take off her shoes and her dress, then pulled a fluffy quilt over her. "Sleep a little, Mother," she said. "I'll send Thelma to wake you in time to bathe before dinner."

Edith turned on her side and put one hand beneath her cheek. Margot started toward the door, but before she could open it, her mother spoke for the first time in hours. Her voice was thin, as if it took more energy to use it than she had to spare. "Margot."

"Yes, Mother."

"He can't help himself, you know."

Margot turned back to the bed, and knelt beside it so she could look into her mother's eyes. "I do know, Mother. I know what he is."

Edith's eyelids drooped. "God help me," she whispered. "I love him anyway."

Margot did something she hadn't done in years. She leaned forward, and placed a brief kiss on her mother's cheek. "Of course you do," she said quietly. "I know that, too."

Edith didn't say anything more, and in moments her eyes were closed, her shallow breathing steady. Margot got to her feet and slipped out of the bedroom, closing the door without a sound.

She went to her own rooms, and used her private telephone

line to place a call to the Red Barn to make certain Frank had landed safely and that someone had picked him up at Sand Point. The switchboard found him for her, and they spoke briefly before she went to take a much-needed bath. She ran the tub as full as she dared, and stirred in some Palmer Salts. She stripped off her wrinkled clothes and lowered herself into the fragrant water with a groan of pleasure, resolving to stay there until something made her climb out.

She heard Louisa crowing down the hall, and Nurse's soothing voice answering her. She heard the quick footsteps of Loena and Leona ascending the staircase, in tandem as usual, and then the slower ones of someone else descending. She heard the distant clatter of pans in the kitchen, and felt a pang of compunction for Blake, who had probably gone straight to work after putting the automobile away. Still she stayed in her bath, washing her hair, scrubbing her fingernails, until the water began to get cold.

She pulled the stopper in the tub, and climbed out, wrapping herself in a fresh towel. She combed her hair, cleaned her teeth, and went to put on a fresh shirtwaist and a pleated skirt. As she smoothed on her stockings and fastened them, she remembered the comfortable trousers she had worn at the Parrish ranch. "I'm going to order some of those," she told her reflection, as she bent to slip on a pair of low-heeled pumps. "Even if I can only wear them at home."

The day was far gone when she finally emerged from her room. She glanced down the corridor, and saw that her mother's bedroom door was closed. She could hear her father there, speaking, though she couldn't hear if Edith answered. She would send Thelma up to draw a bath for her.

With this task in mind, she started down the staircase. She heard voices in the small parlor, voices she didn't recognize, and she hesitated in the hall, wondering who was there. The kitchen door swung open, and Hattie appeared, swathed in a large plaid apron, and carrying a long-handled ladle in her hand. "Oh, Miss Margot, it's you. We're awful glad you're back!"

"Thank you, Hattie," Margot said absently. "I am, too. Who's in the small parlor?"

Hattie's eyebrows flew up, and she took a step closer to whisper, "It's the Morgans, Miss Margot! That little Bronwyn and her mama and daddy!"

"Oh, Lord," Margot muttered. She had supposed they would have to deal with the girl sometime, but she hadn't expected it to be immediate. "Do you know what they want, Hattie? Does Father know they're here?"

"Mr. Dickson is in his study, but Mrs. Ramona is in the parlor with them. I don't think they want anything but their girl back. You weren't here, so you don't know, but Miss Bronwyn found Miss Louisa over there in the park. Miss Louisa done fell smack dab in that wading pool!"

"Yes, Blake told me about that during the drive. And her parents—"

"Come all the way from Port Townsend, looking for her. They found a packet of clippings in her room, all about Benedict Hall, and they guessed where she might be. And here she showed up, just today, at that Ryther Home. They went off to fetch her in their motorcar, and Mrs. Ramona asked them to stay to dinner." She waved the ladle in the general direction of the kitchen. "I best get back to it, Miss Margot, if we gonna have nine people for dinner."

"Oh, yes, Hattie, of course. Go ahead. I suppose I'd better go and meet them." Margot smoothed her skirt as she walked along the hall to the small parlor and pushed open the door.

Ramona jumped up when she saw her, and Margot had the impression she just barely restrained an exclamation of relief. She said, "Oh, Margot, how good to have you home! May I present the Morgans?"

Ramona began formal introductions, and Margot automatically put out her hand. Iris Morgan was fair, slight, and evidently very shy. Her cheeks flushed as she shook Margot's hand with a tentative grip. Chesley Morgan's handshake was brisk. He fixed Margot with a hard gaze and said, "It seems we owe your family a debt."

"I don't know if that's true, Mr. Morgan. On the contrary, I've heard that your daughter was a great help to—" She turned to face the young woman standing beside the divan.

Like her mother's, the young woman's cheeks had reddened. Margot caught a breath in recognition. "Why, Miss Jones! It's Betty Jones, isn't it?"

"What?" Ramona said. She gestured to the girl. "No, Margot. This is Bronwyn Morgan. You know, the girl who—that is, the young woman—"

The girl's eyes rose to meet Margot's, and Margot knew she hadn't made a mistake. Those gold-flecked eyes were unforgettable.

"It's true, Dr. Benedict," Bronwyn Morgan said, lifting her chin and speaking quickly, as if hurrying to get her confession over with. "I'm sorry I lied to you. I didn't know it was you until—well, I didn't know you were Preston's sister. I had already told Mother Ryther I was Betty Jones. I was kind of stuck."

"Never mind," Margot said firmly, taking the girl's hand and holding it in both of hers. "You were a great comfort to a lonely little boy while he was in your care. Nurse Church and I were grateful. It didn't matter what you called yourself."

Ramona said, "Margot, it seems Mother Benedict was right after all. What Preston told her is true. There's a—a child."

"Yes, he told me that, too."

"Did he? Well, it seems—that is—Bronwyn is . . ."

Bronwyn said, "I'm sorry, Dr. Benedict." She gently removed her hand from Margot's grasp, but she held her gaze. "I never meant to cause any trouble for your family."

"Nor have you," Margot said. "My brother already told me about you, Miss Morgan. Although of course I didn't realize we had already met."

Chesley Morgan said stiffly, "We understand this is a shocking situation, Dr. Benedict. Mrs. Benedict," he added, nodding to Ramona.

"It's not so unusual as all that," Margot said mildly. She crossed to the divan, where she seated herself, and accepted a small glass of sherry from Ramona.

"It is for us," Iris Morgan whispered.

Her husband cleared his throat again, obviously a habit. He said tightly, "We raised our daughter better than that, I can promise you," he pronounced.

Just as Iris murmured, "Chesley, please," Bronwyn said, "No. You didn't."

Mr. Morgan's face suffused with scarlet, and he sputtered, "What? What? What do you mean by that, Bronwyn?"

"I mean," the girl said, staring at her hands folded in her lap, "that I didn't know anything about—about men. I knew I shouldn't go out unchaperoned, but that was all. I didn't have any idea about—" Her voice faltered, but she swallowed and pressed on. "About relations between men and women. I had no idea how babies came about."

Mr. Morgan blustered, "Of course you didn't, Bronwyn! Nice girls don't know that sort of thing until they—well, their husbands—marriage is—"

Margot put up a hand. She spoke in the level tone she employed in her clinic, the voice meant to be objective, and which often went a long way toward calming emotions. "You know, Mr. and Mrs. Morgan, I've been in medical practice for several years now. I've lost count of the unmarried girls I've cared for who found themselves in a similar situation, and almost always through ignorance. I admire Miss Morgan's frankness in speaking of these things." She turned to Bronwyn to say, "It's very late to do this, but I have to apologize for my brother's behavior. He should have known better."

"He should have stood by Bronwyn, once he knew," Ramona added fiercely. "I'm quite sure Father Benedict will want to set things right."

"Oh, no!" Bronwyn exclaimed. She flashed her hazel eyes at Ramona, and then at Margot. "I don't want anything! I know it looks like that, but I only came to Seattle because I knew the baby was sent to the Child Home."

At this, Mr. Morgan shot his wife a venomous glance. Margot caught it out of the corner of her eye, but Bronwyn's gaze was fixed on her, and she didn't see it.

"The baby wasn't there, and I was afraid to ask about him. I came to look at Benedict Hall just because I wanted to see where Preston lived. I thought he was dead, you know. The newspaper reports said he died in the fire."

"Bronwyn, dear, if you hadn't come, I don't know what might have happened to my Louisa!" Ramona said. She stretched out her hand to take Bronwyn's. "Dick and I will always be so grateful. We don't need to speak of—of the other thing—anymore. Don't worry about it."

Bronwyn cast her a grateful glance, and then a wary one at her father. Margot, following this, saw Mr. Morgan turn his face away from his daughter. No forgiveness there, she supposed.

It was the story she had heard too many times, with differing details, at the Women and Infants Clinic. It was as if girls made themselves pregnant, and on purpose. She had never once, in her years of practice, known that to be the truth, but fathers and husbands and lovers behaved as if it were. It was why she risked her reputation by teaching birth control.

She saw Iris Morgan furtively touch her daughter's hand. Bronwyn gave her mother a small smile, and when she saw Margot watching them, a braver one. Margot smiled back. She liked the girl's spirit. She hoped Bronwyn wouldn't allow it to be crushed.

CHAPTER 27

Leona and Loena were setting the places around the long table, arranging stemware and chargers, setting out saltcellars, folding linen napkins. Loena looked up from straightening a candle that had tilted in the candelabra, and said, "Oh! Mrs. Edith! You need something?"

Blake heard her voice from the hall, and crossed to the open door in time to see Mrs. Edith point at the place that was set, as always, to the right of her own chair. "Clear this, Leona," she said. Her voice was thin, but steady.

"Ma'am?" The twins stood like two identical redheaded statues, staring at their mistress. Blake paused in the doorway, uncertain what Mrs. Edith's intention was.

"Take the place setting away," Mrs. Edith repeated. "Preston won't be returning to Benedict Hall."

Loena, always the bolder one, bestirred herself, and came around the table to Mrs. Edith. She folded her hands properly over her apron, and said in a gentle tone, "Are you sure, ma'am? You've always kept his place there. All this time."

"I'm quite certain. Remove it, please."

Loena glanced back at her sister, and gave a subtle nod. Still Leona hesitated, chewing on a fingertip and staring in wonder at Mrs. Edith. Loena whispered, "Go ahead, then." Leona dropped her hand, and dried her finger on her apron before she picked up the charger and flatware, and placed them on an empty tray. When this was done, Mrs. Edith turned away. She passed Blake in the doorway without speaking to him, and began a slow progress up the front staircase toward her bedroom.

When she was gone, Leona said wonderingly, "Blake, what happened out there in Walla Walla? We been setting that empty place for three years, and she wouldn't never let us take it away before."

"Never mind, Leona," he said gruffly. "She is your mistress, and you do as she asks. You don't need to know her reasons. Loena, please go and tell Hattie Mrs. Edith might be needing her. I'll help Leona finish here."

The newly reunited Morgan family was staying to dinner, at Mrs. Ramona's insistence. Hattie had put together a cold salmon platter, a salad of tomatoes and sweet cucumbers from the Market, and baskets of fresh bread she had made that morning, "puttin' all my worries into that dough," as she confessed to Blake. He heard her heavy steps ascending the staircase now as Loena came back into the dining room with a stack of cut-glass dessert plates for the sideboard.

Blake cast a critical eye over the table and found everything in order. He started back to the kitchen and saw Hattie just coming back down the stairs. He waited for her to reach the bottom, his eyebrows lifted in question. She put a finger to her lips and pointed toward the kitchen.

As soon as the swinging door had closed behind them, Hattie said, "Mrs. Edith just sittin' up there at her dressing table, cryin' her eyes out."

"Do you know what's upset her, Hattie?"

"Somethin' about Mr. Preston not coming home no more. I mean, we all knew that, I guess, but she never would believe it."

"Should we call Mr. Dickson?"

"No, Blake, don't do that. He can't help her. She just needs a good cry. Everybody need a good cry now and again."

He smiled at her. "Everybody, Hattie?"

She was bending to take a bunch of parsley from the vegetable bin, and she straightened with a little grunt, and favored him with a friendly scowl. "Well, maybe not everybody. I don't s'pose you do much crying, Blake."

"Not in a very long time."

"Well. At least for Mrs. Edith, she should feel better afterward."

"I don't know, Hattie." Blake sighed as he reached for a chopping knife and handed it to her. "You might as well know. There's a child. Evidently, this Miss Morgan and Preston—"

"Oh, I know all about that chile, Blake."

"You do?"

"Oh, yes. I've been hearin' about that chile for a long time. I didn't say nothin'. I didn't believe it." Hattie ran the parsley under the tap, and gave it a quick shake. As she laid it on a clean kitchen towel, she said, "Mrs. Edith been talkin' about that chile ever since Mr. Preston was in the state hospital. He told her there was a baby. Her grandson."

"I wish he hadn't done that."

"Baby could be a great comfort," Hattie said. " 'Ceptin' we don't know where he is. I can't help thinkin' Mr. Preston shouldn't have troubled his mama with it."

"Mr. Preston will always be a worry to Mrs. Edith, I'm afraid."

"Not just to her, Blake. Mr. Preston is a worry to all of us. Every blessed one."

Hattie's dinner was excellent, the perfect repast for a hot summer evening. The company, in contrast, was as awkward as Margot had ever seen. Chesley Morgan and Dickson exhausted their business conversation early. His wife answered any remarks addressed to her in a barely audible voice, and if her husband cast her a glance, subsided instantly into silence. Ramona did her best to charm the Morgans, to draw Bronwyn out, and to include

Edith in any brief flurry of conversation, but she was fighting an uphill battle.

Margot made an effort, too, and received grateful looks from her sister-in-law, but it didn't help much. Long silences stretched around the table, broken only by the sounds of flatware clinking on china, or the gurgle of water being poured. Margot couldn't help eyeing Bronwyn, wondering at the connection between this young woman and Preston.

Children born to unmarried girls were an old story, but this baby—this one was her own flesh and blood. Her nephew. She hadn't wanted to believe he existed. It had been much easier thinking Preston had deceived their mother, spinning the lie to keep her tied to him. He knew he was her favorite. He had always known that. He had never hesitated to use her preference for him to his own ends. But this . . .

Blake sent Thelma in to clear when the main course finally dragged to its end. Blake set the dessert bowls and brought in a large bowl of fresh raspberries, which he served with spoonfuls of sweetened cream. The combination was delicious, but Margot could see that appetites around the table were flagging. Only Dick and Frank ate everything put before them, but then, neither of them knew the full story of Bronwyn Morgan, and its potential impact on the Benedicts. She envied their ignorance in this case. Preston's last words to her as she left him ran around and around in her mind.

She knew she had to deal with the problem of the child. She would have to speak to Father. He wasn't going to like it, but she had promised, and she would keep her word. It was tempting to think that a promise to someone like Preston didn't really count, but that sort of justification wasn't in her nature. The sooner she discharged the responsibility—at least to the extent of telling her father—the better she would feel.

Ramona said, with forced good cheer, "Shall we have our coffee in the small parlor?"

Margot was certain a change of venue wasn't going to help, but she trooped with everyone else down the hall, and took a chair.

Frank, however, excused himself, saying he had a report to look at before morning. He shook hands with Chesley Morgan, nodded to everyone else, and made his escape. In the doorway he glanced back at Margot and winked. She covered her mouth to prevent an unladylike giggle.

The evening did inevitably draw to a close. The Morgans departed, after effusive and repeated thanks, for the Alexis Hotel. Margot remembered, at the last minute, that Bronwyn needed two more diphtheria injections, and received a promise she would go to her own physician for them. Dickson escorted Edith upstairs the moment the front door closed, and Dick, yawning, trudged after them.

Margot turned to Blake. "Blake, I want you to go to bed. If there's anything left, we'll deal with it in the morning."

He said, "Thank you, Dr. Margot. I am feeling a bit tired."

"It's been an endless day. Ramona, you too. You look exhausted."

"Oh, I am. What a ghastly evening! Aren't you just worn to a frazzle? The only good thing about tonight was Hattie's lovely dinner."

"Be sure to tell her that. Rest well, Ramona."

"Aren't you going to bed?"

"Yes, but I need to speak to Father first. I heard him come back downstairs."

"He's in his study, Dr. Margot," Blake said.

"Thank you, Blake. Good night."

They were all turning to go their separate ways, Blake to the kitchen, Ramona up the stairs, and Margot down the hall to Dickson's study, when the telephone on the hall table rang. The sound jangled on Margot's nerves. Ramona paused halfway up the staircase, and Blake, frowning, turned back from the kitchen door.

"Late for a telephone call," he said.

"Shall I answer it?" Margot said, as it rang a second time.

"No, no, Dr. Margot. You go on and speak to Mr. Dickson. I'll answer it."

Ramona went on upstairs, and Margot knocked on her father's study door as she heard Blake pick up the telephone and speak into it. "Benedict Hall," he said in his deep voice. "Good evening."

Dickson rumbled, "Come in." Margot opened the door, but before she could step into her father's cramped, smoky study, she heard Blake speak again.

"Good God," he said. His voice carried down the hall, and it vibrated with shock. "You're quite right, Doctor. That's the most terrible news."

Margot stopped where she was, her hand on the doorjamb, and gazed down the hall to the spot where Blake stood with the candlestick receiver in one hand, the earpiece of the telephone in the other. He turned to face her, and his expression sent a thrill of horror through her body.

She said, "Blake, what is it?"

He spoke again into the receiver, then cradled it against his chest. "Dr. Margot," he said. "It's the sanitarium. I think—" His voice caught, and he cleared his throat. She heard the South in his voice, the old accent that only surfaced when he was truly disturbed. *Ah think.* "I think you'd better call Mr. Dickson to the telephone."

It was Blake's task to rouse Hattie, and to climb to the third floor of Benedict Hall to knock on the maids' doors and ask them to come down. In their dressing gowns, Hattie with a scarf tied around her tousled hair and the twins with their hair in long braids, the staff assembled as requested in the large parlor. Thelma came, too, in curlers and a wrapper and a pair of worn leather slippers. Only Nurse was excluded, allowed to sleep on in the nursery with her charge, but Mrs. Ramona, Mr. Dick, and Mrs. Edith were all there.

Blake noted that Dr. Margot had fetched her medical bag, and tucked it beneath her chair beside the empty fireplace. The house was cool now, the heat of the day dissipated. Mrs. Ramona and Mrs. Edith were both shivering with the shock of the news,

but there had been no time to lay a fire. Dr. Margot made her
mother sit close to her, and watched her surreptitiously throughout Mr. Dickson's grave announcement. The major stood behind
Dr. Margot, his good right hand resting protectively on her shoulder. Blake saw her put up her left one to touch it.

"This is doubly tragic for us," Mr. Dickson was saying. "Thelma,
you weren't with us at that time, but we thought we lost Preston
three years ago, in the fire that destroyed Margot's first clinic.
Now we have lost our son again. This time there is no doubt. Dr.
Dunlap has his—" He had to stop, and swallow a bit of the brandy
Blake had supplied him with.

They all had a glass, even the twins. Hattie, her round cheeks
glistening with steady tears, hadn't touched hers. Everyone else
had cautiously taken a sip. Thelma's was nearly gone. Mrs. Edith
had drunk down her portion straightaway.

"His remains," Mr. Dickson finished. His voice faltered, and
he drank again. "His body will be sent by train. He will—that is,
it will—arrive in Seattle tomorrow night."

Leona and Loena clung together, eyes wide and freckles
standing out on their pale faces. Thelma watched everyone, no
doubt wondering at the drama that seemed to erupt so often in
this house. Blake thought it would be no surprise if she gave notice after this event.

Mrs. Ramona sniffled softly into a handkerchief, her cheek
resting against Mr. Dick's shoulder. Mrs. Edith was dry-eyed, but
her lips were bloodless and her cheeks as pale as snow. She hadn't
spoken a word.

Dick said heavily, "I don't see how he pulled it off, Father."

"He got out of his room. I saw that door, and the lock on it. I
don't know how he managed it, but he broke the lock."

"Did he—leave a note, or anything?"

"He said good-bye." It was Mrs. Edith, speaking in a flat
voice, staring in the empty fireplace.

Every eye turned to her, and Mr. Dickson made a sudden
sound in his throat, as if in protest. He said, "What, dear?"

"Preston. He said good-bye, and I knew." She looked up at

her husband, and then around at the rest of them. "He couldn't live that way. So sensitive."

Blake saw the twist of Dr. Margot's mouth, and the tightening of the major's hand on her shoulder, but neither spoke.

Mrs. Edith said after a moment, almost absently, as if it were now of no consequence, "I took him the sapphire. The one he liked so much. That's probably how he managed it."

Now Dr. Margot sat forward. "Mother—you took it to him? Still with that jagged concrete around it?"

"Oh, yes," Mrs. Edith said. She moved her hand, limply, then let it fall to her lap. "He asked for it specially, so I took it to him. I tried to get the concrete off—you know, so it would look better—but I couldn't."

Blake closed his eyes for a brief moment. He had seen that chunk of concrete, with the old stone embedded in it. He knew Dr. Margot had buried the sapphire, dropped it into wet concrete, and smoothed it down, chain and all. Mr. Preston had pried it out of there, though of course it would never have any value now. He had made use of it anyway, it seemed.

He glanced at Mr. Dickson, and saw that he, too, understood. It would have been enough, that piece of concrete, to smash the lock on Mr. Preston's door. There were no other patients on the third floor of the sanitarium, and there would have been no one to hear the noise as he splintered the wood.

He had helped carry Preston's case to his room when he was first installed there. He knew there was no outer window in the room, but the corridor was lined with them. Once he was out, he had his choice.

As a young man, little more than a boy, Blake had seen someone fall from a roof at the Chatham County Convict Camp. The image had haunted him for years, the hideous sight of mangled flesh and bone and a stunning amount of spilled blood. He tried not to think of Preston that way, but he couldn't help picturing how it had happened—Preston smashing the window, balancing on the sill, drawing a final breath before launching himself into the air, falling to a terrible death on the path three stories below.

It was, as Mr. Dickson had said, doubly tragic. And it was sick-eningly cruel to Mrs. Edith, to Mr. Dickson, and to Hattie, who had loved him despite everything.

Blake wouldn't grieve for Preston. The world was a better place without him. But he could grieve for these people, who had been through so much at Mr. Preston's hands.

This, he hoped, would be the end of it.

"We will make our plans in the morning," Mr. Dickson said gruffly. "I hope you can all get back to sleep. Please tell Blake if a bit more brandy would help you."

Dick said, "Are we going to have another funeral, Father?"

"Private," Mr. Dickson said. He cleared his throat, and looked away. Blake thought, for one awful minute, that he might sob.

"Yes," Dr. Margot said. "Everyone already believes he's gone. We'll leave it that way."

Blake thought of the many trips to the cemetery, when he had driven Hattie and Mrs. Edith there to lay flowers on Preston's grave. The empty grave, with no bones in it, and a meaningless headstone. He was sure Mr. Dickson could arrange things so that Preston could be buried there after all. It might give Mrs. Edith some comfort.

He said, "If you'll permit me, Mr. Dickson, I'll speak to the maids about keeping this—this sad event—confidential. Within the walls of Benedict Hall."

Loena said, "Oh, we know that, Mr. Blake. Don't we, Leona? We wouldn't never say a word to nobody." Thelma nodded along with the twins.

Mr. Dickson said, "Thank you all. Your loyalty is a great comfort to Mrs. Benedict and myself—to all of us."

They began to disperse. The maids climbed to their attic rooms, and Mrs. Ramona went up to check on Louisa in the nursery. Hattie, steadily weeping, plodded off to her room behind the kitchen. Mr. Dickson said, "Well, Blake. I suppose that's all for tonight. Nothing more we can do. We'll speak about the arrangements in the morning."

"Yes, sir. Allow me to say, Mr. Dickson, how very sorry I am for—for everything."

"Of course. Thank you." In a gesture that was wholly unusual for him, Mr. Dickson clasped Blake's arm with his hand, and squeezed it. As he released his grip, Blake saw a telltale shine in his employer's eyes. He suspected Mr. Dickson was taking this harder than anyone.

Mr. Dickson helped Mrs. Edith up from her chair, and kept an arm around her as they walked toward the hall, but Blake had the impression that, this time, it was the wife supporting the husband rather than the other way around.

They had just reached the foot of the staircase when he heard Mrs. Edith say, "We have to find that child, Dickson. Preston's boy. As soon as possible."

CHAPTER 28

Margot and Dick went with their parents to meet the train that brought Preston home for the last time. Dick had arranged for the hearse, a long white vehicle with carved panels and fringed curtains shading the windows. The driver and Blake nodded to each other, and stood back as the coffin was unloaded from the train. It was far simpler than the one they had buried three years earlier. That one had been ebony, with brass handles and curlicues decorating the lid. This one looked as if it might be pine, or perhaps fir. It was a plain brown, with iron fittings.

Curious eyes followed it as the men Dick had hired lifted it on their shoulders and made their way through the King Street lobby with the family following in its wake. Edith had draped a black veil over her hat. Dickson kept his Homburg pulled low over his eyes. Dick and Margot trailed behind their parents. Margot felt drained of all feeling, as if the well of her emotions had run dry. Dick, grim-faced, spoke only when he had to.

When they had seen the casket safely into the hearse, they all climbed back into the Cadillac to follow the hearse to the cemetery. It was a parody of a funeral procession, nothing like the grand one of three years before. It felt hurried and a bit slapdash, but they had agreed that would be best, and would attract less attention.

"No reporters," Dickson had growled.

"No, Father," Dick said. "In fact, it might be best if you avoided the station and let me—"

"No. Your mother needs me there."

"Do you want me to have a word with C. B., then, at the *Times*?"

"Yes. Just tell him—ask him—to make certain no one gets hold of this."

Frank had offered to come with Margot, but she had assured him it wasn't necessary. "Go to work, darling," she had urged him. "It's going to be a rotten day. It's best all of us Benedicts just muddle through it, I think."

He had kissed her, and gone off to the Red Barn with the unmistakable air of someone making good his escape. She watched him go from the porch, where she sat in one of the Westport chairs with her morning coffee. Hattie had come out, surprising her, and when Margot asked her to please sit down, she surprised her further by accepting the invitation.

Hattie lowered herself into the chair, and fanned herself with the hem of her apron. "Miss Margot," she said after a moment, "I bin wantin' to talk to you."

"Of course, Hattie. Do you have something on your mind?"

"It's about this chile. This bitty boy of Preston's."

"I think that's on all our minds just now."

"I think I ought to tell you, Miss Margot, that Mrs. Edith bin tellin' me about that chile for a long time. I didn't believe a word. I thought Mr. Preston—" As she spoke his name, her eyes welled, but she dabbed at them with the corner of her apron, and pressed on. "I'm sorry to say it, Miss Margot, but I thought Mr. Preston done made it up. I never said nothing to Mrs. Edith, but I didn't think there was no chile."

"Nor did I, Hattie. I don't think anyone would blame you for that."

"But now—now we know there really is one, and that pretty Miss Bronwyn is the mama—now what are we gonna do about it?"

"We've been discussing it." Margot cradled her coffee cup between her fingers, savoring the familiar comfort. "I promised Preston, when I saw him last, that I would try to find the boy. Mother is insistent upon it. That doesn't mean we'll be able to, though."

"That Mrs. Ryther, she'll know. She wouldn't tell Miss Bronwyn, but she'll know."

"Yes, Hattie, but—if the baby's been adopted, what do we do? Take him from a family that has come to care for him?"

"I don't know, Miss Margot. I don't know. But I don't see how Mrs. Edith ever gonna be herself again unless we find that chile."

Now, at the Washelli Cemetery, Margot watched her mother's face as the empty casket was hoisted out of the grave, and the one containing Preston's body was lowered into it. Edith watched the coffin descend, and her face was utterly, chillingly blank. Margot's feelings for her mother had always been complex, but pity overrode anything else at that moment. Her mother had lost her favorite child twice. She needed something to live for.

Was it fair to expect a little boy to be that something? It was a challenging ethical question.

The four of them stood beside the grave for a long time, until two laborers, with spades in their hands, crossed the grass toward them. Dick said, "I think we're done here."

Father nodded. Mother took his arm. Her veil fluttered against her face as she walked beside him back toward the gravel parking lot. As Margot and Dick followed, the sound of dirt clods falling on the lid of the coffin carried clearly through the summer evening.

Dick said, "God, that's awful."

"The whole thing is awful."

"It was bad enough, but—suicide. Christ."

"It doesn't seem like a characteristic choice, does it?"

"To tell you the truth, Margot, I wouldn't have thought Preston had the nerve."

"He meant to do it last year, when he tried to—to cut me."

"Yes, but—throwing himself out a window—knowing what it was going to be like—it's not like Preston at all."

"He wasn't the same man, Dick. Living the way he has for the past three years took plenty of nerve, I think. He had nothing left. Nothing he cared about."

"What about the little boy? It seems Preston cared about him."

"I don't know if I believe that. Preston usually had other reasons."

"Maybe it was for Mother."

"Possibly."

"How do we find him?"

Margot said, "I'll speak to Olive Ryther."

"Do you think she'll tell you, that Mrs. Ryther?"

"I don't know. She's not always cooperative. And she keeps terrible records."

"Well, if you need to bring pressure to bear on her, we could speak to the mayor. She needs city licenses and so forth."

They had reached the Cadillac, and Father heard Dick's last sentence. He glanced up from helping Edith into her seat, and Margot felt a pang of fear for him. His face looked gray, with grief or fatigue, perhaps both. Blake had come around to hold the door of the automobile, but Dickson paused with one foot on the running board. "Yes," he said wearily. "I'll call the mayor myself. I promised Edith I'd do everything I could."

Blake straightened abruptly, and fixed Margot with a gaze full of alarm. She said, "Blake?"

He shook his head, and didn't answer, but she knew him too well. As they drove back into the city, she saw tension in the muscles of his neck, and in the hard grip of his gloved hands on the walnut steering wheel.

She rubbed her eyes with her fingertips, and wondered what new trouble was coming.

*　*　*

It was long past the dinner hour by the time the Cadillac returned to Benedict Hall with its paltry group of mourners. Blake opened the back door of the automobile, then opened the scrolled iron gate. He stood beside it as they trudged in silence up the walk to the porch. Hattie had been watching for them, and she opened the front door, nodding to Blake as she closed it.

He got back into the Cadillac, and turned up the drive to the garage. As he crossed the lawn to the rear of the house, he stripped off his driving gloves with deliberate gestures, and tucked his cap under his arm as he let himself in through the kitchen door. He tried to greet Hattie normally, but she took one look at him and said, "Blake! What's the matter with you?"

He gave her a wry smile as he crossed to the wall pegs and hung his jacket and cap there. "I can't fool you, can I, Hattie? Even today."

"Maybe specially not today, Blake. I knew this would be bad, but you look as if you seen a ghost."

"If so, it would be my own," he said. He took his serving coat from its peg and began to put it on. He saw that Hattie had a platter of finger sandwiches ready. "That was a good idea," he said, nodding to it.

"They think they're not hungry, probably," she said. "But they will be. People gotta eat, even when they're feelin' sad."

"That's quite true, Hattie. Very wise."

"They in the small parlor, I expect. You could just take this here platter in, and a pile of little plates. I'll send Loena with some napkins."

"No, don't bother her. I can put it all on a large tray." He pulled on his white gloves, and smoothed down his sleeves.

"All right, then, Blake. You go and serve that, and see if they want anything else. Then you gonna come back here and tell me what's wrong."

She was an irresistible force, was Hattie. The thought made Blake smile despite his anxiety. She was the anchor that kept the ship of Benedict Hall steady in its harbor, no matter how cruelly the tidal waves rocked it. To Hattie, the kitchen was the heart of a house—and perhaps she was right. People gotta eat, as she often said. It was a piece of folk wisdom he couldn't deny.

He settled the family with the drinks cart near at hand, and the platter of sandwiches in the center of the little piecrust table. They had started to take them even before he left the small parlor, which he knew would gratify Hattie.

He pushed through the swinging door into the kitchen, and found she had laid a place for him at the enamel-topped table. There was a thick sandwich of cold roast beef and sliced cheese, and one of her fat homemade pickles beside it, along with a glass of apple cider. He sat down, and opened a napkin across his lap. He hoped he could eat, because he knew she would cluck at him if he didn't.

She sat across from him, a cup of tea before her. "Now," she said, in the tone a mother might use with a naughty child. "You tell me, Blake. And don't go tellin' me it's nothin', 'cause I got eyes, and I know you."

"All right, Hattie." He picked up the glass, and drank half of it straight down. As he set down the glass, he said, "I could lose my job tomorrow. I have done something—outrageous, I think would be the word. Mr. Dickson is going to find out, and there's no way I can stop him."

Her eyes went round, and she leaned forward, her big apron crinkling around her. "Why, Abraham Blake!" she cried. "Whatever . . . ?"

"Oh, Hattie," he said ruefully. "No one ever calls me Abraham except you."

She would not be diverted. She put her elbows on the table and ordered, "Go on! Tell me."

"Well," he said. He touched the sandwich, but didn't pick it up. "As so often happens, this particular road was paved with my best intentions. I didn't see another way, and there was no time." He shook his head. "It was Nurse Church, you see. And her family."

As he explained what had happened, how desperate he had been to think of something, her eyes grew wider and wider, until the whites seemed enormous in the fading light of evening. "You pretended to be Mr. Dickson? Why, Blake! I can't believe it!"

"Nor can I," he said. Now he did pick up the sandwich, and took an enormous bite. Telling Hattie had somehow relieved the tension in his belly, and he found he was ravenous.

While he was chewing, she said, "So, did it work? Were the Churches able to stay in their home?"

He swallowed, and reached for the glass of cider. "I don't know, Hattie. I can only assume. Mayor Brown said that development company can't operate without his approval, so I hope and trust we were successful."

" 'Specially if you gonna get fired over it!" she exclaimed.

"Yes, indeed," he said. "Especially if I'm going to be fired. I'd like to think there was a point to my subterfuge." He took another bite of sandwich, and chewed it while Hattie gazed at him, her lips parted in amazement.

The sandwich was gone, and he had started on the pickle, when Hattie said, "You have to speak to Miss Margot. And do it tonight, before Mr. Dickson finds out some other way."

"I don't think this is a good time," he said. "They're all upset, and they're tired."

"You're upset, too, Blake. And tired!"

He shrugged. "True. But there's nothing to be done about it."

"Oh, yes, there is." Hattie sat back, smoothed her apron, then placed her palms flat on the table and pushed herself up. "I'm gonna fetch Miss Margot my own self. That girl loves you, Blake. She'll be real mad if you don't let her help."

He was too weary to argue with her. She disappeared through the swinging door and in less than a minute reappeared with a frowning Dr. Margot behind her.

"Blake?" Dr. Margot said, crossing quickly to the table, pulling a chair close, and looking into his face. Automatically, she reached for his wrist, even as she said, "What's troubling you? Do you have pain? Nausea—"

Blake, very gently, removed her hand from his wrist, then patted her fingers. "No, no, Dr. Margot. I'm perfectly fine."

"But Hattie said you needed me."

Above Dr. Margot's head, he met Hattie's unrepentant gaze. "Well," he said. "Well. I suppose Hattie is right. I didn't want to trouble you, but—"

"Don't be silly," Dr. Margot said tartly. "I'm awfully glad to find you're not ill. Whatever it is, it can't be that bad."

"Oh, you might be surprised," Blake said, his tone as mild as hers was sharp. "You just might be surprised."

Margot found her father on the front porch, sprawled in one of the Westport chairs with his head back, gazing past the branches of the camellia into the starry night sky. He had a fresh cigar clenched between his teeth, its tip glowing red in the starlight. A slight breeze had sprung up, carrying away the stifling heat of the day.

Margot drew a deep breath. The cigar smoke was fruity and strong in the night air. She settled into the other chair, and stretched her legs out in front of her. "Father," she said. "I'm glad you're still up. I have to tell you something."

He turned his head without lifting it, and squinted through the cloud of cigar smoke. "Good Lord, daughter. Hasn't there been enough?"

"Yes. There has definitely been enough. But there's more to come."

"About the child?"

"No. I don't know any more about him than you do, I'm afraid. This is about Blake, and about his nurse—well, my nurse, too. Sarah Church."

"Fine girl," Dickson said.

"Yes. We all think so." Margot linked her hands before her, and watched her father's face. "Her family lives in one of those northern neighborhoods."

Dickson raised one bushy gray eyebrow. "Covenants," he growled. "Those developers trying to push them out?"

"Yes. You always know everything, don't you?"

"My city. I like to know what's going on."

"The Klan had a hand in this, I understand."

He puffed a cloud of smoke into the darkness, where it hung for a moment like a gray cloud, until the breeze broke it apart. "Goodwin Company, I suppose. They've got a reputation for it."

"Yes. That's the name Blake mentioned."

Dickson lifted his head. "What does Blake have to do with this, Margot?"

"Sarah came to him for help. Her family was given no time— some men came to their home, and told them they had to go. They frightened her mother."

"They can't do that," Dickson said with assurance.

"They did."

"We can fix it. I'll give the mayor a call, and—"

Margot put a hand on his arm, and he gave her a wary glance. "The thing is, Father," she said, in the sweetest tone she knew how to produce, "Blake already did that."

He thundered, "What? What are you telling me, daughter?"

She kept her hand where it was, hoping to keep him calm as she explained. "Time was terribly short, Father. Those men told the Churches they had to go immediately, and Mother went missing that same night. You and Blake had to rush off to Walla Walla, and so—" She pressed his arm with her fingers. "Blake called the mayor, and—" She had to pause for a breath, aware of how preposterous the whole thing was.

Dickson rumbled, "What did he say to Ed that was so awful?"

She lifted her hand, and dropped it back into her own lap. "He pretended he was you. Blake did, on the telephone. Asked for Mayor Brown's help, and—it seems—received it."

Her father was silent, puffing on his cigar. Margot sat listening to the faint clatter of the camellia leaves in the wind, the occasional bump or rustle from indoors as the family settled itself for bed. She had told Blake to go to his own bed, that she would handle this, and now all she could do was to wait for her father to decide how he felt about it.

After two or three minutes had passed, Dickson said, "The Churches still in their home?"

"As far as I know."

"Hmmm." Cigar smoke swirled away on the breeze. "Blake probably thinks I'm going to fire him."

"I suspect that's his concern, Father. You wouldn't, though, would you?"

A strange sound came from Dickson's throat. At first, Margot tensed, because it sounded as if he were choking. Then, as she leaned closer so she could see his face through the haze of smoke, she saw that he wasn't choking, or coughing. He was laughing.

"Is it funny?" she asked, and at the same time felt a giggle rise, as if her father's mirth was contagious.

Dickson took the cigar from his mouth, and guffawed. "Funniest thing I've heard in years!" he said, when he could catch his breath. "His Honor bamboozled by my butler! That's rich!" He went off into another gale of laughter, one that ended in a coughing fit.

Margot was chuckling, too, a relief after the grimness of the day. She patted her father's back until he stopped coughing, and then the two of them sat on in the darkness, grinning at each other. "You smoke too much, Father," Margot finally said, her lips still twitching.

"I know. How do you suppose Blake made himself sound like me?" That set them both off again, snickering like schoolchildren. The tension of the evening bubbled away as if a cork had been pulled from a bottle of something fizzy.

At least, Margot thought, once their amusement abated, some good had come out of these troubled days. When they rose at last, and went into the house side by side, she thought that her father, at least, would recover from the tragedy of Preston's suicide.

She wished she could be as confident about Edith.

CHAPTER 29

Olive Ryther scowled across her cluttered desk. "I don't like my home being interfered with," she said.

"I'm aware of that," Margot said.

Dickson stood behind Margot's chair, his hands in his pockets, his jaw thrust out in his characteristic way. "The city does a great deal for you and your children," he said.

"I do a great deal for the city."

"No one is arguing about that, Mrs. Ryther. You're very well thought of."

"Someone's always coming in here trying to make me do things I don't want to."

Margot tried to speak in a soothing manner. "We only want what you want, and what's best for the children who come to you—the ones you take such good care of."

"I can't be certain this is the child you're looking for," the old woman said truculently. "And it's hardly fair for you to decide you want him now—take him away from his foster family, who have probably become attached to him."

"Mrs. Ryther," Margot said, "we didn't know the child existed until recently."

Her father was less placating. "My son's dead, and now I need to know my grandson is safe. Well cared for."

Mrs. Ryther sniffed. "God cares for these little ones," she said. "We're just His instruments."

"Fine," Dickson said. His voice had dropped, and Margot could feel his temper building, like a lightning storm growing behind her. "I want to know, just the same. I hardly think God would object to that."

The look Olive Ryther directed at him through her spectacles might have withered a lesser man, but Margot knew her father. Such a look would only ricochet off the iron casing that was his normal demeanor, and might cause more damage on the rebound than it had on its original trajectory. Without looking back, she saw by Mrs. Ryther's face, the flicker of the eyelids, the brief pursing of the lips, that she was right.

Mrs. Ryther lifted the felt cover of the book, and adjusted her spectacles on her nose. She turned pages with deliberation, occasionally glancing up to look at the two Benedicts over the rims of her glasses. "So many children," she muttered. "Tossed away as if they were rubbish."

"I can assure you," Dickson rumbled, his voice so low it was nearly inaudible, "that this little boy isn't unwanted in the least. Only unknown."

"Someone should have thought of that."

"Yes," Margot said hastily, feeling her father stiffen at her shoulder. "Yes, that would have been ideal. But the people involved—that is to say, the young girl who gave birth to him—she didn't know anything. Literally."

"You mean Miss Morgan."

"I do."

"Hmm." Mrs. Ryther turned another page. Each page was covered in an uneven, looping hand, and Margot wondered if even Mrs. Ryther could read it. "I don't hold with keeping girls in ignorance. It doesn't help them."

"I couldn't agree more," Margot said with assurance. "Nurse Church and I work hard with the Women and Infants Clinic to solve that very problem. Education is the only way I can see to change it."

"Nurse Church is an outstanding young woman," Mrs. Ryther said. "A credit to her race."

"A credit to her *profession*," Margot said. She said it half under her breath, not sure either of her companions could hear her, but Dickson nudged her shoulder, and she knew he, at least, heard, and understood.

Mrs. Ryther turned another page, and ran her forefinger down a column of entries. "Here," she said, with some reluctance. "This may be the one you're looking for."

Margot stood up, and her father came around the chair to stand close to the desk. Mrs. Ryther turned the ledger so they could see, but as Margot had expected, her handwriting was illegible.

Mrs. Ryther tapped one of the entries. "An infant came to us in the winter of 'twenty-one, sent with a nurse from Vancouver. A sizable cash donation came with him."

"But no names?"

"That's not uncommon. These rich people think they can bury their indiscretions under piles of money."

"Evidently they succeeded," Dickson said.

Mrs. Ryther looked up at him. "Mr. Benedict," she said, "I have no control over what has happened before children come to me. Once they're here, I do everything within my power to care for them, to see they're settled, to see they have a future. It's not easy. Not many families are interested in taking my children."

Dickson shifted from one foot to the other, and cleared his throat. "I understand, Mrs. Ryther," he said. "I apologize for the inference. It's been a terrible time for my family. We've had a—a death. And my wife has not been well."

"You think finding this child will solve your problems?"

"It may," he said frankly. "I don't know for a certainty that it will, but I have to try."

"He's in the Rainier Valley," Margot told Frank, once they were alone in their rooms at Benedict Hall. Their shades were drawn, the windows open to admit a breath of fresh air, but still their small sitting room was stifling. The camellia blossoms had withered and fallen, littering the windowsill with browned petals. Margot had changed out of her skirt and shirtwaist, and rested now in a light dressing gown, barefoot and bare legged.

Frank was in his undershirt, and he had kicked off his shoes and socks as well. His prosthesis glimmered in the rays of the setting sun, and he exercised it reflexively, in a way Margot had gotten used to, bending the elbow, working the fingers. He said, "Mostly farms out there."

"Sarah sees women and babies from that neighborhood. They tend to have big families. Odd that someone would want to take in another child when they already have so many."

"Labor," Frank said. "Farmers, ranchers . . . they need labor. Big families are useful."

"He's not yet three."

"He'll grow. Think of the orphan trains, and all those ranchers." They had spoken of that, of the thousands of little children shipped across the country to be adopted by rural families, not always with happy results.

"What a horrible thought. It's the sort of thing Olive Ryther would hate."

"Maybe she didn't know. She doesn't even know for sure where he is!"

"No. Sarah's asking around. She knows those people so much better than I do."

"Try not to worry about it until you're sure."

"I just wish I could get this settled before I go back to the clinic, and the hospital."

He put out his right hand, and caressed her bare thigh where the dressing gown had fallen away. "For now," he said, "you're still on vacation. Try to let it rest. Nothing you can do tonight."

She was about to agree with this, when her private telephone rang.

"Don't answer it," Frank said, moving his hand to her waist. "You're not supposed to be at home."

"Sarah knows I'm here, Frank."

He circled her waist with his arm, and pulled her closer. "You could be out." He kissed her shoulder, and grinned at her, his eyes very blue in the low light. "We might have gone out to dinner, or be taking a walk in the park."

"Frank." She kissed his forehead, then pulled free. "We might have, but we didn't. If it's Sarah, I don't want to miss her." She had to get up to reach the telephone. She picked it up from the coffee table, lifting the earpiece from its cradle. With a wry smile at Frank, she said, "Dr. Benedict speaking."

"Margot." It was Sarah, and her voice was tight and worried. "I found him. That is, William Jackson found him, and I'm sure he's right."

"That was fast, Sarah."

"It's a berry farm. I haven't seen it, but William looked into it for me. I've treated a few of the children who work there—too many, to tell you the truth."

"How do you know it's him?" Margot carried the phone to the window, where she stood staring out into the dusk, her shoulders already beginning to hunch. Frank must have seen, and he came to stand behind her, rubbing the back of her neck with his good hand. She closed her eyes, and leaned gratefully against him.

"One blond child, about three. All the rest are dark, some of them Chinese, and a couple from the reservation."

"Good Lord, Sarah, how many children do they have there?"

"I can't even tell you."

"Who are these people?"

"They call themselves the Jenks family. I think there were three brothers, and they all came out from someplace in the South."

"What can we do?"

"We'll have to go there in person. If we send William with a message, they'll just send him away again."

"All right. They know you, so it would be good if you come, too."

"Yes, I know a couple of the women well enough, I think, though they won't like seeing me there."

"We wouldn't let you go alone, Sarah."

"No. Not a good idea. Now, the streetcar goes to Columbia City, but this farm is farther east. Do you think Blake could drive us? If we start early, I can be back to open the clinic on time."

"Yes. I can see you've thought this through. I'll go speak to Blake now. And Father. I think he'll want to be with us."

"I'll meet you at the clinic in the morning, then. And, Margot—" Sarah paused. "Margot, I don't think Mrs. Benedict should come. I know she wants to find the child, but from what I've seen—she might be upset."

"All right. We'll be at the clinic at seven, will that do?"

"I'll see you then. I want to thank your father, too, for what he did for my family."

This made Margot smile. "I'm sure you'll have your chance."

Frank insisted on being included in the party the next morning. "I don't want you down there alone," he told Margot, as they rose early and, for once, had coffee and toast brought up to their rooms.

"I won't be alone, Frank," she said. "Blake, Father—"

He shook his head. He spoke in his usual laconic manner, but she could see he meant it. "I'm going with you, Margot."

She saluted. "Yes, Major." He made a face at her.

It was an odd sort of group, Margot and Dickson and Frank in the rear seats of the Cadillac, and Sarah Church in the front with Blake. Blake had tried to insist she sit in the back, but she shook her head. "You know what they're like, Blake. It's better to keep it simple."

"Well, Nurse Church," he said, touching his cap with his forefinger. "I'll let you decide this, but just for once. You remember what I said before."

"I do," she said, dimpling at him. "But I'm quite happy to ride in the front of this beautiful motorcar with you."

Frank looked puzzled by this exchange, but Margot knew what Sarah meant. There was a hierarchy of prejudice among the people they treated at the Women and Infants Clinic. She would have preferred to find that these people were open-minded about racial differences, but she usually found the opposite to be true. The Negresses who came to them were thrilled to have a nurse they felt comfortable with. The others—Italian, Irish— were all too glad to find someone they felt was lower in the world order than they were themselves. Sarah was unfailingly graceful in the face of all of it.

Margot, on the other hand, had snapped at more than one woman who turned up her nose at being treated by a Negress. Her usual line was, "Well, Mrs. O'Donnell, you are welcome to take your custom elsewhere."

The truth was, of course, as both she and the offending patient knew very well, that Mrs. O'Donnell and those like her had no money to take to another practitioner. Margot wasted no energy on their offended expressions and stiff-necked responses, and she refused to tolerate even a hint of rudeness to Sarah.

As they drove south and east from the clinic, Sarah twisted in her seat to explain the situation to them.

"There are three separate families there, as nearly as I can tell," she said. "They have some children of their own, and a number they've taken in. At least, that's what they call it. They've 'taken them in,' which I'm afraid means they give them a place to sleep and food to eat, in exchange for their work picking raspberries and blueberries, and then blackberries in the late summer. They have a day stall at the Market where the women sell the produce."

"We probably have some of their berries at Benedict Hall," Margot said.

"I've seen a number of the children at the clinic for infected scratches, earaches, that sort of thing. Once or twice there have been serious injuries, but those I sent on to the hospital. I've never seen one that didn't have other issues—rashes, bruises, lice. One little one—couldn't have been more than five—fell off a truck and broke his arm. He was supposed to be holding the bushels in place."

"I remember him," Margot said. "I didn't know where he came from, though. A woman came with him to the hospital. I thought she was his mother."

"I don't know which are their natural children and which aren't," Sarah said. "And they won't talk about it. They don't talk much, in fact, and they usually wait until the children are really sick before they bring them to see us. I've had no luck persuading them to bring them all in for vaccinations and general examinations."

Frank said, "Aren't there laws about child labor?"

"Several have passed," Margot said, "but the federal courts ruled them unconstitutional."

Dickson said, "Ought to keep the government out of business. Farm families—"

"If these *are* families," Margot said sharply. "Even so, this is the twentieth century. We don't need children working like mules to put food on our tables."

"You're exaggerating again, daughter."

Margot thrust out her chin at him. "You just don't want to know about these things, Father. So much easier for you—and for me and Frank and all the rest of us—if we don't have to worry about five-year-old children picking the blueberries we eat for breakfast!"

Dickson's mouth pinched tight, and Margot let the subject drop. It was one of the arguments she and her father had pursued for years, but now it was personal, and uncomfortable. She felt Frank's eyes on her, and she touched his thigh with her hand. Despite her assurances that it would all go well enough without his presence, she was glad he was here.

The Cadillac rolled down a narrow dirt road between cultivated fields. Once they had to stop for a cart pulled by a donkey, and two laborers on the bench seat stared at the automobile in wonder. They passed farmhouses set back from the road, square, two-story affairs, surrounded by barns and sheds and kitchen gardens. Once or twice they saw a tractor grumbling along in a field, and along every stream or creek blackberry bushes flourished in great green rolls. The berries hadn't come on yet, but Margot could smell the promise of their sweetness through her open window.

Following Sarah's direction, Blake turned into a rutted, dusty lane that wound through fields planted with something Margot didn't recognize. Frank thought it might be potatoes, but he wasn't certain. "We only grew hay," he said. "Timothy, alfalfa."

The lane opened out, after a number of twists and turns, into a packed dirt yard littered with vehicles in various states of repair. There was a wood-sided wagon with its shafts resting on the ground, and a tangle of harness looped over the frame. There were a couple of rusting trucks, their tires gone, axles sitting on the ground. There was a van that had once been white, and looked as if it might still run. Beyond this bounty was a low-roofed house built in an L-shape, with a complex of laundry poles to one side and a wilting garden to the other. An outhouse with a tilting roof and a larger building Margot guessed to be a washhouse were at the far end of the garden.

In the field behind the buildings, curls of dust rose, and after Blake pulled the Cadillac into a clear spot, and turned off the motor, the sound of another motor carried clearly in the morning air. A woman peered from the door of the washhouse, and a moment later she and two children of perhaps eight made a dash for the back door, the children casting curious glances at the automobile now parked in front of their home. From the front windows, which were low and narrow, Margot saw the twitch of curtains. Someone was looking out at them.

They sat for a moment waiting for the swirling dust to settle, and staring at the motley assortment of structures. Margot couldn't imagine a place more different from Benedict Hall. Sarah pointed to a slanted door that looked as if it was set into the earth. "I think that's a root cellar," she said.

"No electrical wires," Frank said.

"None of these farms have electricity."

Margot said, "Running water?"

"I don't know."

"There's a well beside the washhouse," Blake said. "I'd guess they use the creek, too."

Dickson said, "Sounds like you have experience, Blake."

"Oh, yes, sir. A very long time ago."

Margot hadn't thought, until that moment, of how familiar this place must be to Blake. In his youth, he had worked on the plantation where his parents had been slaves. He spoke of it very little, but she could guess it had been punishing work, and a terrible life, little better than his parents' had been. He rarely spoke of them, either, except to say that his mama had wanted him to make something of himself. He had, of course, but it had taken a staggering amount of native intelligence, initiative, and discipline.

She said, "We'd better see if they'll let us in."

Dickson said, "Why wouldn't they?"

"They don't trust strangers, Mr. Benedict," Sarah said. "Especially not ones who arrive in an expensive motorcar, wearing expensive clothes."

"What do they think, that we're the police?"

Margot said in a dry tone, "Very likely, Father. Try not to shout at them, all right?"

She saw the corner of Frank's mouth twitch. He was the first out of the car, and the first to approach the door of the sprawling house. He used his artificial hand to knock firmly on the door, and as Margot moved up beside him on the cracked wooden stoop, he edged in front of her.

There were voices inside, mostly of women and children. They fell instantly silent upon Frank's knock. Dickson had come up behind them, and he stood below the stoop, frowning. Sarah stepped up beside Frank, and said quietly, "I should speak to them first, Major Parrish."

Margot watched Frank's face as he considered this. He looked both fierce and worried, and the combination made him seem oddly youthful. Her champion. A rush of love for him warmed her heart.

She touched his arm, and said softly, "It should be all right, Frank. Why don't you wait with Father, and let Sarah and me go in?"

"If anything looks wrong—" he began.

Sarah said, "We'll call out, I promise."

He looked unconvinced, but he stepped back, letting Margot and Sarah come between him and the door. It had once been blue, but the paint was peeling now, faded by sun and wind, and cracks ran crazily from top to bottom. Voices had begun to chatter again beyond it, voices in a wide range from high to low. Sarah raised her hand, and knocked again. A single, distinctly male voice rang out, and the other voices fell silent.

Sarah said, "Mrs. Jenks?" There was a long silence. Sarah cast a glance up at Margot, and shrugged.

Margot said, "I'll try. Sometimes the title helps." She knocked, two sharp raps, and said, "Mrs. Jenks? Mr. Jenks? This is Dr. Benedict, from the Women and Infants Clinic. Nurse Church and I need to talk to you."

They waited another moment, listening to the sounds of scuffling and shushing beyond the door, until at last the knob turned, and with a screech of unplaned wood against curling linoleum, the door opened.

A man stood behind a fly-spotted zinc screen, a small man who peered suspiciously at them through a pair of smudged spectacles. He suffered from a nasty case of divergent strabismus, one eye looking directly at the stoop where they stood, the other seemingly fixed on some random point above their heads. Margot said, "Are you Mr. Jenks?"

He squinted up at her. She was at least a head taller and, she suspected, weighed twenty pounds more than he did. "Who's askin'?" he demanded. His voice was as thin as he was, and hoarse, as if he were a heavy smoker. Or perhaps, she thought, he was hoarse from breathing farm dust all his life.

"As I said, I'm Dr. Benedict. This is Nurse Church. We've treated several of your—that is, several children from your farm."

"Whaddya want?"

"May we come in?"

He shifted from foot to foot, and Sarah nudged Margot. It was then that she saw the shotgun he held in one hand. It was pointed at the floor, but that wasn't reassuring. She heard Frank draw a warning breath from his position below the porch. Behind her back, she signaled with her hand for him to wait.

Mr. Jenks said, "We're busy."

Margot snapped, "So are we. We understand you have a number of children here who have never been vaccinated. The county doesn't like such carelessness."

"No law says they have to get them shots."

"Do you still want us to care for them when they get ill? They come to our clinic and are treated at no charge. That's a privilege that can be withdrawn."

Mr. Jenks opened his mouth again, but before he could speak, a woman appeared at his shoulder. She was as thin as he, and Margot was sure she looked far older than her years. A bandana covered most of her hair, which was an indeterminate color. Her face was lined with the effects of sun and wind and, no doubt, endless work. She said, "Otis, please," in a voice so timid Margot could barely hear her.

Mr. Jenks turned on her. "Get back where you belong, Tilly!" The woman took a step backward, but there she stopped. Her head hung low on her neck, like a dog expecting a whipping, but she held her ground.

"Mrs. Jenks," Sarah said. "Dr. Benedict simply wants to see the children you have here."

"Out workin'," Mr. Jenks said sullenly.

"All of them?" Margot asked. "I understand you have some very young children in your—your home. Too young to be laboring in the fields."

"Guv'mint should stay outta our business," he muttered, which was so close to what Dickson had said earlier that Margot had to stop herself from throwing her father a speaking look.

"We just want to see the children," Sarah said calmly. That voice, Margot knew, was the one she used to defuse tension, to soothe upset patients, to persuade children and women alike to allow her to examine them.

"Otis," the thin woman began.

He didn't bother to look at her. "Git back in the kitchen, Tilly."

Margot peered through the screen, past the man's shoulder. Three small faces looked back at her, huddled beneath a cramped staircase. Two of them were dark, one so dark she was sure he must be Indian.

The third, the smallest of all, was fair. In fact, he was more than fair. His hair was such a pale blond that it glowed in the dimness of the house, and his eyes . . .

She would know those eyes anywhere. Light, clear blue, blue as crystal, blue as lake water on a perfect day.

She pointed to the little clutch of children and said, "Open the door, Mr. Jenks, and put the shotgun down. If you don't, we'll have the police out here."

"You cain't do that. You got no reason."

"I'm very good at finding reasons," Margot said evenly. "Open the door. I'm going to examine that child whether you like it or not."

CHAPTER 30

The inside of the Jenks home was considerably bigger than some of those in the East Madison neighborhood where Margot so often treated impoverished families. It was also considerably dirtier. The smell of bacon grease and sour milk hung in the air like a fog. Mr. Jenks, seen without the filter of the zinc screen, had the faintly gray look of someone with a chronic lung ailment. His accent was that of the South, and Margot wondered if he had worked in a coal mine. He may even have been a child laborer himself. The mines were famous for using children, because they were small enough to fit into tunnels where full-grown men couldn't go.

She didn't offer to shake his hand, and she noted that Sarah didn't, either. No doubt Sarah knew he would refuse to touch her. Tilly, as they came into the house, retreated to the kitchen door, her arms wrapped tightly around her gaunt figure. The little clutch of children disappeared the moment Jenks turned around and glared at them. Margot heard other voices from the kitchen, a woman and one or two more children. She asked again, "How many children do you have here, Mr. Jenks?"

"I don't have to tell you nothing, missy."

"Doctor," Sarah corrected him. "This is Dr. Benedict."

He didn't bother looking at Sarah, but addressed Margot again, fixing her with the one eye he could control. "We got three families here," he said. "Big families."

She gazed steadily at him. "I'm not blind, Mr. Jenks. It's perfectly obvious the children I've seen are not all yours."

"How'd ya know that?"

"It's genetics. You're dark-haired and so is Mrs. Jenks, but you have pale skin. You have at least one Indian child, and you have one so fair he couldn't possibly be yours. Do you have a blond brother?"

He shrugged. "We foster some kids. Give 'em a good home."

Margot held up her medical bag in her right hand. "Just the same. Mrs. Jenks—" She turned to face the cowering woman in the doorway. "Will you bring the children to this room? May I go in?" Without waiting for a response, she turned to her left, into a space that was probably meant to be the front room, but was being used as a bedroom. There was one cot, with a quilt and a worn pillow. There were piles of blankets and pillows here and there, but no other furniture. As she drew close to the cot, she caught a glimpse of something in the corner of her eye, something that leaped and disappeared.

Lice. Damn. She and Sarah would both need to deal with that once they escaped this noisome place. They had done it before, but she hated the smell of the delphinium soap, and it always meant scrubbing the bathtub with extra care after using it.

She didn't realize Frank had approached the front door until she heard his voice through the screen. "Mr. Jenks, if you don't put that gun somewhere else, I'll be coming in there."

Jenks, evidently feeling outnumbered at last, grumbled something rude, but retreated down the shadowy hallway, where a door opened and closed. Margot hoped he had gone outside, perhaps into the fields, and would leave them in peace. She said in a low voice, "Frank, it's better you don't come in. Or Father, either. I'm not sure what that man will do."

"What about you?"

"Sarah and I will manage."

"Mrs. Jenks," Sarah said, seizing the opportunity, "could you bring the children now? Dr. Benedict is waiting."

As Mrs. Jenks scurried to gather up the children and herd them toward the front of the house, another woman appeared in the kitchen door. She could have been the twin of the first, a dried-up, undernourished creature in a stained apron. She half hid behind the doorjamb, as if afraid of being seen. A big-eyed toddler in dire need of a haircut and a clean diaper peered around her knees, and she absently shoved him away with her foot, as if he were a dog who had gotten in her way.

Margot's jaw began to ache, and she forced herself to unclench her teeth. One problem at a time, she told herself. But she would have a hard word with Olive Ryther about investigating foster homes before placing children in them.

Mrs. Jenks returned, dragging two small children by the hand, with a third bigger one trailing behind her. "Hurry up," she hissed at him. "Afore Jenks is back."

The bigger child, a boy of perhaps six, was obviously Indian. His hair was black and lank, his skin and eyes dark. Like everyone in that house, he was painfully thin, and he had a rash on his neck. She pulled gloves out of her bag before she unbuttoned the ragged shirt he wore. As she had suspected, the rash extended down his chest and into his too-large trousers.

Sarah said, "I'll get some ointment for that, Doctor."

"Thank you, Nurse. Sweet almond, I think, and follow with some talcum. There's some in my bag. And a clean shirt, if someone can find it. Mrs. Jenks, are you giving this child cow's milk?"

Mrs. Jenks, still gripping the hands of the two littlest children, nodded wordlessly.

"Most of our Indian patients can't tolerate it. It's probably the cause of this rash."

"What'm I gonna feed 'im, then?"

"Anything else. Surely you're giving the children meat and fish, fruit, vegetables?"

"Mostly taters."

"Potatoes are fine. Not mashed with milk, though."

On it went. Margot examined one of the toddlers, and found her mostly healthy, although all the children were infested with lice. When it was the little blond boy's turn, he began to cry the moment she touched him. He looked at Sarah with round, terrified eyes, as if she were an ogre from a nightmare. When Margot tried to press the bell of her stethoscope to his chest, he screamed as if he were being carved into pieces. Mrs. Jenks stood mutely by, doing nothing, saying nothing.

Margot said, "Nurse, will you take Mrs. Jenks and the other children into the kitchen? Show her—and the other woman who's in there—how to use a lice comb, and instruct her on the use of delphinium soap." As Sarah nodded, and picked up her own bag of supplies, Margot added, "See if you can get a look at that other child, too."

When she was alone with the screaming toddler, Margot crouched to look directly into his fiery red face. There was no doubt in her mind that this was the little boy she and Blake had spotted weeks before, but he was dirty now, and thin. It was hard to know whether he was well, with his nose streaming and his cheeks burning. It wasn't hard to see that he was a Benedict.

She pulled her handkerchief out of her pocket, and wiped his face with gentle movements. She murmured to him, the sorts of endearments she used for Louisa when she was in tears, and she pulled off one glove to stroke his sweat-dampened hair. It was much too long, tangled and greasy looking. In fact, if she hadn't been expecting, hoping, to find him here, she might not have known.

But she did know. He looked so much like Preston it was uncanny. As his sobs began to ease, and he could hear her voice and her calming words, his features ceased screwing themselves into tortured positions. She saw the straight, aquiline nose, the narrow jaw that would one day match Edith's clear profile. His hair was so fair it was all but transparent, and his skin, beneath the grime and mucus, was pink and white, the Nordic look only Preston, of the Benedict children, had inherited from their mother.

Genetics. Pray God Preston hadn't passed on his greatest weakness.

It took several minutes for her to soothe the little boy's fears. When his sobs had reduced to hiccups, she set him on the rickety cot, and knelt in front of him so she could look into his face. She said, "What's your name?" but he only blinked at her, as if he didn't understand. She wanted to clean him, and to wash his hair. She checked his scalp with her fingers. Several lice leaped away from her touch, but she didn't find any nits, which was a small blessing.

From the door, Frank spoke. "Is it him, Margot?"

"Oh! I didn't know you were still there."

"Not leaving you alone, I told you."

"Good." She sat back on her heels, regarding the tearstained face of the boy who was undoubtedly her nephew. "Yes, Frank, I'm quite sure this is the one. I'm not sure how to proceed, but I will *not* leave him."

"Your father's pacing out here. I'll let him know. Back in a moment."

"Thanks, Frank." Margot saw movement from the kitchen, and looked up to see Mrs. Jenks standing in the doorway again. The woman cast a fearful glance toward the back of the house, and Margot was sure she was worried about Jenks returning. "Do you have a change of clothes for this child?" Margot said.

She heard the edge in her voice, but she didn't care. She had attended countless patients in poor homes, where there was no money for the doctor, where food and clothing were sparse. This place was somehow beyond that. Living out here, with fruit and vegetables growing all around them, it seemed particularly offensive that the house itself—and these grimy children—shouldn't be better kept.

"Why?"

"We're going to take him away," Margot said flatly. "I'd rather not take him in this." She fingered the filthy shirt that was all the little boy had on.

"You cain't take 'im. Jenks won't like it," the woman whined.

A spasm of pity briefly overrode Margot's anger. Mrs. Jenks looked as if she had hung her head for so long she could no longer lift it. Her housedress wasn't in much better shape than the child's garment, and her eyes were dull, without the slightest gleam of hope.

"Mrs. Jenks, why do you and your husband take these children in?"

"Had another one, but it died. Got two to replace it."

Margot decided to ignore the "it." Choose your battles, she told herself. In as even a tone as she could muster, she said, "Surely the children are too young—especially this one—to work in the fields?"

"Weedin' taters," Mrs. Jenks said. "Them little hands can get right in under."

Margot's brief moment of sympathy burned away under a fresh surge of temper. She pushed herself to her feet, and put her hands on her hips. "This child is not even three years old," she snapped. "Do you send your own children into the fields that young?"

"Don't have any," Mrs. Jenks said, without regret or emotion. "Always miscarry. Anyways, I worked in a mill when I was little. Jenks went down the pit when he was no more'n eight. 'S no different."

"This is 1923. Children don't do adult work anymore."

Mrs. Jenks only stared at her, mute and stolid. Margot repeated, "Do you have clothes for this boy?"

"Jenks won't let 'im go."

"What will he do? Does he use that gun on people?"

Mrs. Jenks's mouth quivered. She said, with a faint note of satisfaction, "Don't got to worry about that, Doctor. He ain't got no shells for that gun. He jist likes to carry it around."

"Very well. A shirt, then, or at least a clean blanket."

Mrs. Jenks came farther into the room, and bent to one of the piles of blankets that dotted the bare wood floor. She straightened with something in her hand that might have been a shirt. At the same time, Jenks appeared from the dim hallway, the shotgun still in his hand. "Whatcha think yer doin'?" he demanded.

The little boy whimpered at the sound of his voice, and clutched at Margot's thigh. She felt the trembling of his hands through her skirt. Mrs. Jenks cringed, clutching the piece of fabric to her.

Margot said, "This child is coming with me, Mr. Jenks."

"No, he ain't. He's mine."

"He is not *yours*, Mr. Jenks. Not in any legal sense. Unless you can produce some sort of paperwork?"

The man's eyes narrowed until his pinched face resembled a weasel's more than a man's. "Bin feedin' him, clothin' him, all that. I'm keepin' him. It's my right."

Margot bent, and swept the little boy up in her arms. He seemed to weigh nothing at all, or maybe it was that her fury at this man, at this place, made her strong. "Get out of my way, Mr. Jenks."

He didn't budge, except to swing the shotgun up. He didn't precisely point it at her, but it wavered in the air in her general direction.

Margot called, "Frank?"

But he was already inside, slamming the screen door open with unnecessary force. Jenks flinched, and spun to face him. Before he could speak again, Frank had the barrel of the shotgun firmly gripped in his prosthetic hand, which Margot knew had a grip of iron. He twisted it out of Jenks's hand with almost no effort. He slid the stock beneath his arm, where Jenks would have to fight for it.

"Let's go, Margot," Frank said, his voice low and hard.

Jenks said, "Whatcha think yer doin'? You cain't—" He took a step toward Margot, but Frank stepped into his path. He didn't speak again, but he looked tall and fierce. Jenks stopped, but he yipped, "Tilly! Git that child!"

Mrs. Jenks was hunched over the bundled cloth in her arms,

clutching it to her solar plexus. She didn't lift her head, but she said in a voice that trembled, "Jenks. Let 'im go. You got them others."

Her husband threw up his head, and shouted at the cowering woman, "Who're you to be givin' orders? Do as you're told!"

The child in Margot's arms flinched at the raised voice, and began to cry again, but softly, hopelessly. She pulled him close to her, tucking his little head under her chin, lice and grease and stains be damned.

She moved past the bulwark of Frank without so much as a glance at Jenks. She pushed open the screen door and strode across the littered yard to the Cadillac.

Dickson was pacing the weedy lane, and he spun to face her. "Is that him? Is that my—" His voice caught, and she saw his eyes redden. "Is that my grandson, Margot?"

"It is. I don't think there's any question."

He came toward her, his hands lifting toward the little boy, but she shook her head. "Father, he's lousy and dirty. Might as well let me be the one to get infected, though we'll all need to bathe when we get home. Blake, do you have a blanket somewhere?"

While Blake moved around the motorcar to open the back and rummage under his supplies, Margot turned around to look at the ramshackle house. Frank appeared on the splintered stoop, the shotgun broken over his arm and his hat pulled low over his brow. He walked at a deliberate pace across the yard to one of the rusting trucks, and tossed the shotgun into its cab.

Dickson said, "How many children are in there, daughter?"

"Far too many, Father. And not in good condition."

"Is there anything we can do?"

"There has to be." Blake produced the blanket, and she pulled off the little boy's filthy shirt. Beneath it he was completely naked. She wrapped him in the blanket, and when Blake opened the door of the Cadillac, she slid in on the seat. "Frank, Sarah is still in the house."

"No, here she comes, Margot. She seems fine. I don't think Jenks is really dangerous."

"Unless you're a child," she said bitterly.

Their eyes met above the little boy's matted hair, and Frank gave her a tight smile. "We'll get them out of there, Margot. Somehow."

Behind him, Dickson growled, "Damn right, Frank."

Margot settled into the plush seat of the Cadillac, and cuddled the child—Preston's child—tightly in her arms. He turned his face into her chest, like a puppy snuggling close to its mother. She felt the sting of tears in her eyes. "Don't worry, little one," she whispered. "You're going home. You're a Benedict, and you're going home."

CHAPTER 31

Margot carried the little boy, who was apparently nameless, in through the back door of Benedict Hall. Hattie, alerted by Blake, came rushing to meet her, and together they labored up the servants' staircase and straight to the bathroom Margot and Frank shared.

"Oh, the sweet little chile!" Hattie exclaimed, though she could see only the greasy and tangled towhead above the folds of Blake's blanket.

"He has lice, Hattie," Margot said grimly. "And he's thin as a stick."

"Old Hattie will get you a bath going, and then fetch some food for the poor little mite. You'll see, baby boy, we'll have you plump as a pigeon in no time!"

"He needs a name," Margot said, as she sat on the dressing stool and waited for the bath to fill. The boy had fallen asleep against her chest, a node of heat drenching her shirtwaist with perspiration. The skin of her neck itched where he had nestled his head, but she thought that was probably as much from the heat as from the lice.

Hattie tested the water with her hand, and then reached toward the boy. Margot shook her head. "No, Hattie, you'd better let me do it. We don't need everyone in the house getting infested."

"Nothin' I haven't seen before, Miss Margot," Hattie said stoutly, but she stood back, folding her hands over her apron. "Go ahead now, let's see if he'll take to that bath all right."

Margot carefully unfolded the blanket, saying, "We're here now, little one. We're going to have a bath. Wake up, but don't be afraid."

His eyes opened stickily, and he looked around at the shining bath fixtures, the thick white towels, the gleaming mirror on the dressing table. When he caught sight of Hattie's dark face, his mouth opened in an O of surprise, but he didn't make a sound.

Hattie's easy tears brimmed in her eyes and slipped over her cheeks. "Oh, my sweet Lord," she whispered. "Mr. Preston's eyes, as I live and breathe! Oh, you little baby boy, you look so much like your daddy, old Hattie can hardly bear it!"

Margot let the blanket fall in a heap on the floor, and gently lowered the child into the warm water. He made a sound as it enveloped him, a slight groan, but whether it was of pleasure or fear, she couldn't tell. She pulled the small cake of delphinium soap from her pocket, the one Sarah had gotten out of the storeroom at the clinic, and showed it to him. "I'm going to wash your hair," she said, miming the motion. "It won't hurt, but it will get rid of those nasty bugs."

He watched with wide eyes as she lathered the soap in front of him, and then began to scrub. She started with his feet, winning a tiny crow of laughter at the tickle, and she worked her way slowly up to his hair. Hattie handed her a cup to sluice his head, and though he sputtered and grasped at her hand when water ran over his face, he didn't cry again. She had to take care to make certain none of the soap got in his mouth. It was nasty stuff.

"He hasn't spoken a word, Hattie," she said.

"Nobody bin talkin' to him, Miss Margot. He'll talk soon enough."

Margot lifted him out of the bath, and Hattie hunkered down before him with a towel. Margot watched as Hattie's strong hands wrapped around the little boy, enveloping him as much with her love as with the soft terrycloth. He lifted one hand to touch her cushiony skin with a curious finger, and she chuckled richly. "Oh, yes, baby boy," she said softly, pressing her cheek against his damp clean hair. "Oh, yes, we gonna have you talkin' up a storm in no time. Old Hattie's got you now, baby boy."

She glanced up, over his head, and said, "Why, Miss Margot! You're cryin'!"

Margot touched her own cheek, and found that it was true. Two tears had escaped without her realizing, and were dripping down her face.

Hattie gave her a wide, white smile. "I haven't seen you cry in years, Miss Margot. Don't you worry now. Everything's gonna be all right."

Margot sniffed, and laughed. "I know, Hattie. I know. It's just—I think of Preston, and that girl—and now this child. Who doesn't even have a name!"

"We'll leave that to Mrs. Edith," Hattie said sagely. "This chile gonna be her boy now."

Hattie was going to carry the child down to the nursery to see if anything of Louisa's might fit him, but when she picked him up, he whimpered, and reached for Margot.

"He's just frightened," Margot said. "Too many changes, too fast."

"I know, Miss Margot. That's okay. I'll sit here with him while you have your bath, then we'll go down together."

"Excellent. Thank you, Hattie. There's a comb there on the dresser. Could you go through his hair, make sure they're all gone? I didn't see any nits, but I could have missed them." Margot stripped off her own clothes while a fresh bath ran. She was relieved not to see any lice as she tossed her skirt and shirtwaist into the hamper. The rest of the household would be unhappy if she'd brought such an infestation into Benedict Hall. She was quick to duck beneath the water and soap her hair.

Within half an hour, both she and the little boy were clean and dressed. Margot wore a beige summer frock of polished cotton, and she covered the child in a nightdress that had been sent to Louisa, which Nurse had folded away until she was big enough to wear it. Nurse cooed over the newcomer. She found a tiny pair of bloomers for him to wear, muttering something about hoping he was past the diaper stage.

Hattie went ahead to prepare the way. Margot carried the boy down the wide front staircase. His little bare feet, peeking out from beneath the nightdress, looked so vulnerable that she almost shed more tears. She tightened her lips, and told herself that her crying wouldn't help anyone. He was, just the same, a pitiful and moving sight.

And an unnerving replica of his father as a child.

Margot, with Nurse following behind, carried the boy to the small parlor, where the rest of the family was assembled and waiting. Dickson and Frank had bathed, and Frank's silver-shot hair still sparkled with damp. Ramona was in an armchair, with Louisa on her lap. Edith sat on the divan, gazing blankly into a sherry glass. Dick stood by the cold fireplace, looking worried, and Dickson had a whisky in his hand.

Blake was standing just outside the door, and he nodded gravely to Margot.

"Did you bathe, Blake?" she asked. She paused in the hall, where she could see the family, though they hadn't yet caught sight of her and her little charge. "Any sign of lice?"

"I did, Dr. Margot," he said, his voice reassuringly deep and calm. "No bugs I could find."

"Good." She cast a wary glance at the gathered family. "Are they ready, do you think?"

"I have no doubt about it," he said.

"They understand he doesn't speak?"

"I asked Hattie to come in to explain. She did an admirable job of it."

Margot cast him a grateful glance. She murmured into the boy's ear, "There are a lot of people waiting to meet you."

He didn't make a sound, but his eyes stretched wide, and she could feel the quick flutter of his heart beneath her hand. He clung to her, his legs around her waist and his head turned into her neck. She said, "There's no need to be frightened anymore. This is your family."

She stepped through the doorway as she said this, and every eye turned to her.

Dick exclaimed, "My God, he looks just like—"

Ramona breathed, "Oh! What a darling!"

Louisa cried, "Baby!" and slid abruptly from her mother's lap to race across the room to Margot. She seized Margot's skirt in her two fists so she could tip her head back and look up. "Baby!" she said again.

"Yes," Margot began. "Yes, this is your cousin. We don't know his name, but—"

Edith spoke, in a clear, light voice that carried above the flurry of exclamations. "His name is Charles," she said. "For my father. I always meant my first grandson to have my father's name."

Though Louisa reached up to seize the boy's bare foot, Edith intervened. She pulled Louisa's hand gently away, and said, "We mustn't frighten him, Louisa, dear." She held out her arms, and said, "Margot, may I hold my grandson? I've waited such a long time."

Mute with wonder at the transformation in her mother, Margot loosened the boy's grip on her, and transferred him carefully to Edith's arms. He looked up at his grandmother, and instantly buried his face against the cream silk of her bodice. Edith pressed her cheek to his fair head, and closed her eyes. "Poor little Charles," she murmured. "You've had such a bad time, but it's all over now. You're safe. You're home."

*   *   *

Margot and Frank and Dick joined Dickson in his cramped study after dinner. Ramona had gone up with Nurse and the two children, and Edith had gone with them to be certain all was well. Margot sat on the stool, her arms around her knees. Dick took the other chair, and Frank lounged against the door, smiling at Margot above his brother-in-law's head.

"We'll need another nurse," Dick said to his father. He crossed his legs, and accepted a cigar from Dickson's hand. "If we're really going to do this."

"Is there any doubt?" Margot asked. "I haven't seen Mother so engaged since—well, you all know."

"Yes," Dickson said. He snipped the end off his cigar, and took a match from the silver matchbox. With the cigar between his teeth, he said, "Damned good to see Edith smile again. Worth any cost."

"We can turn the guest bedroom into a second nursery," Margot said.

"Build a guesthouse for company," Frank offered. "I can help with that, sir."

"That's a hell of a good idea, son," Dickson said. "Plenty of room in the back garden."

Dickson and Dick both lit their cigars, and smoked in contented silence. It was past time to go to bed. Margot was returning to work at the hospital in the morning, then on to her clinic. The men had their offices to go to. There was a sense, though, of savoring the moment, of appreciating the importance of today's events. They would have an impact on everything to do with Benedict Hall for years to come.

There were legal matters to be handled. Dick and Ramona were going to start adoption proceedings, declaring the child a foundling. Since Mrs. Ryther's record keeping was all but nonexistent, and since the Jenks family had no legal claim on the child, they felt the adoption would go ahead without incident. Charles Dickson Benedict—or Charlie, as Frank had already started calling him—would be theirs, if the single obstacle to their plan could be surmounted.

None of them knew what Miss Morgan might want, now that the child had been found.

"Ramona will make a telephone call to her tomorrow," Dick said. "She and the young lady became friendly, and she thinks she's the best person to give her the news."

"She doesn't have any legal standing," Dickson said. "There's no proof."

"Moral claim, Father," Dick said.

"Good for you, Dick," Margot said softly. "I know it's hard to face, but it's only right."

"Not my affair, perhaps, but I agree," Frank said. "Face it now, or you'll always worry."

Dickson blew a cloud of smoke toward the ceiling. "I just can't bear the thought of Edith being disappointed. Feels like she's coming back to us at last."

Margot leaned forward, and put a hand on her father's knee. "It does feel like that, Father, and it's marvelous. Let's try not to worry until we learn what Miss Morgan has to say."

"Spoken like a doctor," Dick said with a dry chuckle. "Try not to worry while we wait for the test results."

She smiled. "Yes. A taste of my own medicine."

At last they parted, though reluctantly. Margot bent and kissed her father's cheek. "Sleep well, Father," she said.

"You, too, daughter. Frank."

"Good night, sir."

Dickson stayed on in his study for a time, and Dick walked up the staircase with Frank and Margot. At the landing, Margot said, "You're very generous to take in Charlie as your own son, Dick. I think Preston would—well, despite everything—I think Preston would thank you."

"Doubled my family in one stroke," Dick said with a grin. "There wasn't any question, really, Margot. He's ours."

"Lucky little boy," she said.

"I hope so," Dick said. "I guess we'll find out tomorrow."

CHAPTER 32

In the days since returning to Morgan House with her parents, Bronwyn had done little but pace in the garden, gazing out at the Sound, remembering what it had felt like to be on her own. Nothing had gone well, and yet she had been independent in a way she never had before. She knew, within an hour of coming back to Port Townsend, that she would never be free if she stayed.

She had barely stepped her foot through the front door before her father commanded her not to leave the house alone. Her mother watched her every move, and found excuses to follow her when she went into the study or the music room, or outside into the garden. Mrs. Andrew cast her sly glances as she served her meals, as if gloating over her fresh imprisonment. Betty Jones scurried around after her as if keeping Bronwyn under control was her personal assignment. Perhaps it was. Bronwyn wouldn't have been surprised to learn that her father had set Betty to be her watchdog.

Johnnie had learned of her return and slipped a note through her window. She found it on the floor of her bedroom, fortunately spying it before Betty could. Despite his fury on the day she left Port Townsend, his note invited her to meet him at the Cellar.

She wasn't going to go. She was done with speakeasies. She would drink no more Fallen Angels. She was weary of men thinking she was fast. She couldn't go on being Port Townsend's most infamous ruined girl. She hadn't decided what she was going to do about that, but she intended to do something. She paced, or perched on the stone bench under the hot August sun, staring at the ripple and shine of the water as she pondered.

She and her mother sat down to lunch in the dining room, the two of them at one end of the long table. Mrs. Andrew brought in their salads, and filled their glasses with iced lemonade. She set a small basket of rolls between them. Iris said in her hesitant way, "Some butter, please, Mrs. Andrew?"

The cook heaved a gusty sigh, and stumped off toward the kitchen.

"Mother," Bronwyn said. "Why don't you get rid of her? She's always rude to you."

"Oh, no, dear," Iris said, glancing at the door to the kitchen as if afraid Mrs. Andrew had heard. "I don't want to make a fuss. She's just—"

"Why shouldn't you make a fuss? She's your employee!"

The door swung open, and Mrs. Andrew appeared with a butter dish. The butter was deeply scored in the middle and marked here and there with bread crumbs, as if it hadn't been refreshed since the night before, or had been used in cooking. She plunked it in front of Iris without speaking, and turned back toward the kitchen.

Bronwyn said, "Mrs. Andrew," in a tone of such sharpness that the cook stopped in her tracks, looking back in surprise. Her mother stared with parted lips as Bronwyn pushed the butter dish across the table. "Take this away and bring a clean one."

For a long, pregnant moment Mrs. Andrew glared at her, and Bronwyn thought she might just refuse.

Iris said faintly, "Bronwyn, dear, this is . . ." Her sentence ended in a vague gesture that hovered between agreement and denial.

"It's not. Do as I ask, please, Mrs. Andrew."

The cook sniffed, but she came back to the table, picked up the offending butter dish, and disappeared. When she returned a moment later with a cut-glass bowl in which an untouched pat of butter rested, she set it in front of Bronwyn, and raised her eyebrows.

"Thank you, Mrs. Andrew," Bronwyn said, in what she thought was a creditable imitation of the way Ramona Benedict spoke to her staff.

Mrs. Andrew's mouth pulled down as if she had tasted something sour, but she muttered, "You're welcome, miss."

When she was gone, Iris said, "Bronwyn! I've never—I mean, she's always so—"

Bronwyn covered her mother's hand with her own. "I know, Mother. But she works for you. She should do things the way you like them."

"She'll complain to your father."

"Let him fire her, then."

"He hates household arguments, Bronwyn. He likes everything to be quiet and calm when he comes home from the office."

Bronwyn released her mother's hand. "What's he going to do, Mother? Kick you out?"

"He just—he gets so angry."

"Let him be angry. Let him storm about like a spoiled boy! It all blows over eventually."

"Bronwyn!" Iris covered her mouth with her hand and stared at her daughter above her splayed fingers. "I don't know what's come over you!"

Bronwyn smiled at her mother. Iris's eyes sparkled with gold in the clear sunlight, and her artfully painted eyebrows arched over cheeks marked with only the finest of lines. "You're so pretty, Mother," Bronwyn said. "And so sweet—too sweet. You mustn't let them treat you so."

Iris lowered her hand, and though she picked up her fork, she only held it in her fingers, staring at the salad as if it had no appeal for her. "I'm a coward," she said. Her eyes lifted again, and her gaze caressed her daughter's face. "But you're not, Bronwyn. You never have been."

"Mother," Bronwyn said. She hadn't touched her salad, either. She drew a deep breath, and blurted, "I have to tell you something."

Iris set down her fork again. "I've been afraid of this," she said.

"Afraid?"

"Yes. I think you're going to leave again."

"I have to," Bronwyn said simply. "But this time, I hope I'll have your blessing."

The ring of the telephone made them both startle. "Oh!" Iris said. "Who can that be?"

It was true, the telephone sat mostly silent on their hall table. When Bronwyn had been in school, before everything had gone wrong, it had been much used, Bessie and Clara calling almost every day. Even Iris's friends rarely telephoned these days, creating a sense of isolation at Morgan House. It was Mrs. Andrew's task to answer telephone calls, although Bronwyn had always hated hearing her snap, "Morgan House," into the instrument, as if whoever it was had interrupted her in some vital task.

The ringing ceased, and both Bronwyn and Iris gazed at the door to the dining room in anticipation. Mrs. Andrew appeared, smoothing her apron with her hands. "The telephone is for Miss Bronwyn," she said sullenly. She added, "It's some woman says she's calling from Benedict Hall. Long distance."

Bronwyn and Iris exchanged a glance, and Bronwyn pushed back her chair. She hurried out to the hall, and took up the telephone in her hands. "Hello?" she said breathlessly.

"Bronwyn, dear?"

She recognized the voice instantly. "Mrs. Benedict—Ramona! How are—that is, how kind of you to call."

"Bronwyn, I have news for you. Some of it is wonderful, and

some of it is terrible. I hate to tell you over the telephone, but I feel I must."

"Yes?" Bronwyn's heart began to pound, and her hand on the receiver trembled so she was afraid she would drop it.

"I hope you're not alone there at Morgan House."

"No, m-my m-mother is here."

"Oh, that's good. Is there a chair where you can sit? I think that would be best."

Bronwyn tottered back to the dining room after managing, somehow, to say good-bye to Ramona Benedict. She groped for the back of her chair, stunned nearly to swooning by what she had heard.

"Bronwyn? Dearest, you're white as a sheet!" Iris leaped up, and encircled Bronwyn's waist in a surprisingly strong grasp. She helped her pull out her chair and sit, then moved her own chair close so she could chafe her wrists. She called out, "Mrs. Andrew! I need a cup of good strong tea, and quickly." In a quieter voice, she said, "We'll put a tot of brandy in it, Bronwyn. There's some in the sideboard, I'm sure. Now, take a few deep breaths. When you're ready, tell me what's happened."

Bronwyn did as her mother suggested, breathing, sipping the tea with its bite of brandy until the spinning of her head began to slow. Iris held her hand, patting it, warming her cold fingers between her palms. "There now," she said. "You have a bit of color. Goodness, Bronwyn, I thought you were going to faint!"

"I did, too," Bronwyn whispered. She cleared her throat. "Oh, Mother. You won't believe what's happened."

Bronwyn was glad, now, that she had made a clean breast of everything that had happened when she fled Port Townsend. Her parents knew all about her search for her child, about the death of the baby from diphtheria, and about her rescuing Louisa Benedict from the wading pond at Volunteer Park. They knew she had allowed Mrs. Benedict to take her all the way across the state on a train. They knew Preston Benedict was alive, restrained in a sanitarium. They knew he had attacked her, and that she had fled on foot and taken refuge in a church, to be sent home courtesy of funds from the charity box and the kindness of an unusual little man.

When she told her mother of Preston's suicide, the horror of it made her tremble anew, and she gulped at the brandy-laced tea to calm the pounding of her heart. Iris said, "Oh, dear heart. It's terrible, but you must let it go. His life sounds—oh, my goodness. Truly, it sounds as if his life was already over."

"Yes, Mother, but you remember how he was—it's horrible!"

"It's always sad when a young person dies. But this one—he did terrible things."

"I know. And all this while, I still loved him."

"You thought you did."

"Isn't that the same thing?"

There was no answer to this. Bronwyn steeled herself to tell her mother the rest of it. She took a deep breath and said hoarsely, "They found him, Mother. They found my baby."

CHAPTER 33

Margot left the clinic early, leaving Angela in charge, with instructions to send any urgent cases to Seattle General. Blake was
waiting for her with the Cadillac, and they drove up Madison to
Broadway in a tense silence.

"How's Mother holding up?" Margot finally asked, as they
turned up Aloha.

"I believe you would call it a brave face, Dr. Margot. She
spends every moment with Master Charlie when he's awake, and
when he's sleeping she's on the telephone, ordering children's
furniture or setting an advertisement for another nurse."

"The rest of them?"

"Worried, I think. No one is saying much."

Margot could feel the anxiety when she stepped into the front
hall, as if it were something cooking in the kitchen and filling the
house with its distinctive aroma. As she was removing her hat
and taking off her gloves, Hattie came through the swinging door
and stood twisting her apron between her hands.

"Tea is all ready for when they come," she said. "And lemonade."

"Thank you, Hattie. Do you know where Mother is?"

"She ordered up some clothes for Master Charlie. She's in the nursery sorting them out."

"When are the Morgans due?"

"Any minute now, Miss Margot. Any minute. I got some little sandwiches and cookies, but I don't think anybody gonna eat much."

"Louisa will," Margot said. "And Charlie."

This brought a tentative smile to Hattie's face. "I do love having little ones in the house. Makes it feel like a home."

"Yes, it does."

"You think that Miss Morgan gonna want to take Charlie away?"

"Oh, I hope not. We'll just have to hope for the best. Is Father coming? Dick?"

"No." Hattie's smile faded, and she smoothed the wrinkles she had put in her apron. "No, Mrs. Ramona said this is a thing for women. I heard Mr. Dick ask her to make him a telephone call first thing."

"Thank you, Hattie. I'll just wait in the small parlor."

As Margot walked down the hall, she heard Blake's deep voice from the back porch. In the small parlor she found Ramona standing at the window, parting the lace curtains with a fingertip so she could peer out. She glanced up with a guilty laugh. "Oh, Margot! I'm glad you're here. I'm just so anxious—I wish they'd get here, and we could get this over with."

"It might not be so simple, Ramona," Margot said. "I hope you're prepared."

"Well. As prepared as I can be, I guess." Ramona took a few restless steps toward the divan, then turned back to the window.

"That's all you can do." Margot felt the same anxiety, despite her warning. She forced herself to sit down on the divan, pretending calm, but when Ramona said, a moment later, "Oh! there they are!" she was up again, moving to a different chair, ruffling her hair with her fingers, then trying to smooth it back into place. Ramona turned, and as they caught sight of each other, they both laughed.

"We're a pair, aren't we?" Ramona said.

"This is the right thing to do."

"Of course it is. There's no doubt about that. It's just—we've already fallen in love with him. And Mother Benedict . . ."

"I know. I'm amazed at the change in her."

The door opened, and Blake said, "Mrs. Morgan. Miss Morgan."

Ramona smiled suddenly, her pretty face lighting as if she had never felt a single qualm. She crossed the room with her hand out and spoke with her usual charm. "Mrs. Morgan, how good of you to come. Bronwyn, dear, it's lovely to see you again! My mother-in-law will join us in a moment."

Margot greeted their guests, and Blake went off to fetch the tea things. By the time he came back, with Thelma at his heels, the ladies had arranged themselves around the piecrust table. Both the Morgans were pale, their unusual eyes following everything with the same nervousness the Benedicts had been trying to manage. Ramona poured the tea, and Margot passed the silver tray of sandwiches. Everyone took something, but as Hattie had predicted, no one tasted a thing.

Ramona said, "I can't imagine how you got here so quickly, Mrs. Morgan."

"Oh—" Mrs. Morgan's eyes flickered uncertainly to her daughter. "Oh, you see, Bronwyn—"

"I know someone with a boat," Bronwyn said. "One of the Mosquito Fleet. He was at the dock and brought us straight to Seattle."

"How kind," Ramona said. "How fortunate."

"Yes," Bronwyn said. Her mother stared wordlessly at her teacup.

After Blake and Thelma withdrew, Margot said, "We want you to know, Miss Morgan, that though we found Charlie in—"

"Charlie?"

"My maternal grandfather's name. My mother always wanted to call her first grandson after her father."

Bronwyn took a small, shivery breath. "It's a nice name," she said softly.

"We had to call him something, you understand. If he had another name, we never could discover what it was. This place—this farm—where he was living, the conditions were very poor. He's unharmed, though, as nearly as I can tell."

"The only real problem," Ramona said, "is that Charlie doesn't speak."

"He doesn't?" Mrs. Morgan's eyebrows rose. "Is there something wrong with him?"

"There's no reason to think that," Margot said. "I've occasionally seen children in whom speech comes quite late, and he's not three yet."

Bronwyn broke in. "No one talked to him, Dr. Benedict," she said sadly. "He was just another baby among a dozen babies."

"That's probably a good explanation, Miss Morgan," Margot said. "Our cook said the same thing. There's no reason to think he won't catch up, with time. And with patience."

Ramona set down her untouched tea. "I expect you would like to see him." Margot hoped she was the only one who heard the reluctance in her voice.

Mrs. Morgan tried to say something, but it seemed her mouth was too dry to speak. She took a sip of tea, and cast a beseeching glance at her daughter.

Bronwyn put up her chin, and Margot's heart contracted at the emotional struggle so evident on the girl's face. Bronwyn's lips trembled, but she tightened them, and said, "Yes, please, Ramona. If you don't mind."

"Of course. Just wait a moment." Ramona, Margot thought, was doing a better job than she of hiding her anxiety. She rose gracefully, smiled at both the Morgan ladies, and went out of the room.

Margot said, "Miss Morgan, I can see how difficult this is for you. And for your mother."

Mrs. Morgan turned her face to Margot, and Margot saw that her eyes swam with tears. "My grandchild," she said. Her voice caught, and broke, and she dropped her gaze again. "We made a terrible mistake. My husband—"

Bronwyn said, "My father was furious. He gave us no choice."

Margot's heart sank. It was possible these two expected to carry Charlie away with them. That they wanted to reverse the course they had set three years before. If that was true, Edith—and now perhaps Ramona as well—would be devastated. As the door opened, she stood up, feeling somehow she could be stronger if she was on her feet.

Ramona came in first, holding the door for her mother-in-law. Edith, with more color in her face than Margot had seen in ages, carried Charlie in. She tried to set him down, but he clung to her, and wouldn't let go. Though he didn't make a sound, his eyes were wide with alarm, and Margot felt the emotions swirling through the room rise to the drowning point.

Charlie was properly dressed now in boy's clothes. He wore a white shirt with a Peter Pan collar, and a pair of knee pants with suspenders. He had long socks that stretched to his knees, and a pair of white leather shoes. He was beautiful, soft and fair and slender. How could anyone resist such a child?

Mrs. Morgan was weeping silently, making no move to touch the boy. Bronwyn got up, and crossed to Edith. She didn't try to take Charlie from his grandmother's arms, but she did touch him, just her fingertips grazing his fluff of pale hair, running down his back, stroking his bare knees.

She said, "He looks so much like Preston, Mrs. Benedict."

Margot stiffened, unsure how her mother would react to this, but Edith bestowed a peaceful smile on Bronwyn. "You're right, my dear. He looks exactly like my son did at this age. Isn't it the most marvelous thing? My Preston is gone, and I can never have him back. But now there's Charlie."

Ramona crossed to the divan, and sat down close to Mrs. Morgan. "I think," she said quietly, "that it's a wonderful thing for so many people to care about a child. Don't you?"

Mrs. Morgan wiped her wet cheeks with a lace-edged handkerchief. "You're all so kind, Mrs. Benedict," she said. "I'm sorry about—well—it's too kind of you to understand."

Ramona said, "Of course I understand. I'm a mother, too."

Margot said, "You'd better sit down, Mother." Bronwyn stepped aside so Edith could move to the armchair. When she was seated, Charlie nestled close against her. His wary gaze took them all in—Bronwyn, her mother, Margot, Ramona. Margot said, "This must be confusing for Charlie. Not so long ago he was living in very different conditions."

"I feel terrible about that," Mrs. Morgan said.

"You couldn't have known."

Edith said, "The important thing is that Charlie's safe now."

"Yes," Ramona said. She sat up very straight, and turned her face up to Bronwyn, who was standing behind Edith's chair. "Bronwyn, I think we should be frank about the situation. My husband and I would like—no, we would dearly love—to adopt Charlie and raise him as our Louisa's big brother."

No one could miss the surge of color in Bronwyn's face, nor the fading of it a moment later. Her eyes were stretched so wide Margot thought they must hurt, and she saw the girl's throat muscles contract. Nevertheless, Bronwyn's voice was steady as she answered. "Are you asking my consent, Ramona?"

Ramona glanced at Margot for guidance. Margot nodded, but she didn't say anything. There was no need. Ramona was doing beautifully.

Ramona turned her face back to Bronwyn and said quietly, "I suppose we are, Bronwyn. We would always wonder, if we didn't consult you, what your wishes might have been."

"So kind," Mrs. Morgan sniffled again.

"Yes," Bronwyn said. She stepped around the chair, and knelt before Edith and the little boy. "Yes, you could have gone ahead without a word to us. I wouldn't have blamed you in the least."

For a long moment, she looked into Charlie's small, anxious face. He shrank back at first, huddling closer to Edith's body, but when Bronwyn made no move to touch him, he relaxed. He looked into the eyes of the mother he never knew, and Margot had the fanciful idea that an understanding passed between them.

In time, Bronwyn drew a deep breath, and pushed herself to

her feet. She turned to Ramona. "I feel as if I love him—but I don't really know him, do I?"

Ramona gave her a sad smile. "Well, dear, I love him, too, and I only know him a little bit better than you do."

"Perhaps," Margot said, "you need some time, Miss Morgan. To think about what all this means—to you and to your family."

Bronwyn suddenly pressed the palms of her hands over her eyes. Margot thought she was crying, but it appeared, when she dropped her hands, that she had been gathering herself. She drew a long breath and released it before she said, "Thank you, Dr. Benedict, but I don't need time. I knew before I came today, really."

She looked around at the group of women, the hopeful, worried, tearful faces. "Charlie has found his home," she said. "I couldn't have asked for anything better for him. And I need to grow up myself before I can be anyone's mother."

Mrs. Morgan emitted a single sob, and buried her face in her handkerchief. Ramona put an arm around her shoulders. "You won't object then," Ramona said softly, smiling up at the girl. "Charlie will be our son, and you won't mind."

"I'll be proud," Bronwyn said. Her eyes glowed with unshed tears. "Perhaps, once in a while, you could send me news of him."

"Of course," Ramona said.

Edith said, "You can come to see him, if you like."

"No," Bronwyn said. "It would be too confusing. He needs . . ." She waved her hand, indicating the entirety of Benedict Hall. "He needs to understand that he's home. That this is where he belongs. That he won't be taken away, ever again."

Bronwyn held her composure through the polite farewells, the thank-yous, the promises of letters and so forth. She and her mother shook hands with everyone, and Bronwyn took a last look at Charlie, but without trying to touch him or, as she longed to do, give him one kiss. She gripped her hands together in the backseat of the Cadillac as Blake drove her and her mother back to the Alexis. She bade Blake farewell and walked with her mother into the hotel and up to their room. She didn't cry until the door was closed and they were alone, and then she lay on the bed and sobbed for a very long time.

When she quieted, Iris brought her a glass of water and a damp washcloth. She stroked Bronwyn's hair, and murmured nonsense words of comfort. When the shuddering aftermath of tears subsided, Bronwyn sat up, wiped her face with the cloth, and took one final sniff.

"Are you all right?" her mother asked.

"Yes," Bronwyn said. "I am."

She spoke the truth. The tears were the final step, the last act of the saga of Preston Benedict and herself. Their child was safe, and in the best possible care. She had no more secrets to protect. There was only one final thing to be done, and she would do that now, while she and her mother were alone.

She swung her legs off the bed, and went to stand by the window, looking down at the automobiles and horse carts maneuvering around one another on First Avenue. Tomorrow, Captain Albert would carry her and her mother back to Port Townsend, but after that . . .

She turned to face Iris. "Mother, I'm going to go to Oakland."

Iris looked up at her with surprise and consternation. "Oakland! Where is that?"

"It's in California."

"California! Why, Bronwyn? What put that in your head?"

"It's Mills College. They have a very good dance program. I'm a little old to start, but I want to try."

"Your father . . ."

"It's a women's college. He should approve."

"Oh, Bronwyn. California is so far away!"

"Just a train trip, Mother. You take the train directly from Seattle to San Francisco."

"But how did you find this college?"

"I looked it up in the library. I've already applied."

"But you could go here, couldn't you? The Cornish School accepted you."

"The Cornish School is only a few blocks from Benedict Hall. I would always be tempted to go there, to see the—to see Charlie. That's not a good idea." Bronwyn sighed, and turned back to the window. "I think it's fair to ask you for this, you and Daddy. To ask you to help me. But if you say no, I'll find my own way. I've waited too long as it is."

Below her in the street, the traffic was thinning. A single horse, pulling an empty wagon that had probably held vegetables or perhaps barrels of fish, clopped wearily by. The sun had gone down, and only the very tops of the highest buildings now glimmered with its waning light. From this angle, Bronwyn couldn't look up the hill toward Millionaire's Row, but she didn't need to. She would never, as long as she lived, forget Benedict Hall, or the surprising people who lived there.

Behind her, Iris matched her sigh. "You're right, of course, dear."

Bronwyn, startled, spun to face her mother. "I am?"

Iris rose from the bed, and went to the mirror to take up a comb. She began to smooth her finger-waved hair. "I don't know what Chesley will say. We'll just have to convince him."

Bronwyn went to stand beside her mother, and their eyes, so much the same, met in the mirror. "He might shout, and stomp around," Bronwyn said.

"Then I'll probably cry," Iris said. She shrugged, and smiled into the mirror. "But that won't change anything."

Bronwyn hugged her mother's shoulders. "Thank you," she whispered.

"I'll go to Mills with you. See you're settled. You won't mind that, will you?"

Bronwyn dropped a kiss on her mother's temple. "I wouldn't want it any other way."

The mood in Benedict Hall was more relieved than jubilant. Ramona and Edith took Charlie upstairs, and Margot could hear them in the guest bedroom, planning what changes were needed to turn it into a second nursery. Blake returned, having dropped off the Morgans at their hotel and then picked up Dick and Dickson from their office. He had to make a second trip for Frank, who was delayed by a meeting with Bill Boeing. By the time Blake and Frank pulled into the driveway, the whole family was gathered in the small parlor for a celebratory drink. Louisa was in her mother's lap, and Charlie was standing at his grandmother's knee, sucking on a forefinger, his small face intent as he watched and listened.

Dickson said in his gruff voice, "Is that boy ever going to talk?"

Edith said, "Dickson, shush. Give the child time."

"How much?" he said, gesturing with his whisky glass. "Louisa has been talking a blue streak for months already."

They all heard the front door open and close, and a moment later, Frank's tall figure appeared in the doorway. Louisa squealed, "Fa!" and threw herself from her mother's lap to barrel across the room and grip Frank's legs. Laughing, he bent to pick her up.

"Uncle Fa, Louisa," he said, nuzzling her curly hair. "Uncle Fa."

"Fa!" she crowed again.

"See what I mean?" Dickson said.

Charlie watched as Frank crossed to the divan and settled onto it with Louisa on his lap. Frank smiled down at the boy's solemn little face. "Good evening to you, Charlie," he said.

Charlie stared up at him. After a moment, with something like ceremony, he removed his finger from his mouth. His forehead furrowed, and his lips worked, forming and re-forming, until he finally pronounced, "Fa?"

Margot was startled into laughter, quickly suppressed. Edith smiled with fond pride, and Dick and Ramona exchanged a glance.

Frank said, "That's right, Charlie. I'm Uncle Fa."

"Fa!" Louisa repeated, kicking her heels against Frank's thigh.

Charlie glanced at his cousin, then back to Frank. He blinked once, then pronounced with great care, "Un-co Fa."

"Good man," Frank said with a nod. "Well done."

Charles Dickson Benedict gravely returned Frank's nod before he replaced his forefinger in his mouth.

ACKNOWLEDGMENTS

I am indebted, as always, to my first reader, Catherine Whitehead, and to the other members of the Tahuya Writers Group: Brian Bek, Jeralee Chapman, Niven Marquis, and Dave Newton. Heartfelt thanks go to my editor, Audrey LaFehr, for helping me shape and direct the Benedict Hall novels. Thanks also to Martin Biro, her assistant and an editor in his own right, for his quick responses to my questions and worries (authors always have worries!). Peter Rubie at FinePrint Literary Agency has been faithful and helpful.

I wish I could also express my gratitude to a physician and a nurse, two people I never had the opportunity to meet, but whose personal libraries provided me with resources perfectly suited to my needs. The book *Manual of Emergencies*, published in 1918 by J. Snowman, MD, bears the beautiful copperplate signature of one A. Gerend, a physician. *Materia Medica for Nurses*, by A. S. Blumgarten, MD, published in 1924, was once the property of Kathleen M. Hayes, a nurse who, according to the handwritten inscription in the book, practiced in a hospital in Berwick, Mississippi. I'm so grateful these volumes came into my hands, and I will always treat them with the reverence they deserve.

Medical help and advice came from Dean Crosgrove, PAC, and Nancy Crosgrove, RN, ND. Help with historical details was provided by Professor James Gregory, of the University of Washington History Department, and by James Sackey, of the Northwest Railway Museum in Snoqualmie, Washington. I'm especially indebted to work done by the Seattle Civil Rights and Labor History Project for information on restrictive neighborhood covenants.

Perhaps most importantly, my thanks go to my readers. I have loved writing about the inhabitants of Benedict Hall and the people whose lives they touch. Thank you for sharing this journey with me. Without readers, writers would be talking to themselves. We might go on doing it, but it wouldn't be nearly as satisfying.

THE BENEDICT BASTARD

Cate Campbell

About This Guide

The suggested questions are included
to enhance your group's reading of
Cate Campbell's *The Benedict Bastard*.

Discussion Questions

1. In the late nineteenth and early twentieth centuries, many upper-class girls were deliberately brought up in ignorance of sexual intercourse and its consequences. In the industrialized societies of the twenty-first century, with the proliferation of television, movies, and books on every topic, is this even possible? Is there such a thing as too much information?

2. Child labor laws were passed in the United States Congress in the first two decades of the twentieth century, but were struck down by the Supreme Court because they denied children the "freedom" to work. A quatrain by Sarah N. Cleghorn in 1916 illustrated the problem and incited an angry public response:

   > The golf links lie so near the mill
   > That almost every day
   > The laboring children can look out
   > And see the men at play.

   Is there still a problem with child labor? At what age is it acceptable for children to work, and for how many hours in a day?

3. The concept of what is or isn't obscene varies for different eras and different cultures. The Comstock laws in the early twentieth century made it illegal to publicly discuss contraception, ruling such topics obscene. Margot Benedict, in her medical practice, struggles against the Church and the established medical community in order to supply women with information. Is there still reluctance, in the present day, to open discussions about preventing pregnancy?

4. The Ku Klux Klan was active in the Pacific Northwest in the 1920s, and influenced the establishment of restrictive neighborhood covenants. These covenants persisted for decades, only becoming illegal after the civil rights movement and the ensuing reforms. What effects did such restrictions have on cities like Seattle in creating racially segregated neighborhoods? Have cities recovered from those effects a century later, or do echoes of them remain?

5. The Benedicts use their money and influence to protect their family and dependents. Preston is confined in a sanitarium rather than being sent to prison, and Sarah Church's family is allowed to stay in their home when less well-connected people are not. Do you think the Benedicts abuse their power in some instances? Do they consider themselves above the law?

6. The word *bastard* has different meanings, in the English language and in the story of this novel. To which of them do you think the title of *The Benedict Bastard* refers?

7. In the book *Send Us a Lady Physician,* Regina Morantz-Sanchez writes, "More than one historian has portrayed the years between 1900 and 1965 as dark ones for the progress of women in medicine. . . ." Margot Benedict makes reference to the problem, and on her brief visit to Montana, learns that herbalists often stand in for physicians, particularly in treating women. Why do you think the progress women in medicine were making in the late nineteenth century halted, and even reversed? Is there still a male bias in medical practice?

8. Vaccinations were quite common by 1923, though many people didn't trust them. In what ways does that distrust mirror the controversy surrounding vaccines in the early twenty-first century?

9. From the mid-nineteenth century until the last one crossed the country in 1928, the Orphan Trains are estimated to have carried more than a quarter of a million homeless or abandoned children, including infants, from New York to rural communities in the Midwest and West of the United States. The results were, as you might expect, mixed. Was such a disposition of children the best idea for its time?

10. In what ways do you think the position of children in society has changed since the 1920s? Are all of the changes positive?

11. Margot Benedict finds value in the herbal treatments Jenny Parrish administers, and is interested in their application to her own medical practice. In the present day, this is sometimes called "integrated medicine," a relatively new term. What fresh ideas that Margot is willing to consider—ideas outside traditional medical practice—have been put into regular use today? Do herbalists still have a place in health care in the twenty-first century?